False Light

False Light

CAROLINE LLEWELLYN

LITTLE, BROWN AND COMPANY (CANADA) LIMITED
Boston • New York • Toronto • London

First published in the United States by Scribner

This Canadian edition published by
Little Brown Canada
148 Yorkville Avenue
Toronto, Ontario M5R 1C2

Canadian Cataloguing in Publication Data
Llewellyn, Caroline
False Light
ISBN 0-316-55702-1 (bound) ISBN 0-316-55813-3 (pbk.)
I. Title
PS8573.L.45F35 C813'.54   C96-931446-9
PR9199.3.L.53F35

Designed by Erich Hobbing

Printed in Canada

For
Sarah Frizzell Williams

Chapter 1

The darkroom was his sanctuary. He would come to it in the black hours, or after the frenzy of the act, seeking release. When he bolted the door and switched off the light, he felt at peace. Once inside, he could hear only the sounds of his work, the rhythmic slop of the developing bath in its stainless steel pan, the running water as he rinsed away the dissolved chemicals, or the whir of the extractor fan. Nothing could disturb him here. It was the safest place he knew.

Tonight, however, he found no tranquility with the simple extinguishing of the light. It was as if he had brought in with him some residue of the evening's occupation, to which the room was sensitive.

Ordinarily, he was careful on these occasions to remove every trace of the outside world before he entered. He would strip off his clothes and bundle them up for burning later, when it was dark, on the rubbish heap in the garden. Then he would shower for a long time, paying particular attention to his fingernails, which he would carefully clean with a brush. Afterward, he would put on fresh clothing, usually a clean white shirt and cotton trousers. Only when he considered himself immaculate would he cross the darkroom's threshold.

But this time, in his eagerness for the image, he had come straight from the cliffs, pausing only to wash his hands at the kitchen sink. They were trembling now as he removed the film from the camera.

He knew he ought to wait, but the climax that he sought came only when he could see what he had done. Everything led up to the moment of looking. The completion of the photograph meant the act it pictured was finished. Until then, he himself was incomplete.

He must look. When he saw, he would be free again, for a little while.

With his eyes closed, he loaded the black-and-white film into the developing tank. What was the point of keeping them open in a darkness so absolute? If necessary, he could process the film entirely without light—the steps were second nature to him, and his materials were always kept in perfect order. He could stretch out his hand in the darkness to whatever he required with the certainty he would find it in its proper place.

He had practiced the same discipline over his actions earlier this evening. The necessity to punish never interfered with his self-control. Everything had been thought through, prepared, nothing left to chance. The site had been carefully selected for its complementary qualities of concealment and, from certain vantage points, spectacular revelation; lenses and angles had been considered; the time chosen for optimum light.

Even that other variable, the human element, had conformed. But he had known she would come. People were as predictable as the process taking place under his fingers, as long as one knew precisely what one was doing.

This reflection calmed him. As he rinsed and fixed the film, all his actions were smooth and consistent.

While he worked, he recalled the events on the cliff in a series of images that duplicated those on the film. This was a crucial part of the process. He found it not only cathartic but somehow intrinsic to the final picture. If he had been able to talk to anyone about it, he would have described it, with a certain humor, as the emotional development of the latent image.

When the film was dry he made his contact sheet and examined it for the frames most likely to produce the best enlargements. All the frames showed the same subject, shot from various angles and distances. He printed a number of them in varying sizes, experimenting with papers, filters, and exposure times, until he was satisfied.

Now he was free to indulge in the mental re-creation of the act that had led to the making of these images. The memory was pleasurably uncomplicated by the many factors he'd had to keep in mind during the act itself. Not that the successful resolution of these technical problems hadn't given him a great deal of satisfaction. But they had distracted him from achieving the release he needed. That only came now, as he lost himself in these final, immutable images.

With a sigh like a whisper, he slumped in the chair.

After a while, he got up and unlocked a small steel filing cabinet hidden beneath a movable counter. He placed the photographs, each protected by a sheet of pure white tissue paper, vertically in the cabinet, with cardboard separators between them.

Later that night he burned the negatives, contact sheet, and test photos, along with his clothes. The acrid smoke left a gray smear against the silver tones of the moonlit sky, like a careless thumb. As he raked the embers, he reflected on his mistakes. He would do better the next time.

Chapter 2

In Sloane Square taxis darted like water beetles through the rain, paused briefly to disgorge passengers in front of the Kazanjian Gallery, then sped off again, their black carapaces glittering under the streetlights.

A brightly lit black-and-white poster shone in the gallery's rain-streaked window. It showed a rounded mass of stippled light rising from vast shadowy depths, an image mysterious yet familiar. Underneath this enlarged reproduction of an 1851 daguerreotype of the moon were printed the words LIGHT YEARS: AN EXHIBITION OF EARLY VICTORIAN PHOTOGRAPHS. A yellow banner pasted to the bottom of the poster announced that tonight was the exhibit's opening, with an auction to benefit The Society for the Preservation of Antiquarian Photographs.

Dana Morrow came out onto the pavement from the nearby Underground station, saw the rain, and groaned. It hadn't occurred to her to bring an umbrella. Not an hour ago it had been a mild May evening with swallows skimming the rooftops and a cricket game on the common behind the house in which she was staying for the summer.

She dashed toward the Kazanjian Gallery with her head bent and one arm raised above it to keep her hair dry, colliding at the entrance with a man who had paused to collapse his umbrella. He waved aside her apologies, then opened the door and stood back to let her pass through ahead of him.

As she glanced up to thank him, she took in a lean, angular face with an aggressive-looking nose and mouth and dark-browed blue eyes. The fleeting thought that he was attractive gave way to alarm at the sight of the crowd inside the gallery. She would have to hurry or she would never get a seat.

A noisy crush of Londoners, ranging from the fashionably dressed to the scruffy, thronged the circular marble-floored foyer. Dana surrendered her ticket, checked her coat, and registered for the auction. She was given a catalog and a small paddle, which she was told to raise when she wanted to bid. She then went up the curving staircase to the auction room on the second floor, where she managed to claim an empty seat in the middle of a row of chairs near the front.

She riffled unseeing through the exhibition catalog as she tried to quell her rising excitement. A neophyte, she nevertheless knew enough about auctions to realize how easy it was to be carried away. She couldn't really afford to be here at all; the cost of the ticket alone had put a dent in the week's budget. But there was only one item she wanted and she had no intention of bidding beyond her limit for it.

A notice of the exhibition had appeared in that morning's *Independent*. When she read that the exhibit would include photographs by Henry Arlington Hobhouse, and that a rare portrait of the photographer's first wife would be among those for sale at the charity auction, she had abandoned her breakfast and gone straight to the gallery for the open preview. An attendant had directed her to the small room where the photographs donated for auction were hanging.

There she had seen the portrait of the young woman she had virtually lived with for the past three months.

Like a mid-Victorian Madonna, Marianna Hobhouse stared gravely out from a small oval frame with her hands pressed to her breast and her large dark eyes cast upward, as though fixed on some heavenly vision. Light haloed the mass of dark hair, which was parted in the center and looped back from a face beautiful in the fashion of her time, straight-browed and smoothly oval.

Surrounded by larger and more obviously appealing prints, the photograph had appeared at first glance insignificant. A small faded monochrome barely four inches high, it was badly foxed in one corner, with several scratches across its lower half, and its undecorated gilt frame was spotted with age.

None of this mattered to Dana. In fact, she hoped the photograph's defects would work to her advantage. The unprepossessing appearance might deflect attention to more striking photographs, and the condition could affect the amount those who were interested would be willing to pay. As for herself, she cared only that it was a picture of the elusive woman whose story she was beginning to believe might be as sinister as it was tragic.

An excited rustling, like birds settling to roost, filled the auction room. Dana looked up to see the auctioneer walk onto the dais. A hush fell on the crowd. Dana found that she was trembling.

The auctioneer began by exhorting the audience to remember that it was here to support the work of The Society for the Preservation of Antiquarian Photographs, a group devoted to rescuing old photographs from destruction.

"You will have the satisfaction not only of helping to preserve our past," he said in a suave, persuasive voice, "but of owning a tangible image of that past. Be generous, and you may find that your generosity is rewarded. The old chestnut tells us that a photograph is worth a thousand words. A number of the photographs here tonight are certainly worth a thousand pounds, and may someday be worth a hundred times that amount."

Smoothly, he disposed of lot after lot. To her dismay, Dana found that the bids were generally much higher than she had anticipated. Either the charitable impulse was loosening wallets, or old photographs had achieved the status of art objects.

At last, he arrived at the photograph of Marianna Hobhouse.

"Ladies and gentlemen, we come now to lot twelve, 'Fixed by Light.' This is an original albumen print of 1863 by the noted photographer Henry Arlington Hobhouse. It is signed, titled, and dated by the photographer. It is believed to be of his first wife, Marianna, and we know of only one other photograph of this rather mysterious woman.

"Although perhaps not of the remarkable quality of the best of Henry Hobhouse's portraits, some of which are certainly the equal of those by Julia Margaret Cameron, this is a fine example of his ability to capture the spirit of his subject. And I use the word 'spirit' deliberately. Those of you who have seen the photograph in the viewing room may have discerned a certain, shall we say, spiritual quality. If so, you may congratulate yourselves on your perception. Marianna Hobhouse was in fact a well-known medium in her day, consulted by such eminent Victorians as Sir Edward Bulwer-Lytton and Elizabeth Barrett Browning. Her career is believed to have ended in some sort of scandal, which was suppressed, and she went mad. She died shortly afterwards in an asylum."

Dana found herself resenting this gossipy, tabloid summary of Marianna's life, resenting even the mention of that life. Over the course of the past few months she had come to feel that the medium's story was somehow her—Dana's—own personal property, her discovery, and that no one but she had any right to speak of it until her work was done and the story published.

She recognized this as possessive nonsense, the jealous territoriality of a researcher too involved with her work. The auctioneer was simply doing his job. And anyone knowledgeable about Henry Hobhouse was likely to know something about Marianna.

All the same, she wished he hadn't made Marianna so interesting. This looked to her like a fairly literate crowd, if you could judge that sort of thing by the number of people in sweater vests and eyeglasses. What if someone here were sufficiently intrigued by what he had said to think of pursuing it? Writers were always looking for material. . . . This was paranoia! She willed herself to relax.

"I think you will agree with me," the auctioneer was saying, "that Marianna's story makes this photograph of particular interest. Shall we start the bidding at two hundred pounds?"

A paddle in the front row shot up.

The auctioneer nodded. "Do I hear two hundred and twenty?"

Dana raised her own paddle. Her limit was three hundred pounds, an extravagance in terms of her instructor's salary at New York University but one she felt she could justify in this case. However, various voices soon raised the bidding well beyond that amount and she was forced to drop out. A sick chill of disappointment told her just how much she had wanted the photograph.

A well-dressed Japanese man bid four hundred pounds, and was immediately trumped by a woman swathed in a purple scarf sitting near Dana. From somewhere at the back another man bid four hundred and fifty, a fellow American to judge by his voice. The Japanese returned with five hundred.

"Five hundred and fifty," Dana shouted.

She was crazy to be doing this, she told herself. An untenured lecturer with student loans to pay off had no business spending close to eight hundred dollars on a photograph. But the thought that someone else might win Marianna had become unbearable.

The paddle in the front row went up again.

"I have six hundred," said the auctioneer. He looked expectantly at Dana, as if he sensed her potential for reckless behavior.

"Seven!" she obliged, feverish, almost light-headed, with her own daring. The more her chances of owning the photograph were threatened, the greater her need to possess it seemed to become.

In a matter of moments the bidding reached a thousand pounds, while the number of bidders narrowed to three: the woman in the purple scarf, the American somewhere at the back, and Dana.

Purple Scarf bid eleven hundred pounds, and Dana countered with twelve. Then Purple Scarf's companion, a florid-faced man in his fifties, leaned over to whisper in her ear. The man in the back was silent.

"I have twelve hundred pounds," the auctioneer urged. "Do I hear thirteen?"

Dana felt ill. Barely a week into her stay in London, she had with a single phrase squandered nearly a fourth of the grant meant to support the entire summer's research.

"Thirteen." It was the man in the back.

When her body sagged with relief, Dana realized how frightened she had been. However, she and her work were safe now. All she had to do was keep still.

But a small warning voice inside her was saying, It's what you don't do that haunts you, the chances you let slip that you regret. Marianna's soulful, enigmatic face rose up before her. She thought of what it would mean to have that face in front of her while she worked. . . .

Purple Scarf shook her head angrily at the man with her. "Fourteen hundred," the woman snapped out, wielding her paddle like a flyswatter intended to squash opposition.

Act now, pleaded the interior voice.

"Fifteen hundred!"

She had to force the words out, and her breathlessness turned them into a gasp. As a ripple of amusement went through the audience, faces looked her way. She could feel her own face flame with embarrassment. Fifteen hundred? the auctioneer repeated. She nodded; she could not speak.

That's enough, she told herself sharply as Purple Scarf came to her rescue with a bid of sixteen hundred. Not only do you sound foolish, you are foolish. The book matters far more than any photograph, no matter how seductive. Without money, the book won't get written, and without a book you won't get promoted, and that will be the end of your short academic career.

The bidding war between Purple Scarf and the American quickly escalated far beyond anything she could possibly have fooled herself into believing she could afford. At least she would not be left wondering if she had quit too soon. All she could do now was hope that the winner would allow her to use a reproduction of the photograph in her book. She tried to assess her chances of success from the faces of the two contestants.

Purple Scarf had a sharp, expensively maintained profile under upswept blond hair. She sat leaning forward, chin out, thin red mouth tightly compressed. As the price reached two thousand, her companion again muttered something in her ear. She frowned, then raised her bid to twenty-five hundred.

Immediately Dana turned around to locate the American. She hoped he would look more approachable.

"Twenty-eight hundred," he called. He was standing by the door, a dark-haired man in his early thirties dressed in a loose, wheat-colored linen jacket over a white shirt and jeans. It was the man she had bumped into outside the gallery. He stood with his hands in his pockets, leaning with one shoulder against the door jamb, at his ease. Like someone comfortably prepared to stand there all night until he got what he wanted.

"Three thousand," the woman in the purple scarf returned, but it seemed to Dana that her voice was slightly less self-assured.

"Three thousand, five hundred." The man's voice, on the other hand, was as calm as it had been all along. It sounded as though he could go on forever. Perhaps his rival felt this, for she abruptly gave up, throwing herself back in the seat with a little shrug, as of sudden boredom with the game. Her companion attempted to pat her shoulder but she batted his hand away with the paddle.

Dana was amused by her own relieved reaction to the American's triumph; the thought of Marianna's photograph in Purple Scarf's hands had become decidedly distasteful. And a fellow countryman, she thought, might be more inclined to agree to her request for a copy.

The auctioneer congratulated the winner and moved on to the next item. As Dana negotiated her way along the narrow row to the center aisle, she saw one of the auctioneer's assistants go up to the American. The two stood together for a moment while the assistant wrote something down in the notebook she carried. Before she could reach them, however, their short conversation ended and the man left the room.

By the time she herself came out into the hallway he was nowhere in sight.

She stood for a moment at the top of the stairs looking down into the central well of the foyer, but she could not see him among the crowd below. Presumably, however, the auctioneer's assistant had been recording his name, and he would return to pay for his prize later, when the auction was over. One way or another she should be able to find out who he was. In the meantime she would go and say good-bye to Marianna.

Chapter 3

Dana bought a glass of white wine from the bar set up on the far side of the foyer, then made her way through the crowd into the main exhibition room.

When she had first seen them, that morning, the luminous monochromes hanging on the walls had been a revelation to her. She had not known photographs could be so beautiful. Subtle, serene, they glowed softly in tones of sepia, silver, and golden brown, with the iconic presence of the antique. They had seemed to her then like whispered messages from some more noble, vanished age, poignant with loss.

Tonight, in the presence of the colorful mob that jostled and babbled, drinks in hand, the photographs were somehow diminished. Too delicate to compete with so much visual distraction, they had withdrawn into their shimmering shells like underwater creatures exposed to the sun.

But now, as she edged her way through the room, a pair of photographs she hadn't noticed before caught her eye. Serene was the last word that anyone would apply to these.

Each showed an intently smiling woman with disheveled hair and clothes and wide staring eyes whose pupils were completely ringed by white. If there was happiness in those smiles, it was of a kind better left unexperienced. Their gaze was so disturbing that Dana found she had to look away.

According to the catalog, the two women had been inmates of the Surrey County Asylum during the 1850s. The asylum superintendent, she read, a Dr. Hugh Diamond, had been one of the first to propose the photographic documentation of psychological reactions and mental abnormalities, and had taken many of his patients' photographs. Had Marianna Hobhouse come to look like these women, Dana wondered, with the same fixed smile and vacant eyes? She felt a faint revulsion at the possibility.

She made a note in the back of the catalog to remember Dr. Diamond and his inmates for her research. As she moved away she saw two fashionably dressed women pose obligingly for a photographer. She smiled to herself when she realized that the photographer was placing his unsuspecting subjects in such a way that Diamond's patients would appear with them in the picture, commentators on the social scene.

With relief, she escaped into the small room where the auction photographs were hanging. Here, farther from the food and drink, there were fewer people and, consequently, less noise and jostling for position.

At the sight of Marianna's photograph, she felt a sharp pang of regret. She tried to comfort herself with the thought that perhaps the attribution was mistaken, that it was not Marianna after all. But she knew that it was. The face too closely resembled the one other photograph of the medium she had seen in a published collection of Henry Hobhouse's work, and it had the same slight but noticeable asymmetry. Moreover, the title, "Fixed by Light," was a phrase Marianna had used to describe the way she felt during her trance states.

Marianna's enigmatic gaze was lifted toward the light that flowed down into the photograph from some invisible source. Unlike other mediums, she had conducted her seances in well-lit rooms. The spirits, she had written, "yearn towards our light as we do theirs." In her face, Dana could see no sign of the madness that would engulf Marianna a few years later. The thin cheeks and hollowed eyes hinted at her frailty, and the asymmetry at the mild form of epilepsy from which she might have suffered, but compared to the faces in Dr. Diamond's portraits, Marianna's seemed healthy and sane. On the other hand, Dana told herself, lunacy wasn't necessarily visible in the features.

As she contemplated the photograph, she let her thoughts range over what she knew of Marianna's life. Apart from its tragic end, that life had not been so very different from those of many other young women of her class and time. Dana had begun to piece together the details from various official documents, including the reports on Marianna's case by the Commissioners in Lunacy, who reviewed the situations of asylum inmates, and from Marianna's own writings—a privately published pamphlet and her letters to the commissioners.

The sickly, sensitive daughter of a wealthy London merchant, Marianna had seen her mother and three brothers all die of fevers within a few months of one another in 1852, when she was thirteen. Fearful for his only remaining child, her father had kept her "like a pheasant under glass," as she put it in one of her letters, cosseted, protected, and imprisoned. Her account of the life she had led, cloistered to the point of claustrophobia in the dim, shuttered rooms of the gloomy family home in Stanhope Place, reminded Dana of Elizabeth Barrett Browning's description of her sealed and airless chamber in Wimpole Street, where the dust lay like sand underfoot.

At seventeen, Marianna had discovered her gift. Seriously ill with a fever, she had fallen into a trance during which the spirits of her dead mother and brothers appeared in a cloud of light and spoke to her, recalling her to life. After this, she wrote, her mind became "a sort of whispering gallery" that enabled her to hear the voices of her dead loved ones. As she lay recuperating from her illness, she felt a sudden, violent trembling in her right hand and a simultaneous compulsion to write. The outpouring of words onto paper proved to be another way to talk to her spirits and to escape the confines of her straitened life. She spent hours at her writing table, questioning the spirits and recording their answers. Overjoyed by these miraculous signs that his wife and sons remained with him even after death, Marianna's father encouraged her in her communication with them. He would not, however, allow her to leave the parental home or to see anyone other than the few friends and relatives who were invited to participate in Marianna's seances.

"Do you think she was a fraud?"

The familiar voice that broke into Dana's thoughts made her start. Wine slopped over the side of her glass onto her dress, a caramel-colored jersey bought on sale just before she'd left New York, expensive but impossible to resist because it made her light brown hair look blonder. But she suppressed the curse that rose to her lips, for the voice belonged to the new owner of the photograph, who had come up unnoticed beside her.

"I'm sorry, I didn't mean to startle you. Here, use this." He took a crumpled handkerchief from his jacket pocket and gave it to her. "It may not look it, but it's clean." Contrite, he offered to pay her cleaning bill.

"That's not necessary," she said stiffly, flustered by his sudden presence and her own reaction. "White wine won't leave a stain."

While he held her glass and catalog, she blotted up the wine—and found herself registering details. The piercing blue eyes; the longish auburn hair, so dark that from a distance she had mistaken it for black; the prominent nose and firm, humorous mouth; and the appealingly low-key manner, which seemed in keeping with the agreeable voice. All these confirmed her first impression, that this was an attractive man. But a significant part of that attractiveness, she realized, stemmed from a slight but distinct contradiction between the manner and the acute blue gaze, which suggested a power deliberately restrained.

She exchanged the damp handkerchief for her glass of wine, slipping the catalog into her shoulder bag, then glanced again at Marianna. Had she been a fraud? Had she resorted to the tricks unscrupulous mediums used to gull their victims? At the beginning of her research, Dana had often asked herself these questions. But by now she was persuaded that Marianna had genuinely believed in her spiritualistic powers. The trance states and automatic writing may have been self-induced, but not with the intention of deceiving others. Marianna had used them to escape the circumstances of her life.

"No," Dana replied at last, "no, I don't think she was a fraud. Do you?"

"Aren't the words medium and fraud synonymous?" He sounded more curious than accusatory.

"That depends on whether the medium believes in what she's doing." She drank some of her wine, to quell a slight nervousness; after all, he had the power to refuse her request to use Marianna's photograph.

He said lightly, "A cynic might say that all a medium believes in is her client's money."

"But then it's easier for a cynic to understand avarice than faith, isn't it? Besides, Marianna never took money for her seances. She didn't need to. She was a rich woman." Dana was tempted to add, but did not for fear he would think she was lecturing him, that money had rarely been the motivation of middle-class mediums.

"Not a fraud, then. Just delusional?"

"Or someone extraordinarily gifted who didn't conform to conventional expectations."

"It's too bad you weren't her lawyer, or her doctor. You might have kept her out of the asylum. The ones she had didn't do her much good."

"That's not surprising. Given that her husband chose them."

Immediately, Dana regretted the words and her sharp tone. It was a sign of how involved with Marianna she'd become that she had responded so defensively to his comment. But she viewed Henry Hobhouse as Marianna's nemesis, the person most responsible for her destruction.

This man, however, might have an entirely different take on the Hobhouse marriage, might see Henry much as Marianna must have seen him at first, as her rescuer. Dana tried to gauge from his face if he was offended by her response; she could not afford to annoy him.

His expression seemed merely interested. "You think Henry was too 'conventional' to understand Marianna?"

"Perhaps." She was being deliberately disingenuous. In her opinion, "conventional" was far too mild a word to describe Henry Hobhouse. Marianna's relationship with Henry might appear to some to be the classic story of a young woman trading one form of benign but confining paternalism for another, but it struck Dana as a much more sinister tale.

Not that Henry himself was obviously sinister. Photographs taken in middle age showed an unexceptional man, heavily bearded, with a long, serious face and watchful eyes, handsome but humorless. A bachelor almost twenty years Marianna's senior, he was just beginning to make a name for himself as a photographer, after years spent working unsuccessfully as an engraver, when he came to Stanhope Place to photograph her father. He and Marianna married a few months after that first meeting, on her eighteenth birthday. Dana was convinced that the marriage was yet another attempt by Marianna to free herself, one that had led, ultimately, to a more devastating imprisonment.

Dana said none of this to her companion, however. By now, she was beginning to worry that his remarks, combined with the purchase of the photograph, might mean that he was interested in Marianna's story himself, might even be writing about her as well.

Warily, she observed that he seemed to know a lot about Marianna Hobhouse.

"That makes two of us."

She decided to be frank, but not completely. "I've been doing some research on British female spiritualism in the nineteenth century. For a book. Marianna intrigues me. That's why I wanted the photograph."

"I'm sorry to have been responsible for disappointing you." The steady gaze seemed genuinely regretful, as if he understood that the picture mattered to her. Of course she had undoubtedly made that plain enough with her idiotic manner of bidding.

"Don't be. You saved me from myself. The price was way out of my league."

"Prices were too high generally. But then it was in a good cause, and the auctioneer was very skillful." He gave a wry smile. "You know the saying, that an auctioneer's a man who announces with a hammer that he's picked your pocket with his tongue."

She laughed. "You seemed a lot calmer than I was about having your pocket picked."

"That's because it wasn't my pocket. I was acting for someone else."

"Oh." Although this relieved her concern that he might be a competitor, it meant that once again Marianna's photograph seemed to recede before her. Then, because she had nothing to lose, she said that she hoped the new owner would allow her to reproduce the photograph in her book.

"You can ask him," he replied noncommittally. "His name's Quentin Finn."

"The photographer?"

He nodded.

Momentarily at a loss, she grappled with the implications of this new development for her research. Quentin Finn not only owned Kerreck Du, the house in Cornwall to which Marianna and Henry Hobhouse had retreated after the mysterious scandal, in the spring of 1870, but a considerable collection of Henry Hobhouse's photographic work and papers. She was intending to write to him, to ask his permission to consult the collection, which she hoped would include material on Marianna. But Finn, who was usually referred to by his last name alone, had a formidable reputation both as a photographer and as an eccentric, and was known to be as fiercely protective of the collection as he was of his privacy.

"Finn will never let you near the Hobhouse material," an academic acquaintance in London who knew him slightly had warned her. "Henry Hobhouse's photographs may be Victorian kitsch to the rest of us, but not to Finn. He's a descendant, you know. A great-grandnephew or some such thing. He bought Kerreck Du and everything in it years ago from an elderly cousin who'd kept it like a shrine. The word is he's planning some sort of book on Hobhouse, to show he's a neglected genius. Finn is very careful about who he allows to see the Hobhouse collection. Afraid of poachers, I suppose. On the other hand, as it's not Henry himself you're interested in. . . ."

However, Quentin Finn's purchase of Marianna's photograph suggested to Dana that he might be as interested in the medium as she was. If this was the case, she thought, he might be even more reluctant to allow her access to his collection. But her hopes rose slightly when her companion now offered to speak to Finn on her behalf. "Though I can't promise that it'll do much good. Finn tends to be wary about things like that."

She thanked him, and then, because something about his pronunciation of certain words made her curious, added impulsively, "You're not American, are you? I mean, I am and I thought you were, too, but the way you speak . . ." Aware that she was floundering, she stopped, embarrassed.

"I'm Canadian. I ought to have introduced myself." He held out his right hand. "My name's Daniel Finn. Quentin Finn is my father."

"Dana Morrow." As they shook hands, she remembered reading that Quentin Finn had come originally from Vancouver.

There was a pause in which neither spoke. It lengthened, but not uncomfortably. She began to feel more optimistic about her chances with Quentin Finn. If he was anything like his son, he might be more approachable than reports had suggested.

"Look," Daniel Finn began abruptly, "about the photograph—" He broke off as a young woman in a black trouser suit approached them.

"Daniel!" she said, reproachful. "I've been looking for you everywhere."

She had a cool, self-possessed beauty and flawless white teeth, revealed by the quick social smile she directed at Dana. Leaning forward, she peered at Marianna's photograph. "My God, Daniel—thirty-five hundred pounds for that! It looks like the cat sicked up its dinner on it. I certainly hope Finn thinks it's worth it." Then she linked her arm through his. "Come on, darling, there's someone I want you to meet."

"Just a minute, Lynn." He took a pen and a piece of paper from his jacket pocket, scribbled something on the paper, and gave it to Dana. "This is Finn's address, and my London number. I'll talk to Finn, but you should write to him as well. Tell him why you want the photograph and maybe a little about yourself. If you don't have any luck with him, let me know."

"Thanks, I will."

As they moved away, Dana heard the other woman ask Daniel Finn what that was all about, but not his own reply. What had it all been about, she wondered. More than a photograph?

Chapter 4

Daniel Finn rode his motorcycle furiously along the deep-cut, ferny lane that led to his cottage, a nineteenth-century schoolhouse a quarter of a mile from the Cornish hamlet of St. Mawl. The Yamaha bounced over the ruts, swerving to miss the low branch of an overhanging hawthorn.

Ordinarily, Daniel enjoyed the ritual of each arrival at the Schoolhouse, navigating his way slowly along the undulating lane through rich green shadows splashed with red campion and foxgloves. He liked the little drama of the approach, the way the lane suddenly shook off the last leafy tentacles of briar and hedgerose to emerge without warning onto the wide treeless headland above the sea where the long, low rectangle of the white-washed Schoolhouse stood.

But now he was impatient to get out on the cliffs with his camera, to salvage something from the day. A strenuous ten-mile hike along the coastal path would exorcise the anger—mostly with himself—roused by the argument with Lynn that morning and aggravated during lunch at Kerreck Du. Dana Morrow had been expected to join them. When she failed to show up, his father had lapsed into the morose abstraction to which he seemed increasingly prone.

The retrospective exhibition of Finn's photographs at the Chapel Gallery in Trebartha would open in three days' time. Now that the months of preparation and work were coming to an end, Finn was showing signs of reverting to the behavior that had followed Solange's death a year ago. Daniel had hoped that Dana Morrow's research into Marianna Hobhouse's life might interest Finn enough to provide a distraction from the inevitable letdown.

True to the promise he'd given her at the auction just over a week ago, Daniel had broached the subject of Marianna's photograph. To his surprise, Finn not only had already agreed that Dana could reproduce it but had gone so far as to invite her down to Kerreck Du. This was precisely what Daniel had hoped he might do. Not so quickly, however; not while life at Kerreck Du was almost as turbulent as it had been when Solange was alive.

The dismay provoked by Finn's swift response to Dana had made Daniel realize that his intercession on her behalf hadn't been entirely altruistic. Her slender, gray-eyed presence lingered in his mind, a piquant combination of uncertainty and self-possession. Details recurred: a curve of cheek and fine-boned wrist; the smooth pale skin, with its faintly olive cast; light on the golden brown hair; and her look, direct, immediately connecting, yet with the sense, too, of something guarded. He wanted to see her again, but not at Kerreck Du. He wanted Finn to help her, but not to become overly involved with her. As it was, his father's wayward curiosity had obviously been aroused. Thwarted, as it had been at lunch, it would only become more intense.

Damn, he thought. Damn, damn.

The bike jolted violently over a deep rut, and he took the last hundred yards with the sudden caution of a man who remembers that the nearest garage is five miles away. As he came over the rise onto the wide, grassy headland, he saw Lynn's gray Volvo still parked by the barred gate at the end of the track that led to the Schoolhouse. His heart sank. He had been so sure she would be gone.

He pulled up beside the Volvo and sat there on the motorcycle with the engine running. Lunch at Kerreck Du had ended early; she might not be expecting him back yet. He could simply ride away again and spend the rest of the afternoon at work. He had the Pentax, after all, in the bike's saddlebags. It would not give him the sharpness of the Leica, but that camera, his favorite, was in the Schoolhouse.

But he could not bring himself to leave. Flight seemed both cowardly and, if Lynn had seen or heard the Yamaha, cruel. And sooner or later they had to face the fact that their relationship wasn't working. If not here, then in London.

The sudden, acute conviction that he couldn't take another

argument with Lynn made him cut the engine and dismount. He opened the gate and wheeled the motorcycle up the track toward the Schoolhouse.

In the days when the local population had been large enough to support one, the tiny white building had been the local dame school. Now St. Mawl's few children were taken by bus to Trebartha, three miles down the coast. Two years ago the Schoolhouse had come up for sale. The fact that Finn had let him know had in itself predisposed him to the place. When he saw it, isolated, neglected, devoid of any attempt at modernization, he had known at once that it was perfect.

No effort had ever been made to soften its plain facade or the starkness of its exposed position on the bare headland. The wind blew unchecked from the sea, rippling the long grasses into green and yellow waves that lapped against the foundations. A wild rosebush grew crookedly against one wall. There was no other house in sight. The single architectural feature that distinguished both the exterior and the large plain room inside, that made them beautiful, was an enormous double-lancet window of leaded glass set into the south wall. It let in a flood of light, and, as Lynn was quick to point out, a vicious draft.

The Schoolhouse was Daniel's refuge, offering him the simplicity that his city life lacked. In London, his days were busy with his freelance digital photographic work for a wide range of clients, work that interested him and paid well but left little time for a private life. His studio cum flat, in the vast top floor of a converted warehouse, was filled with his work, the detritus of his travels, and the computers and other technological tools of his trade. During the working day, which often extended well into the night, he shared the space with assistants, clients, models, and friends.

Here at the Schoolhouse he could be alone, and he had only himself to please. Often the mere sight of it was enough to restore his peace of mind. Deadlines, commitments, questions of taste or cost, would all drop away. Each time he came down from London or returned from his travels he wondered if in his absence the place would somehow have lost its power over him. But he found it always the same, whatever the season, whatever the weather.

In the past, however, he had come by himself. This time, Lynn was with him. She had persuaded him, at a time when their relationship seemed promising, that they should spend a week's vacation here. It was primitive, he warned her. That didn't matter, she blithely replied, it would be an adventure. He then reminded her of the recent deaths of two women on the cliffs. There was talk locally of murder. Would that worry her? No, she replied, she had no intention of walking by herself.

But their affair, which had begun so well, had quickly become complicated by arguments. At first he couldn't understand how these fights started. He blamed himself, accused himself of clumsiness or insensitivity, and did his best to woo Lynn back to him. Gradually, though, he began to realize that Lynn actually enjoyed their arguments, that in some way they excited her and that she deliberately provoked them.

A few days before they were to leave for the Schoolhouse, another quarrel had erupted out of nowhere. When he failed to respond in his usual way with the expected blandishments, Lynn told him angrily that she was going to Dorset instead, to visit friends.

His relief was immense.

Two days after his arrival at the Schoolhouse, however, Lynn had turned up, repentant and at her most seductive and amusing, wanting to make up the quarrel. As before, they'd ended up in bed, and for a few peaceful days he deluded himself with the illusion that she had changed. Then, that morning, they had argued again. For the last time, he told himself now, as he settled the Yamaha onto its kickstand by the front door and went inside.

Lynn was standing in the light from the lancet window, consulting a map spread out on the wooden trestle that served him both as desk and dining table. She wore the dress she'd traveled down in, a tube of pale yellow whose color was a match for her hair. An actress with a small but growing reputation, she had a sure sense of dramatic detail, visible now in the lighting and in her choice of props. Her suitcase, with her raincoat laid across it, stood on the floor beside her.

"I thought you'd be later than this," she said in a toneless voice, without looking up. "I was going to leave before you got back." But he didn't believe her. She had been waiting, he thought, for one last scene.

He said, "Lunch broke up early."

"Not a success, then?"

Despite the question, her voice held no curiosity and her eyes remained on the map. Her face in profile, aloof, severely beautiful, aroused in him something of the old impulse to photograph it, although he had long since learned that its air of cool self-possession, which once had seemed so mysterious and detached, masked a personality at odds with her looks.

"Finn was in a lousy mood. The guest he was expecting never showed up." Generously, because he could afford to be generous now, he added, "You were right to stay away."

They had quarreled that morning over Finn's request that they come to lunch at Kerreck Du. Lynn said she had no intention of spending their last day together in that madhouse. With very few exceptions, she went on, the ménage at Kerreck Du struck her as a particularly disagreeable group of people. Pascale was so silently efficient you hardly knew she was there and John Malzer was rather sweet, but the American girl Karen was a bitch, the beautiful Tim a bore, and the Yugoslav couple the best advertisement she'd seen for the single life. How Nadia Tatevic could justify her ignorance of English after a year here was simply beyond her, especially when her child spoke it so well. That the Tatevics' daughter had turned out so charming was merely proof that changelings existed. But worst of all was Finn's self-appointed patroness. If she had to listen to yet another panegyric from Estelle Pinchot on Finn's artistry, she would strangle the woman. "You know of course she's besotted with your father?" she had continued.

Yes, he'd replied. Although it was really John Malzer that Estelle wanted, he thought. And not for the usual reasons. "She's only renting down here now, but she's been threatening to buy a house."

"How does Finn react to that?"

"With terror."

She'd given a brief, humorless laugh. "Serve him right."

Daniel had understood this to mean that Finn ought to be less free with his embraces. He touched people, put his arm around them, caressed them, because it was in his nature to make physical contact. But it sometimes led to misunderstandings.

Unstated but implicit in Lynn's criticism was a dislike of Finn she concealed from everyone but Daniel. He sometimes wondered if his father's sin, in this instance, was the uncharacteristic one of omission rather than commission. Finn, who flirted with everyone, male as well as female, had not flirted with Lynn. If it had been possible to say anything on the subject, he might have tried to tell her that Finn was acting out of consideration for his, Daniel's, feelings. Although he wasn't so sure that this was the truth. Finn rarely considered anyone else's feelings, Daniel's least of all.

As he agreed for the most part with her assessment of the inhabitants and hangers-on at Kerreck Du, he had not tried to persuade her to change her mind about lunch. He hadn't even bothered to tell her that most of those she disliked wouldn't be there. All he'd said was that he would go alone.

But she had wanted him to stay with her. When he'd refused, citing a promise to Finn, she became furious, threatening to leave at once for London, instead of the following day as planned. He'd simply walked out the door, fed up.

Now she folded up the map and turned to face him.

"So."

He met her gaze but did not speak. The silence between them lengthened. At last, with a rush of words, as though conscious that this was a fence to be taken head-on and very fast, she said, "It's over, isn't it? That's why you let me stay. So I'd realize."

There was the hint of an appeal in her voice, a suppressed plea to tell her she was wrong. The temptation to deny the truth, to placate her, was still there, but this time he resisted it.

"I thought I knew you, Daniel, until I came here. But I'm not sure who you are anymore. It's as if you've turned into someone else. Finn changes you somehow. I wish you'd tell him to go to hell, just once."

He shrugged. She ought to know by now that he had, frequently, to negligible effect. He and his father had long ago worked out a modus vivendi and if it seemed unequal to outsiders, well, that was their problem, not his.

Her eyes narrowed and she stared at him in angry appraisal. "You know, you really should choose another line of work. Get a life, as that tart Karen would say." He saw now that he wasn't going to escape the scene after all. "I'm not denying you're a brilliant photographer, Daniel. It's just that following in the footsteps of a famous father is asking for trouble. And you make the odds worse by coming down here. Though you're clever enough to avoid comparisons." Pointedly, she looked around at the bare white walls. He did not hang his own work here, but not for Lynn's reason.

For such an intelligent woman, he thought, she could sometimes be phenomenally stupid. Her words didn't anger him, however; she no longer had the power to anger him. All he felt was an incipient boredom, which expressed itself in a small internal sigh. She was wrong, he might have told her, his work had nothing to do with Finn's, was entirely different. Only the label, photographer, applied to them both.

But arguing with her was pointless. He did not want their relationship to end in a quarrel; he simply wanted her to go. He ought to have known, however, that his failure to respond would anger her.

She looked around the room, as if searching for further ammunition. And found it easily. "You know what you've got here, don't you?" Her voice was accusing. "A bloody hermit's cell."

He supposed it was true enough. He'd added only a rudimentary kitchen and a bathroom that could double as a darkroom to the single large room. The furnishings were plain, even spartan, and there were few creature comforts to encourage visitors to linger. A scarlet Oriental rug provided the only color; otherwise, white and gray predominated. There was nothing on the walls simply because no photograph, no print or painting could equal the huge window with its view of the ever-changing sea and sky.

"It suits me," he observed mildly, when he saw she would not be satisfied with silence. Only after the words were out did it occur to him that they were cruel.

She picked up her suitcase. "You make it all too obvious that you think I'm excess baggage."

Although he knew it was a mistake, he couldn't help but smile at this. "I've never thought of you as a baggage, Lynn."

"Don't condescend to me! You know perfectly well what I mean." Then she shrugged. "Oh, what's the use."

She refused to let him carry the suitcase but made no objection to his accompanying her to her car. She put the suitcase in the

Volvo's trunk, slammed it shut, then stood for a moment by the car door, looking across the headland toward the sea.

"It's beautiful," she said, after a moment's silence. "But I think it's the loneliest place I've ever been. Perhaps I'd feel differently, if I'd come here when we were happy."

There was nothing he could say to this. Their unhappiness, he believed, was not of his making.

"Or if it didn't seem so haunted."

He thought at first that she was referring to the two women whose cliffside deaths had occurred a few miles down the coast, outside Trebartha. She had admitted to feeling some fear after all, despite the earlier bravado.

But she had something else in mind.

"It's time you stopped mourning Solange, Daniel. She wasn't yours anymore anyway."

As a parting shaft, it was stunning. He could only stare at her, amazed that she knew, as his face stiffened with the effort of masking his emotions.

Something must have shown in his eyes, however. She flushed, and her own eyes were suddenly uncertain, as though she recognized that she had gone too far. Abruptly, she got into the car, switched on the engine, and reversed with a harsh grinding of gears. She lifted her hand in a cursory farewell, and then, without looking at him again, drove away.

Whatever regret he might have felt was effectively banished by this last example of her need to hurt him. Desperate now to get out onto the cliffs, he went back to the Schoolhouse and changed hurriedly into hiking clothes and boots. He was about to leave, Leica in hand, when the phone rang. Tempted at first not to answer, he gave in and picked up the receiver only to hear Estelle Pinchot's piercing, slightly breathless voice on the other end. She had been ringing Kerreck Du, she announced, but there was no answer. Would Daniel be kind enough to tell her where Finn was?

How the hell should I know, he wanted to ask her, but did not. Estelle was obtuse when it came to the feelings of others, but was easily hurt herself and very quick to take offense. Politely, he said that he had no idea where Finn was.

"Well, never mind. I'm sure he'll be back by teatime. He knows

John and I are coming over then. John has an absolutely brilliant idea for the exhibition. Finn will love it."

Privately, Daniel doubted that. John Malzer was a clever man with a pronounced flair for mounting provocative exhibits, but Finn had a clear conception of how he wanted his work shown. Nothing would be allowed to interfere with that.

"We'll see you at teatime, then?" Estelle was asking.

"I'm afraid not. I have some things that need taking care of."

"What a pity. I had so looked forward to seeing Lynn again. Such a lovely girl. Now if only Pascale—"

He interrupted with a muttered excuse about an appointment, and hung up. He had no desire to discuss Lynn with Estelle. Or to listen to her comments on Pascale. He knew exactly how she felt about his father's sister-in-law. Like many others, he thought, she misunderstood the relationship and misjudged Pascale.

A few minutes later he reached the cliff path, a pale ribbon of beaten earth, which wound through thickets of scented yellow gorse and around great, grass-mantled outcroppings of rock, high above the sea. At the foot of the cliffs, broad streaks of liquid emerald and turquoise swirled around the black rock, frothed with a foam of creamy lace. As he hesitated, debating his direction, a solitary gull swooped down to perch on a nearby fence post, facing the sea's horizon like some watchful coast patrol.

His usual route was westward, toward Trebartha and beyond, to photograph the Stacks, whose rocky pillars rose from the sea in bizarre patterns that shifted with the changing light. But now, prompted by Lynn's last words, he took the path to the east, in the direction of Kerreck Du. This time, he thought, if he looked long enough, hard enough, at the place where Solange had died, he might succeed in cauterizing the wound so thoroughly that he would seal it shut forever.

Chapter 5

In a maze of narrow Cornish lanes sunk so deeply in their hedge-banks that the branches of beech and elm arched overhead like a green sky, Dana acknowledged to herself that she had lost her way.

She gave Quentin Finn's map a last, skeptical glance. It no longer seemed trustworthy, and the directions to Kerreck Du scribbled in its margin now looked deliberately illegible. Twice she had retraced her route and set off in a new direction only to find herself once more at the same crossroads. The decision to walk from the bus station in Trebartha had been a mistake. She ought to have taken a taxi, despite the expense. But the fine morning and the temptation to wander lanes once frequented by Marianna Hobhouse had been too appealing to resist.

Well, she had certainly wandered, and meanwhile the fine morning had become a warm and humid afternoon. Her shoulders ached from the weight of her knapsack and her shirt was clinging stickily to her skin. She pushed her hair off her damp forehead. It was nearly two, long past the time she was expected. Resigned, she shrugged off the heavy pack and sat down on a moss-covered log. The air smelled of fern and wild garlic; sunlight and birdsong spilled down through the fretwork of branches. Time had ceased to matter, now that she was late, and for a little while she let the lane's narrow green world hold her in its spell.

As she massaged the muscles in her shoulders, she felt as if more than the weight of the pack had slipped from her. The foreign yet familiar countryside and the prospect of the work that lay ahead had somehow combined to ease the burden of the last two years. What did it matter that she was lost, or that she might never gain access to the Hobhouse collection? She had been right to come.

Through half-closed lids, she stared drowsily down the green tunnel. A nimbus of filtered light played over the ivy-smothered trunk of a dying elm. It might almost be the sad ghost of Marianna Hobhouse, she thought, yearning toward her on the current of mutual sympathy that the young medium had believed could resurrect the dead. That current would flow far more strongly here than in dim library stacks and carrels. It was tugging at Dana now.

Dana knew what it was like to suffer as had Marianna the early death of a parent and an unborn child, and the failure of a marriage. She knew, too, that Marianna's sufferings were a part of the medium's attraction for her. While Dana's own marriage disintegrated, she had been writing a paper about the Brownings, Robert and Elizabeth, a study of the way in which each poet had responded to the rise of spiritualism. She had once imagined that their intellectual and emotional harmony—in all things but spiritualism—was not so very different from hers and Stewart's, her former husband. Brutally disabused of this illusion, she could only see the Brownings' domestic bliss as an ironic commentary on her own marriage. She put her paper aside, incomplete.

Casting about for another project, adrift and unhappy, she had by chance come across a brief account of Marianna's mediumship and incarceration. Intrigued, she dug deeper. Bit by bit, Marianna's story took hold of her. Something in it seemed to cast a light on her own.

Dana looked around. It was odd, she thought, how in even the loneliest places—perhaps especially in such places—you could persuade yourself that you were watched. But in the last half hour she had seen no one, and no car had passed her. Kerreck Du was on a peninsula, remote, isolated from main roads. Trebartha, the nearest town, was now, according to a signpost she'd passed, more than four miles away. Apart from the occasional roadside bungalow or farmhouse glimpsed through a hedgebank, or the steeple of a church in a valley, she saw few signs that anyone at all lived in this countryside.

To reassure herself of her welcome, she took out Finn's letter and read it again.

It was a reply to her own requesting permission not only to duplicate Marianna's photograph but also to visit Kerreck Du and to consult the Hobhouse collection. She had given her academic bona fides—her instructorship at NYU, the fellowship financing the summer's research in London—and explained that she was writing a book on the role played by female mediums in nineteenth-century England. Marianna Hobhouse's tragic story, she'd said in her letter, perfectly illustrated the complicated issues involved. A visit to the house in which the medium and her husband once had lived, a look at her papers, and at anything else that had belonged to her, would help to illuminate certain aspects of that story.

In her letter, Dana had tried to make it very clear that Marianna was her focus. Her book would attempt to conjure up Marianna's spirit, she wrote, half-facetiously, to make her come to life for modern readers. The Victorian medium had languished in her more famous husband's shadow for too long. Henry Hobhouse's photographic work, while admittedly remarkable, only interested her insofar as it touched on his wife's life.

As Marianna's life had been short, thirty-one years, and as much of Henry's work had come after her death, Dana hoped that Quentin Finn would see her research as no threat to his own.

He wrote back by return post.

Come, the brief, elliptical note replied. Her project interested him. He promised nothing, but was open to persuasion. He named a date five days off and said that unless he heard otherwise he would expect her then, for lunch. She should stay at Kerreck Du; the house always had room for one more, if the guest had a tolerance for chaos. His signature was the single syllable, Finn, in a spiky blue script with the "F" hugely dominant.

Underneath, as though in afterthought, he had written slantwise across the page, "If you want a spirit to speak, you know, you must give it a bowlful of blood."

Melodramatic words. But Quentin Finn's reputation as a photographer once had rested on an ability to shock and provoke, to titillate with images that hinted at the unthinkable. That talent might express itself in other ways as well. And she herself had referred to Marianna Hobhouse's spirit.

As she returned the letter to its envelope, three children appeared around a bend in the lane, a small boy and a girl in her early teens pushing a baby in a stroller. Dressed in T-shirts and shorts, the two older children trudged toward her with their heads down. Their attention was fixed on something the boy held in one hand. As they drew closer, Dana heard the manic music of an electronic game.

A woman with a backpack was nothing out of the ordinary in this part of the world, whose coast was a lure for hikers, and the boy's eyes flicked over Dana and back to his game. He was about seven, with freckled, rabbity features and lank brown hair. The girl's gaze lingered with a female curiosity. The baby was slumped down in the stroller, asleep, and at the sight of the small form, Dana felt the familiar pang of loss.

She asked the children if they knew a house called Kerreck Du.

The girl nodded, biting her lip, while the boy lifted his head to give Dana a sideways, almost furtive, look from under sparse lashes. He switched off the game, as though she had become more interesting.

"That's where those foreign loonies have their orgies," he said to the girl, before she could speak. He gave orgies a hard g, so that for a moment Dana thought he was speaking of the Queen's favorite dog.

The girl frowned at him, blushing. "That's all a load of rubbish, Ernie." Her contemptuous tone was a grownup's, her mother's perhaps. Obviously the boy's sister, she had the same short nose and raised upper lip. "Never mind him, he's only little," she told Dana. "He doesn't know what he's talking about."

"I do." He glared up at her, indignant. "Mick told me. He saw 'em in Tantry's Cove, the folk who live there, and they didn't have no clothes on either. Any clothes on," he amended carefully. "They were having an orgy. And taking pictures of it. Mick said." As if that clinched the matter, he turned away from the girl to stare at Dana.

"You American, miss?"

"Don't be so nosy, Ernie," the girl told him sharply.

"Only I was wondering," he went on, ignoring her, " 'cos they're foreigners, too, those people."

The girl shushed him by clapping her hand over his mouth. He struggled briefly, then fell silent, diverted by the sight of a toad. It was sidling away toward the opposite hedgebank. He went to examine it while his sister described the way to Kerreck Du.

"Go straight on," she told Dana. "There's a shortcut, 'bout a quarter of a mile on the left. It's a footpath through a wood, and it comes out onto a hillside field, behind the house." With a bitten fingernail, she traced the route on the map. "Otherwise, you got to go back the way you come and take the second lane at the crossroads. See." Dana had already rejected this lane because it seemed to be heading in the wrong direction. But the girl assured her it would eventually bring her to the main drive to Kerreck Du, hidden from the lane in a little valley that ran down to the sea.

"It's a bit of a ways, the lane," she warned. "The path'll be quicker."

The boy, meanwhile, had found a stick and was prodding experimentally at the toad. His sister was on him at once, jerking the stick from his hand and pulling him back.

"What do you want to go and do that for? It'll spit poison at you, the nasty thing!"

It was the boy's turn to be contemptuous. "Nah, they don't do that. That's just stories."

"Come on," she urged. "Mum'll be getting worried."

His small face lit up with an oddly malicious smile. "She'll think the gull got us." He glanced at Dana, as if expecting some response to this from her.

"Don't start on that," the girl told him fiercely.

"I'm the gull," he jeered, flapping his arms up and down at his sister. "Peck, peck, pe—" Once again his words were stifled by her hand over his mouth.

"You just shut up, Ernie!" Gripping him firmly by the upper arm, the girl began to drag him after her as she pushed the stroller with the sleeping baby ahead of her with her other hand. He cast a last longing glance at the toad, which was making its clumsy escape into the hedge, and let himself be hauled along. Dana picked up her pack and swung it over her shoulder. She would try the footpath; anything to avoid retracing her steps a third time.

As the children turned a corner, the boy wrenched free of his sister's hand and shouted back at Dana.

"Mind the naked loonies!"

His sister collared him and they vanished. It was a joke, his retreating laughter seemed to say, a joke at Dana's expense.

As she walked along, she wondered what Quentin Finn would make of the boy's description of his home. It might have amused him once, when he had apparently cultivated his outrageous reputation. But now? Reformed rakes were reputed to be the greatest puritans, and puritans weren't known for a sense of humor. But perhaps his reformation wasn't yet complete.

Curious to know something about the man she was going to meet, she had spent several hours scanning a clutch of magazine articles written about him over the years. She hoped he would prove to be approachable, but what she learned from the rich fund of gossip, reminiscence, and critical appraisal was intimidating rather than encouraging. In hyperbolic journalese at least, Quentin Finn sounded formidable.

A young Canadian expatriate in sixties London, he had made a name and a small fortune as a photographer with an uncanny ability to charge his pictures with a powerful current of sexual energy. By all accounts, he had not confined this talent to photography. "Everyone found him seductive," confided a former model and lover. "Except fathers, of course."

He inspired what seemed to Dana extravagant quotes. "He's drawn to the demonic. He'll find it in the most angelic subject." This from a picture editor he'd worked with. "Some people say he gets the soul and sometimes he doesn't give it back," said an ex-assistant, who described Finn's work habits as "diabolical—I don't think the man sleeps." A former crony, recalling various adventures together, put it less romantically: "Finn goes to prove that old cliché, that all good photographers are crazy."

His own words, Dana found, could be just as provocative. "Photography's been described as a brothel without walls," he'd announced to an interviewer in one early profile. "So call me Madam." And, a decade later: "You know what the sixties were all about? Nostalgie de la boue. My pictures made the mud look good."

Beautiful women, the natural subjects of most of his work for fashion magazines, were transformed into icons by his camera. He preferred working with women, he said, because his photographs were most successful when there was "a certain mutual appreciation" between himself and his subject. But he also gave a sinister glamour to males in his grainy, high-contrast black-and-white portraits of working-class heroes, notorious sociopaths, and the bell-bottomed offspring of England's aristocracy.

All the while, Dana discovered, he had also been making monochromatic montages of dreamlike images utterly unlike his commercial work. Surreal pictures of urban and domestic buildings invaded and reclaimed by the natural world. Of floating trees whose exposed roots spread above children asleep among ferns. Of women's bodies evolving, dryadlike, into or out of some aspect of the landscape.

This landscape, the one around her, Dana thought now, looking about. Like his forebear Henry Hobhouse, Finn used the countryside near Kerreck Du as inspiration for his work.

Technically expert—he was described as a "magician with the enlarger"—Finn composed these photographs in the darkroom from a number of different negatives, producing prints with seamless precision; again, like Henry Hobhouse. Beyond giving them titles, Finn refused to interpret them. "I like enigmas," he'd said. "The photographs—and characters—which interest me most are those that sustain their mystery."

Viewed as a product of the sixties' taste for phantasmagoria, and disdained by critics who admired "straight" photography, his combination prints were largely ignored for many years. "Finn's trick pics," an unfriendly critic labeled them after an exhibition in the late seventies, and went on to suggest that Finn had fallen too much under the influence of his Victorian ancestor, Henry Hobhouse.

Leafing through a book of Finn's work, Dana had found these black-and-white photographs beautiful and disturbing, their tones opulent, the subjects both complicated and evocative. One in particular leaped out at her. Her own recurring childhood nightmare materialized in the image of a small child standing in a vast empty space that might have been an attic, where the walls bulged with the pressure of some unseen presence.

By the mid-eighties, Finn had given up most of his fashion and advertising assignments to concentrate on his composite photographs. These gradually began to gain more widespread critical approval and were now coveted by collectors and museums. Their value was enhanced by the fact that, after making three prints, Finn destroyed the negatives used to create them. "You have to know when something is finished, and let it be," he said. "I don't want to be tempted to go back."

At the same time, a once chaotic and highly visible personal life apparently grew settled and private. He withdrew from the public eye and began to acquire a reputation as a recluse, by tabloid standards. An early, short-lived marriage to a childhood sweetheart had produced Daniel, his only child, who was now, Dana learned, a successful photographer himself. That marriage had been followed by a period of rampant and notorious hedonism, which had given way in turn to a long series of apparently monogamous relationships. The last of these, with a young Frenchwoman, had resulted in a recent second marriage when he was fifty-seven. But this marriage, too, Dana read, had been brief. Solange Finn had died in a fall near Kerreck Du a year ago, shortly after her twenty-seventh birthday. She and Finn had been married only nine months.

One result of Dana's research into Finn's life was to make her slightly fearful of the man, and wonder more than ever about the son. Increasingly, she found herself hoping she would meet Daniel Finn again. But not here at Kerreck Du. She would need all her self-possession simply to deal with Finn.

In a few minutes, she came to the wood, a mixed stand of oak, beech, and ash with a thick undergrowth of briars and vines. It was bordered by a crumbling wall whose stones were laid herringbone fashion, zigzag layers tufted with ferns and yellow vetch. A rickety wooden stile across the wall marked the footpath, but there was no sign to indicate that it was a public right-of-way. Nevertheless, she climbed over it.

The footpath plunged at once into the wood and she soon found herself enveloped by a dense thicket. The aqueous light was soft with green shadows, rich with the vegetable smell of rotting plants and the frenetic chattering of birds. The path was overgrown in places, as if rarely used, and she had to push aside the overhanging bulk of old man's beard and tangled mats of ivy.

She wondered if she was trespassing on private land, and felt uneasy. But she suppressed an instinct that urged her back to the lane. She was too easily deflected, Stewart had often told her during their marriage, by her fear of invading privacy, or of encroaching on someone else's property, intellectual or otherwise. You had to overstep the bounds every now and then, he had argued, especially in academia. In his opinion, the most successful researchers were trespassers by instinct and inclination. Keep Off signs, visible or invisible, just told you where the pickings were. They were incentives to get there first. Eventually, with the affair that had ended their marriage, Stewart revealed just how wide a latitude he had given himself.

She, on the other hand, had been raised to observe boundaries of all kinds, and the lessons of her childhood were strong. But she wondered at times if she had learned them too well. Courtesy so easily masked cowardice; respect for other people's privacy was one way of escaping pain.

The path became clearer as she walked on, and in a few moments she saw what appeared to be the edge of the wood a little distance away to her right, with glimpses of wide blue sky beyond. Eager for open space and a view of the sea, she left the footpath.

She had gone only a few yards when she heard laughter, softly mocking, like a long-delayed echo of the boy's but unmistakably female. It came from somewhere ahead, where the wood ended.

Chapter 6

Cautiously, Dana moved through the thinning trees. In a moment, she was standing among some saplings at the edge of a mossy bluff, overlooking a clearing. At the base of the bluff was a green hollow roughly fifteen yards across, tree-fringed, with a small brook running through it. Lush with grass and wildflowers, the hollow was sun-drenched and silent. It was not deserted.

Lying on the grass across the clearing some twenty feet below her, she saw a man and a woman, naked and apparently asleep. They were stretched out on their stomachs, close together but not quite touching, with their faces turned to each other. Sunlight fell on white flesh, luminous as glass. Enclosed within the luxuriant green oval of the hollow, their young and slender bodies seemed etched on the grass like some voluptuous cameo.

Then she saw the sword.

It lay between the naked couple, long and unmistakable, the polished steel of its broad flat blade gleaming sharply in the sunlight. At the sight of it, she felt the rock tilt suddenly under her feet. As she stepped back, reaching out to grasp a sapling's trunk for balance, the picture of the sword-divided pair multiplied around her like an image in a shattered mirror.

"Shut your eyes, goddammit!"

The man's harsh voice seemed to come from beneath her. She thought at first he meant her, the command a remedy for her vertigo, and she obeyed. Gradually, behind her closed lids, the dizziness receded. When she looked down again, she saw that someone else had joined the sleepers, who were now awake.

It was Quentin Finn. His beard and the graying dark hair that fell thickly across his forehead partly hid his face from her but she recognized the man from his own pugnacious self-portraits of the later years. Around his neck hung a camera; another, she saw now, stood on a tripod directly beneath where she was standing.

He had not been speaking to her but to the couple, hadn't seen her at all, in fact, and was violently berating them now for spoiling the shot. The young man sat up and covered his groin with a protective hand while the girl only rolled onto her back and stretched. Then she propped her head on one hand and gazed up at Finn, apparently unconcerned by her nudity and his abuse. With her free hand she fluffed up the short red-gold hair that aureoled around her head in a frizzy mass. Her partner was the beauty, physically speaking, with a smooth perfection of face and form, but she drew the eye. She had the provocative nonchalance of Manet's Olympia, sexuality alfresco, for a price.

But it was Quentin Finn who dominated the scene. And not simply because he was clothed and standing, and shouting.

Burly and broad-shouldered, he paced the clearing while he raged at them. His energy was palpable and disturbing. He violated the serenity of the place, like a satyr erupting into some drowsy pastoral scene, but he also brought it vividly to life.

Chewing on a stalk of grass, the young woman calmly observed the tirade while her partner grew visibly more agitated. "Christ, Finn," he interrupted at last, his well-bred English voice high-pitched and petulant, "how do you expect anyone to relax cuddled up to a sword? I'd like to leave here with all my extremities intact, thank you very much."

Finn halted in front of him. "And that, Tim my love, is precisely why you must not move. Otherwise, I might be tempted to use the sword on one extremity in particular." He spoke evenly, with the teeth-gritted emphasis of an adult to a recalcitrant child.

The girl laughed—the same laugh Dana had heard earlier—while her partner drew up his knees and looked around, possibly for some sort of protection, or his clothing. "Sod this! I didn't come here to be threatened. . . ."

"Relax, Tim," the girl drawled lazily, rubbing one bare foot up and down his leg. "Finn's only kidding. And anyway, it's so small he'd have a hard time finding it." She was American, but the faint

British precision contracting the broad vowels hinted that she might be as much an expatriate as Finn.

"Bitch." The young man scowled at her and withdrew his leg from the reach of her foot. He muttered something about wanting to know what the sword meant anyway.

"It's a symbol. You know, like phallic." The girl spoke with a lazy patience that had to be offensive to him, although he only glowered at her and said nothing. "Or maybe it stands for disease or fear of commitment or the wrong mouthwash. You read into it what you like, okay?"

She was taunting them both, but Dana had the impression everything she said was really directed at the older man.

He seemed indifferent, however. His anger had evaporated and he was concentrating now on some instrument in his hand that might have been a light meter. Mildly, he said, "Shut up, Karen, and lie down. Both of you. On your sides this time. While you talk the light's changing."

Obediently, the woman rolled over onto her left side and stretched her arm out to her partner, patting the grass. He would not look at her, however.

"Come on, Timothy, let's get it over with," Finn urged, his voice coaxing, humorous. " 'Lay your sleeping head, my love, human on her faithless arm . . .' "

"Faithless doesn't begin to describe it," the younger man said sullenly. But he took up his position beside her and closed his eyes. Silent, he became beautiful again.

As Dana continued to look down on the trio across the glade, Finn squatted beside the girl and moved her arm to place it along her flank. He manipulated the fingers of her hand, shaping them, curving them up from the open palm until they formed the shape he wanted, a gesture expressive of abandonment or relinquishment. She lay passive, feigning sleep, while he worked on her. Then all at once her hand broke free and, with the fingers still curled in the position he had chosen, clawed upward at his face. Before the nails could touch his skin, he grabbed the wrist and forced it down again to her hip. There it remained, immobile. All this occurred with no words spoken.

Then Finn stood up, raised his camera, and began to circle

them slowly, snapping off photographs. He moved lightly, the broad shoulders hunched and his back bent over his work. There was something almost necromantic about his movements, Dana thought, as though he were following some magic ritual.

Abruptly, he stopped. "Right. That'll do. Bring the equipment back to the house, will you." Leaving them there, he strode off down the wooded slope.

"Fuck you, too, Finn," the girl called after him, but softly, almost wistfully. Then she stretched out one hand and ran it along her partner's hip. With a groan in which anger and desire were mingled, he rolled over onto her.

Dana turned away. As she went back to the footpath, she heard the girl's laughter, coarser this time but with the same mocking note as before. It seemed that she had found the naked loonies.

Chapter 7

The thieves' severed heads, their eyes closed, sat in a row on the flat cross-pieces of crude wooden arches in what might have been a farmyard littered with buckets and straw. The neck of each was wrapped in a scarf. As though it were still possible for the poor devils to catch cold, Thomas Attery thought with grim amusement. Between the heads and a line of pine trees in the background hung a nightmare scarecrow, the crucified, gas-distended body of a murderer.

Thomas gazed at his latest acquisition with the satisfaction of a man who has just attained a long-sought prize.

The eight- by twelve-inch albumen silver print, taken by Felice Beato in Japan in 1870 and entitled "Hanging Man, the Execution Ground," was to his knowledge unique. There was only one other print in existence, in a university collection in America, and it was hand tinted. His monochrome was the true original, he reflected complacently, faithful to its glass negative. He had paid a great deal for the photograph, far more than he'd originally planned to spend, but it was worth every penny.

He removed his glasses to peer at the print more closely. It really was brilliantly composed. As he pondered the mysteries of the picture, he carried it to his study. His wife had chosen the house for its large garden when they had moved from London to Trebartha for her health ten years before, but he had acquiesced in the purchase because of the study. Together with a large anteroom it occupied its own wing, separated from the rest of the house by a short hallway, and had become his domain, as the garden had been hers. He could not recall his wife ever trespassing in the study.

The mild climate of Cornwall's south coast had not lengthened his wife's life, and she had died within two years of the move. The garden was now a sporadically tended wilderness frequented by the neighborhood cats. The guilt he felt at its decay was offset by the irritation aroused when he remembered how she would berate him for his supposed indifference toward the natural world simply because he disliked gardening. She'd had a bad habit of generalizing from the particular, a habit he considered specifically female.

His wife had been large and imposing, handsome in a rather masculine way. He himself was a small, almost diminutive, man of fifty-two with a spare, elegant figure and neatly made features. Age had drained him of color, fading the closely cropped hair to gray, mottling his skin with liver spots, but it had given him an air of pale distinction. He accentuated this with his choice of clothing, invariably a black silk turtleneck under a light gray woolen or linen jacket. Behind his gold-rimmed glasses, his pale slanting eyes with their specklike black pupils were as shiny and opaque as a bird's, observant to a degree that many people found unsettling. He knew the effect his gaze sometimes had, and rather enjoyed it.

He went into the anteroom, which served as his office. Here he conducted, by computer, telephone, and fax, his business as a financial investor. He preferred to work at home, and alone.

Unlocking a connecting door, he stepped inside the study, and as he did so his eyes made their automatic, thorough inventory. So familiar was he with the collection of nineteenth-century photographs hanging on the walls and arranged on shelves and tabletops that he would have known at once if one were missing.

Another man might have chosen to decorate the study with an overstuffed accumulation of Victoriana in an attempt to evoke the era of the photographs. When asked why he had not done this, Attery always replied that his collection spanned sixty years; to chose one style over another would imply a partiality for a particular period, while the jumbling together of various periods was simply not to his taste.

Instead, he had furnished the study with plain, modern pieces in light wood and natural fabrics. Coarsely woven, wheat-colored linen covered the walls; a soft, diffuse light filtered in through shades of translucent rice paper covering the windows and large skylight. Immaculate, serene, the room was as free from clutter as it was from dust and dangerous sunlight. There was nothing to distract the eye from the photographs themselves, and nothing to harm them.

The photographs represented a number of early processes—daguerreotypes, calotypes, and salted paper prints among others—and a range of tones, from the rich siennas of a carbon print through the golds and mulberries of albumen to the silvery gray of platinum. The smallest was a carte de visite by an anonymous photographer, the largest a 22- by 30-inch composite by Rejlander.

For all their variety, the photographs were united by a common theme. Death, explicit or implicit, was the subject of each.

Carefully, Thomas hung the Beato on the empty place reserved for it on one wall. Then, stepping back to view the effect, he stood for some time with one hand cupping his elbow and the other rhythmically stroking his chin, assessing the place of this new jewel in the collection.

The pursuit of these early photographs, fragile and elusive as butterflies, offered Attery pleasures, as well as risks, which he found in no other aspect of his life. It was filled with mysteries and unexpected adventures, and required tenacity as well as the lightest of touches.

Turning from the Beato, he moved among his treasures, handling them with a delicacy born of long practice and necessity. He picked up a daguerreotype of a remarkably beautiful child who looked as if she were asleep. Victorian viewers would know by her crossed feet, the photographer's signal, that she was not sleeping but dead. A careless hand could wipe away her image, he thought now, as easily as death had her life. A daguerreotype was best looked at with its case not fully opened, in private and by lamplight. One should approach it like a secret.

While he stood musing, the telephone on his desk in the anteroom rang. Resenting the distraction, he went to answer it.

"Attery here."

"It's Clement. I just wanted to let you know that a roll of twenty-four Fujicolor came in yesterday. Amateur work but some nice shots. All the same subject, and she's a beauty. In her teens, by the look of her."

"I'll come by tomorrow morning, around ten."

"There's something else," the other man said quickly, before Attery could hang up. "My rates are going up, as of now." When he remained silent, Clement hurried on, a whine creeping into his voice. "I mean, I could get the sack for this. It's just not worth it, what you're paying me now. Not with my cousin having his share and all."

"How much more do you want?"

Clement named an amount. After a moment's deliberation, Attery acceded. "But I won't go higher than that. If you push for more, I'll simply have to find another source."

There was a derisive snort on the other end of the line. "You'd be hard put to find one with an undertaker for a cousin."

The fellow was undoubtedly right, Attery thought as he put down the receiver. It amused him to imagine Clement's unknown cousin at his work, unctuously suggesting to his bereaved customers that they might wish to take snapshots of their dear departed, to remember them by. He could recommend some one who would do an excellent job of developing the film, someone who would respect their privacy. You could never be too careful with those big labs, could you now? The hint would be enough to send the grieving family member to Clement. Few would know that in the large labs the processing was done mechanically and the results checked by computer. Human eyes rarely saw the finished product.

Thomas stood by the telephone, wondering whether he ought to break with Clement. He was wearying of those amateur images of death, so crude compared to the exquisite works of art in the next room. He no longer felt that furtive, addictive excitement the photographs had once provoked, and the traffic with a man like Clement now seemed to him sordid rather than adventurous. The photographs themselves had become strangely repetitious. One look, he now found, was enough.

Moreover, there was the problem of Karen Cody. He'd always known it was dangerous to use a supplier in Trebartha, but he had been tempted by the remarkably fortuitous offer that Clement, hearing of his collection, had made privately to him. Then, two weeks ago, Karen had come into the shop where Clement worked just as Thomas was collecting his prints. With her American pushiness, she had asked to see the photographs, and when he refused had begun to tease him about why he was hiding them from her. Momentarily ruffled, he had handled the matter badly, growing irritable while Clement looked on, his expression thoughtful.

He wouldn't put it past Karen, he thought now, to have bribed Clement into telling her about the photographs. Or Clement, to have accepted. Since the incident in the shop, Karen had been acting as though she knew some shameful secret about him.

Thomas had reason to worry about more than the revelation of his penchant for candid snaps of corpses. Several disastrous investments, combined with the exorbitant prices of some recent purchases, including the Beato, had forced him to dip temporarily into clients' funds. Unwisely, he had dipped most heavily into Finn's account. And now Finn was asking questions.

But this was a temporary lack of fluidity, he told himself. He had no doubt that he would shortly be able to cover the diversion of funds before answers to those questions became unavoidable.

There was a knock on the front door. It would be John Malzer, come to collect him for the drive out to Kerreck Du for tea. His own car was in the shop for repairs. Eager to show John the Beato, he was glad of this reason to get him to the house. John was the one person, Finn apart, who would truly appreciate the photograph.

As he went to the door, Thomas acknowledged to himself that he had missed his young friend. Consumed by the preparations for Finn's retrospective, John had excused himself from their weekly Wednesday dinner together and had generally been unavailable for the long walks and conversations Thomas had come to depend upon. And it seemed to him that the little spare time John did have was increasingly claimed by Estelle Pinchot, who left his side only to dance attendance on Finn.

He was too perceptive a man not to be aware that much of his dislike of Estelle stemmed from the fact that she reminded him of his dead wife. Her fey, girlish enthusiasm, which masked an iron determination to have her way, and her use of money as a sweetener when people began to sour on her whims, were precisely like his wife's. He hated to see John taken in by her. But at least he would have this time alone with his friend before her inevitable descent on Kerreck Du. When he opened the door, however, he found Estelle there on the stoop with John.

Thomas rarely showed his emotions, and it was easy enough to disguise his dismay now with a smile of welcome as he invited them in. Estelle bustled into the house with a clashing of gold bangles, talking. As John followed her, he gave Thomas a small shrug of a smile, as if to say, What could I do?

"We've been discussing the hanging of one of Finn's photographs," Estelle told Thomas, as she mouthed kisses past each of his cheeks. Her scent was always too strong, he thought, with a small inward shudder of revulsion. "I thought if we all drove to Kerreck Du together, you might help us come up with a way to persuade Finn. You're always so reasonable, Thomas."

He moved away from her, pretending that a picture on the wall beside the stairs needed adjustment, but she followed him. She had a thin, restless body that was rarely still and a deceptive—and to some appealing—air of vulnerability, a patent eagerness to be liked. A resolutely blond woman in her early fifties with delicate, faded features that were overpowered by the brightness of her hair, she was always perfectly groomed. She was wearing a pale green linen dress banded around the neck, cuffs, and hem with some material in a darker green. The color, he noted, was unkind to her fair, aging skin.

"I'm astonished anyone but Finn has a say in what goes where," Thomas said, turning to John Malzer. "Hasn't he insisted on making all the decisions himself?"

"Mostly," Malzer said. "The important ones. But we're allowed some say over the trimmings." He smiled at Attery. A large and slightly plump man of twenty-eight with dark brown hair falling over his collar, he had a round, boyish face and brown eyes. One eyelid drooped slightly, giving him a perpetually sleepy, confused look that Attery found oddly touching. Like a boy's, his shirt was rumpled and partly pulled free of his baggy corduroys. Attery longed to tidy him.

Estelle announced she wanted to powder her nose before they left, and went off to the guest lavatory. It was on the tip of Thomas's tongue to complain about her presence to John, but he curbed the impulse. He knew he must be circumspect. Estelle had given a great deal of money to sponsor the exhibition of Finn's work at John's gallery—far more then he, Attery, had. Finn's photograph of Estelle's daughter, Barbara, was to appear in the exhibition; she had modeled for him before her death from a drug overdose three years ago. John considered it one of Finn's masterpieces. Unknown to Finn, he had gone up to London several months ago to persuade Estelle to lend it for the retrospective. To Thomas's fury he had returned to Trebartha not only with the photograph but with its owner, who immediately took a house nearby on a short-term lease. Finn's own reaction to Estelle mystified Attery. Ordinarily no respecter of patrons or silly women, he treated her with far more kindness, in Thomas's opinion, than her behavior warranted.

Malzer turned to him. "Where's this prize you were telling me about?"

Thomas hesitated. He would have preferred to wait until he had John to himself, but this might be the only chance he would get until after the preview night of Finn's exhibition. "I've already hung it with the others." He turned to lead the way to the study.

The younger man put a hand on his arm. "On second thought, Thomas, perhaps I ought to see it another time. Estelle won't appreciate your collection."

"She's occupied," Thomas pointed out. "And this won't take long." Anyway, it might be amusing to observe Estelle's reaction to his photographs, he thought. She was notably squeamish about the unpleasant realities of life.

Malzer's response to the Beato was everything Thomas expected. He recognized not only the photograph's extraordinary qualities but also Thomas's skill in acquiring it. After expressing his admiration, he paused and said, "This must have cost a bomb, Thomas. If you went to Sorenson for it."

Thomas shrugged. "More perhaps than I ought to have paid. But I had to have it. You can understand that."

Before the other man could reply, Estelle joined them. She seemed unperturbed by the photographs, gazing around with an air of polite interest, which surprised Thomas until he remembered that without her eyeglasses she was extremely nearsighted. It was another sign of the woman's vanity, he thought, that she refused to wear them.

She went up to a large portrait nearby and peered closely at it. "Who is this gorgeous creature?"

To Thomas's amusement, he saw that she was staring at Nadar's portrait of Étienne Bazin.

Leaving Malzer to enjoy the Beato, Attery went over to Estelle's side. The subject of the photograph was seated against a plain gray background, a cloak draped over one shoulder, scowling slightly at the camera. Angelically handsome, with dark, flowing curls and romantic features, he might have been a George Sand hero.

"He is quite wonderful, isn't he?" Attery agreed. "That's a particularly fine example of a Woodburytype. Quite an interesting process—"

"Oh don't waste your explanations on me," Estelle interrupted. "I never understand that technical mumbo jumbo. All that matters to me is the result. And he's lovely."

"On the outside only, I'm afraid." Attery went on to explain that Étienne Bazin had been a minor actor at the Comédie Française. It was thus that the famous photographer Nadar, who was making a series of portraits of actors, had happened to photograph him. "As an actor, Bazin was apparently second-rate. But at his true métier he was remarkably successful. He was a first-rate murderer."

Estelle frowned and peered again at the photograph, then moved back a step.

For two years, Attery continued, from 1859 to 1861, Bazin had terrorized Paris, luring more than a dozen women to their deaths. In a grotesque attempt to create his own personal catacomb, he had carried the bodies of many of his victims into the tunnels that ran below the city. After his capture, the police had found nine corpses in a crypt shaped like a miniature amphitheater, in a remote and almost inaccessible part of the catacombs.

"In one of those ironies of history, Nadar happened to be photographing nearby. He was one of the first photographers to experiment with the use of artificial light."

"The police asked Nadar to photograph Bazin's catacomb for purposes of evidence. That's the result." Thomas pointed to a neighboring photograph, a grisly companion piece to the portrait. It showed the female victims arranged around the small amphitheater as though in some grotesque theatrical.

Estelle put her hand to her mouth. Then, without looking at either man, she said she would wait for them outside, in the car, and hurriedly left the room.

Malzer said, "She's on edge. This business with the Gull, it's made her nervy. I'd better go out to her."

A spurt of rage washed over Thomas as he watched his friend follow Estelle from the study. His eyes met those of the murderer. A pity, he thought with grim humor, that Bazin wasn't around now; he would have liked to introduce him to Estelle.

As Thomas climbed into the backseat of Malzer's car, Estelle turned around to him and said, "That was absolutely revolting, Thomas. I don't understand how you can bear to look at those pictures of yours." The soft, slightly sagging features were reproachful.

Repressing a sharper response, Thomas said, "I find it instructive to consider the ways we look at death. Or don't look."

She was staring straight ahead now, so that he could see only the carefully curled helmet of gilt hair. After a moment she said in a small voice, "Why should we want to look at something so painful? Unless, in some way, we're offered hope. And I fail to find anything hopeful in the picture you just showed us."

"Your enthusiasm for Finn's photographs surprises me then," he retorted. "I would hardly describe them as hopeful."

"But they *are* life-enhancing," John said mildly. "And Estelle has a very acute eye for that quality in a work. I would even call it a sixth sense."

Thomas saw Estelle turn to give John a grateful look. He could almost feel her preening herself. Really, John's flattery of the woman could be quite nauseating at times.

"You know Finn's working on a new composite for the exhibition, Thomas," John said over his shoulder, as though he sensed the older man's annoyance and wanted to turn the conversation. "It's some sort of homage to Hobhouse's series on the Tristan legend."

"I don't understand why Finn should bother with a German opera," Estelle said.

"Actually, it's a Cornish legend," John told her quickly, in time to prevent Thomas's sharper response.

"Oh. Well, I know the names, of course, but I have to admit I'm really not that familiar with the story." She was gazing in the mirror of her compact, about to apply fresh lipstick in a shade of bright tangerine that Thomas found particularly objectionable.

John took his eyes from the road to glance at her. "It's wonderfully romantic, Estelle. You should read about it."

She glanced coyly up at him from the mirror. "I'd much rather hear it from you, John."

"Well, it's quite simple really. King Mark of Cornwall sends his nephew Tristan to bring Iseult from Ireland to marry him. But on the voyage Tristan and Iseult drink a magic potion by mistake and fall passionately in love. Iseult has to marry Mark, of course, but she and Tristan go on meeting in secret. When they're betrayed, Mark decides to burn Iseult at the stake. Tristan rescues her in time and they escape together into the wood. Mark discovers them sleeping there with Tristan's sword between them—"

"The poor, deluded fool thinks this means they aren't actually having sex," Thomas interjected. Thomas, who himself considered the story a black comedy of errors and lust, was amused by his friend's attempt to make it innocuous for Estelle.

"So he spares them," John continued. "But they never really overcome all the obstacles in their way and Tristan dies thinking Iseult doesn't love him anymore."

"But before that happens," Thomas pointed out, "they've had it off in trees and on muddy riverbanks and on beds covered in flour. Watched by an evil dwarf and several stupid barons."

Estelle pursed her freshly lipsticked mouth. "I believe you'd make even *Romeo and Juliet* sound sordid, Thomas. And I still don't understand why it should interest Finn."

At times Estelle was willfully obtuse, Thomas thought. Aloud, he said, "What could be more compelling than sex and death? Especially for a man like Finn. And after all if you live here you can hardly avoid the story." He rattled off a list of place names, all of them possibly referring to the story of Tristan and Iseult, finishing with the cove in front of Kerreck Du. "Tantry's Cove is a corruption of Tantric. Which was just another name for Tristram or Tristan or whatever you like to call him."

She put the cap on the lipstick. "You'll have to give me a local history lesson, John. I really do want to know more about the place now I'm living here."

Thomas said, "I thought you were going back to London?"

"I waver. John tells me I musn't worry so much. But living alone as I do . . ."

"I won't allow you to leave us, Estelle." John's left hand relinquished its grip on the steering wheel and reached out for hers. Thomas watched as a fond smile made her features, in his opinion, more than usually foolish.

"Did you see the morning paper, John?" he asked spitefully, knowing it would upset Estelle. "They've finally identified that woman. The one who was killed on the cliffs last month."

John nodded. "Yes, I heard. No one reported her missing because her neighbors thought she'd gone on holiday."

"The article made it out to be somehow a blessing, that she and the other victim weren't locals. Am I supposed to sleep better knowing the killer attacks only outsiders?"

"Well, it might be a relief to believe the murderer came with her." John signaled, then turned off the road onto the drive that led down to Kerreck Du. On their left, the wood that crowned the hilltop gave way to a sloping field of waving grasses as the silvery roofs and gray walls of Kerreck Du came into view, nestled into the small green saucer of land between the hill and the distant cliffs.

"And with the first victim? That's stretching it a bit, surely?" Thomas gave a short laugh as a thought occurred to him. "Perhaps the murderer's a local who hates tourists. If so, the police will have to round up half of Cornwall for questioning."

"Are the police certain the attacks are related? I thought they were calling the first death an accident."

"For Heaven's sake!" Estelle broke in. "Can't you talk about anything but murder and death?"

From the silence that immediately descended on the car, Attery reflected, it seemed they couldn't. But they had arrived at Kerreck Du at last.

Chapter 8

The footpath brought Dana out of the wood onto the crest of an open green hillside. Folded into the gentle combe below, the slate roofs of Kerreck Du shimmered softly in the sunlight. The house sat at the head of the little valley looking down toward a small cove with steep cliffs on either side. From the hilltop, she could just make out a thin wedge of blue sea sparkling between the cliffs. The granite Georgian rectangle and its long, low outbuildings might have been a cluster of oddly shaped boulders flung inland by some storm-churned tidal wave. To the west of the house, a stream flowed along the valley's trough toward the cove, its slender thread glistening like mercury against the green.

She was startled to see the place in color. She had pictured it in monochrome, shades of black and gray, the way it looked in the old photographs taken by Henry Hobhouse.

As she started down the hillside, a human figure suddenly took shape near the mouth of the cove. Tumbling like wind-driven fleece, the speck of white ran toward the house. On the breeze came a thin wailing cry, sharp as a gull's.

Dana watched, mesmerized. It was an eerie re-creation, in reverse, of Marianna's flight from Kerreck Du, wearing only the white cotton dress of her seances, on the stormy October day when she learned of her husband's intention to commit her to the asylum. Her pursuers had found her standing at the cliff's edge with her long dark hair streaming and the thin dress soaked and clinging to her small, shivering frame.

The sudden evocation of this image, and the keening cry, both frightened and compelled Dana. She was tempted to turn around, go back to the path, back to London. Instead, she found herself hurrying down the hill.

The figure soon disappeared from sight, presumably into the house, but the formless cry grew steadily stronger as Dana neared Kerreck Du. By the time she reached the gravel drive, it had crystallized into a bizarre reproach.

"Fiend!" a woman was shouting over and over. "Fiend!"

A pair of wide wooden gates set in a stone wall stood open. Dana went through into a large cobbled courtyard ringed by the wall, the north side of the house, and a cluster of outbuildings. Two cars and a small tractor were parked in an open-sided shed; a child's pink bicycle lay on the cobblestones.

The woman's voice was coming from somewhere inside the main house, now loud, now faint, as though she were racing from room to room. But her accusation might have been hurled at the silence for all the response it provoked. There were no answering voices, no one came running to see what the matter was. Apart from the two of them, the place seemed deserted.

The theatrical scene in the woods prejudiced Dana, made her suspicious now and slow to react. She thought she heard an operatic note in the voice as flamboyantly dramatic as the gaudy fuchsias that spilled from a hanging basket against a whitewashed wall. For all she knew she might again be an onlooker at another of Kerreck Du's private performances.

As she hesitated, the woman shrieked some words that were recognizably names, among them Tim's, that of the naked young man in the hollow. Teem, she pronounced it, and Dana realized then that by "fiend" she must have meant Finn.

A side door of the main house stood slightly ajar. Before Dana could move, the door banged wide and an overweight woman in a white cotton sundress burst clumsily into the courtyard. Brown eyes bulged from a face mottled red, and strands of her badly dyed, flyaway blond hair stuck to her face with sweat. When she saw Dana, she surged forward, babbling in a foreign language that sounded Slavic.

"What's wrong?" Dana asked, taking a wary step back to elude the grasping hands.

But the woman did not speak English, and the same question in French and German only caused her face to contract with despair while her hands dropped to her sides. She groaned, and then abruptly turned away and lumbered across to one of the outbuildings, flung the door open, and vanished inside. Dana started to follow, but the woman reappeared almost at once with a large coil of nylon rope slung over one shoulder. Before Dana could evade her again, she gripped her arm fiercely with a large-knuckled hand and began to pull her across the courtyard.

Something had happened down in the cove, that much was clear. When Dana managed to make the woman understand that she would come with her, the look of desperate entreaty that screwed up the round face eased and she released Dana's arm and ran down a narrow passage that led to the front of the house. Dumping her backpack by the door, Dana went after her.

A low stone wall divided the clipped grass of the front garden from the rough ground beyond, where the path descended toward the cove. After twenty yards or so, the path forked. One branch continued down to the cove while the other rose steeply up a field of waving grass to the clifftop, parallel with a barbed wire fence. Instead of continuing on to the cove, as Dana expected, the woman swerved off toward the cliffs. Dismayed, Dana cursed herself for not having forced some sort of explanation out of her while they were still near a phone.

At the summit of the path, a wooden stile crossed the fence. On the other side, the footpath continued eastward along the grassy lip, some five feet from the edge. They had reached the highest and steepest section of the cliff.

Level with the eye, sea birds wheeled in the wind, while two hundred feet below lay the little cove visible from Kerreck Du, a crescent of biscuit-colored beach bisected by the hillside stream running out across the shingle to meet the sea. Part of a vast bay, the whole length of the coast on either hand was scalloped with similar coves formed by smooth green headlands that jutted out into the water.

Scrambling over the stile, the woman dropped to her knees and crawled toward the edge of the cliff. A few feet from the verge, she slipped the coil of rope from her shoulder and flattened herself on the ground, inching forward until she could look over. What she saw there seemed to reassure her. A tremulous smile lit up her face when she glanced around, motioning at Dana to join her.

A bad fall during a rock-climbing course in her teens had left Dana with a weak left ankle, as well as a fear of heights that she had never quite conquered. Sweat pricked her skin as she crawled to the brink, careful to keep well out of the woman's reach. Nothing in her behavior so far inspired in Dana the confidence that she would behave sensibly at the edge of a cliff.

Following the line of the woman's pointing finger, Dana looked down.

At first she saw only the cliff face dropping away to the beach far below. Rivers of bracken flowed down its flank to meet the bare rock at its base, where huge boulders turned their scarred flat cheeks skyward.

"Elvina," the woman called softly.

The response was a whimper, the sound of a terrified child.

Dear God, Dana thought when she saw her. Pinned to the cliff some fifteen feet below them, the little girl stood facing the rock with her thin arms splayed wide. From above, it was easy enough to miss the small blond head half screened by the plants that sprouted around her. She looked about eight or nine years old, a slight figure dressed in a yellow T-shirt and jeans.

One hand clung to a bush, the other to the rock itself. She appeared to be standing on a broad tussock of pink-blossomed thrift, a few feet above a stony ledge about eighteen inches wide which projected out from the cliff. A yard or so to her left was a slide of loose stones, like shale, in which another bush lay, torn out by the roots.

Dana assumed she'd climbed from the ledge to the tussock using the bushes as hand grips, and then, when one of the bushes gave way, became trapped where she was either by fear or by an injury. How had she gotten so far? The ascent seemed too steep for anyone so young to attempt, let alone achieve. She might have climbed down, but Dana could not believe any child of that age would go willingly over the edge of a precipice as dangerous as this one. Here at the top, the cliff face was almost vertical.

Apart from that wordless sound of fear, the girl remained silent and motionless. She did not raise her head to look up, nor did she reply when her mother spoke to her again in a crooning, anxious voice. But she seemed in no immediate danger, as long as she did not move.

The woman sat up and began frantically and inexpertly trying to fashion a loop in the end of the nylon rope. "Here, let me," Dana said, holding out her hand. With a dazed look, the woman gave her the rope.

While her fingers automatically formed various knots, Dana debated how best to use the rope. They could throw it down to the child, but their aim would have to be true and she would have to let go of one handhold in order to catch it. If it snagged on a rock or a bush they might not get a second chance. And if she lost her balance she would almost certainly fall.

Ideally, someone should take the rope to her, or be there with her to catch it and put it around her. Unless she was injured, she should be able to climb back up with help and the rope's support.

Dana uneasily scanned the drop below her. Her training had taught her that a climber ordinarily descends a cliff facing outward, sitting down if possible, with the back toward the rock in order to see. Pressure holds, counterforce, and a low center of gravity should keep the body from pitching forward. But the steep grade of this cliff at its summit would make a forward-facing descent initially impossible. The rescuer would have to face the rock, blindly feeling her way from hold to hold with hands and feet. Only the rock itself could be used for support—bushes and bracken might be too shallowly rooted for safety—although the evidence of the shale slide made even the rock unreliable.

Climbing up would be easier, but to approach the child from below, it would be necessary to go back along the path to the cove and then locate a safe route up the cliff. This would take much longer, longer perhaps than the child could endure.

But there was no choice. To climb down was beyond Dana's powers. She was too afraid.

Was there still time to run back to the house and telephone for help, then look for Quentin Finn and the others? Even as the question took shape, the answer became irrelevant.

The tussock on which the little girl stood suddenly broke loose and fell with a clatter of stones to the ledge below. The hand clutching the rock lost its grip. And for one terrible moment it seemed she would drop away from the bush like an unfledged bird.

"Elvina!" The mother's cry was a shriek of despair. Dana's own scream caught in her throat.

The child was saved by the gymnast's skill young girls often have. Despite the harsh jolt to her body, her left hand held on to the bush and with a twisting lunge of her shoulders, the right swung up to join it, so that both hands were grasping the branch. One sneaker-shod foot, scrabbling wildly against the rock next to it, somehow managed to find a niche to support it, taking much of the weight from her arms. The other foot dangled limply in the air like a rag doll's.

Through it all, she kept eerily silent. But beside Dana, the mother sat groaning loudly with her fists crammed against her mouth, rocking like someone in pain.

Dana thrust the rope at her, pushing the free end into her hands. She tried to make her understand that she was to keep it until the signal came to throw the loop end down. Then she swiveled around on her stomach and felt with one foot for a toe-hold. When the woman realized what she was about to do, the hysteria in her bulging eyes gave way to a violent hope.

Only the thought of the child, and a wave of adrenaline that chaneled through her veins like a tidal bore, conquered Dana's fear of the void at her back and propelled her down the rock. Pressing herself into the stone, she searched for crannies and fissures wide enough for her fingers and the toes of her shoes. With each precarious toehold, she could feel her feet shift slightly inside the rubber-soled walking shoes.

Above, the mother resumed her frantic crooning. The tone of her voice made it clear she was urging the child not to let go, telling her help would be there.

But how long would it be before the child's weakening grip failed, or her weight pulled the roots of the bush away from the stone? And when the inevitable happened, what then? With luck she might land on the ledge, but if she panicked she would almost certainly tumble off.

Dana forced these thoughts away. Afraid to look at the small dangling body, terrified she would see it fall, she kept her eyes on the cliff face immediately beside and below her, searching for handholds. Jagged rock and branches of gorse gouged at her skin, blood ran onto her lips from a cut on her cheek.

Then, as her right foot came down on the ledge at last, the chanting above changed to a shout. Instinctively, she turned to look for the child.

She realized her mistake too late. She ought first to have checked that the ledge was clear of debris, for in turning she brought her left foot down on a chunk of the stony earth from the broken tussock of thrift. The shoe slipped off the rubble and the foot twisted beneath her. Her grip and the width of the ledge kept her from falling, but she knew by the pain that her ankle was injured.

Simultaneously, she saw the child's body hanging beside her, the small feet level with her waist. With her own feet now flat on the ledge and her right hand clamped to a spur of stone, she grabbed her, wrapping her left arm tightly around her thighs.

A tremor ran through the thin little body. Rigid at first, the child slowly relaxed, although her hands kept their hold on the branch. Above them, the mother was screaming, but Dana hardly heard her.

"It's all right," she told the girl, knowing the words were as much for herself, for that part of her wanting to cry. "You're safe, it's all right."

But the child did not let go.

"Elvina? Is that your name?" As she looked sideways up at her, trying to coax some response from the averted face, she saw that a camera hung from a strap around the child's neck. "Do you speak English, Elvina?"

"Yes," came the almost inaudible response.

"Open your hands." She spoke slowly, enunciating each word. "I won't drop you."

"I can't." It was an agonized whisper. She had gripped the branch so tightly and for so long, Dana realized, that her hands had virtually locked themselves around it.

The screeching of gulls, disturbed by their presence, the crashing of waves, and the hot sun off the rock, which brought out the sour-sweet smell of the child's body and the scent of the gorse around them, made Dana dizzy. And the pain in her ankle was growing steadily worse. Unless she shifted her weight off it soon and changed the position of her left arm and shoulder, which were raised at an awkward angle in order to hold the girl, the effort required to help her climb either up or down would be beyond her.

Struggling to keep desperation out of her voice, she began to make small talk, to try to relax the child. "I see you have a camera. Did you climb up to take photographs of something?"

At last the little girl turned to give Dana a slanting downward look. Anxiety puckered her forehead and her lower lip was swollen and bleeding, as though she'd bitten it. She nodded her head. "The bird." She said what might have been its name in her own language.

Small flames were flickering through Dana's ankle and upper body muscles. If the child wasn't able to let go of her own accord in the next few minutes, she would have to find some way to prise her fingers free. The strain of holding her like this was swiftly becoming unbearable.

"Where did you see the bird?" Dana asked.

"There." Automatically, the child took one hand from the branch to point. Realizing with a little sigh of surprise what she had done, she released the other. Her body slumped suddenly against Dana's. The extra weight threatened to throw Dana off balance and topple them both, but at once the child slid down Dana's flank to the ledge. She seemed blessed with an instinctive ability to save herself.

Dana helped her to turn slowly around and sit down, cross-legged, her back to the rock, then eased herself down beside her.

All the while she had simply tuned out the noise from above. The original shout that had misled her into thinking the girl was about to fall had continued, with variations in tone, until it had ceased altogether. Now the mother called out her daughter's name. They looked up to see her ecstatic face. She loosed a torrent of words before vanishing from sight.

"My father is coming," the little girl said. Relief and apprehension both were in her voice.

They sat panting and weary, the child with her head low and her hands tucked up against the front of her T-shirt. In the wake of the receding adrenaline, Dana's senses seemed exposed, almost painfully sharp. Everything—the cries of the sea birds, the rough, pebbly feel of the ledge under her palms, the light that glittered with such fierce, blinding brilliance on the sea—resonated with new significance.

She closed her eyes and raised her face to the sun. Its heat on her skin felt benign, a mark of grace.

When she opened her eyes again, she found the child staring intently at her, the only visible sign of distress a sheen of unshed tears. She smiled, and the girl smiled back, blinking the tears away. They shared the complicitous smile of those who know they have gotten away with something remarkable.

With the pressure off her ankle, the pain had begun to ebb, replaced by a dull ache. When she asked the child if anything hurt, she held out her hands, palms up, in reply. The fingers were curved like small claws and the flesh was a dead white from lack of blood. "Also here," she added, touching her shoulders.

As Dana tried to explain that cramp and returning blood were the cause of the pain, which would gradually ease, the mother called out. They looked up to see her flanked by two men. One was Daniel Finn.

All three lay prone as they gazed down so that only their faces and the upper parts of their torsos were showing. The face of the man to the woman's left was lantern-jawed and so large as to seem almost outsize. He stared down at them with the somber intensity of an Easter Island statue, his eyes buried deeply under the jutting ridge of his brow.

"Elvina!" he said hoarsely.

"Papi!" The child's emotions, until now so contained, poured into the passionate flood of words that followed. Worried that she might lose her balance in her agitation, Dana put a hand on her arm.

The man's expression gradually softened as he listened to his daughter. From time to time he glanced Dana's way. When the child fell silent at last, he and his wife both began to speak, but it was his voice that prevailed, gruffly overriding the woman's shrill tones. After questioning the girl, he turned to Daniel Finn. A brief, inaudible colloquy followed. Daniel Finn then called down to ask if Dana was all right.

Dana explained that she'd injured her ankle, and the two men conferred once more. Daniel Finn told Dana that he was going to climb up to them, then disappeared from sight. Meanwhile, the woman began to talk to her daughter, her voice veering wildly between caressing reassurance and querulous reproach. Elvina kept her gaze fixed on the horizon, where a ship's toylike outline was moving slowly to the west.

As Dana massaged her ankle, she took stock of other damage. A vicious scrape against the rock had left one cheek raw and throbbing; blood from a variety of cuts and scratches stained her shirt and trousers, which were torn beyond repair. None of it mattered. She felt at peace with herself in a way she had not for a long time, as though an obscure failure had been redeemed.

In a few minutes, Daniel Finn appeared on the beach below. He scaled the cliff with an experienced climber's ease, moving so quickly that she assumed he was using a familiar route. He hoisted himself up onto the ledge beside Elvina, tousled her hair, extracting a smile, then looked across her head at Dana. In the sunlight, Dana saw that his blue eyes were lightly flecked with green.

Gravely, he said, "I see now why you missed lunch."

"That had more to do with my map-reading abilities. I'm afraid I got lost."

"Kerreck Du isn't the easiest place to find. In any case," he went on with the same mock formality, "I'm delighted to see you again."

Deliberately, she leaned forward to look at the drop below her, then back at him. "Not half as delighted as I am to see you."

He smiled. "We can argue the point later, when you're not at a disadvantage." He went on to say that he would help Elvina climb down but that in Dana's case it might be wise to send for more help. "There's a rescue team in Trebartha. If your ankle's badly injured, it would be safer to use them." His tone made this an observation rather than a directive, and plainly left the decision to her.

The ankle felt marginally better and she was already tired of the ledge. "If you don't mind, I'd prefer not to wait for them."

"Whatever you like. It's up to you." She thought she heard relief beneath the calm manner, as though he was as eager as she to be quit of the ledge. "Mico," he called to the other man, "throw down the rope."

He caught it easily with one hand and placed the loop around Elvina's chest, carefully testing the fit. Then, his voice gently reassuring, he explained to her that he would take her down and then come back for Dana. "Ready?" he asked, when he'd made certain she understood his instructions. She bit her lip, then nodded. He smiled and said a phrase in what sounded like her own language, at which she gave a small, shy laugh.

His skillful negotiation of the cliff face made it obvious that Elvina was in good hands. Even her mother, watching now from the sands at the base of the cliff, must have realized this for she waited quietly, without histrionics. Once the pair was safely down, she folded her daughter into her arms so completely that from above the girl was invisible. When she released her, she took the stance of mothers everywhere, hands on hips, head thrust forward, as they scold their children.

As Daniel settled beside her after a second ascent, Dana could feel the heat from his body on her arm. For a few moments he sat silently gazing down at the beach, his hands braced flat on the stone and his legs dangling over the edge. He seemed neither winded nor particularly exhausted, but abstracted. A slight contraction of his forehead, and something about his detachment in the face of the drop below him, gave her the impression that he was focused on more than just catching his breath.

In profile his face was more sharply defined, its edges harder. The nose had a pronounced Roman curve, and the line of the eyebrow paralleled the long, firm line of his mouth. It was a singular face, aloof yet appealing. Perhaps, she reflected, it was that suggestion of a breachable reserve that made him so attractive.

She began to think she'd noticed enough about him, and focused instead on the way the waves broke in creamy shawls on the little beach below.

With a faint exhalation of breath, he sat back. "So," he said, turning toward her, "where do we go from here?"

This sounded so much like the echo of an inner question of her own that she asked, confused, "What do you mean?"

"The climb. Which way would you prefer? Up or down?"

There was a glint of humor in his eyes but his manner remained opaquely courteous.

"Up, then." An ascent would mean less time spent using the bad ankle. With his help and that of the rope—which he had gathered up on the way back and which now lay coiled between them with its upper end held invisibly by Elvina's father, like a fakir's prop—it shouldn't be too difficult.

She was wrong, and more than once might have ended up dangling from the rope if it hadn't been for Daniel's quick intervention. His hand reached out for her almost before she realized she was in trouble. By the time she struggled up over the edge of the cliff onto the grass, long minutes later, she had acquired not only an increased appreciation of the horizontal but also an elusive sense that her own rescue had left her somehow at risk.

Elvina and her mother were waiting by the stile. The woman rushed forward and crouched down beside Dana as she sat recovering on the grass. Passionate and incomprehensible in her gratitude, she clutched Dana's hand while tears and words gushed out of her. The child turned away and began picking at the splintered wood of the stile.

"Nadia!" her husband said sharply. A few terse words in their own language caused her to flush a deeper red and stumble to her feet. She stood in sullen silence while he made a pompous little speech to the effect that the Tatevic family was forever in Dana's debt. His heavily accented English was very good, even idiomatic. The fluency was verbal, however, not physical. His jaw had a stubborn, unyielding angularity that mirrored the heavy brow and the rigid posture of his big body. And his expression struck Dana as more pained than grateful, as if he resented owing her anything, even his daughter's life.

Daniel, meanwhile, had picked up a camera case that was hanging from one of the fence posts and was searching through it. Mico Tatevic had a camera around his neck. It was like an identity tag, Dana thought; at Kerreck Du, even a child had to wear one.

Tatevic began to repeat the speech, with variations, to Daniel, who deflected the bulk of it with the observation that Dana's injuries needed looking after and that they ought to get her back to Kerreck Du.

He knelt down on one knee beside her, holding a small cloth. It was a lens cleaner, he said, but new and unused. "That cut on your face has grit on it. Hold still." He took her chin in his hand and turned her face toward him. His touch was light and slightly cool on her skin. Briefly, their eyes met. For some reason, the image of Quentin Finn manipulating the young woman's hand came into her mind. She looked away, across the field, while he dabbed at the cut with the cloth, his fingers deft and gentle.

As he worked, Dana remembered some words of Marianna Hobhouse's. Flesh touching flesh was a conduit for the spirit, the medium had written. The linked hands around the seance table allowed the spirit of the dead to flow through the fleshly channel. Impurities such as sin or doubt clogged the channel, might even block it entirely. Naturally, spirits flowed most easily from and to the pure in heart.

Dana no longer asked herself if this was nonsense, just as she no longer asked herself if she believed in ghosts. But, she reflected now, her own spirit must be exceptionally pure, for it seemed to be flowing very freely toward Daniel Finn.

The two men helped her up. As she could not walk on her own, they supported her each with an arm around her waist while her hands rested on their shoulders. Elvina trotted off ahead, as though eager to get away from the cliffs, or the grown-ups, as quickly as possible.

On Dana's left, Mico Tatevic might have been a wooden crutch for all that she was conscious of his body. But Daniel Finn was tangibly flesh and blood. The ridge of his shoulder muscle under her hand, his own hand on her waist, the hard line of his hip against hers, emphatically told her so.

They came at last to the gate. The severe beauty of the house's flat stone front was softened by a small, white-columned portico. Wide stone steps led down to the terrace where wicker chairs circled a cloth-covered table. A blue- and white-striped blanket was spread out on the grass nearby and a bright pink blazer, a shade darker than the poppies in the wooden tub by the steps, hung over the back of one of the chairs.

Daniel gave a mock groan. "The tea ceremony. La belle dame sans merci must have arrived."

"Who?" asked Mico Tatevic.

"It's what Finn calls Estelle. Because she's relentless."

Yes, she was there, Tatevic replied, with a grim smile. It was why he had come to the cliffs. "Estelle does not say thank you, but she likes to hear it. Often." Only when Daniel laughed did Dana realize that Tatevic had made a pun. She was surprised; he hadn't seemed a man capable of humor.

"One grows weary of being grateful," Tatevic added, in his harsh voice. Then, quickly, as though afraid that the other man would misunderstand, "But never to Finn. He doesn't oppress us with all he has done for us."

"You know how he feels about your work, Mico. You—" Daniel Finn broke off, and Dana felt his arm tense along her back. His father had come out of the house.

Daniel asked them to wait where they were and then walked quickly toward his father, intercepting him before he could reach them. The two spoke intently together, but all Dana could hear was a furious "What the hell was she doing there?" from Quentin Finn. He listened to his son's reply, shrugged, then wheeled around and came toward them, striding ahead. Behind the beard his face was unreadable. Nadia Tatevic called Elvina to her side and placed one hand on the child's shoulder.

He stopped in front of the little group and his eyes swept over them.

One of his more recent, and less friendly, interviewers had written that in late middle age Finn's was the face of a "bare ruined choirboy." Dana saw now what he meant. The boyish good looks had gone to seed: the full-lipped mouth was a libertine's, the pouchy cheeks were broken-veined, and the skin just below his eyes was plum-colored, dark as a bruise. But the eyes themselves denied the ravaged face. They were a clear light blue, youthful and piercingly bright, and they seemed really to see, not merely to look. Their curiosity was a child's, hungry for knowledge. It was as though a grain of innocence lingered somewhere in all that worldly sensuality.

He looked down at Elvina. Nadia Tatevic pulled the child closer while her husband said quickly, "Elvina's very sorry, Finn. She knows it was wrong, what she did." For the first time, Dana heard real anxiety in his voice.

"But you're all right?" Finn asked the child, who nodded. He smiled at her and Dana saw that even on a child the impact of that smile was considerable. Then he clapped Mico Tatevic on the shoulder. "Well, thank God, eh? That's all that matters. And what about you?" he asked in almost the same breath, turning the searchlight gaze on Dana. She felt its force as a challenge, but to what she could not have said. "Daniel tells me you're a heroine. But you've hurt your ankle?"

"It's just a sprain. Nothing serious."

"Can you walk on it?"

"No."

He glanced at his son. "We'd better get Dr. Penelly to look at it. Give him a call, will you, and ask him to come out. He owes me a favor. And tell Pascale to get antiseptic and some bandages."

Daniel nodded. He was turning to go when Finn added, "Oh, and Daniel . . .?"

"Yes?"

"Estelle's inside. Organizing. Pascale's not in the best of tempers. See if you can spread a little oil, will you?"

"There's Estelle now," said Mico Tatevic suddenly, before the other man could reply.

Dana saw a woman in green with bouffant gilt hair come out of the house onto the terrace, carrying a heavily laden tray. She was looking down, frowning nearsightedly as she concentrated on the steps and uneven flagstones. Sunlight glinted off her dangling gold earrings and the bangles that circled her wrists. Carefully, she placed the tray on the table. She picked up the teapot, then raised her head and saw them for the first time.

"There you are!" she called out, lifting her free hand to wave. The bangles clashed together. She was about to set the teapot down when she noticed Dana. Simultaneous with her cry of alarm came the crash of china on stone.

But it was her words that startled Dana.

"Oh God!" she moaned. "The Gull!"

Chapter 9

Later, when it became important to remember, Dana was able to reconstruct the scene that followed the woman's cry. From what had seemed at the time a chaotic miscellany of unfamiliar faces and overlapping voices, she retained a vivid picture of Kerreck Du's inhabitants and guests.

Nothing, it seemed in retrospect, had escaped her notice.

She heard Finn swear under his breath, saw the quick glance between father and son, saw Nadia Tatevic bend and whisper into her daughter's ear and the child respond with a sentence that caused the mother's face to darken. And she felt Mico Tatevic, whose arm still supported her, grow rigid, as though his only reaction to the cry was to become even less yielding.

"What happened?" the woman was frantically asking. "Don't tell me there's been another attack. I couldn't bear it."

"Relax, Estelle," Finn said, visibly struggling to conceal his irritation. "Elvina got into some trouble and needed help. That's all."

He and Tatevic helped Dana across the grass to an old-fashioned wooden lawn chair on the terrace, while Daniel went indoors to call the doctor. Estelle Pinchot hovered where she was, by the table. The tea had splashed up onto her skirt, flecking the green fabric. She began dabbing ineffectually at the spots with a napkin.

As Dana sank gratefully onto the chair, four people emerged together from the house. It occurred to her then that more than half a dozen people had just come out of a house that not so very long ago had seemed empty. Had the house really been deserted when Nadia Tatevic called for help? Or had Nadia exhausted her credibility by too many similar alarms, and been ignored?

Two of the men were unfamiliar. She learned later that the older was Thomas Attery, Finn's business manager, and the other was John Malzer, the gallery owner. But she immediately recognized the young couple with them.

Finn's models were clothed now, and like a male peacock's his plumage made hers look dull. Tim Sundy wore a pink-striped silk shirt over white trousers, and his blond hair fell in a smooth unbroken line to his shoulders. Karen Cody, on the other hand, was dressed in a plain beige shift. However, when she stepped forward into the sunlight Dana saw that her dress was not so dull after all, for the thin fabric made it plain that underneath she wore nothing but panties.

"What happened, Finn?" Thomas Attery called from the portico, eying the smashed crockery on the flagstones. "Daniel said there'd been some sort of accident."

Dana heard more curiosity than concern in his voice, and he looked at her through his gold-rimmed glasses as though she were an interesting specimen brought up from the beach. The razored cut of his iron-gray hair gave a slightly brutal air to a face that otherwise struck her as overly refined and bloodless.

"I'll explain in a moment, Thomas," Finn replied, as he adjusted the back of the lawn chair. Very softly, so that only she could hear, he asked Dana if she would prefer to go inside. "You don't have to take part in this Mad Hatter's tea party, you know."

"It seems safe enough," she said, turning slightly to look up at him, "now that the teapot's broken."

The blue eyes glinted with amusement. "I don't think anyone would mistake you for a dormouse."

Karen meanwhile had come slowly down the steps. Something of the languid sensuality she had shown in the hollow still lingered about her. The short red-gold hair fell in a tousled mass around her face and her movements had an indolent, sleepy grace. With the toe of one sandal, she prodded at a piece of broken china on the flagstones. Sotto voce to Tim but loud enough to be heard by everyone, she drawled, "I knew Finn would have to throw something at Estelle someday."

"Shut up, Karen!" John Malzer pushed past the others and put one arm around Estelle's shoulders. With an almost filial solicitude he asked if she was all right. He had the look, Dana thought, of a little boy not grown up but simply enlarged, with a child's soft features.

At that moment a slim, middle-aged woman in black came around the corner of the house, carrying a flat basket filled with flowers. It was his sister-in-law, Finn told Dana with what sounded like relief. As he made introductions, Dana found it difficult not to stare at the other woman. Pascale Silvy had the face of a Modigliani, extraordinarily narrow, elongated, and impenetrable, with eyes like black olives and a sharply pointed chin. It was a face that revealed nothing its owner did not wish it to.

"You can see Dana needs looking after, Pascale," Finn was saying. "Daniel's gone to call Dr. Penelly for her ankle, but in the meantime will you deal with the visible wounds." To Dana, he said, "Pascale's a natural healer. They'd have burned her as a witch three hundred years ago."

For the face alone, Dana thought.

"Finn flatters me," Pascale told her, in a strong French accent. "Antibiotic ointment is my only secret." Her voice was warm and attractive, so attractive that the unsettling face at once seemed less jarring.

"Come on, Pascale," Karen said impatiently, "aren't you going to ask what happened? If not, I will." She turned expectantly to Dana, but Finn brusquely told her to give Dana a chance to recover before pumping her for details. Then, succinctly, he described what had occurred.

Uncomfortably aware of the general gaze during Finn's account, Dana glanced at Nadia Tatevic, wondering how much of this she understood. The woman was standing alone now, slightly apart from everyone else. The afternoon light, which shimmered on the grass and made the white pillars of the portico gleam like marble, fell harshly on her bulky figure. It seemed to isolate her further, like her language.

When Finn finished talking, Karen mimed an exaggerated wonder. "Incredible," she said, placing the accent on the first syllable, as though to suggest she meant it literally. "I thought I was the only woman around here who hadn't been scared off the cliffs by the Gull."

This third reference to the gull, in combination with Estelle Pinchot's cry and the words of the boy in the lane, convinced Dana that they weren't speaking of a bird. She remembered the way the boy's sister had shushed him, and the terror in Estelle's voice.

"Yes, yes, we all know how brave you are, Karen," Thomas Attery was saying, his voice very dry. "Although foolhardy might be a better word. But then the risks you take don't tend to be altruistic, do they?"

While Pascale went off for the ointment, Finn issued rapid orders. He dispatched John Malzer for an icepack to put on Dana's injured ankle, Tim for a pillow to put under it, and Karen to fetch sandwiches from the kitchen. He told Mico Tatevic that he wanted a word with him and, before he drew the other man aside, added, "And will someone for God's sake please clean up this mess." There was a little flurry of activity as everyone hurried to comply.

Only Thomas Attery and Nadia remained aloof. He sat down in a chair, crossed one leg over the other, and lit a cigarette. She stood at the farthest edge of the terrace, looking toward the sea. Her shoulders slumped forward, straining the fabric of the crumpled sundress across her thickset back. She struck Dana as somehow forlorn, and rather sad. If not for the language barrier and her ankle, she might have gone to the woman.

Or, she reconsidered, perhaps not. There was something frightening about Nadia Tatevic, about even her gratitude.

While Elvina gathered up the larger bits of broken china in a dustpan, Estelle Pinchot made inexpert efforts with a broom, then stooped down with a clashing of gold bracelets to pick up the teapot spout. She carried it on her palm, like some precious artifact, to Quentin Finn.

"It was dreadfully silly of me, Finn, to react so hysterically," she told him, breaking into his conversation with Tatevic. "Was the teapot very valuable?" She clutched the spout between her fingers and gazed up at him. The mixture of girlish contrition and flirtatiousness on her face verged on the grotesque. Dana saw Pascale's olive-eyed glance rest coldly on the older woman as she passed her with the tube of ointment. It was not a friendly look.

"Very," Finn replied gravely, as he took the spout from Estelle. "Woolworth's best." He dropped the spout into Elvina's dustpan. "Don't worry about it, Estelle. Tea's never been my cup of anything. And we can do better by our heroine."

Smiling, he looked across at Dana. She understood then why he had been so successful with women. His eyes and the tone of his voice singled her out and made a direct, apparently unguarded statement. She interested him, they said. She was almost certain, however, that the interest was more complicated than Finn's reputation might lead her to think.

Karen Cody set a tray of sandwiches and cake down on the table, while Tim settled a pillow under Dana's ankle. "You've made Finn very happy," Karen told Dana. "You've given him a reason to drink—" she let a beat elapse "—champagne in the afternoon." This provoked a stifled laugh from Tim, who glanced over at Finn.

Finn seemed not to hear, however. He was talking now to Thomas Attery and John Malzer, who had returned with the icepack. But Karen's elliptical comment registered with Pascale, for the Frenchwoman paused as she applied the antibiotic to Dana's cheek, resuming only when Karen finished her sentence. Then she sat back and gazed critically at Dana's face. "The cut will heal quickly," she said, capping the tube of ointment. "It's not deep."

At that moment, Daniel returned with the news that the doctor was on his way. "He's a climber himself," he told Dana as he collected some ham and cress sandwiches and a small bottle of mineral water from the table. "When he found out it was a rescuer that needed him, he said he'd come straight over." He gave Dana the plate of sandwiches and put the mineral water on the flagstones by her side, where she could reach it easily. As he sat down in a chair next to her, he asked how her ankle was.

"Better, I hardly notice it now. There's too much to distract me."

He smiled. "And confuse you?"

When she nodded, he went on briefly to describe who everyone was. The Tatevics, she learned, had left the former Yugoslavia and come to Kerreck Du a year ago, sponsored by Finn. Mico was a remarkable photographer, he added. Karen and Tim were designers who made clothes for several expensive London stores and for their own small shop in Trebartha; they modeled for Finn in exchange for his contacts with the London fashion world. Thomas managed Finn's money, while John owned a gallery in Trebartha that was about to exhibit a retrospective of Finn's work.

Estelle, meanwhile, had been whispering intently to John Malzer. As he listened to her, he sat chewing on his lower lip while he cracked his knuckles. Dana found herself flinching at the sound. When he shook his head at some question or other, Estelle turned to Daniel to ask where Elvina's accident had taken place. She put her hand to her mouth when he told her. "Oh, no, how dreadful. Poor Finn. I must . . . " The words trailed vaguely off as she looked around.

Finn was going up the steps to the house. "Look after Dana, will you, Karen?" he called before he went inside. "She missed lunch and she'll be hungry."

She made a mock salaam at his back. "I live to obey, master."

"Finn!" Estelle called out, hurrying after him.

"He should give that one a few orders, too, while he's at it," Karen said. "Sit. Stay. Play dead."

Malzer leaned forward and took a sandwich from the plate on the table. "You don't give orders to rich patrons."

"Not until the last check's cleared at any rate," Thomas Attery said with a thin smile. He took off his eyeglasses and rubbed the bridge of his nose.

Dana turned to Daniel. "What did she mean, another attack?"

"A woman was killed in a fall from the cliffs near Trebartha a few weeks ago. Some people think she was murdered."

"She was the second woman killed along the coastal footpath recently," Attery told her. "Estelle's convinced herself that there's a maniac out there somewhere." He motioned with his glasses toward the cliffs.

"Third woman, if you count Solange," said Karen, without looking up. She was occupied in arranging crackers in a complicated pattern on a plate that already held several sandwiches and an enormous wedge of pâté. "If women keep falling off the cliffs around here, we're going to be overrun by bored husbands bringing their wives down for a nice walk. 'One more photograph, sweetheart, a little closer to the edge. Just a little farther. Perfect . . . Oops!"

Tim Sundy snickered, but several of the others looked uncomfortable. The legs of Daniel's chair grated on the flagstones as he stood up. "Excuse me a moment," he said to Dana, and went into the house.

"Oh God, did I put my foot in it?" Karen asked with mock innocence. "Pascale, I hope you don't think . . ." The Frenchwoman shrugged, as if to say it was unimportant. Karen then placed a large slice of chocolate cake on the already overloaded plate and brought it to Dana. "Finn said you were hungry."

"Thanks, but I already have something to eat." She held up the plate Daniel had given her.

"Oh I'll bet you'll manage both," the other woman replied, placing the plate on her lap.

Pascale took the extra plate from Dana and set it beside the mineral water on the flagstones. She watched Karen walk away, then said to Dana, "I'm told that she and Tim are having problems with their business. That's not to excuse her behavior, only perhaps to explain it."

But Dana was distracted by the sight of the Tatevics, who were standing at the edge of the terrace glaring at each other over their daughter's head. His Easter Island face had grown longer and more forbidding, while she seemed on the verge of tears.

Pascale too had noticed the Tatevics. She called to Elvina to come and have some cake before it was all gone. The child tugged at her father's arm, and he nodded. He came over with her while his wife sat down disconsolately on the blue-and-white blanket spread out on the grass.

"I saw an extraordinary thing today," Tatevic said suddenly in his loud guttural voice as he helped himself to cake. He went on to describe how he'd watched a great black-backed gull playing with a fish it wanted to eat. The fish was too broad to fit in the bird's gullet and so the gull kept tossing it up, trying to work out a way to swallow it. Meanwhile, a herring gull approached and did its best to snatch the fish away.

"Now, the great black-back is a big bird, very powerful. A ferocious killer," Tatevic told them. "But the herring gull also is a large and savage bird. However, the black-back ignored it at first, treated it as a nuisance, no more. But the herring gull persisted. It became excited and would not leave the black-back alone. Then, without warning, the black-back turned on it and struck it once with its beak. The herring gull cried out and then flopped over, dead. And the black-back calmly returned to playing with the fish, as if nothing had happened.

"Do you know what I thought?" Tatevic asked, looking slowly around at them all. "I thought, this is how a certain type of person kills. Casually, to rid himself of a nuisance who prevents him from enjoying his pleasures. Or coldly, when he has persuaded himself that it is not murder to kill for a cause."

In the silence that followed, he took his cake and went to join his wife and daughter on the blanket.

"We really must teach Mico the art of British small talk," Attery said with an acid smile.

As if Tatevic's story had in some way excited him, Tim went back to the subject of the women's deaths. He refused to believe they were the act of a killer, he said. Accidents were bound to happen if inexperienced tourists were foolish enough to go hiking alone. "The police aren't saying it was murder."

"The papers are," Karen said. "Or as good as." She turned to Dana and added conversationally, "You probably don't know about our local murderer. They're calling him the Gull. Do you know why?"

"Do be careful, Karen." Pascale Silvy motioned with her head toward Elvina. "You never know how much she understands."

Karen leaned forward and in a low, confidential voice said to Dana, "You see, he gouged out the eyes of one of his victims. Just like a gull." She sat back, wiped the icing from the cake knife with one finger, and put the chocolate-covered finger in her mouth. Slowly, she sucked it clean. The finger came out of her mouth with a little pop.

Despite a lurch of nausea at the description, Dana continued to eat her sandwich. She was beginning to loathe Karen Cody.

"Don't be such a ghoul, Karen," Malzer told her. "Birds might easily have done it. After all, she wasn't found right away."

"And aren't you being sexist?" Thomas Attery was lighting another cigarette. "Even the papers aren't saying that this putative murderer is a man."

Karen stared at him, her eyes bright with malice. "Maybe they have the same trouble some of us do figuring out genders."

As she spoke, Mico Tatevic walked over to the table for a napkin for Elvina, passing in front of Attery. It was just possible, Dana thought, that Attery did not hear the remark. His face registered nothing more than a mild boredom as he smoked his cigarette.

"Estelle wanted to know if the women were interfered with," John Malzer was saying. "The poor woman can hardly sleep at night for worrying."

"Someone should 'interfere' with Estelle," Karen told him, with emphasis on the euphemism. "That might cure her sleeping problems."

Malzer wrinkled his forehead. "Do you have to be so nasty, Karen? After all, she's made Finn's exhibition possible." He glanced around at the Tatevics, then continued in a lower voice, "And I happen to know she's been very generous to Mico and Nadia."

"The exhibit's happening because Finn wants it to," Karen said. "If it weren't her money it would be someone else's. As for the Tatevics, she only supports them because Finn persuaded her that Mico's a genius and because she likes to play Lady Bountiful. She couldn't care less about refugees."

During this exchange, Dana noticed that Pascale Silvy sat with her head slightly bowed and her hands folded on her lap. The short, feathery dark hair revealed the shapely curve of her skull and accentuated the graceful neck. In profile, with the too-narrow shape of her face hidden, she had become beautiful. Her role at Kerreck Du puzzled Dana. She had neither involved herself in the others' squabbles and dissensions, as an intimate friend might, nor made any effort to deflect them with the tact of a hostess. Her only intervention had been on Elvina's behalf.

When Finn came out carrying two large foil-capped bottles by their necks, followed by Estelle with a tray of glasses, Pascale raised her head. For an instant, as she stared up at him, Dana saw a look like sorrow on the Frenchwoman's face. It vanished at once as she stood up to help hand out the glasses.

Tim Sundy took the pink linen blazer that was hanging on the back of a chair and put it on. It was beautifully cut, Dana noticed, with long, scrolled lapels and folded cuffs. In response to John

Malzer's admiring comment, he said that he had designed it for a client, then decided to keep it himself.

"That's bad business practice, Tim," Thomas Attery warned. "Like an alcoholic pubkeeper drinking up his profits."

The younger man flushed. Before he could respond, Karen said coolly to Attery, "At least they're *his* profits. He doesn't waste other people's money." He let this pass in silence, as he had her previous jibe, but behind the glasses his slanting black eyes stared at her with such unblinking concentration that she flushed and looked away.

Finn raised his glass and proposed a toast to Elvina's rescue and to Dana. There was a general murmur along the lines of "hear, hear," followed by a silence as everyone drank. The silence extended itself, and Dana gradually became aware that they were looking in her direction. Was she expected to make some sort of speech? she wondered. Then she realized that Nadia Tatevic had come up and was now standing next to her, staring down at her with unsmiling intensity. For an unsettling moment, Dana thought she had somehow offended the woman.

Then, abruptly, Nadia crouched beside her, took her hand between both of hers, and pressed it to her breast. Among a confusion of feelings, including profound embarrassment, Dana felt a terrible pity for her.

" 'A Mother's Gratitude,' " Karen said with elaborate sarcasm. "What a great shot. All these photographers and nobody's taking it?"

Karen's tone must have given Nadia the gist of her remark, for she was suddenly on her feet. Two long strides brought her to Karen. The girl flinched back, as though expecting a blow, but before anything could happen Finn slipped an arm around Nadia's waist and turned her toward her husband, who hustled her away.

At that moment the doctor arrived.

Chapter 10

Finn stood with the others on the terrace as Denholm Penelly examined Dana Morrow's ankle. While she submitted to the doctor's probing fingers, Finn studied her, fascinated as always by the power a particular form could have over the eye. The curve of her shining hair against the pale skin of her jaw, a certain innocence in the intelligent gaze, and her composure, these made him think of that photographic cliché, the chambered nautilus. Implicit under the smooth nacreous beauty were convolutions and secret places that resisted scrutiny. Or provoked violation.

He had been right, he thought, to invite her to Kerreck Du. The wave of boredom and despair that inevitably threatened to engulf him whenever he was away from his work had receded.

Daniel had obviously been surprised by his willingness to let her look at the Hobhouse materials. But Daniel so rarely asked him for anything that his intervention on her behalf had made Finn curious about her. And then, if he was honest with himself, he welcomed the chance to unsettle Lynn, whom he found the least attractive of Daniel's women friends. Something in Daniel's voice as he spoke of Dana Morrow, a studied dispassion, had made Finn think she might be a threat to Lynn.

But there was another reason, stronger than either of these. From the little that Daniel had told him about the woman and her attempt to buy the photograph of Marianna Hobhouse, he sensed that she, too, had an obsession. Fellow obsessives had always intrigued him.

Both Daniel and Pascale had wanted him to wait until after the exhibition to invite her to Kerreck Du, but he preferred to have her here now. He liked a ferment around him. He did his best work in the midst of turmoil, when things were slightly out of control, tending to chaos. Unstable elements seemed to him the most interesting.

He looked around the terrace at the others. Most of them, he thought, were precisely that: unstable elements whose ostensibly civilized surfaces concealed an infinite potential for disruption. Karen, the least able to control her tongue, was the obvious example, but even the best-behaved, John for instance, allowed glimpses of a darker self. Even Pascale.

Daniel alone remained unfathomable.

Finn felt the usual mixture of irritation and affection at the sight of his son, who sat slightly apart from them all on the low terrace wall. For some years now, Daniel had eluded him. His growing ability to detach himself with polite good humor from almost any situation maddened and confounded Finn. Sometimes he longed to provoke some sort of response from Daniel—pain, fury, reproach—anything rather than that implacable self-restraint. When he remembered the enthusiastic eighteen-year-old boy who had left his mother's home and come to England to seek him out, he felt a pang of something that might have been regret or guilt, if either were an emotion he ever allowed himself.

In a post-Freudian age there could never be simplicity in close relationships, he thought, least of all with one's child. What was he to make of the fact that Daniel had chosen photography as his work, but a form of the craft, digital photography, that he himself despised? Should he see it as a subtle form of opposition or as an attempt not to trespass?

As for those other suspicions, the jealousy . . . He thrust the thought away, refused to face it. What was the point?

"It's nothing to worry about," Penelly was telling Dana Morrow. "A sprain, that's all it is." He took a removable cast from his bag and fastened it around her ankle with Velcro straps. She should be able to walk on her own with the support of the cast, he told her. "A day or two of rest and the ankle should be fine. You're lucky no bones were broken."

"Not to mention necks," she said. "There must have been a guardian angel out patrolling the cliffs today." She smiled shyly, glancing around at them all.

An awkward silence followed. Finn saw her eyes cloud over as she realized that her words had somehow been wrong.

"That's because we do as the Bible tells us," he said to her. "We entertain strangers. You never know when they'll turn out to be angels in disguise."

The elaborate gallantry had been automatic, a way of dealing both with the silence and with his own pain. But her look was uncertain, as though she suspected him of laughing at her, and Daniel's glance was wary. Well, to hell with them, Finn thought irritably. He rubbed the back of his own neck, kneading the spot that troubled him. A pinched nerve or a bruised muscle, he supposed. He ought to tell Penelly, but the man would have him back on the examining table.

Penelly snapped the lock of his bag shut and stood up. "Mind you keep off that ankle as much as possible for the next day or two," he told Dana Morrow. "And let me know at once if the pain doesn't subside.

"Attractive young woman, that," he added privately as Finn walked with him to his car. "If a trifle tactless. Or perhaps she doesn't know that Solange died just there."

"Oh for God's sake, man, of course she doesn't! I haven't put a marker up, 'In this place, Solange Finn fell and broke her neck.' "

"No, of course not," Penelly said equably. Finn sensed the shrewd brown eyes on him, assessing him. After a moment Penelly asked him casually how things were going.

"Back to normal. Or what passes for."

"Splendid. The pills are helping then?"

Finn made a noncommittal noise. He had stopped taking the pills months ago. Despite the occasional black pit, he preferred the uncertain terrain of his real inner life with its promise of peaks to the safe, flat landscape of bland well-being created by the medication. Besides, he'd missed the whiskey too much.

"Any more memory blanks?" Penelly asked as he got into his car.

"I don't think so. But then how the hell can I be sure?"

Penelly looked up at him through the open window. His round, tortoiseshell glasses echoed the shiny dome of bald head fringed with brown hair, the bulge of tubby belly resting against the steering wheel. He seemed to Finn all circles and curves. "You must be under a fair bit of pressure," he said, "with this exhibition of yours coming up."

"Pressure's not a problem. In fact, I find it useful." Would the man never go?

"All the same," the doctor persisted, "you'd better come in to the office one of these days. You missed our last appointment, you know."

Finn did not tell him that he had gone instead to a specialist in London, someone too far away to lecture him with regularity.

Penelly switched on the ignition. "I must be off. Some fishermen netted a body along with their mackerel this morning and the police in Trebartha want me to have a look at what's left. Which isn't much, apparently. They're worried this chap the papers are calling the Gull might be responsible."

Finn could feel the knot in the back of his neck tightening. "Is that likely?"

"Not very. People like to stir themselves up. Not enough to do, if you ask me." Penelly raised his hand in farewell and drove off up the hill.

Finn's head was aching now as well. He needed a drink. In one of his violent about-faces, he wished all of his guests to the devil. Time wasters, that's all they were. Why in God's name did he saddle himself with them? Pascale was right, the house was much too full of people these days; he needed calm to complete his work for the exhibition. As he strode back around the house, he swore to himself that he would get rid of the lot of them.

But he found Dana Morrow and Daniel alone on the terrace. She was standing, holding on to Daniel's arm, as she tested the support of the cast. He was staring down at her bent head. Finn recognized the look on his son's face, as well as the unfamiliar emotion that immediately possessed him at the sight of it. I'm jealous, he thought with surprise. But of what?

They glanced up and saw him. The others had gone off in various directions, Daniel said. Pascale was taking Dana's backpack to the guest room, Estelle was washing up the tea things, and the rest were looking at Mico's latest work.

"So then," Finn said to Dana Morrow, "what shall we do with

you?" He heard his own bad temper and saw Daniel's eyebrow lift fractionally.

She seemed unoffended, however, and replied simply, "Let me begin my research." Something about the eager tone of her voice, as if the day were new and unmarked by injury or weariness and her own strength were infinite, gave him the bitter sense of how much he himself had once been capable of. Still was, goddammit.

"Right," he said with a sudden return of energy, offering her his arm. "We'll take you to Henry's glasshouse." Glasshouse, he explained, was a Victorian term for a photographer's studio. It was in the north wing, which was used for guests. "Your room's right across the corridor. Just as well."

Henry Hobhouse's glasshouse had been preserved exactly as the photographer had left it by the piety of his great-niece, old Miss Hobhouse. The first time Finn had seen it, more than twenty-five years ago, he had made up his mind to buy Kerreck Du. On that day he had felt as though he had stepped into a past age and met a kindred spirit.

Built to Hobhouse's design, the glasshouse was a wood-paneled, oblong room with a northeast wall composed entirely of windows, and a slanting ceiling punctured by huge skylights. There were several pieces of William Morris furniture—a desk and chair, two wooden stools, a large armoire, and a bookshelf that held Hobhouse's published work—as well as the remnants of Hobhouse's equipment: various cameras from different periods, a box of glass plates, even a collapsible, portable darkroom on a wheelbarrow.

As in a theater, a system of pulleys worked curtains and a series of canvas backdrops. A large fireplace was set in one wall; another wall was thick with Hobhouse's framed photographs; and the third was covered by an enormous painted screen on rollers.

The screen was a magnificent object. Her uncle himself had made it, old Miss Hobhouse had told Finn proudly when he went up to it for a closer look. It depicted a finely detailed interior view of a great baronial hall thronged with people in Victorian-medieval dress. Instead of painted figures, however, Hobhouse had used hand-colored photographs of his contemporaries, cut out and varnished into place. In the center of the picture, isolated from the others, stood a young couple with bowed heads. Gazing at it, Finn had realized that some sort of confrontation or trial was going on and that the pair were outcasts.

The photographs on the wall also showed staged medieval scenes in the pre-Raphaelite fashion, all clearly part of the same story cycle. Faces from the screen appeared in the photographs, many of which seemed to portray some surreptitious transgression, a reconciliation, or a punishment.

On that long-ago day, he had recognized that the contents of the glasshouse represented a man in the grip of his own private obsession. Then, the room had fascinated him; now, it frightened him.

He went ahead to unlock the glasshouse, while Dana Morrow stopped to wash up in the bathroom adjoining the guest bedroom. Daniel waited for her in the hallway. In a few minutes, both came into the glasshouse together. Her immediate smile of delight reminded Finn of Daniel's reaction when he had first brought him here. He had known then that some sort of relationship would be possible, after all, with that boy of eighteen who had been a stranger to him.

One of Hobhouse's first cameras stood on a tripod near the door, a wet-plate mahogany monster shawled in its black cloth. Dana put her hand out to touch it. "A piece of a vanished world," she said, almost to herself.

"Dead and buried, thank God," Finn said roughly. He hated sentimentalizing about the past. Most people had no idea what early photographers went through to make a picture, he told her. "Their hands turned black from chemicals. Their clothes stank of them. Sometimes the poor buggers fell ill and died of them. Wonderful tones the wet plate gave, and lovely detail. But it was a diabolical method.

"The equipment needed to produce and develop a single glass plate might weigh over a hundred pounds," he went on. "And all of it had to be lugged about with you if you traveled beyond your doorstep. Camera, lenses, glass sheets, tripod, tent-darkroom, chemicals, gallons of water, test tubes . . . You had to coat your plate, expose it, develop, and fix it all within minutes. Never mind what might be going on around you. A storm, for instance, or a war. Fenton set up his photographic van in the middle of a Crimean battlefield. Hobhouse took pictures of London from a balloon. Developed them in the air while he puked up his breakfast from vertigo."

Dana Morrow smiled. " 'Mystic, awful was the process.' "

He stared at her, momentarily disconcerted by the suspicion that she was mocking him and by the familiarity of her words. Then he gave a bark of laughter as he remembered their source, Lewis Carroll's parody of Longfellow, "Hiawatha Photographing." "So you know something about it after all," he said to her.

"Only the funny nonsense the poem describes. Not what you've just told me, how they suffered."

Again he suspected her of irony, although her face was grave. He liked this about her, he thought, that she kept him off balance.

"We shouldn't forget that their subjects sometimes suffered, too," Daniel said. "Julia Margaret Cameron's maid was forced to lie on the floor for two hours clutching the porter's ankle. Pretending to be Guinevere pleading with Arthur."

"That's one of the things I find so interesting about the Victorians," Dana replied. "Their love of dressing up and playacting. Using disguises as a way of hiding and revealing what they really felt."

"Signs and symbols," Finn said. "That's what it boils down to. It always does. If you know how to look, you'll know what to see. Nowadays we've impoverished ourselves imaginatively, so we take everything at its face value. Then bitch because we're bored." Abruptly, he pointed to the Hobhouse photographs behind Dana. "What about them? Do you know what they're playing at?"

She stared at them for some moments, then turned back to him with a tentative smile. "Tristan and Iseult?"

She was quicker than he had been to see it. It had taken a knowledgeable friend to point out the story line of the photographs. He had been more interested in what he understood their message to be.

"What they're really about, of course," he said now, aloud, "is death."

On his left, he saw Daniel suddenly turn away and walk over to the desk, where the piles of Hobhouse documents lay: papers, manila envelopes, and small archival boxes. He pulled out the chair for Dana. "You should be sitting down."

"Because that's what Tristan and Iseult is really about," she responded with that eagerness of hers as she sat in the chair. Then she went on, like the clever student she'd undoubtedly been, "Togetherness isn't what the lovers want, because for each of them it's the other's absence that makes the heart grow fonder. And the best sort of absence is death. Reality can't get in the way then, and the loved one is always with us. There can be no jealousy."

"Exactly," Finn said to her. "Hobhouse understood that." And more, he thought. His photographs showed Iseult and Tristan's complicities, their deceptions, the foolishness of the cuckold, King Mark. Only their deaths romanticized the lovers; in life they had been lustful, deceitful, even ludicrous at times, covered in flour or mud.

Dana said, "It's such a perverse notion of love."

"But very human, don't you think?"

"Maybe. Though I'd hate to get mixed up with someone who felt that way." She looked again at the photographs, then leaned forward slightly, frowning. "There's something familiar . . . " With an exclamation of surprise, she pointed to a photograph in which Iseult was being led with bound hands to a pyre. "That's Marianna Hobhouse, isn't it?"

"Her head, anyway," he replied. "Marianna had died years before Hobhouse took the Iseult photographs. These are combination prints." He explained that combination prints were photographs that used a number of different negatives to achieve a single picture.

She glanced up at him. "Like your own?"

He nodded; the differences were legion but unimportant.

She stared at the other photographs in which the figure of Iseult appeared. In many, Iseult's face was either hidden or obscured, but there were several that indisputably showed Marianna Hobhouse. "But why did he portray her this way?" she asked him. "Was she . . . ?" She stopped in midsentence, flushing.

He shrugged, suddenly bored with the business. "Maybe you'll find the answer in those," he said, gesturing toward the papers on the desk.

But she was still looking around. "Marianna's photograph, the one from the auction . . . ?" Again she hesitated.

He glanced at Daniel, who shrugged, as if to say, It's your decision. Well, he thought, why the hell not? It would have to come out sometime, and it might as well be this woman as anyone. She wasn't like the others who'd come sniffing around.

He went over to the locked cabinet, opened it, and took out a large, leather-backed Victorian photograph case, which he brought over to the desk. Inside were two monochromes. One was the portrait of Marianna that Daniel had acquired for him at the auction. Facing it was another, taken when Marianna was younger, perhaps soon after she'd married. In this photograph, however, she wasn't alone but in the company of a middle-aged woman and a boy of about nine or ten.

He heard Dana Morrow's sharp intake of breath. She looked up at him almost fearfully, as though she were afraid he would deny the evidence of her eyes. He nodded in confirmation. The other woman was Elizabeth Barrett Browning, and the boy with her was Browning's son.

The poet's drawn, intelligent face, with its cheeks half hidden by ringlets, its humorous mouth and eyes wearied by illness, was unmistakable. She and Marianna were seated together on an ornately carved sofa, their heads inclined toward each other so that they were both looking at the camera in three-quarter profile. Browning's son stood beside her, dressed like a young cavalier, with long curls falling to his wide lace collar. His hand rested on the poet's shoulder, while she cradled Marianna's left hand in both of hers on the stiff black width of her skirt.

"I've never seen this before." Dana Morrow's voice was wondering.

"It's never been reproduced."

She stared at him, and he could see an amazed hope growing in her eyes. Softly, she said, "It's like a miracle, to see this. Oh, I knew that Elizabeth Barrett Browning had been to one of Marianna's seances. That was partly how I came to be interested in Marianna. But this suggests that the two women were closer than I thought. You see, Elizabeth promised Robert Browning she wouldn't involve their son with her spiritualist friends. So for her to allow him to be photographed with Marianna must mean that their friendship went beyond Marianna's talents as a medium."

She told them that Robert Browning had been so fearful of future ridicule of Elizabeth for her spiritualist sympathies that he had attempted to recover all her letters and writings on the subject in order to destroy them. "He might even have destroyed this photograph, if Elizabeth had owned a print of it."

Finn shrugged, largely indifferent to everything but Robert Browning's desire to spare his wife's memory. Biographers now were like jackals, he thought, sniffing at their dead or wounded prey. He did not want their bloody snouts rooting through his own life. All he intended to leave behind were his pictures. Let biographers make of them what they would.

Daniel pulled a stool up to the desk, then leaned forward to explain to Dana what the various piles contained. Daniel knew more of the details, Finn reflected, than he himself did. During Daniel's second visit to Kerreck Du, when he was twenty-one, he had worked hard to resurrect Henry Hobhouse's life, rummaging through tea chests stored in the attics, unearthing papers, photograph albums, memorabilia buried in trunks and forgotten. At the end of each day, he would come to Finn to tell him what he had learned. Eventually, Finn had ceased to listen. In those days, he hadn't much cared about the details of Hobhouse's personal life. Only the photographs themselves had mattered.

Originally he had been drawn to Hobhouse's work because Hobhouse too had so clearly felt compelled to work with symbols. As a young man Finn had liked to create mysteries. In his middle years he had wanted to solve them. Now he had come to believe that there were no solutions, not ultimately. Only further mysteries.

The greatest mystery, to him, had been Solange. Why, of all the women he might have had, had he chosen her? No, not chosen. There was no question of choosing to love Solange. He simply had.

He looked around the room. They had made love here, in the glasshouse. It had been a summer's evening, the first time, thick with heat and a sultry smell off the sea. They had opened the glasshouse windows one by one, like impatient children with an

Advent calendar. She had slipped easily from her clothes, first for his camera and then, as the light darkened to night, for him. Her skin had been soft, but beneath the tender flesh her bones had felt fierce and hard. They had seemed unbreakable then, bearing his weight with ease.

Their last time together stayed with him like a bruise that would not heal. That night, rain had blown in with the wind through the open windows. Laughing, she had complained that the damp in the rug on which they were lying would give them rheumatism in their old age. But she would be happy then, she had said, to have that ache in her bones to remember their lovemaking by. When his own bones troubled him now in damp weather, it seemed to him that they were mourning her.

He had photographed every inch of her, compulsively, as though he had known that he would lose her. He had photographed her in every light. Now he wondered if the light in which he had seen her, studied her, possessed her, had failed him, if it had been essentially a false light. It had revealed so much about her, but it had not, ultimately, revealed the truth.

"Man is led to believe a lie, when he sees with, not through, the eye." Like everyone else in the sixties, he had read a little William Blake—enough, as he realized later, to misunderstand him. For years he had carried these few words, scribbled on the back of a canceled cheque, in his wallet. They had been a guiding principle for his work. But Solange had made him forget their wisdom.

A sudden revulsion of weariness and impatience swept over him now. He knew from experience that he would need the aid of a good stiff scotch, several in fact, to combat it. Glancing toward the desk, he saw that Daniel and Dana were oblivious now to his presence. He turned and left the room.

Chapter 11

Daniel watched the faint outline of his father's reflection flicker silently across the wall of glass windows and fade from view. He knew when Finn had left the room by the change in atmosphere. It was like a low-pressure system lifting.

Finn's moods were increasingly black. Perhaps the retrospective was stirring up thoughts of his own mortality or memories better left suppressed. Perhaps he had somehow learned that Solange . . . No, that was impossible, Daniel told himself; he would know if that had happened.

If Solange were alive, she would have dismissed the idea of a retrospective as self-indulgent egotism and an absurd waste of energy. Worse, as a sign of age. Why look back? she would have asked Finn. What did he need to prove?

When John Malzer had proposed the exhibition of Finn's work, Daniel himself had expressed no opinion about it one way or the other. And Finn hadn't asked, as though he sensed Daniel's reservations. They were both careful to avoid subjects that might lead to disagreement or recrimination. Which left them, Daniel thought, with so little of interest to talk about that they were often silent with each other.

Sometimes a look was enough to convince Daniel that Finn loathed the sight of him. Then it was all he could do to keep silent. He would force himself to walk for miles along the cliffs until the impulse to wash his hands of Finn had died away. When he was calmer, he would tell himself that it was in Finn's nature to find it easier to be angry with the person he believed he had harmed than to feel guilt. But how could he convince his father that no harm had been done, when so much between them was banned?

Beside him, Dana was looking over the list he had made of the contents of the various manila envelopes and archival boxes stacked on the desk top. The open photograph case with Marianna's two photographs stood in front of her, directly above the cleared space where she had placed her own notes. The bell of gold-brown hair swung forward to hide her face, bent over the list. He found himself wanting to smooth it back from her cheek.

She glanced up from the piece of paper, disappointment in her eyes. "It's all Henry."

"On the list, yes. But Marianna's in there too." He gestured at the piles on the desk. "It's just that Henry's more obvious, so he gets recorded."

"And he was the survivor. So he got to fiddle the records."

"If he did, time gave him a hand with it. The records were a mess." To find the small trove on the desk, he told her, he'd had to winnow through numberless cartons of junk, trunks of clothing mixed up with letters and bills, and drawers stuffed full of ancient receipts and scraps of paper scribbled with incomprehensible notes.

"I felt like a stableboy in the Augean stables. At one point I wouldn't have minded diverting a river to get rid of it all." He could still smell the musty stink of the trunks with their rotting leather bindings and the faint but distinct scent of tea in the wood of the chests. "But I was twenty-one and stubborn. I wouldn't give up. It took all winter, but I finished." He remembered the triumph he'd felt, the weary elation, as though he'd managed at last to wrestle a slippery opponent down to the mat.

"Your father must have been impressed." She smiled, and he noticed then that one front tooth was slightly crooked, a flaw that for some reason made her even more attractive.

"Baffled, more likely," he replied. "He couldn't understand why I kept at it." Why had he? he wondered yet again. To prove to Finn that he could be just as relentless, just as determined? That he was his father's son? Or simply to show him that he had his uses after all?

At eighteen, he had dared to dream that Finn would teach him how to be a great photographer. He'd come to London for that express purpose, despite his mother's warnings that he was wasting his time. He had learned early on that her judgment was as unreliable as her presence, but in this she had been right.

"Go home," Finn had told him. "Get an education. I've always regretted I didn't." He would pay Daniel's fees, he added, so long as he worked at some sort of job in the summers. Then, maybe, he'd see what he could do for him. . . . With that shred of encouragement to urge him on, Daniel had gone to university, spending all his free time taking photographs. When he next came to Finn, four years later, he had a degree in history and a portfolio.

In retrospect, Finn's reaction to Daniel's photographs had been generous. "Not bad," he'd said, glancing through the portfolio as he ate a stand-up lunch during a break in a fashion shoot. Daniel knew now that in fact they had been terrible, with one or two exceptions: a dramatic, contrasty portrait of his mother laughing, which wasn't entirely derivative of Finn's own early work, and a shot of a beach on a holiday weekend in which he'd used a long shutter speed to blur the figures and give the sands a desolate quality despite the crowds.

"But," Finn had continued as he closed the portfolio, clearly impatient to get back to work, "I work alone and I never let anyone into the darkroom with me. No exceptions." However, he had a friend, a photographer named Malcolm Eldredge, who might be willing to teach Daniel a thing or two.

As it turned out, Malcolm had known a thing or two about computers as well as cameras, and Daniel had learned more from him than perhaps Finn had intended he should. His father's creation of the final image using darkroom techniques began to seem outmoded, an artistic dead end. The future lay elsewhere.

All the same, when his apprenticeship was over, he had refused Malcolm's offer of a job as his assistant and had gone back yet again to Finn. He was astounded now by how unsquelchable he'd been. As though he'd wanted to force Finn to acknowledge by deed as well as by word that they were father and son.

By this time, the brief hermitlike stage of Finn's life had begun and he'd left London to live full-time at Kerreck Du. There was a No Trespassing sign now planted firmly in front of his life as well as in front of his darkroom. Daniel sometimes thought that only Finn's curiosity had prevented his being tossed out on his ear. Something about his persistence in the face of so little encouragement must have caught his father's interest. Daniel would swear that paternal feeling had nothing to do with it.

He told Dana some of this, more than he meant to. She listened intently, a pencil held loosely between two fingers while her hand rested on the desk, as though the material she'd been so eager to examine had temporarily ceased to compel her. While he spoke, he observed the delicate turn of her wrist, the polish on the nails of her small, strong fingers. A darkening bruise on the back of the hand. He had been attracted to her from the start, at the gallery, and had felt that attraction again, more strongly, out on the cliffs. Now he acknowledged to himself that he wanted her more intensely than he'd wanted anyone in a long time. But he wasn't going to reveal that here, at Kerreck Du.

"Finn had no idea what to do with me," he told her, careful to balance the account, to describe Finn's patience in the face of what must have seemed an assault on his privacy. "Out of desperation, I think, he told me to inventory Hobhouse's photographs and then look for others that might have been stored away. He said maybe I could learn something from Henry."

"And did you?"

He heard the sharpened curiosity in her voice but kept his response deliberately vague. "From and about, both. He was a brilliant photographer, technically and artistically. And a complicated man. Maybe even a little crazy." When he had expressed as much to Finn, Finn had said Hobhouse's personality and private life were irrelevant; all that mattered was the work. But then Finn knew at first hand what it was like to have people interpret the work in terms of the life.

Dana frowned, tapping the pencil against the desk with her thumb. "I don't think he was crazy at all, though he was the one they should have locked up. Not Marianna."

"I don't mean crazy in a lunatic sense. Obsessive's a better word. When conditions were right, his obsessions produced art. And when they were wrong . . . well, they still produced art, but misery along with it."

She tilted her head to look at him, her gray eyes narrowed. "And what were the wrong conditions?" she asked. "Marriage to Marianna?"

"Maybe. Eventually, anyway." He looked away from her, out at the small wasteland of brambles and weeds that had overtaken the garden beyond the glasshouse. Sooner or later, he thought, marriage seemed to produce the wrong conditions. He pushed the stool back from the desk and stood up. "I should let you work."

He was about to leave when it occurred to him that she ought to have something under her injured foot, which was resting on the floor. As he upended a wastebasket and placed it under the desk, he said, "You know, I've always wondered why Marianna's father consented to the marriage. Who was Hobhouse after all? A failed artist turned photographer, twenty years older than Marianna and penniless. You'd think her father would have insisted she hold out for something better."

"Unless she had epilepsy," Dana said quietly, lifting her foot onto the wastebasket.

Surprised, he asked her how she knew this.

"It's an educated guess. But it seems likely, from her own descriptions of her symptoms. Hearing voices, seeing visions; falling into dreamy states; uncontrollable trembling. She would see her mother and brothers surrounded by light. Or have a vision of paradise. That's how she described a certain place she saw over and over again. She wrote that the ecstasy she felt then was almost unendurable."

Marianna's epilepsy wasn't the more acute kind with grand mal seizures, she explained, but a milder version, in which the sufferer experienced an altered state rather than a loss of consciousness. "It's called temporal lobe epilepsy."

"I've heard of it." Prompted by interest in Lewis Carroll's photographic work, he told her, he'd once read a biography of the writer, which had described Carroll as a sufferer from this form of epilepsy. He remembered the biographer's explanation that a scar on the part of the brain controlling feelings and memory, which resulted in misfiring electrical charges, might have caused Carroll's seizures.

Dana was familiar with Carroll's story. "Both *Alice in Wonderland* and *Through the Looking Glass* describe seizure states. The sensation of falling down a hole, of shrinking or expanding. Alice's emotional turbulence, her panic attacks and fits of temper. The bliss she feels when she's floating. They're all symptoms."

She twisted around in her chair and pointed to the wall where Hobhouse's photographs were hanging. "Look at Marianna's face in that middle photograph over there," she said. "The one that shows her full-face. There's a symptom there, too."

He walked over to the photograph that portrayed Iseult on her way to the pyre. He saw at once what she meant. Marianna's face was strikingly asymmetrical, as Lewis Carroll's had been. Along with other symptoms, Carroll's biographer had written, this was an indication of damage to one side of the brain.

He said, "Do you think Marianna's epilepsy explains her spiritualism?"

She hesitated for a moment before she answered. "Some people would argue that it does. The doctors who signed the papers committing her to the asylum certainly did. A lot of nineteenth-century doctors compared the characteristics common both to spiritualism and epilepsy—the trances, bodily contortions, and unconnected language—and explained the medium's religious ecstasy as a clinical condition.

"I suppose even the automatic writing that we associate with mediums could be seen as a symptom," she went on. "Temporal lobe epilepsy often results in a compulsion to write. Hypergraphia, it's called. Marianna produced reams and reams of automatic writing, and she kept diaries and notebooks all her life. Most of her writings have vanished—Henry probably destroyed them after she died. But she published a pamphlet about her spiritualist practices, and it survived. And we have her letters from the asylum. They suggest that there were other reasons why Marianna became a medium.

"I can only judge Marianna's beliefs by her actions," Dana continued. "And those seem to have been sincere. She believed in the reality of the spirits. Anyway, I don't think there is a single, or simple, explanation why women like Marianna became spiritualists. When you look at what was happening in the midcentury—"

"You mean Darwinism? That big monkey wrench thrown at established Christianity by *On the Origin of Species*?"

She smiled at the pun. "And all the discoveries in science."

"Which made people want scientific proof of immortality."

"Yes, exactly. And a seance seemed to offer that. Or at least visible proof, anyway. Especially a seance with manifestations. Not that Marianna ever went in for that herself," she added quickly. "There weren't any ectoplasmic apparitions or ghostly hands at her table. But complicated issues about women's roles were a factor, too. How women fitted in to a society that was changing so dramatically. Issues of power and freedom."

He knew that women had outnumbered men in mid-nineteenth-century England. "Which meant that marriage wouldn't have been an option for a lot of women."

"And the alternatives for middle-class girls were pretty dismal. Governess, stay-at-home old maid? Not a lot of power or freedom there."

"But a medium . . . ?"

"Had both. And if you were a private medium, like Marianna, you had respect as well. Spiritualism let women have an active professional and religious role that was denied them in almost every other sphere."

Talking to Dana reminded Daniel why he had chosen to study history at university, quixotic as it had seemed at the time. Her enthusiasm was infectious. And she made him feel that his interest mattered to her, that they were sharing a process of discovery. It had been a long time, too long, he told himself, since he'd had this sort of conversation with a woman.

Returning to his original question, Dana said, "If Marianna was an epileptic, she wouldn't have been very marriageable. Her father might have considered Henry the best she could do." Her voice, so full of energy only moments before, grew noticeably duller as she spoke. She looked down at her hands.

He wondered if she was feeling pain from her ankle, and told himself that he should leave and let her get on with her work. But it was so easy to go on talking like this, watching her face in profile, the dark lashes half closed now over her eyes, the curve of her mouth. She was finely made, with delicate features, but he could see strength there, too, and a supple resilience.

"What do you think Marianna saw in Henry?" he asked.

She turned then and gave a small, rueful smile. "Maybe she mistook him for a liberator. From all accounts her father kept her a virtual prisoner after her mother and brothers died. He might have been trying to protect her from the fevers that carried the others off. Or he might have been afraid that she would have a seizure in public and disgrace him. Whatever the reason, she spent most of her time shut up in her father's house.

"It's ironic, her father dying only a year after the wedding. If she'd waited, she would have had her independence and her own money, too. As it was, she lost everything."

"No one could accuse you of taking the romantic view. But the money was hers, wasn't it?"

She shook her head. "This was before the Married Women's Property Act. It was as much his as hers—more his, given a husband's power then."

"You make it sound as if you suspect Henry of foul play to get his hands on her father's money."

"Not then. Her father apparently died of a fever, like his wife and his sons. Their plumbing was probably responsible for all the deaths. Septic tanks installed in the garden next to the well killed off a lot of middle-class Victorians. They never realized that the indoor plumbing they were so proud of was doing them in."

In that case, Daniel said, it could be argued that Hobhouse had saved Marianna's life by taking her away from such a lethal family home. "But what did you mean, 'Not then'?"

She only shrugged. "I shouldn't paint such a grim picture. Maybe she enjoyed married life in the beginning. In one letter, she wrote that when they were first married Henry encouraged her as a medium. Famous people began to come to her seances. Charles Dickens, Fanny Trollope, Elizabeth Barrett Browning." Her gaze lingered on the photograph. "Henry photographed some of them, and his reputation grew. But the more successful he became, the more he began to feel that her spiritualism was somehow shameful. Eventually he tried to stop it."

"Maybe he was only trying to protect her. Maybe he foresaw she'd be exposed, that there'd be some sort of scandal." Daniel was playing devil's advocate for Henry, but he was curious to know how far Dana's obvious partisanship of Marianna went.

"We don't know that the scandal necessarily had to do with her being exposed as a fraud. That was only the rumor. Anyway, whatever the scandal was, it gave Henry the opportunity to put an end to the seances and hustle Marianna down to Kerreck Du. Where he soon claims that she's gone mad and has her committed to an asylum. Obligingly, she dies shortly afterward. And the rich widower takes up where he left off, growing richer and more famous."

"You don't like Henry."

"I don't like the way everything turned out so well for him and so badly for Marianna."

"Not all that well for Henry, if he loved her."

She raised a disbelieving eyebrow. "Sure."

"There's some evidence he did. The early pictures he took of her, for instance. Even those." He nodded at the pictures on the wall. "They're the work of retrospective jealousy, wouldn't you say?" Not that jealousy necessarily implied love, he was quick to add.

"They're saying she was unfaithful, those photographs, aren't they?"

"I think so, yes."

"Then the cause of the scandal might not have been some accusation of fraud, but because she was having an affair." She bit her lip, her brow furrowed. She looked tired now, and the pale skin under her eyes was shadowed. He was suddenly, guiltily, conscious of how much she had been through.

"You should rest," he told her. "All this can wait."

"But I haven't even begun. . . ." She made a vague gesture toward the heap. Then, acknowledging her weariness, she allowed herself to be persuaded. They locked the glasshouse door and he helped her across the hall to the guest room.

She was very quiet, a little remote, as he showed her where things were. She thanked him politely, with a trace of formality. But then, just before he left her, she said almost pleadingly, "I don't believe it, you know. It's another one of Hobhouse's fantasies about her. It's how he wanted to see her: the mad, unfaithful wife. So he wouldn't have to feel guilty."

As he closed the door, Daniel felt as if he were deceiving her, keeping the truth about Marianna from her. But he was curious to see if she would come to the same conclusion. He would tell her what he knew, eventually, but not yet. He wanted the shared journey of discovery to continue.

Chapter 12

After leaving Kerreck Du, John Malzer deposited Thomas and Estelle at their respective houses, then picked up a chicken curry at the Indian take-away by the quayside in Trebartha. Like gray palisades of stone, the sea walls sheltered the little harbor where fishing boats, dinghies, and pleasure craft rested at anchor in the twilight. On the slipways and jetties, lobster pots and faded orange nets waited for the next day's meager catch, and an enormous rusting iron anchor lay on its side near some rotting pilings, a reminder of better days.

Malzer drove slowly back to the Chapel Gallery through narrow, stony streets, so steeply sloping that the buildings seemed to stand on one another's roofs. Overtaken by sudden weariness, he yawned widely. He had been forced to linger with Estelle longer than he had intended. Now that the time had come to part with her daughter's picture, she'd told him, she felt as though she were losing Barbara again. This was not intuition, he was sure, but simply a sentimental bid for sympathy. Providing the expected reassurances had exhausted him. Only his plea of the pressure of work had persuaded her to release him from having dinner with her.

But it was worth all the trouble, he reflected as he glanced at the large wrapped parcel on the seat beside him. He had never really doubted that Estelle would give the photograph to him; she had simply wanted to spin out the courtship, make him dance attendance on her a little longer.

He rested his left hand on the wrapping, and for an instant almost persuaded himself that he could sense the powerful image beneath it. "She had the uncanny ability to project dissolution," Finn had once said of Barbara Pinchot. "In both senses of the word. You only had to look at her to know she was spoilt, somehow corrupt, and that she was coming apart. It gave a nervous edge to her photographs." John would never forget these words, or the way Finn had said them, clinically, almost indifferently.

The car labored up the steep street until at last it reached the crest of the hill. The gallery came into view immediately ahead on the left, its odd jumble of buildings outlined by the waning light in the west.

The sight of the Chapel Gallery often gave him an almost sensual thrill of pleasure. He liked to think that its unique structure and complicated past reflected his own periodic reinvention of himself. Tonight, however, he seemed to see the place with a stranger's eyes, as if it no longer belonged to him. He took the odd sensation to mean that he was already detaching himself.

After he had parked the car, he stood for a few moments contemplating the bizarre facade, consciously impressing it on his memory.

The gallery was made up of three architecturally distinct parts, each built in a different century for a different purpose. "All they have in common," Thomas had once said to him, "is their creators' contempt for the poor sods who inhabited them." What a perfect symbol, he'd continued in his waspish way, of that obstinately dissident Cornish trinity: church, state, and military.

Although privately amused by Thomas's witticism, Malzer did not include it in the little history of the gallery he sometimes gave to interested visitors. There was no point in unnecessarily offending people.

The gallery's oldest section had begun life as a small eighteenth-century Nonconformist chapel set at the crossroads. Hence the name, which was also a private joke of his own. Next to be built, in the mid-nineteenth century, was a row of workers' cottages, erected some fifty feet from the chapel by a Methodist mayor of Trebartha in fulfillment of an election promise. Devoid of beauty apart from the silvery sheen of their slate roofs, the three tiny attached cottages were squeezed onto the remaining bit of level land before it dropped sharply away to the harbor. John had once seen an early photograph in the local historical society's collection, which showed the chapel's unadorned square of granite, as grim as the message preached within it, lowering over the mean little huddle of cottages. To Malzer, it looked like a bully with his victims.

At the end of the nineteenth century, poverty drove the cottages' occupants to Canada and Australia in search of work, while the success of Methodism resulted in a larger, and even uglier, chapel down in the town. A local farmer eventually bought the abandoned chapel and cottages as a wool barn and fold for his sheep. Then, during World War II, the army requisitioned the property for obscure reasons of its own and erected a Nissen hut. The long half-cylinder of corrugated metal linked the chapel to the cottages. Local rumors speculated that German prisoners of war would be housed in the conglomeration of buildings, but the expected prisoners never arrived. After the war, the property had a brief, unsuccessful life as an inn before it reverted to storage again, then lay derelict for years. Potential buyers were discouraged by a preservation order on the chapel, by the decrepit state of the buildings, and perhaps by their sheer ugliness as well.

But John had seen their possibilities. Seeing possibilities, and persuading others to see them too, was his gift.

The property was affordable, interesting, and from his point of view, perfectly sited. He had been looking for a building near Trebartha but not actually in the town itself; something set apart but accessible to tourists. This seemed to answer all his requirements. The closest houses were down the hill, several hundred yards away. Only their rooftops were visible. And across the road was the car park where visitors and tourists were obliged to leave their vehicles before walking down the precipitous streets into the town. No one who came to Trebartha could miss the place.

He hired roofers but did much of the conversion work himself, and all of the wiring. The largest space, the chapel, became the main exhibition room, its plaster walls painted white. In the long hump of the Nissen hut he built a plywood labyrinth of open-plan cubicles at different levels linked by gently sloping ramps covered in industrial carpeting. Visitors would enter the foyer of the gallery by the hut's double doors and make their way up the incline and through these tiny viewing rooms to find themselves suddenly in the large open space of the chapel. The first two cottages served as his office and living quarters, the third as a storage area with darkroom.

At some point, probably during the army's tenure, and for some unknown purpose, large metal ducts had been installed along the ceilings through the three cottages and the Nissen hut. By painting those that were visible in the exhibition areas a bright yellow to contrast with the white walls and black carpeting, he had cleverly made them seem an integral part of the gallery's idiosyncratic design.

There was a high gloss to the interior of the gallery when Malzer finished his work, but it was only skin deep. He had used the cheapest possible materials. But as long as the place passed inspection he was content. He wasn't building for the ages; three or four years should do nicely. Although there was much that he liked about his creation—the enclosed feeling, for example, the sense of privacy, almost of invisibility, that it gave him—he could see it burn to the ground tomorrow without regret. He had no attachment to physical objects, whatever their size, and he felt a certain contempt for those who did.

A cool wind from the sea brought him out of his reverie. It was dark now here on the uplands, and he was suddenly cold and very hungry. Taking the curry and the parcel from the car, he went to the first door of the cottage wing, his private entrance.

Inside the small bed-sitting room cum office, he switched on the lights and propped the wrapped photograph on the sofa bed, shoving aside a mingled heap of newspapers and clean laundry. To his left, a doorway in the middle cottage's shared wall led to the kitchen and bathroom. The third and farthest cottage could be entered only through its own door.

The kitchen smelled faintly of sour milk and a full waste bin. There was a half-eaten container of yogurt on the counter and two days' worth of dirty dishes in the sink, but he ignored these. He poured the curry onto a plate, took some leftover salad and a beer from the refrigerator, and carried them back on a tray to the other room. His desk doubled as a table. As he ate, he reflected on how quickly his plans had developed, more quickly than he could have hoped. Four years had been an overly pessimistic estimate. Already he had his eye on a space in London for another, larger, gallery.

Once he had wanted to be a photographer himself. He'd been an art student at a London polytechnic at the time. Quentin Finn's work became an inspiration, the man himself a kind of god in his imagination. The passionate intensity John gave to anything that compelled him he now gave to a study of Finn's work. Then one day he heard that Finn would be teaching a master class to a selected few, application by portfolio. The girl he was living with persuaded him to let her take his portfolio around to Finn's studio, to get a jump on the other students.

Weeks went by. His portfolio remained with Finn and, although he heard nothing, this gave Malzer hope. At last, a month later, the class list was posted. Malzer's name was not on it.

An emotional crisis with the girl compounded his furious, crushing disappointment. She left the portfolio, which she'd retrieved from Finn, along with her good-bye note, on their bed. He did manage to persuade her to change her mind, but it ended badly nevertheless. And a few days later he learned that Finn had used some of his photographs in the master class as examples of photographic ineptitude. Finn hadn't identified their source, but the fellow student who told him this had recognized his work. The photographs suffered from "a sentimental squint in the photographer's eye," Finn had said. It had been one of his kinder comments, the student confided with some glee.

Malzer took his portfolio to Tower Bridge and sailed the photographs one by one out over the river. Then he quit the polytechnic.

He was grateful to Finn, he liked to tell himself, for without that boot in the pants he might never have discovered his true metier. He never mentioned this incident in his past to anyone, and he continued to profess himself a devotee of Finn's work.

When they'd first met, eighteen months ago in Trebartha, he had made the mistake of telling Finn himself that he had watched his development as an artist with profound admiration. He knew Finn would never connect him with that "squint-eyed" portfolio. And anyway, he had changed his name from the one he'd used in his art school days.

Finn's response had been characteristically caustic. He had crossed his forefingers at Malzer, as though to ward off a hex, and said, half-humorously, "Don't you know that it's the admirer and the watcher who provoke us to all the insanities we commit?" The way he'd said it made it sound like a quote. John knew from the titles he gave his photographs that Finn liked obscure quotes.

The Chapel Gallery had been an immediate success. Malzer had a showman's flair for revelation. He knew how to mount an exhibition that whetted the viewer's appetite with glimpses of strategically placed pieces. And he quickly established a reputation among the local artists as someone willing to work tirelessly on their behalf. His connections with several London gallery owners meant that a successful exhibition at the Chapel Gallery often resulted in a subsequent show in London.

He rarely photographed for pleasure now, but he did take pictures of the pieces he exhibited in the gallery for publicity, catalog, and insurance purposes, as well as black-and-white tourist shots of the town and countryside, which he made into postcards and sold. As he preferred to do his own developing, a darkroom was a necessity.

When he had learned that there would be a retrospective of Finn's work in London in September, he persuaded Finn to let him mount a smaller version at the Chapel Gallery first. A trial run, so to speak. They agreed it would open at the end of May, when a week of school holidays brought a tourist influx to Trebartha.

He wanted the best pieces, he told Finn, but also representation across the years. He mentioned a photograph he'd once seen. Was it available? It had been vandalized, Finn said shortly. Were there other versions? One, Finn replied. But the mother of the girl who had modeled for him now owned it and he would not approach her. However, he agreed that John could try his luck. So Malzer went up to London, met Estelle Pinchot, and persuaded her not only to lend the photograph but to fund the exhibition. This was a stroke of brilliance, he felt. He promised her that Barbara's photograph, which was undoubtedly Finn's masterpiece, would be the centerpiece of the exhibit.

Malzer looked across the desk at the parcel on the sofa bed. Propped upright, with the light shining on the smooth brown paper, it had an expectant quality, almost as if it were waiting for him. He pushed aside his half-eaten dinner.

At that moment the doorbell rang. For an instant he was tempted not to answer, to pretend he wasn't in, but of course whoever it was—and he could guess who it would be—would have seen his car and the lights. Resigned, he stood up. Before he went to the door, he put the parcel away in the wardrobe.

It was Thomas Attery, as he'd expected. He knew the other man had been frustrated by not being able to meet alone with him for the past few days.

"Thomas!" he said, injecting delight into his voice. "Come in, come in."

Thomas seemed pleased with his welcome, almost shy. He looked around, then clicked his tongue and said in the dry manner that Malzer by now knew was used to disguise his feelings, "Really, John, you live like a student." He sounded like a fond but exasperated parent speaking to his child; it was a voice he used only when he and Malzer were alone together.

"I keep the gallery clean and tidy," Malzer replied mildly. "That's all that matters. D'you want something to eat? Or a beer?"

Thomas shook his head. "A drink, but not here. You finish your dinner and we'll go down to the Pickled Herring." The Pickled Herring was the name of a pub in one of the back streets near the harbor which was frequented by the local artists' colony.

While Malzer went back to his curry, Thomas removed a crumpled shirt from one end of the sofa bed and sat down. A dismissive sweep of one hand took in the squalor of the little room. "I'll never understand how someone with your gift for mounting an exhibition can have so little interest in your own surroundings."

Malzer had heard him say this too often to respond. He watched with suppressed amusement as the other man took the shirt across his lap and smoothed out the arms, neatly folded it, then set to work on the rest of his laundry. Thomas looked somewhat haggard, he thought, the gray in his skin more pronounced, with a fine crepelike webbing around the eyes as though from lack of sleep.

"Well, what did you think of Finn's latest?" Thomas asked him after a moment. Dana Morrow, he explained, when Malzer pretended not to know what he meant.

Anyone who interested Finn interested him, Malzer was

tempted to reply. Estelle had complained to him that the woman was a nuisance, turning up just now when Finn had so much on his plate, but he disagreed. If Finn was in love with her, or simply sleeping with her, then her presence made everything that much more interesting.

But he said only that she seemed a nice enough girl. "Pretty. In a quiet way. But what makes you think there's anything going on between them?"

"Why else would he let her into the holy of holies?"

This was John's assumption, too. He forked up the last of the curry, chewed for a moment, then observed with a thoughtful air, "She coincides nicely with this Hobhouse period of his, doesn't she?"

For the past few months, Finn had focused exclusively on variations of themes in Henry Hobhouse's work. No one had seen the results yet, but he had promised two or three of the best to Malzer for the exhibition, along with companion pieces by Hobhouse himself.

"Hobbyhorse, you mean," Thomas said dryly. "And we know why he's riding it, don't we. You only have to look at those old photographs of Hobhouse's wife. She was the image of Solange. Looked far more like her, in fact, than Pascale does." He took a sock, found its mate, and stuffed one inside the other with a savage emphasis. "If Marianna Hobhouse's character was anything like her doppelgänger's then no wonder Henry locked her away."

Thomas had not liked Solange. Shortly before her death, he had confided to John that he was sure she was prejudicing Finn against him. It was obvious to John, although Thomas did not say so explicitly, that he feared losing Finn as a client. His most important client.

Seeing Malzer's empty plate, Thomas stood up. "If you're ready?"

Malzer acquiesced only because it would be easier to extricate himself from Thomas at the pub than here. He liked the Pickled Herring chiefly because tourists tended to avoid the place. Unlike its competition, it made no effort to charm them with fishing nets and old lobster pots strung from the ceiling or facsimile posters of smugglers' broadsheets. And strangers who wandered in often faced a silence that was sufficient to send them back out the door again.

Inside the pub, Thomas steered him firmly to an empty table, acknowledging familiar faces with the barest of nods, then went to the bar for their drinks. Malzer was amused rather than annoyed by Thomas's proprietary manner; he wasn't in the mood for collegiality tonight anyway. And he was curious to know what was on Thomas's mind. He soon found out. Midway through his glass of port, Thomas launched into a diatribe against Estelle.

"The woman's a hysteric," he concluded, draining the last of his port.

"She's excitable," Malzer agreed quietly. "I suppose it's understandable. She feels very guilty about her daughter's death. It wasn't ruled a suicide, but it seems pretty clear that it was close enough as makes no difference."

Thomas's reaction was characteristic. "Well, no wonder," he said immediately, "with a mother like that. And if that was a plea for understanding, I'm afraid it's wasted on me. I still don't see why Finn tolerates the woman."

Malzer hesitated, then said, "Perhaps he feels badly about Barbara's death as well."

"Why should he?"

"She was modeling for him when it happened. He was doing a lot of nudes at the time. Perhaps in her unstable state it wasn't good for her."

Thomas gave him a shrewd look over the rim of his glass. "Perhaps she was more than a model to him."

"Oh, I don't think Estelle suspects him of that. She'd hardly support this exhibition if she did." He added slowly, as if against his will, "Although I have to say I've sometimes wondered about Finn and Barbara myself. . . ." He gave a soft, rueful laugh. "I wouldn't want to be in Finn's shoes if Estelle herself began to wonder. She'd take a cleaver to him."

"In other words," Thomas said with a small air of triumph, "you agree with me that she's unbalanced."

He let that pass.

"How did you learn all this?" Thomas asked then, his voice curious. "From Estelle?"

He nodded. "Sometimes she confides in me."

"You poor man." The voice became acid. Then, irritably, "Must you crack your knuckles? You'll get arthritis, you know."

John folded his hands in his lap. "You'd find she's not so bad," he went on in a moment, "if you got to know her better."

Thomas gave an exaggerated shiver. "I sincerely hope I won't have to know her any better. Perhaps the Gull will oblige me by doing her in."

When Malzer let out a small, audible sigh, Thomas leaned forward and placed a hand on his sleeve. "Sorry, John. I know you deplore that sort of talk." Then, reverting, he added, "Must be the chapel upbringing. Didn't you say once you were a chapel boy?"

Again Malzer did not reply. Thomas knew very well that he had never said any such thing. It wasn't a bad guess, though; Thomas was no fool. He'd once told Thomas that his past was so boring he'd forgotten it. Not quite the truth, but near enough. His early life as a foster child in a series of temporary homes was something he did his best not to think about.

He finished his orange juice in a gulp. "I've got to get back."

"Now I've offended you," Thomas said contritely.

He looked so cast down that Malzer took pity on him. "It's not that. It's just that I've work to do. But if you're going tomorrow night, we might drive together." At Thomas's blank look, he added, "Finn's dinner party, remember?"

"Oh Christ, I'd forgotten. I suppose I'll have to go. Although at the moment I suspect Finn would prefer I stayed away." With the air of someone making a difficult confession, he added, "The truth is, several investments have gone sour in rather a large way. I had to tell him today, just before we left. He took it well, considering." Hastily he added, "This is just between you and me, of course."

It was so unlike Thomas to confess to any trouble whatsoever that Malzer assumed the loss must have been considerable. In response, he leaned forward and touched Thomas's shoulder. This was a calculated gesture; he had never deliberately touched the other man before. "Don't worry too much, Thomas. You're so clever with money you're bound to recoup it. And the price of Finn's photographs is going up all the time. He's hardly going to starve."

Thomas's response was an almost pathetic smile of gratitude. Then, with a rush, he said, "I'm more worried about myself, if I'm frank. There's a dealer in London. I owe him rather a lot."

"The Beato?"

Thomas nodded. "I had to have it."

"How much?" Malzer asked. When Thomas told him, he began to understand the extent of the problem.

Later, as he walked back up the hill, Malzer reflected that Thomas was showing the distinct signs of someone losing control. He felt a twinge of pity mixed with contempt. He prided himself on his own discipline. Unlike Thomas, he thought, he could wait for what he wanted.

He took the photograph, still in its wrappings, into the former chapel. He liked to imagine the fire-and-brimstone sermons that had once been preached in this room, their contrast with the cool white boxlike space. Retribution was a creed of his own. All the same, it amused him to think how those preachers might have reacted to the use he now made of their place of worship. Beauty was a relative term, but it had been anathema in any incarnation to those early Methodists. He could imagine their response to the picture he was about to hang.

Stripping away the paper, he settled the large photograph into place and stood back. Technically and visually it was a tour de force. The tones moved subtly from the creamy white of a pearl through soft grays to a rich, velvety black; the joins of the parts were seamless and invisible. But its power over him went beyond the aesthetic.

In the photograph, the slim figure of a young woman stood naked in a long hallway that receded behind her into darkness. A narrow stream ran down the hallway beneath her feet, where the floor should be. Her hands were at her sides, palms out; one foot was placed slightly in front of the other. Her dark hair fell forward, hiding her face, as she gazed down at her reflection in the water, a headless shadow. On either side were open doorways and in each stood the same girl, sometimes nude, sometimes clothed, in different positions and in decreasing size, but always watching that central figure, her double. Overhead, in place of a ceiling, was a wide, cloud-filled sky.

As he gazed at it, he remembered an Agatha Christie novel he'd once read in which the characters had discussed reasons why someone might want to keep a photograph. Poirot had given the reason Malzer himself favored: to keep the desire for revenge alive.

Chapter 13

Dana woke from a deep sleep confused and disoriented. She sat bolt upright, terrified, with no idea of where she was or why her body was hurting so badly. Only when she saw the brace on her ankle did she remember, and sink back again with relief into the pillows behind her. She noticed then that a tray with covered plates was sitting on the bedside table. Someone, probably Pascale, had brought her dinner. Or was it breakfast? The window curtains were drawn and the room was dim, lit only by the small lamp on the chest of drawers. A glance at her wristwatch showed her that it was after ten. Dinner, then.

Her arm and shoulder muscles were aching now along with her ankle. Groggily, she reached for one of the painkillers the doctor had left with her, then lifted the tray onto her lap, uncovered the plates, and slowly began to eat the cold roast beef and salad she found there. Still half asleep, she knew that she was hungry but hardly tasted the food. Images from the day tumbled before her mind's eye, like those of a dream, their meaning unclear but somehow profound.

To distract herself, she looked around the bedroom, which she'd hardly noticed earlier. Pleasant but rather small, the room was furnished with dark, nineteenth-century furniture that seemed too large for it. As well as the bed, there was a chest of drawers, an armchair covered in bargello work, and a bookcase filled with the kind of books a guest staying only a night or two might want: collections of short stories, poetry, essays. The stack of magazines on the bedside table, a mix of fashion, literary, rock, and gossip, suggested that Firm played host to all types. Dark blue velvet curtains were drawn across the single casement window.

There was no rug on the dark wood floor and Dana found this, combined with the furniture and the mildly claustrophobic feel to the room, also suggestive. Guests at Kerreck Du, whatever their predilections, weren't to be made so comfortable that they were tempted to overstay their welcome.

Still, the bathroom with its huge, claw-footed tub and piles of soft towels was undeniably luxurious, and the long, deep, soporific bath she'd taken had soothed away the worst of the aches. Afterward, intending only to rest, she had stretched out on the bed, falling asleep almost before her eyes closed.

The dessert on the tray was a crème caramel. As she spooned up its syrupy remnants, she realized that the earlier feeling of disorientation had given way to restless excitement, combined with an acute unease.

The excitement was easy enough to explain. The portrait of Marianna together with Elizabeth Barrett Browning was in itself more than she had hoped to find at Kerreck Du. Added, tantalizingly, to that remarkable photograph were those of Henry's Tristan and Iseult series, in which Marianna so disturbingly featured. Most promising of all, there was the waiting heap of documents, which, in light of the photographs, might hold dramatic revelations of their own.

As for the uneasiness, that had its source in everything she'd seen and heard earlier on the terrace, including the sinister discussion of the Gull. She was drawn to Kerreck Du and its possibilities, but instinct urged her to finish her work here as quickly as possible and leave, to avoid becoming embroiled in the turmoil of other lives and infected by their fears.

There was another source, she acknowledged to herself, for both the excitement and the unease—Daniel Finn. Their conversation in the glasshouse, and her immediate sense of rapport with him, reminded her of past illusions, those naive expectations she'd once had of what her marriage would be. One long passionate conversation with a man who loved her, sexually, intellectually, spiritually, as deeply as she loved him. A relationship in which neither partner sought to dominate or subjugate the other. A marriage, in fact, like Elizabeth and Robert Browning's, with shared passion, shared power, shared knowledge.

Stewart, a reknowned authority on contemporary drama, had been older, sophisticated, culturally with it, and physically attractive. He had seemed to her to embody perfection.

She shifted uncomfortably in the bed as she recalled that impossibly romantic fantasy of love. A line from a forgotten poem came into her head: "We've fed the heart on fantasy, the heart's grown brutal from the fare." She hoped her own heart hadn't become brutal, but it wasn't as trusting as it once had been.

Then, like an antidote to the pain, came the memory of that moment when she had reached out for Elvina's fragile body and held it against her own. Once again she felt the amazed joy that had swept through her when she realized that the child was safe. No matter what harm she might have done, to herself and to her marriage, by her self-indulgent wishful thinking, she now had one great unreflecting act to set against all her failures.

She put the tray back on the night table and swung her feet over the side of the bed. Gingerly, she rested her weight on her right foot, then slowly stood up. Her left ankle hurt, but not as much as she thought it would. She slipped on her sandals, took the key to the glasshouse from the top of the chest of drawers, and, keeping one hand on the walls for support, went out into the hall. It was close to eleven, but so long as sleep eluded her, she might as well begin to satisfy her intense curiosity about that pile of documents.

The long pink cotton T-shirt dress that doubled as her nightgown fell almost to her ankles, modest enough if she should meet someone. But as the glasshouse wing was separated by the kitchen from the rest of the house, she wasn't likely to. Nor was it likely that she would disturb anyone.

In the glasshouse, she sat down at the desk and stared for a few moments at the open photograph case. "Secure the shadow ere the substance fade," Elizabeth Barrett Browning had written, urging a friend to have photographs made of loved ones before they died. In an early example of advertising acumen, her exhortation had been expropriated and used to sell daguerreotypes. But the poet had also sought ways to secure the shadows of those whose substance had faded long before, among them her dead mother and drowned brother. With that hope, she had come to Marianna.

Dana set aside a certain part of the material. She wouldn't read letters tonight; those could wait for the morning. Rested, she would be able to concentrate better. Then, closing her eyes, she let her hand decide, hovering above the remaining papers and boxes spread out on the desk, like the planchette above a Ouija board.

Her hand came to rest on the smooth surface of a flat gray archival box. Inside, she found an old photograph album with red morocco covers stamped and gilded with a pattern of intertwined vines. Turning the pages, she saw that the album contained close to two dozen photographs, each on a single page framed by a gold line and protected by a sheet of tissue paper, each signed by Henry Arlington Hobhouse and dated 1870, the year of Marianna's death. Group portraits of two to four people, all the photographs had been taken in the same small, richly decorated room hung with tapestries and heavy curtains. A small shiver of excitement stirred inside her.

Hobhouse's subjects were visibly rapt with some profound inner experience. Most were seated decorously enough at a small table; a hand outflung or clutched against the breast was the most extravagant gesture. The drama—for these were intensely dramatic pictures—was created by the faces alone and by Dana's sense that she was looking on at a private act: a seance. Or rather a series of seances, each conducted by Marianna Hobhouse.

The medium appeared in every picture. Often the other faces were turned to her, and this, taken with her slender, upright bearing and the unadorned white dress, made it seem as though she were a priestess at some rite.

Those with her looked as though they were under a spell, their heads thrown back or bowed on their chests, eyes staring wildly at nothing or closed, faces contorted as though by ecstasy. Dana wondered how the photographer had been able to persuade his sitters to surrender themselves so unself-consciously to the camera.

The photographs exerted an irresistible, almost hypnotic, pull on her eye, and not just for their subject matter. Details were lushly sensuous, textures palpable. The rich nap of the velvet hangings shrouding the room, the sheen of bombazine and satin, the soft, cotton-batten bulk of an old man's long white beard, all were caught with a painterly brilliance. Where light touched an object, usually at the center of the picture, it glowed. But the edges of many of the photographs were indistinct, the hangings blurred to a dense mist.

These effects combined with the size of the seance room to create the enclosed, suffocating atmosphere of a hothouse. Victorian city dwellers had been used to shutting themselves up in overdecorated rooms with the windows sealed and swathed against the diseased, soot-laden air, but Dana wondered if the subjects had found the little room as claustrophobic to inhabit as she did to observe.

Most of those with Marianna were women. Men were present in only two of the photographs. In one, the man was elderly and was accompanied by two elderly women. But in the other, the last photograph in the album, Marianna was alone with a young man whose face was partly turned away from the camera but who looked to be not much older than twenty.

As she stared at that last picture, she felt drawn into the soft depths of the little room. She wanted to be there, to submerge herself with the pair so that she could understand what had passed between them at that moment. She looked up, away from the photograph, at a leaded window with its dark diamonds of glass outlined in black. She was sitting in a pool of light from the desk lamp but the room around her was dim and shadowy and the curving glass that arched above her head was black. The weight of its darkness, and the silence, seemed to press down on her.

She thought of how Kerreck Du sat alone in its little valley, with the dark woods and the sea surrounding it, of how in Marianna's time it must have seemed at the world's end, and of Marianna crying out that the light was gone, and that her sin had killed her powers. But what was that sin? What had happened between the time that her husband took these photographs and the October day on which she died?

Chapter 14

Estelle Pinchot's bedroom was lavishly comfortable. Its apricot-colored walls, glowing softly in the morning sun, suffused a light that was kind to the skin; the fitted cream carpet was soft underfoot; the chintz-covered divan piled with cushions invited indolence. The four-poster bed, hung with a tasseled canopy, felt snug and warm on rainy nights.

This seductive room, with its opulent modern bathroom tiled in pink and white, was one reason she had chosen to rent the house when she first came to Trebartha three months ago. It had seduced her with its promise of ease and enveloping warmth. The master bedroom in her London house had never achieved quite this degree of comfort. There, she rarely felt warm enough.

It had seemed so secure at first, this pretty house with its view from the bedroom window of the harbor. It held no memories to reproach her. She had liked its elegance, the way it presided from its height over the little town below, secluded from the road behind the high hedge of shiny-leafed escallonia. She had never imagined that a horror like the Gull would make her nights miserable with terrifying dreams, or that the house would come to seem too big for a woman living alone, too isolated, especially after dark.

She opened the mirrored doors of her closet and rummaged among her clothes, pulling out dress after dress, holding them up for the mirror's judgment—this one too bright, the next too dark—then thrusting them back. Several slid from their hangers onto the closet floor. She left them there. Mrs. Pargeter, her daily, would hang them up again. At last she chose a pale pink mock Chanel suit and a cream-colored blouse to go with it.

As she struggled with the zipper on the skirt, which had

snagged on her slip, she decided to act on her wish that John Malzer come to live with her. Those cramped bachelor quarters of his at the Chapel Gallery were dark and squalid. As far as she could tell, he spent almost nothing on himself or on creature comforts; all his money went into the gallery. And one shouldn't live over, or in his case beside, the shop like that, never free from work. Here, she would point out to him, he could have his own entrance, privacy, independence. She would look after him, but he would be at liberty to come and go as he pleased.

Dreaming a little, she stood there with one hand idly caressing the slippery silk of the blouse while she imagined how it would be. She would pamper him with the small luxuries he loved to have whenever he visited her, the anchovy toast and petits fours, a fire in the grate. She would iron those rumpled shirts of his. Smooth back the curls from his forehead. Be the family, the mother, he'd never had. . . .

She put her hand to her throat as she realized where her thoughts had led her. A hot flush crept over her body. She knew she must never, ever, reveal these thoughts to John; they might frighten him away from her.

No, the line to take was her appreciation of their mutual sympathy and understanding, which transcended age and gender, and his extraordinary talent, a rare plant that she would nourish. She must persuade him of her willingness to support his gift, to trust him absolutely.

Everyone believed that she was infatuated with Finn, when it was really John she cared for. But she was quite content to be seen as a patron of John's gallery, sharing only his admiration for Finn's work. The others almost certainly understood their friendship in these terms. The truth, of course, was far more complicated and more interesting. At the thought of this, their shared secret, she felt a sudden thrill of pleasure.

She was quite sure that no one was laughing at her for making a fool of herself over a younger man, as they laughed at Thomas. At the thought of Thomas Attery, a frown creased her forehead. Such a desiccated stick of a man, like some insect, as though all the juices of life had been sucked from him. And that dreadful collection of his . . .

The snagged zipper pulled free of the slip at last, and she finished dressing. As she slipped on her small jeweled wristwatch, along with her bracelets, she noticed that it was already ten o'clock. She must hurry. There was so much to be done.

She was breaking eggs for an omelette when Mrs. Pargeter arrived. Mrs. Pargeter had come with the house. The owners had written her hours into the lease and were paying her out of what Estelle considered to be an excessively high rent. She would have preferred to choose her own help, but the woman was unarguably efficient, if too prone to gossip about local affairs and overly familiar.

"You look a bit peaky this morning," she said now to Estelle as she removed the bicycle clip from her right trouser leg. She always came by bicycle. She and her family lived in a cottage on the main road, a mile away. Each time Estelle passed the place the front garden seemed to be swarming with rackety children. Three were the Pargeters' own, the youngest not yet out of diapers. The rest, she assumed, were neighbors' children, lured there by the rusting automobiles and motorcycles in various stages of repair that littered the yard. The oldest, a girl, seemed sensible enough, but Mrs. Pargeter's tales of her son Ernie's exploits confirmed Estelle's opinion of small boys and their unattractive habits. Mrs. Pargeter was unaccountably proud of Ernie, who featured largely in her conversation. She rarely mentioned the daughter.

Estelle ignored the comment on her appearance. Mrs. Pargeter was hardly an arbiter of good looks. How dumpy the woman was, Estelle thought now; she might be quite attractive if she'd only make a little effort and lose some weight. But that hair, flying out every which way as though she couldn't be bothered to brush it, and those dreadful nylon blouses in the candy floss colors that clashed with the red lipstick she wore.

"I'm not surprised," Mrs. Pargeter continued, oblivious to Estelle's silence. "About your looking peaky, I mean. What with this Gull business. It's enough to give anyone nightmares, let alone a woman living on her own." As Mrs. Pargeter tied on her apron she began to tell Estelle about an encounter her Ernie'd had with a young woman looking for Kerreck Du. "An American. She was lost. Well, you know how they are. Always rushing about with no idea where they're going."

It must have been Dana Morrow, Estelle thought.

"Ernie set her straight," Mrs. Pargeter was saying. With a clatter, she took a mop, bucket, and rags from the cupboard. "Warned her about the Gull as well. Mind you, from what I hear she'll find more than enough to alarm her at Kerreck Du."

As she made it a point never to discuss personal matters with the help, Estelle thought perhaps Mrs. Pargeter might not be aware that she herself went often to Kerreck Du. That seemed unlikely, however, given the woman's apparently vast knowledge of local affairs. She compressed her lips, but said nothing. On the cooker, the butter began to sizzle in the pan. She poured in the beaten eggs.

"Well, they're artists, aren't they, the folk at Kerreck Du?" Mrs. Pargeter continued. "And all artists are mad. That's what Fred says. The Gull's probably an artist, he says." Artists were frequently the subject of Mrs. Pargeter's meditations. They infested Trebartha like head lice, she'd once told Estelle. This image had immediately evoked Ernie in Estelle's thoughts; Mrs. Pargeter was undoubtedly intimately acquainted with head lice, had been her silent reaction.

Fred was Mrs. Pargeter's husband. In the summers, he sold snacks to tourists from a ramshackle van in the public car park above the town; winters, he worked as a mechanic at a local auto shop and, Mrs. Pargeter had hinted, drank. Estelle had met him once, a rabbity-faced man with a ragged mustache and grease-stained jeans.

Her own husband, Bertrand, had worn a mustache, but it had been as trimly tidy as Bertrand himself. She rarely thought of Bertrand now; she didn't like to. His memory aroused in her a mixture of shame and guilt. She knew that she ought to have stood up to him. He had been a bully, and worse, and she had been a coward. She had failed to protect their child from him.

Widely admired as a successful businessman and civic leader, Bertrand at home had been a martinet with a penchant for petty domestic tyrannies whose only point was to demonstrate his power over his wife and daughter. The thermostat must never be set above 64, even on the coldest days, although they could well afford to run it perpetually at 80 if they'd wanted to. His breakfast egg was to be boiled for no more and no less than three minutes and ten seconds—once he'd thrown it against the wall when she'd overcooked it. His shirts must be washed and ironed only by her—laundries always used too much or too little starch.

This despotism, combined with the inexplicable rages and sudden, capricious acts of largesse for which he expected beaming gratitude, made their home miserable. One moment he was screaming at the eleven-year-old Barbara for her failure to clean under her nails, the next he was buying her unsuitably sophisticated and very expensive clothes, shutting himself up in her bedroom with her while she tried them on. He'd been proud of her beauty when she was a little girl, had made too much of it, Estelle thought, taking her to the factory, showing her off. Once, in Estelle's hearing, he had observed casually to an acquaintance that it must be difficult for a woman whose own good looks were waning to see her daughter's increase.

Barbara's adolescence had changed all that. Puberty transformed the pretty child into an awkward and unlovely girl. She grew too fast, had pimples, was fat. Bertrand lost interest in her; he was ashamed of her and took no trouble to hide it. He left her alone.

Estelle had expected Barbara to be as relieved as she was when Bertrand's attentions ceased. But to Estelle's dismay, Barbara clearly missed them. She tried desperately to win him back with a pathetic flirtatiousness. Bertrand responded by teasing her cruelly about her looks. When she cried, he grew disgusted, then angry. In retaliation, she began deliberately to deface herself. Nose rings belonged on bulls and pigs, was Bertrand's outraged response, and green was the natural color of grass, not hair. Estelle could do nothing. Barbara seemed to blame her more than she blamed Bertrand.

"Mind now, you'll burn it!"

Mrs. Pargeter's sharp warning brought Estelle's attention back to the omelette. She tipped it out onto a plate and escaped into the dining room, leaving Mrs. Pargeter in possession of the kitchen. The omelette was leathery, almost inedible, but she hardly tasted it. She ate mechanically, still held by her memories.

At seventeen, after a terrible row, Barbara had disappeared. For more than a year they had no word of her; Estelle's only consolation was that her child was safe from Bertrand. When she reappeared, she had metamorphosed once more, and was beautiful. She revealed nothing about her life during the past year, except to say that she was now working as an artists' model, but hoped soon to get fashion work. The childhood game of dress-up behind closed doors resumed, with a difference. Now she seemed to have the whip hand in her relationship with her father, and to know it.

Six months later, Bertrand had died of a stroke. Barbara's only response was a tight little grimace of what might have been pain, or satisfaction. She moved out of the house again but would not tell Estelle where she was living. From time to time she came by to collect some piece of clothing or a cassette she wanted, but she rarely lingered. At each visit she seemed to have grown thinner, her beauty more luminous and vulnerable.

Then, on a blustery March afternoon as the light was going from the sky, Estelle came back from a shopping trip at Harrod's to find a policewoman waiting in an unmarked car outside her house. Quentin Finn was also in the car. They were bringing her the news of Barbara's death.

Barbara had come to his studio for a photographic shoot, Finn told her gently, but it had been clear to him she was in no shape to work. He was about to send her home in a taxi when she had collapsed. She had died in the ambulance on the way to the hospital. Estelle did not hear the details of the cause of death, relayed by the policewoman. She took in only the fact of the death itself.

After the policewoman left, Finn had stayed with her until her brother and his wife arrived; she wasn't close to them, but they were all the family she had. The next few weeks were now mercifully blurred together in her memory. Strangers returned Barbara's few belongings from the squat where it seemed she'd been living, but Estelle did not ask them any questions; she was too afraid of their answers. The private funeral was attended, as Estelle had requested, only by relatives and a few close friends. Then followed the long days of oblivion while she sat alone in the house, refusing all offers of comfort and help.

One morning, as she had been idly flicking through the pages of a woman's magazine, she had come across an article about a psychic frequented by society figures. Although Estelle rarely went to church she had a vague, if wavering, faith, which was more a yearning toward something she could not have put into words than a belief in established religion. She wasn't sure quite where Bertrand and Barbara were now, but she did believe that on some celestial plane their spirits still existed. She had no desire whatsoever to encounter Bertrand again, but she desperately wished there were some way to see Barbara, to gain from her some sign of forgiveness.

She had gone to the psychic. The woman, who was reassuringly well-groomed and expensive, did sense her longing for a departed loved one but was far too abstract in her responses to satisfy Estelle. All she would say was that Estelle should expect a marvelous sign of hope in the near future. Estelle came away from the experience without the comfort she sought, but feeling nevertheless that she had taken one small step in the right direction.

To her astonished joy, the sign predicted by the psychic had been given almost at once. The next day Quentin Finn rang to ask if he might come round to visit her. He wanted her to have a photograph he'd made of Barbara.

When she saw the photograph, and realized that this man had understood her child better than she had, she had begun to cry. Finn took her in his arms then and somehow she found herself telling him what she could not have brought herself to reveal to anyone else. He had not tried to comfort her with useless words, he had only held her. He had felt so warm, so very warm, at a time when she seemed to be freezing to death.

There had been no one moment when the simple embrace turned into something more complicated. She remembered it as a natural, inevitable progression and the act itself as less sexual than consolatory. She had craved his warmth and he had given it. And, like some anodyne drug, it had for a little while taken away her pain.

Chapter 15

The morning sun flooded the glasshouse with light. Dana once again settled at the desk with her ankle resting on the wastebasket, then spread out the material she had brought with her from London. Everything from her files the least bit relevant to Marianna's story was here. Her notes; a copy of Marianna's pamphlet, "Fixed by Light: Or How the Dead Can Come to Us Again," published privately in 1867; and photocopies of Marianna's few surviving letters, written from the asylum to the Commissioners in Lunacy, protesting her incarceration.

With her mind's eye, Dana reviewed the brief chronology of Marianna's life: the death of her mother and brothers in 1852, when she was thirteen; the discovery, four years later, of her spiritualistic gifts; her marriage at eighteen to Henry Hobhouse, in 1857; increasing fame as a medium during the 1860s, but also two stillborn children and gradual disenchantment with her marriage; and finally, in 1870, scandal and death. The known facts tantalized and frustrated Dana with all they implied but failed to reveal.

With her materials arranged on the desk in front of her, Dana began to feel in control again. Last night's emotional tumult had frightened her, but now she recognized it for what it was, the combined result of the day's chaos of images and fresh impressions, the strain of the unfamiliar, exhaustion, the side effects of the medication, and physical pain.

This morning, with her energies restored, eager to work, she barely noticed the slight ache in her ankle. She intended to dismiss from her mind everything but the matter at hand. Nothing and no one would be allowed to disturb her morning, not even Daniel Finn.

As she reached for the packet of letters that Daniel had told her she ought to look at first, the familiar excitement rose up inside her. She was about to read words from a past sometimes more real to her than her own. A dead past perhaps, but one that might be quickened again into life by words like those in her hand.

Attached to the packet were some penciled notes Daniel had made when he'd found the letters, either for himself or for Finn.

Letters to Henry Hobhouse found in an accordion folder labeled 1870. It was packed in a tea chest with dozens of other folders, each crammed full of business correspondence for a particular year. Everything else in the folder—and in the others—concerned Hobhouse's photographic work: sales, exhibitions, the purchase of equipment and supplies, that sort of thing. No personal letters, which seem to be almost nonexistent for this period anyway. These letters were so out of place in the folder you have to think someone—Hobhouse?—deliberately hid them there. No wonder.

That cryptic last sentence apart, the folder's date alone signaled to Dana that the letters might hold revelations: 1870, the year of Marianna's incarceration and death in the asylum to which Henry had committed her.

Carefully, she pulled the top letter from its yellowed envelope and unfolded it. The handwriting that flowed neatly from border to border was small and embellished with elaborate capitals. When she saw the signature at the bottom of the page, she caught her breath. "Theophilus Veasey." The physician into whose care Henry Hobhouse had committed Marianna.

There were ten letters in the packet, all written by Veasey. As Dana began to read them her first excited anticipation gave way to an increasing horror and pity. When the last letter dropped from her fingers to the desk, she sat back, stunned. The truth was more complicated, and more banal, than she had at first conjectured. It confirmed the implications of the photographs hanging on the wall beside the desk. And it confirmed her suspicion that between them Henry Hobhouse and Theophilus Veasey had destroyed Marianna.

It was Henry she found guiltier. Of all the doctors who might have treated his wife, he had chosen one guaranteed to view her mediumship as proof of insanity. That choice had surely been deliberate.

In her research, she had time and again come across Theophilus Veasey's shrill voice inveighing against female spiritualists. He had written widely on the perceived link between mediumship and weak or diseased minds—she could lay her hands on a dozen examples in the files in front of her. One particularly egregious passage leaped out at her now: "It is a well-known fact that mediums become haggard idiots, mad, or stupid."

Veasey's first letter to Henry hinted at what was to come. It was dated September 30, 1870, the day after Marianna's arrival at Beacon House.

My dear Hobhouse,

Mrs. Hobhouse arrived yesterday in the early evening. After supper, as she seemed much affected by the journey and little disposed for conversation, I suggested that she might like to retire at once to her chamber. We have given her a large and comfortable room with a view of the Island, as you requested. She became agitated upon learning that the keeper must sleep in the room with her, that the door would be locked and the light extinguished. We require this of all our patients, for obvious reasons. More than anything else, she protests the nighttime darkness, but I have explained that for fear of fire we cannot allow candles or lamps to burn all night in the patients' rooms.

Today, Mrs. H. is much depressed in spirits, with a pronounced melancholy marked by restlessness and a desire that a light be always close by her, perhaps because the day is overcast and somewhat gloomy. She speaks very little. There are at present eleven other women at Beacon House, all ladies of good family, quiet, and harmless. Perhaps she will discover a friend among them.

Some ill-informed persons may find debateable the question of whether Mrs. H. is or is not of sound mind, but in my opinion, you are wise to commit her to our care. Allow the disorder to advance and it will become a chronic malady! When a woman surrenders the privilege, and abrogates the duty, of

*shaping her belief according to the evidence of senses trained
and instructed by experience, she endangers her sanity.*

*Mrs. H. clings to her delusions with a pertinacity that might
seem incredible were it not well known that under the influence
of Spiritualism the human mind—in particular the female—
can fall into an abyss of mysticism from which it is virtually
impossible to rescue it. Your wife is prone to Hysteria, and in
one or another of its Protean forms, this is doubtless the disease
which more than any other provides the most abundant crop of
fruit to the Spiritualists.*

*Alas that this once cultivated and pure woman has sunk to
such a state through the evil of mediomania. I assure you that I
will endeavour to treat the evil to the utmost of my abilities.*

Your obedient servant,
Theophilus Veasey.

Mediomania. Dana knew the word well. To numerous physicians of Marianna's time it had been synonymous with uteromania, the ancient and ignoble theory that an "off-balance" womb contributed to female hysteria. Female sexuality itself was suspect. Dr. Veasey went so far as to claim that perverse sexual indulgence was often responsible for convulsive fits and trances. Mediomaniacs, he wrote, were "proverbially erotic, egotistical, and religious."

Like a self-appointed witch finder, Veasey had virtually campaigned for the committal of mediums to asylums. "That day is upon us," he wrote in one treatise, "when we must vigorously root out those who spread this virulent mental malady which so debauches our social order." Women, he argued, were most susceptible to the lure of spiritualism because of their innate passivity and lack of masculine willpower.

Any temptation on Dana's part to laugh at the absurdity of all this was tempered by the knowledge that a diagnosis of mediomania often had dire consequences. Doctors used nasal feeding, rectal examinations, and enemas as part of the prescribed treatment for women suspected of the disease. The more "hysterical" female patients were put under the control of male keepers. Veasey himself once boasted of successfully treating a female patient prone to trance states with potassium bromide to rid her of her spirits. Among its other uses, potassium bromide had been employed as a sedative, and in photographic emulsion. "The chemical rendered her corporeal structure so gross," Veasey wrote, "that the spirits refused further use of it for their manifestations."

Dana shifted in her chair, and a twinge of pain shot through her ankle. She hardly noticed, she was filled with such anger and disgust at the thought of what Marianna might have suffered under Veasey's care.

All but three of Veasey's letters to Henry Hobhouse had been sent from Beacon House, the small private asylum he had established as a profitable sideline to his practice.

Dana had read several descriptions of the place. A substantial red brick villa in the village of Trevena, on the north Cornwall coast, it had catered to "eccentric" ladies of good families with large fortunes. Its location was dramatic, high on the cliffs, with a view of the sea and of a small island, connected to the mainland by a causeway, which held the ruins of an ancient castle. Dr. Veasey commended the benefits of the sea air for his patients.

Ozone apart, there were other reasons why the patients' families might have found Beacon House appealing. For all that she herself might loathe its proprietor, Dana knew that he had been a respected member of the medical establishment and had, by all accounts, an impressive manner, calm and patriarchal. And the place itself was isolated. In 1870, Trevena was a tiny village with neither train nor telegraph, its population dependent on farming, fishing, and quarry work. The roads were bad, and in the tiny cove surging tides often smashed beached boats to pieces.

Beacon House was a place to which relatives could consign their loved ones with a good conscience, yet secure in the knowledge that it would be extremely difficult for the loved one to trouble them.

But Dana knew that middle-class families with pretensions to culture might have chosen Beacon House for quite another reason. The ruined castle on the island was Tintagel, the legendary stronghold of King Mark, birthplace of King Arthur, and scene of the two kings' wives' adulteries. Intrepid tourists made pilgrimages to Trevena, many inspired by Tennyson's "Idylls of the

King." In 1900, in what one guidebook would later describe as "a flash of marketing genius worthy of twentieth-century promotional methods," Trevena changed its name officially to Tintagel. Was it a comfort, Dana wondered, to know that the family loony resided in such poetic surroundings?

She had suspected that Veasey himself had probably been the reason for Henry's choice of asylum. Now, in light of the photographs that hung around her on the walls, she was struck by the irony of that choice. The man who twenty years later would portray his long-dead wife as an errant Iseult had confined her within view of the scene of Iseult's adultery. Had Tintagel itself inspired him to link Marianna with Iseult, and later to take artistic revenge on the memory of a troublesome wife? Or had he chosen Beacon House precisely because it looked out at Tintagel? If so, he must already have believed Marianna unfaithful. Had jealousy over some affair, as much as the desire for her money, prompted him to have her declared mad? Veasey's letters now convinced Dana that this was closer to the truth.

But, she reflected bitterly, whether the motive was avarice, jealousy, or a genuine belief that his wife was mad, it had been easy enough for Henry to have Marianna declared insane. In 1870, twelve years before the Married Women's Property Act was passed, a wife was at her husband's mercy. Marianna's rights were no greater than those of children, criminals, and lunatics. Henry had needed only a lunacy order signed by two certifying doctors in order to have her committed against her will.

Marianna had written to the Commissioners in Lunacy describing how she had come to be an inmate of Beacon House. Dana took out her photocopy of the letter and reread it.

> For all but the last year of our married life, my husband acquiesced in the practise of my gift. He never before showed by any sign that he disbelieved in it. However, when our marriage became so unhappy that I wished to end it, he pretended for his convenience that from the first he had doubted me.
>
> On the morning when I told him that I would leave him, he turned round and said to me, I do believe you are mad. Soon afterwards we received separate visits from two doctors,

acquaintances of Mr. Hobhouse. At the time, I believed these visits to be purely social occasions, and did not realize that I was under examination by these gentlemen. With their complicity, Mr. Hobhouse was able to condemn me to this lingering death in life, this moral torture among maniacs. My limbs, even my life, are now at the mercy of my keepers, my liberty at that of my incarcerator.

In my life I have wanted only to cultivate a reverent desire for what is pure, good, and true. I have taken to heart the blessed St. John's words, "Beloved, believe not every spirit, but only ask the spirits whether they are of God." St. Paul told us to pray for the gift to interpret the spirit voices which come to us and I have kept his commandment in my heart at all times. Rather than be deceived in the slightest degree, I have prayed that I might lose the hand that holds the pen, and the eye that sees the sacred light.

Alas, my prayers were answered and I am punished for my sin. But I deny that I am mad. Were I the most deluded woman in England—were Spiritualism avowedly and exclusively witchcraft—I have a right to my liberty.

Once confined to Beacon House, Marianna's only legal recourse was the Commissioners, who were required to visit patients in asylums every three months. Letters to the Commissioners from inmates had to be forwarded unopened. In one of her letters to them, written on October 10th, 1870, Marianna described her days and nights at Beacon House.

In the daylight hours, I read and write or go for walks about the garden. I listen to the deep-throated hum of the sea, a music steady and sure, sounding as if the pivot upon which the world spins round were grinding out its bearings there below the cliffs.

My companions, poor creatures, sit in smiling silence or chatter like the gulls, puffins, petrels and terns which populate the cliffs. These birds, believed to be the spirits of those shipwrecked on the rocks, are called here black souls and white. The souls at Beacon House are less fortunate than they, condemned to their earthly prison without wings to escape.

At nine o'clock I am locked in my room with only a candle to light my preparations for bed. The harsh sound of the key grating against the lock is a painful reminder that the seeming liberty of my daylight hours is an illusion. Shortly afterwards, the key is turned once more to ensure that the candle is extinguished, and yet again an hour later to admit the night-keeper. My sleep is broken by the groans of my neighbours in the adjacent rooms and by the snoring of my keeper. I would ask to dispense with this person were it not that under no emergency of danger or illness could help or egress be obtained until the morning rounds, and were it not for the unrelieved darkness of the room.

I can bear everything but the dark.

Marianna went on to write that a pond in the garden which received the house sewage made the air "pestilential," and that the house, although impressive enough to look at, was full of "rottenness and uncleanness." Veasey himself was often away, she said, leaving his patients to the mercy of their keepers.

Although Veasey was legally obliged to forward Marianna's letters to the Commissioners, letters to other addressees could be opened and held for the Commissioners' visits, at Henry's request. One of Veasey's letters to Henry made it plain that Henry had requested this. But another, written by Veasey a week later in late October, made it equally plain that several of Marianna's letters apparently had escaped this censorship, with devastating consequences.

Dear Hobhouse,

Today a most troubling incident has occurred, for which I blame myself. I have been too generous, too trusting. In my defense, however, I must say that your wife had shown herself to be both tractable and obedient. In short, she beguiled me into believing that I might allow her safely to take walks into Trevena unaccompanied, for purposes of exercise and recreation. Fortunately, conscious of your concerns, I instructed Mrs. Biddicombe, her keeper, always to follow her and to report any unusual or troubling behavior to me.

This afternoon, shortly after dinner, Mrs. H. set out for her daily walk. The weather being somewhat tempestuous, with a boreal wind, she was closely shawled and bonneted. It was the day of the annual cattle fair and in consequence a large number of people had come into the village. Mrs. B. found it difficult to keep her patient always in view and to distinguish her from other women similarly costumed. For a short time, she lost sight of her and it was only after a search of some twenty minutes that she at last caught sight of her again, emerging from the Shorncliff Arms.

You can imagine her consternation when she saw that Mrs. H. was not alone, but in the company of a young gentleman. They were so deeply engaged in conversation, Mrs. B. later reported to me, that they seemed unconscious of the people around them. Mrs. H. appeared much agitated, several times turning away from the young man, who would hurry after her and place his hand upon her arm. After a short colloquy, they directed their steps towards the Island.

They descended the ravine by its narrow rocky road to the gatekeeper's cottage, which lies in the little valley below what is popularly called King Arthur's Keep. Not knowing whether to watch, as instructed, or to return to Beacon House for advice, Mrs. B. followed the couple until the path became too treacherous for one of her girth. Mrs. B. is a stoutish woman. As well, the strength of the wind made the footing more than usually hazardous. She did not attempt to go on, but observed their progress from a distance and awaited their return.

The young man having obtained the key to the castle precincts from the gatekeeper's daughter, the pair proceeded to cross the isthmus to the Island. When next Mrs. B. caught sight of them, they had come out onto a small plateau above the sea. Upon observing what might have been an embrace or a struggle, Mrs. B. hurried back to Beacon House. Fortunately, I had just that moment returned from my duties in London. Immediately, I summoned Edgar, who assists me when a patient becomes overly excited, and rushed to the Island. We met the guilty pair as they came up the path towards the village. My fears were confirmed when I recognized Mrs. H.'s companion as P.B., the young man over whom she holds such sway.

At first, he blustered and threatened to carry her off with him

*in the carriage which awaited him at the hotel. However, Edgar
is not a man many would choose to quarrel with, and between
us we persuaded P.B. that it would be better to allow Mrs. H. to
return with us to Beacon House. When she saw that he did not
intend to persevere in his determination to take her with him,
she too acceded. Although visibly distressed, she returned quietly
enough. It was only upon entering the house that her self-control
gave way and the Hysteria manifested itself. It being late afternoon and the lamps not yet lit, the house was somewhat dark.
This seemed to agitate her; she cried out for light and would not
be comforted even when a lamp was brought.*

*Although Edgar endeavoured to persuade her to go upstairs to
her room, she resisted, lapsing into one of her fits. During the
subsequent struggle, she tumbled down the stairs. Mercifully, her
injuries were slight, some bruising of the hip and a cut on her
forehead. Only after I administered a dose of Potassium Bromide, which I find to be efficacious on such occasions, did she
quieten and at last sink into slumber.*

*After making a number of inquiries, I learned that a kitchen
maid, suborned by the patient, had been regularly taking letters
to the post office. Needless to say, the girl has been dismissed.*

Dr. Veasey went on to write that the incident forced him to
reconsider his acceptance of Marianna as a patient at Beacon
House. He accused Henry of misleading him about the relationship between Marianna and the mysterious P.B. It seemed, he
wrote, "warmer" than Henry had led him to believe. "This mani-
festation of the depraved instincts so frequently to be found in
those suffering from mediomania suggests to me that your wife
may not be fit company for the other patients here," he concluded.

Another letter followed two days later. It began on a curious
note.

*I have received a letter from our distinguished mutual
acquaintance, whom I had informed of the unfortunate matter.
He is understandably concerned and begs me to do all in my
power to prevent Mrs. Hobhouse from initiating a recurrence of*

the meeting. I have assured him that the emotional incontinence attendant upon Mrs. H.'s condition will be restrained. For his part, he assures me that he will take the young man in question to France for several months.

The penultimate letter, written the next day, was brief.

Your wife became very ill in the night. She was with child— for some five months by my reckoning—but is no longer. A sorry business. If you had knowledge of her condition, you ought to have told me. She herself will not speak of it, nor of anything else, but calls perpetually for light, although the room is sufficiently lit. Fever has set in and I fear she is weakening rapidly. I suggest you come at once.

The final letter was a formal note of condolence on Marianna's death.

Chapter 16

Daniel strode up the path from the cliffs toward Kerreck Du. Sea birds wheeled in the windy blue sky, like bits torn from the ragged clouds. When he glanced up, startled by the shriek of a gull directly overhead, the high morning sun dazzled his eyes. He raised his camera, tracking the bird as it sailed through the sky, then snapped off a series of shots at a lucky conjunction of arched wings with a trio of triangular clouds.

He was struck by a vivid image from the past, conjured up by the steepling effect of wings and clouds. A pair of hands clasped in prayer or supplication. Solange's hands. Pearly pink flesh on seemingly boneless fingers, they belonged to a saint in a Cranach painting, or to a Venus. He had once tried to evoke their erotic power, that perverse combination of the sacred and the profane, in a photograph.

"What you have here are living oxymorons," he had told her as he arranged them under the light. She'd made a face and pulled away. "That word doesn't sound very nice, Daniel." When he explained, she laughed and began to unbutton his shirt. "Well, if that's how you see them," she said, pushing the shirt from his shoulders, "I won't contradict you."

The memory developed to its sharpest focus, then blurred and dissolved.

He stumbled on a stone in the path. One hand went up automatically to protect the camera and he realized then that he'd dropped the lens cap. She still had the power to trip him up, he thought, could still make mischief.

As he retraced his steps, scanning the ground, he speculated on the use he might make of the hands, as a form of exorcism. He imagined them in a montage with wings and clouds, angled one above the other in a pure blue sky like arrowheads pointing at heaven. It might do for that nature conservancy poster.

Or for a greeting card, he amended with sudden disgust. Why was it that his memories of Solange produced only clichés?

The black plastic cap lay like a bull's-eye in a patch of red clover. As he stooped to pick it up, his stomach rumbled with hunger; he'd been out since five with only an apple for breakfast. At the Schoolhouse he always rose early to photograph while the light was new. Down here he rarely had an agenda, rarely thought of his clients' needs. He let his eye alone make choices, regardless of whether or not a subject was useful. Sooner or later serendipity produced images, like the gull, that he could incorporate into his work.

Approaching the house across the lawn, he heard music coming through an open living room window. He knew it must be Nadia Tatevic; she often practiced the piano in the mornings. Afternoons, she gave Elvina her lesson. She was playing a Brahms piece he recognized, one of the variations on a theme by Handel, taking it very fast, almost frantically. Music, it seemed, was her only refuge here; she would not learn English, talk to others, or make friends.

There were times when he found himself warming to the woman as he listened to her music. It could make him forget how difficult she was. But the frenzied quality of her playing now was too much like an echo of her personality.

He went up the portico steps to the door, which stood open. For the first time in two years, he realized, he was actually eager to cross the threshold. Ordinarily, he felt something close to dread. Only a mixture of pride, self-imposed sense of duty, and fundamental optimism compelled him to come, as though his visits mattered. Today, however, the compulsion was straightforward enough. He wanted to see Dana Morrow again.

He tried to analyze why he found her so compelling, why her particular constellation of qualities spoke to him so strongly. Her obvious courage combined with her hesitancies, that grave seriousness lightened by flashes of humor, her delicate beauty, all these moved him, made him want her. Already, he knew, he was partly possessed by her.

"Daniel!"

He looked around. Pascale had come into the hall behind him, a basket filled with vegetables from her garden over one arm. She raised her head to him and they kissed on either cheek. Her olive skin beneath his lips was smooth and cool.

"At last we have a chance to talk," she said. Taking his hand, she drew him into the kitchen, warm with the smell of baking bread. She grimaced as she closed the door to shut out the music. "Quel fracas!"

"But more socially acceptable than murder, wouldn't you say?" The violence of Nadia's playing seemed to him directly linked to the way she had looked at Karen Cody lately.

Pascale laughed. "You think it's catharsis, that noise? Perhaps you're right. Although I don't know why we should be obliged to suffer for Karen's sins."

While she washed and put away the vegetables, he made coffee, glad of this chance to talk alone with her. It was only from her that he gained a sense of how his father was doing. And he genuinely enjoyed her company; her acerbic, perceptive comments amused him, kept him off balance.

He poured the coffee into mugs, the way they both liked it, so strong and black that it smelled like smoke. She set her mug beside a cutting board and began to chop leeks for soup. Expertly, she moved the heavy knife along the stalk until there was a little heap of white discs at one end of the wooden board. As always, she refused his help.

He sat down on a stool nearby, and looked around. Sunlight gleamed on scarred, polished wood, on the battered pots that hung above the stove, on glazed jugs crammed full of wooden spoons or dried herbs. The large, light-filled kitchen was the oldest room in the house and his favorite, with a beamed ceiling, rough-cast plaster walls, and the original wood-fired bread oven, in which Pascale baked daily.

"I'm famished. May I?" He pointed to the loaves cooling on the counter. When she nodded, he took the smallest and tore it into pieces, drizzling honey over the hot bread. He offered her a chunk, but she refused it.

"I ate earlier, with Dana Morrow. She's in the glasshouse now, and has asked to be allowed to work undisturbed." She gave a small smile. "It's understandable, after yesterday."

Then he wouldn't see her this morning after all. He was surprised at the strength of his disappointment. "How's her ankle?" he asked, after a moment.

"Well enough to walk on. Finn invited her to stay for the exhibition. So I think for her it was a lucky break." Her voice was very dry.

"You suspect her of faking?"

"I don't say that."

"You don't have to." He drank a little coffee. "She's not, I'm certain of it. And anyway, why would she bother? How could Finn turn her away after what she did?"

"Why should he be grateful?" she countered matter-of-factly. "Mico and Nadia are Elvina's parents, not Finn."

"All the same . . ."

With the edge of one hand she swept the pile of leeks into a bowl, then turned around to face him directly. Her unusual face was like some carved African mask, he thought, long and severe, beautiful in its singularity. "They take advantage of him."

"Mico and Nadia? Maybe. But I don't think he minds. Mico's work justifies it. You know Finn always has a motive for his acts of charity."

"That absurdity about entertaining angels?" She gave a short laugh. "Devils, perhaps. I sometimes think they are more to his taste." Then, as she turned away to reach down a measuring cup from its hook in a cupboard, she added, "But I meant all of them, not only Mico and Nadia. They all want something from him."

It was probably true, he reflected as he chewed on the last piece of bread and honey. John Malzer had badly wanted the exhibition to happen; the publicity would be very good for his gallery. Karen and Tim wanted Finn's connections with the London fashion world. Estelle wanted his attention.

"What about Thomas?" he asked. "He makes Finn's life easier, doesn't he?" Finn had little patience for the business side of his work.

Pascale shrugged dismissively. She did not like Thomas Attery. Daniel didn't much like the man himself. He was too cold. Just the sort, Finn said, who kept his head when money was the issue. It was Thomas's skillful investment of Finn's money for the last ten years that allowed Finn to refuse advertising work.

"Thomas would like to manage all Finn's money," she said as she took potatoes from a deep cupboard drawer, tumbling them into a colander. "I think your father begins to realize that he must trouble himself more about such things."

This confirmed what Daniel suspected, that lately Finn seemed a shade less confident of Attery's talents. Gossip in Trebartha claimed that Thomas was buying from a particular London dealer known to specialize in arcane, and extremely costly, photographs. If he was purchasing the photographs for himself, where was the money coming from? Although comfortably off, he wasn't a rich man.

Pascale's voice broke into his thoughts. "Your father should be left alone to do his work. All these people, they distract him."

Although her tone remained cool, this, for Pascale, was tantamount to an outburst. Something had made her bad-tempered. He wondered if she was jealous of the latest distraction. Finn was clearly interested in Dana Morrow, but Daniel sensed it was not for the more obvious reasons. His father rarely bothered to disguise his physical interest in a woman; although his approach was never crude, it was always frank.

That was in the past, however, before Solange. As far as Daniel knew, there had been no woman since. Except, perhaps, Pascale herself—although how far their relationship went was hard for him to judge. He could see that each needed, depended on, and, to some degree, exploited the other. Beyond that, he had no idea.

What he did know was that although Solange had revitalized his father's work, Pascale was better for him, if only because she took care of him.

Solange had been beautiful, seductive, volatile, impetuous, unreliable, and utterly undomestic. While she was chatelaine, Kerreck Du exuded a wild haphazard glamour, but promised meals frequently failed to appear, hired help quit, disorder grew. It was either feast or famine, he thought, depending on her mood or occupation of the moment. Fearless and insatiably curious, she had lived at full throttle, expecting Finn to keep up with her.

Mostly, his father had. But he had worn himself out, and begun to drink again, in the attempt. His darkroom had saved him from her worst excesses.

Pascale had been visiting at the time of her sister's death. Afterward, she had simply stayed on. While Finn disappeared into his darkroom for days on end, she had taken everything into her hands. She had in a sense saved Finn, Daniel reflected.

And, he acknowledged, she had saved his relationship with Finn. She was their translator, interpreting them to each other. It was as if the work she did for a living—translating English texts into French for university publishers—had given her a sense of the meanings that lay not only behind the written word but behind spoken words and actions as well. It was largely because of her that he and Finn still saw each other, still managed to retain the fragments of the relationship they'd begun to build before Solange.

As for their own friendship, his and Pascale's, that was based on an unspoken complicity: the desire to protect Finn and his memories of Solange.

Pascale said quietly, as if she'd read his thoughts, "I wish it had not happened just there, Elvina's accident." She meant, in the place where Solange had died.

He couldn't say the same. In some peculiar way he did not fully understand, and could not explain to her, the child's rescue had helped him overcome his own horror of the place. Looking down, as he sat beside Dana on the ledge, he had seen only rock and gorse. The grisly image of Solange's broken body, which had seemed imprinted there, had vanished.

"How did Finn react, when he learned of it?" Pascale asked him. She was peeling the potatoes now, and the skin curled away from her knife in an unbroken spiral. Her movements were always supremely economical.

"More angry than upset. He'd told Mico not to let Nadia and Elvina go to the cove alone. Not while those women's deaths remain unsolved. But Mico and Nadia refuse to warn Elvina about the Gull. They say she has enough to worry about as it is. I can see their point."

She said something in French he didn't understand.

"Translation?"

"Nonsense to sell newspapers, this talk of murder and gulls. It makes us cowards."

"For once you and Karen agree." He was sure Pascale's contempt was genuine. Karen Cody's bravado, on the other hand, struck him as more equivocal. He suspected her of pretending to feel less frightened than she really was in order to bait Estelle Pinchot.

"I will be glad when life returns to normal," Pascale said, with a small exasperated sigh.

"Normal? With Finn?"

She laughed. "Yes, all right. But I prefer his version to anyone else's."

Quietly, he said, "His version is always changing. He never goes back, Pascale."

Her look was sharp. "What are you saying?"

"There's something Finn likes to quote, that in order to be happy we need hope and enterprise and change. Bertrand Russell, I think."

She gave a snort of derision. "The philosophy of a much-married man. I wonder how many Mrs. Russells had to listen to that as he left them."

Now Daniel laughed. "You're a cynic, Pascale."

He occasionally wondered why she had never married. Perhaps responsibility had come too young, had soured her on family life. Her mother had died when she was sixteen and Solange was two. Their father, a professor of English literature at the Sorbonne, had turned the raising of the younger child entirely over to the older. A social life, advanced degree, freedom, all these Pascale had apparently forgone willingly.

Now she said, "How could I not be a cynic about marriage? I only have to look around. The Tatevics, for example. She is determined to be unhappy." She put a nugget of butter into a skillet. There was a small pause as they watched it sputter around the pan. He wondered if she, too, was thinking of another marriage, Finn's to her sister. Then, in a cautious voice, she said, "So Lynn has gone back to London."

He laughed. "You're usually more subtle than that, Pascale." Nevertheless, he told her what had happened between Lynn and himself. Although she rarely asked personal questions, he often found himself telling her things he discussed with no one else.

In a sober voice, he described Lynn's final accusation, that he was mourning Solange. "I don't know how she knew about our affair."

"Karen told her. Lynn asked me if it was true—I suppose her opinion of Karen was much the same as mine. I said she must ask her questions of you."

This was typical of Pascale, he thought, as he carried his mug to the sink. She was scrupulous about respecting his private life. He might confide in her, but she never assumed this gave her the right to speak for him. It was equally typical of Karen, and he felt a spurt of anger at this fresh evidence of her malicious tongue. Someone someday . . . he began, but left the thought unfinished. Karen never sustained his interest for long.

Did he plan to stay for the opening of Finn's exhibition, Pascale was asking.

"I don't know." He let water run over the mug for a moment, then set it on the drainboard before he continued. "We always seem to be on the verge of an argument, Finn and I. The last thing he needs right now is more aggravation."

"That's very considerate of you." Her voice behind him was tart.

Stung, he looked around at her and said with more heat than he'd intended, "Do you think I don't want to stay? All he has to do is say he wants me here. That's all." He felt the old frustration rising in him. And even as he spoke, he was aware of how the words sounded, like an adolescent's self-pitying plea for reassurance.

Calmly, she tipped some wine into the skillet. "But you have to be here to see it."

He knew immediately what she meant: that Finn wouldn't say the words directly, but might give a sign. Signs were, after all, he thought with an ironic inward smile, Finn's stock in trade.

"I have a life of my own, Pascale," he said, turning to go. "I can't hang around here looking for signs and portents."

"Then you may miss seeing wonders," he heard her say as he left.

Chapter 17

Wonders indeed! Frowning, Pascale stared through the kitchen window as she watched Daniel cross the courtyard. How melodramatic those last words of hers must have sounded to him. That sort of verbal extravagance wasn't her usual style, nor was the meddling. Solange had taught her too well the fatuity of unasked-for advice.

She turned away from the window and went back to her cooking. Ordinarily, she enjoyed her conversations with Daniel, but this one had left her uneasy. Her own contributions now struck her as bad-tempered, and his as enigmatic or uncharacteristically obtuse. The atmosphere at Kerreck Du, thick for days with tensions that each had tried to ignore, seemed finally to have infected them both.

Why, she wondered bitterly, did he think it necessary to utter that gnomic warning? Surely of all people he must realize that she knew Finn had to move forward. The past wasn't safe. All she wanted was to keep Finn safe, especially now, in this dangerous time.

As she chopped parsley and chives for the soup, diced stale bread for croutons, loaded the dishwasher, Daniel's remark continued to nag at her. Was he implying that Finn might move forward without her? She refused to believe it. He simply meant that once the preparations for the exhibition were complete Finn would find something else to consume him, that she should be prepared for this. Well, she could prepare herself for anything. Except for leaving him. She could not, would not, go back to the wasteland of her former life.

At eighteen, Solange had begun to drift away from her into a series of love affairs. As a child, she had told Pascale everything;

now she became secretive. Pascale was almost grateful. She no longer wanted Solange's troubling confidences. They lacked the naive charm of childhood and began to seem self-indulgent, and the insights they gave her into her sister's adult nature disturbed her. She blamed herself; she had spoiled Solange. But when, at twenty-five, Solange moved from Paris to London, she felt abandoned. It was at this time that her own love affair, a long, hopeless relationship with a married teacher who would not leave his perpetually ailing wife, dragged to its exhausted end. She reconciled herself to a solitary, passionless middle age.

Then one day Solange telephoned from London to announce that she was married. "You musn't be angry with me, Pascale," she cajoled in her little-girl voice. "We didn't tell anyone. Not even Daniel, Finn's son. We didn't want a fuss."

How could she be angry, Pascale replied calmly, if Solange was happy? This was disingenuous. She knew her sister's capacity for disastrous choices, and what she had heard about Quentin Finn's reputation did not reassure her. However, when she met him a few weeks later, she decided that her sister had chosen wisely after all, that this man might be the safe haven she desperately wanted for Solange. He was charming, intelligent, a man of experience, the quasi-father Solange was always seeking in her lovers. He was tender with her, patient and tolerant, although Pascale sensed that it was not in his nature ordinarily to be any of these things.

She sensed something else, something that terrified her. She could easily fall in love with her sister's husband.

Eight months later Solange called again, this time from Kerreck Du. It was well after midnight, and her voice held a familiar reckless note, the frantic excitement that often heralded some emotional debacle. After a rambling, one-sided conversation in which she described her latest enthusiasms and the pleasures of married life, she told Pascale she wanted her to come for a visit. When Pascale hesitated, she said darkly, "You must come. I need you." She refused to explain.

Pascale arrived at Kerreck Du the following week to find the house in disarray. People came and went at odd hours, meals were taken on the run, microwaved or cold, and the latest housekeeper had left without giving notice, driven away, Pascale learned, by the bacchanalian behavior of a recent group of houseguests. Solange was like a spring with a seemingly infinite capacity to spiral in ever more complicated convolutions. Finn himself, distracted perhaps by the recent arrival of the Tatevics, appeared indifferent to the chaos.

Despite the urgency of her telephone call, Solange seemed reluctant to talk to Pascale, seemed almost to avoid her. Finn may have noticed, for he proposed that the three of them go up to London together, take in a play, visit friends. An exhibition of contemporary photographs had just opened, he said, which included several of his own works. He was curious to see it.

At the last moment, however, Solange begged off. She felt a cold coming on, and wanted a couple of days of peace and quiet. She was going to take the phone off the hook, lock the door, and crawl into bed with a pile of magazines. She insisted they go without her.

In London, Pascale found that the strain of meeting Finn's abstraction with an equal measure of detachment exhausted her. She was worried about Solange. Her night was disturbed by the kind of dreams she'd had when Solange was a child, dreams of her sister in danger. The next morning she awoke determined to return to Kerreck Du. When she telephoned Solange to let her know, she found the phone, as promised, off the hook. There was no time to try again if she was to catch the early train that would get her back to Kerreck Du by nightfall.

Finn seemed relieved by her decision. Either he too was worried about his wife, or the responsibility for his sister-in-law's amusement was weighing on him. He would try Solange again at some point during the day, he said, to let her know Pascale was returning.

The taxi brought her through heavy rain to Kerreck Du at dusk. No lights showed at the front of the house, although there was a light in one of the windows of the stable cottage where the Tatevics were living. The splash of the rain and the cries of rooks from the trees on the hill were the only sounds. In the dim twilight, the house seemed closed in on itself, unwelcoming, its flat gray facade cloaked in ivy and silence.

She paid the driver, then picked up her suitcase and went to the door. Finn had given her his key.

In the silence of the front hall, she heard a faint, muffled thudding, like distant thunder or the beating of her own heart. She thought at first it might be the furnace, but the radiator was cold to her touch. When she called out her sister's name, there was no answer. As she went upstairs to look for her, she began to worry that she might be truly ill.

The squalid disorder of Solange's bedroom startled her. The bed was torn apart and clothes lay scattered everywhere. Someone had made a handprint in the film of spilled dusting powder that covered the glass top of the dressing table. She put her own hand down and saw that the print was smaller and therefore not Solange's, for theirs were the same size. Puzzled, she stared at it for a moment, then brushed it away.

She searched from room to room without success. When at last she entered the hallway that ran from the kitchen to the glasshouse, she realized that the steady thumping was music, the thud of hard rock. It grew louder as she approached the closed door of the glasshouse.

For a long moment she stood with her hand on the brass doorknob, hesitant, almost afraid. Then she opened the unlocked door and went into the room.

The blast of music that met her, a sickening fug of incense and heat, the unreality of the scene before her, all these confused her. But even as her mind rejected the truth, her eyes were noting the details. The pale bodies of the two naked women sprawled stomach down across cushions on the floor. The mirror, taken from the wall and laid flat on the floor, a large oval of glass between them, so that they seemed to be gazing down, female twins of Narcissus, into a pool. And on the mirror's surface, like a snail's track, a long white line of powder.

Solange and Karen were lying opposite each other, dark head to light, each with a straw in one hand. So intent were they on the mirror and the cocaine that they failed at first to notice her. They were giggling like secretive children huddled together over sodas, intent on some forbidden game.

Karen was the first to see her. A sideways tilt of the head, followed by a narrow-eyed smile, was her only reaction. When Solange looked up, Pascale was already turning around to leave.

Behind her, she heard her sister cry out like someone in pain, but that didn't make her stop or go back. She had reached the kitchen when Solange came stumbling after her, half-dressed, hysterical. Fear disfigured the beautiful face, so that the babble of words seemed to come from an ugly stranger.

Desperately, Pascale clamped her hand over the mouth. "Shut up!" she screamed into the stranger's face. "Shut up, shut up!"

Her sister's reaction sobered Solange. With a whimper, she pulled her face free of Pascale's hand and collapsed onto a chair. "Don't you see," she whispered, "it doesn't matter. She doesn't matter. Finn doesn't matter. Only you count, Pascale." She paused, and then with a travestied smile so grotesque that it made Pascale feel sick, added, "Mon semblable, ma soeur."

Baudelaire's words were meant to deflect Pascale's anger, to make her laugh, as they had always done in the past. A trick learned at twelve. This time, Pascale slapped Solange. "We are not alike. What went on in there," her voice trembled as she pointed down the hallway to the glasshouse, "disgusts me, makes me physically ill."

"But you won't tell, will you? I don't want Finn to know." Pale with fright, Solange's face wore the hollow-eyed look of childhood that always made Pascale want to weep.

"Of course I won't tell. But that one will." She jerked her head at Karen, who was standing now in the doorway watching them. How much the other woman had understood was uncertain; they were speaking in French. "Oh, Solange, how can you be so stupid? You told me once all you wanted was someone to love you. You have that here. Why destroy it?"

Solange gave a sullen shrug. "Because I've discovered it bores me."

"My God! Will you never grow up?" It was hopeless, she thought. To Solange, the safe haven was only a trap.

Finn came back from London in a rage. He had been to the exhibition, he said, only to discover that his photographs had been vandalized. Someone had sprayed some sort of dilute acid on the glass. By the time it was noticed, it had already seeped through onto the print. No one had seen it happen.

Like a child resolved to make up for her sins, Solange soothed away his fury and comforted him. A calm had settled over her, the serenity that always followed some particularly outrageous act. The old hope began to revive in Pascale; perhaps this time Solange had learned her lesson.

But two days later Solange was dead. And in the midst of her grief, Pascale acknowledged a grain of relief. She no longer had to fear for her sister.

Solange's death froze that last image, the loving, tender wife, in Finn's mind, and trapped Pascale in the lie. Pascale told herself that she could make reparation for the deceit, and for Solange's betrayal, by caring for Finn. That was the form her love for him would take. But her decision to stay on at Kerreck Du meant she had to swallow Karen's presence and the anxiety it provoked. If Finn learned the truth, he might accuse Pascale of conspiring to betray him, might come to hate her. There was nothing she would not do to prevent that. She was fairly certain, however, that as long as Karen wanted something from Finn she would keep quiet.

And so she was forced to collude silently with Karen as she did with Daniel, for different reasons, to keep the truth from Finn. But she hated Karen so fiercely that at times she longed for her death.

To escape these thoughts, and the persistent, unpleasant sound of Nadia's playing, she switched on the radio. A report on the Channel tunnel was followed by the local news.

"There is a further development in the case of the most recent victim of the murderer that tabloids are calling the Gull. Police have at last confirmed that the dead woman, Rita Becker, thirty-eight, of Leeds, was murdered. The findings of the autopsy also confirm that Miss Becker was not molested sexually, as some had speculated. A body found yesterday by local fishermen has now been identified as that of a young woman lost overboard in a sailing mishap near Fowey on Tuesday. A sudden squall . . ."

Pascale stood with a wooden spoonful of soup in one hand, listening. She meant to let the scalding broth cool before tasting it. Instead, without thinking, she put the spoon to her lips. She cried out with the pain and then, in sudden disgust, she threw the spoon into the sink, lowered the heat under various pots, and went out to the garden. No matter that she had spent an hour digging there already this morning; she took her trowel and knelt down to work, plunging her gloved hands deep in the loamy soil.

She might escape the world and its tragedies, but today there was no escaping her thoughts, even here in the garden, where ordinarily she found peace.

In the days after Solange's death, her discovery of the abandoned remnants of Kerreck Du's walled-in kitchen garden had seemed providential. The herbs and flowers that filled the window ledges of her Paris apartment had been a poor substitute for the garden she'd always dreamed of making. She went to work at once scything away the long grass, rooting up brambles and nettles, barrowing manure from a tractorload dumped in the drive by a neighboring farmer. From the same farmer she bought a few chickens, black-and-white wyandottes. She made a pen for them just outside the garden wall.

And she set about bringing order to Kerreck Du. She paid the bills that Finn ignored, shopped and cooked, dealt with visitors he wouldn't see, calls he wouldn't take. Wordlessly, he signed the checks she left on his desk, ate the meals she provided, accepted her ministrations.

The physical effort that all this required drained her of sorrow and anger, and of reflection. The arrogance of her actions—the implicit message that she would now live at Kerreck Du in her sister's place—did not occur to her until much later. She was simply doing what had to be done.

If Daniel found her behavior intrusive, he hadn't shown it. Instead, he made it clear to her, to everyone, that he was grateful for her presence. For that, she loved him. But only later, when he told her how Finn and Solange had met, could she appreciate just how remarkable his own behavior was. To discover, then, that he too knew the truth about Solange—and was as determined as she that Finn should not—was an overwhelming relief.

Meanwhile, Finn continued to mourn Solange in silence. He spent the summer days in his darkroom, emerging only at night, as though he couldn't bear the light of day. Pascale brought his meals to the darkroom door, knocked, and left, returning later for the tray of dirty dishes. In the early hours of the morning, she often heard his footsteps echoing down the hallways as he wandered about the house.

By midsummer, the garden was lush with flowers and vegetables. A rogue vine sprouted from a stray seed sent its thick twisting stem ramping wildly over the chicken pen's wire mesh top, while the gradually widening leaves screened out the sun. In September pale green gourds, luminous in the dim light, hung like giant pears through the wire above the chickens that pecked and strutted, oblivious to the danger.

One evening Finn asked, almost formally, if he might join her for dinner. His face was ashen and the light gone from his eyes; each word seemed to cost him an effort. During dessert he confessed that even the darkroom had failed him. "I couldn't work. Kept seeing bugs, hundreds of them, out of the corner of my eye. Damn distraction. Photographer's maggots, they're called. They come when you spend too long in the dark."

His defeated look frightened her. When she spoke, she kept the tone of her voice light and deliberately teasing. "It's time you saw a real bug again." She pushed back her chair and stood up. "Let me show you."

He allowed her to lead him outside, into the greenly golden sun of a warm September evening rich with the scent of hay and roses. Gnats and tiny seeds of grass were swimming in the limpid air. He blinked, like someone surfacing after weeks underground. She meant to take him into the garden, but he stopped by the chicken run, mesmerized.

In the shadowy light, their stems invisible, the gourds seemed to float on the thick aqueous air. A slanting ray gilded the swollen flank of the largest, so that it glowed and pulsed with life. Directly below, a drowsy chicken settled itself more comfortably in its dust bowl, faintly clucking a protest.

Finn made a sound in his throat, part laugh, part grunt of recognition. He muttered something to her about his camera and turned on his heel. A few minutes later he came back, squatted down beside the pen, and began to photograph. He stayed there until the light was gone. It seemed to break the darkroom's spell over him. He began to work outside again, to see people, to live.

Never in so many words did he remark on the garden and house, on all that she had done for him. He simply accepted it. Without discussion, they had slipped into their present way of life. She spoke regularly with her Paris neighbor about her apartment, continued her freelance translating, and went up occasionally to London to meet old friends. Otherwise, she renounced her Paris life. From time to time, as a way perhaps of expressing what he could not say in words, Finn gave her photographs, valuable photographs, his own work and that of others. But he never asked why she stayed.

Most people, she supposed, believed they were lovers. They might have been. There was a night three months ago when a kiss of affection, carelessly given, had sweetened to something more. And then, with a mundane cruelty, the telephone rang and she made the mistake of answering it. The woman on the other end gave her name as Estelle Pinchot, said she was an old friend of Finn's from London. Might she speak to him?

"Estelle Pinchot?" she said, holding out the receiver to Finn. She hoped he would shake his head, tell her to put the woman off. Instead, he stood for a moment frozen-faced. And then said he would take the call in his room. She had waited in her own room for long hours, but he never came.

The sun now was hot on her shoulders. She sat back on her haunches and took off her gloves, wiping the sweat from the bridge of her nose with the back of one hand, then stood up and stretched. The ache in her bones, in her being, had become so familiar that she noticed only its absence.

"I thought I'd find you here."

Startled, she looked around to see Finn standing at the gated entrance to the garden, as though conjured up by her thoughts and by the strength of her yearning. The scowl on his face frightened her.

"I'm sorry, Pascale," he began quickly, irritably, before she could speak, "but we've got the whole bloody lot coming for dinner tonight. John, Estelle, Thomas, Tim, Karen. Estelle just rang to ask when they were expected. I'd completely forgotten I'd invited them."

Relief made her smile. It was like him to forget; he was often careless about social obligations that held no appeal for him. She moved toward him, stepping carefully over the onion plants. "It's all right," she said. "I remembered."

"Thank God. Do you also remember why in the name of Heaven I asked them?" Now that he knew she would cope with this latest nuisance, his irritation was giving way to a rueful contrition. She knew the pattern.

"To forestall Estelle's plan that we give a large party here after the opening to celebrate," she said dryly. "You told her you preferred an intimate dinner with special friends beforehand. The others were present, so of course you were obliged to include them."

" 'Special friends'?" He raised an eyebrow. "I must have been drinking."

"Perhaps a little."

"Vous l'avez voulu, Quentin Finn, vous l'avez voulu," he quoted, shaking his head in exaggerated remorse. His accent was atrocious.

She laughed, as he intended she should, then began to reassure him, for she knew that he was miserable at the prospect of an evening spoiled as a result of his own impulsiveness. She told him what she planned to serve. They discussed wines, and whether to eat the meal at the table or as a buffet. Buffet, he decided; that way victims could escape their tormentors if need be.

"Perhaps the victims enjoy their torments." She was thinking of Mico and Tim with Karen.

For some reason, this made him pause and look at her. Then he lightly touched her right cheekbone with the edge of his thumb. It was a painter's speculative gesture, an appraisal of his work, as if to gauge what might be needed. "When all this is over, the opening and the folderol that goes with it, you must have a holiday, get right away."

He had used the singular, she thought despairingly. You, not we. But when she spoke, she kept the hurt from her voice. "I might go to Paris."

"You want to go back?"

The sudden look of panic on his face, which she interpreted as fear she might leave him, comforted her a little.

"For a visit. I must decide about the apartment, whether to let it or not." She wondered if Rita Becker of Leeds, the Gull's victim, might also have left her home "for extended periods" because she was under the spell of some man. But you are not a victim, she told herself. Vous l'avez voulu.

"And then," she went on, "there are a few things I would be

happy to see again." But at that moment she could not remembe
what they were.

There was another pause, before he said, "I've been a selfish so
of a bitch, Pascale."

"You, selfish?" she replied, raising her head to smile at him
"Never!"

He grinned then. "You can't imagine what a relief it is to b
with someone who has no illusions about me."

She looked down at her hands, pretending to wipe a bit of drie
earth from one palm. "No, I have no illusions," she said softly. Bu
he had gone forward to open the door for her, and was no longe
listening.

Before they separated, she thought to ask if he had invite
Daniel for dinner as well. He shook his head. "He wasn't dow
here at the time. Why don't you ring him up?"

Why don't you, she was tempted to reply. "Daniel might refus
when he hears who is coming."

"He'll come." Finn's voice was sardonic. "After all, Dana Mor
row will be one of the guests." When she stared blankly at him, h
said, "He's halfway in love with her."

"How can you know that?"

He shrugged. "Intuition. That's why I invited her down here."

She remembered Daniel's voice earlier, in the kitchen, when h
had defended Dana Morrow from her accusation of shammin
her injury. Of course, she thought. But how remarkable tha
Finn had understood so much, far more than she had, and had acte
on it. . . . Then, suddenly, she was furious. Only he would imagin
he could give people to each other, like God! Do you think that yo
can put them together like one of your photographs? she wanted t
shout at him. Love isn't a darkroom trick, you know.

And then it struck her that perhaps he was trying to make u
for past sins. But it wasn't necessary, she could tell him, Danie
had never loved Solange.

It was impossible to say any of this, however, and so she sai
only that she would let Daniel know about the dinner party.

Chapter 18

At seven o'clock that evening, Mico Tatevic was out on the cliffs with his camera bag over his shoulder and the Leica hanging against his chest. Nadia's shrill cries of reproach were still ringing in his ears. He had fled from the house to escape them. They had been directed for the most part at herself but also at him, and even, unforgivably, at Elvina. She had sent Elvina early to bed again tonight as a punishment for yesterday's disobedience in climbing the cliff. He'd gone out the door while she was still upstairs, overseeing bedtime prayers. Prayers, he thought bitterly, in whose power Nadia persisted in believing.

He was almost grateful to her for forcing him to come out here. The light lay like a photographer's dream of clarity on the silent landscape, sharpening the distant hills, sculpting the granite stacks down the coast, which were ordinarily fuzzed by haze, into cubist blocks, intensifying colors.

For all its photogenic brilliance, the light struck him as equivocal. Unnatural in its intensity, it gave the landscape a threatening resonance, almost a ghostly aura. It was a charged light, he thought, a light in which anything might happen. Its possibilities excited him.

He crossed the stile to the coastal path and gazed down on the place of Elvina's rescue. A sick breathlessness took him when he thought of this second narrow escape from death. She was looking for the honey buzzard, she'd explained afterward. Nadia blamed him for that, as he blamed her for not watching more carefully over their child. She confessed to dozing off on the beach. She'd slept badly the night before, she told him, accusation harsh in her voice; he'd been so late coming to bed. As always.

This was deliberate. He felt the irritable remains of love mixed with pity for his wife but no longer any desire, and the sight of her sullen back hunched away from him in the bed filled him with guilt. Her hysterical rages—at what was happening to their country, to their child, to them—had killed her tenderness and his desire for her. Sometimes her anger made him hate her, made him deceive her.

He had betrayed not only his wife, Mico thought despairingly, but his country and his friend as well. The guilt of these betrayals was an intolerable burden made bearable only by work. The work must justify them. But the more he worked, the angrier Nadia grew and the worse their home life became. He felt like a rat forced to run on some terrible wheel that would carry him up into light only to send him down into darkness again.

He stopped and swept a hand down over his face. He ought never to have abandoned his country. But Nadia and Elvina could not have left without him, and he could not have condemned Elvina to grow up as part of the cycle of harm and revenge that plagued their country.

From the valley behind him came a solitary cuckoo's call. He turned and walked along the path toward Trebartha. As his eyes automatically scanned the cliffs and sky for possible subjects, an interior voice recited the familiar litany: You were someone in your own country, but now you are different; you are no longer the one you believed yourself to be; and so the acts you commit belong to that other person, the one you have become.

The only time he felt himself, his old real self, was when he took pictures. Then he could believe that nothing had changed.

After ten minutes of hard walking, he saw the path curve sharply ahead to skirt a narrow inlet in the cliff face. A screen of gorse and scrub hedged the drop here, and the deeply shadowed rock shelved up in a concave arc beside the path, like a toppling black wave. He was struck, not for the first time, by the desolation of the spot.

Another photographer, Finn perhaps, could have made something of it, he thought. But that was not his own style.

In a few moments, the path crested the cliff again and he found the place he was seeking. Here, on the other side of the fence, two fields rolled side by side down a gentle hill, one a fallow swath of rippling grass, the other cropped by sheep to a felted nub. The lurid scar of a gorse hedge separated them. Screwing a telephoto lens onto the Leica he crouched down to wait in the bracken beside a fence post.

When a pair of yellowhammers flew from the hedge, the vivid yellow head and breast marking the male, his patient concentration was rewarded.

The cock was in swift pursuit of the hen. In a twisting flurry of gold-streaked feathers, she managed at first to evade him, skimming across the long grass, then spiraling up into the sky. But he bore relentlessly down on her, tiring her, until at last he forced her to the ground, to mate with her invisibly in the long grass near the hedge. Close by, a single foxglove spiked the hedgerow like a blood-tipped spear.

Cautiously he stalked the pair, keeping low and downwind, with the foxglove as his guide for the eye of the lens. He found them easily, the male's yellow head a splash of cadmium in the green. While he pressed the shutter over and over, the cock paraded around the passive hen, his wings and tail spread in triumph and his crest erect.

He knew these would be extraordinary photographs. Exultation flooded him. This was what he lived for, this rush of joy in his work. It made the ephemeral pleasure of his coupling yesterday with Karen seem a mere reflexive spasm by comparison, the strutting satisfaction of an animal instinct.

With a sudden burst of determination, he told himself fiercely that he could become that other lost self again, even here, despite all that had happened. The first step was to break with Karen. He owed that much at least to Nadia. He did not love Karen, and he certainly did not like her. He only desired her. For his part, their affair was nothing more than an impulse of the flesh. As, undoubtedly, it was for her.

This resolution made, his spirits rose. The light seemed to simplify everything, to reduce complicated structures to their clearest outlines so that they were no longer ambiguous or elusive but plain to the eye and easily grasped.

He capped his lens and sat down in the grass, then took his

notebook from the camera bag and in his own form of shorthand recorded the chain of decisions made for each photograph. The film used, the light readings, lens chosen, aperture and shutter speeds. Then, pillowing his head on his arms, he lay back. Above him floated small white clouds, their underbellies tinged with gray. He closed his eyes. The smell of grass and earth filled his nostrils. From the hedge, the male yellowhammer began to sing in quick, hard notes ending in a long wheeze. Elvina had once told him the English words to its song: "Little bit of bread and no cheese."

Elvina. His wounded child. Insidiously, inevitably, the memory of the day that had scarred her tender life, perhaps forever, seeped through the defenses he tried to erect against it and flooded into his mind.

An afternoon late last spring, its oppressive humidity unrelieved by intermittent thunderstorms. He and Nadia were at home, arguing. Some trivial argument about socks, how he left them dirty for her to find under the bed, how she never paired them after the wash but only dumped them in a tangled mass in his drawer. When their shouting drew Elvina from her bedroom, clutching her doll, Madonna, to her chest, they told her to go upstairs to her friend Alia's apartment, two floors above their own. Again in memory, he saw her small figure hesitate, unwilling, heard his own impatient command that she obey at once.

He and Nadia were still quarreling half an hour later, when the shells started falling. For an instant he was deluded into thinking that the dull booming was another roll of thunder, but when their building trembled he knew immediately that the guns in the hills must be trained on the part of the city in which they lived. And then, as they ran out into the hallway, a shell smashed into their own building, somewhere above them. He felt the blow as a massive shudder of concrete and steel. Plaster rained down on them while chunks of concrete fell from the walls.

"Elvina!" Nadia screamed. He shouted at her to go down to the basement but she ignored him, wrenching open the heavy fire door to the stairwell so violently that it slammed with a bang against the wall. Pushing her aside, he took the stairs two at a time.

The door to Alia's apartment sagged open, blown off its upper hinges by the blast. In that frozen moment on the threshold, while his eyes searched frantically for Elvina, he took in the bizarre details that would later come back to haunt his dreams. A single cloud surrounded by blue sky where the living room wall used to be. The overturned sofa bristling with the splintered shards of glass and crockery driven into it from the shattered china cupboard. And an arm white as a cast protruding motionless from under a toppled bookshelf that spilled out its broken-backed load, an arm mercifully too large to be a child's.

He waded through the debris, shouting Elvina's name. Plaster dust coated everything, floating thickly in the air. Hoarse with the dust, his voice rasped out like the harsh croak of a crow. Then, miraculously, she appeared from a bedroom, white as a ghost with the dust or with fear, her mouth opening and closing but no sound coming from it. She stood there in the doorway silent and unmoving with one hand holding the dangling doll and the other stretched toward him. As though some chasm had opened up between the two of them over which she could not cross.

With a groan of relief, he gathered her up in his arms and gave her to Nadia, who managed somehow to get her out of the building to safety while he struggled to free the bodies of Alia and her family from the rubble. Only the father was alive, barely, and he died in the operating room. Alia, her sister, and her mother had all been killed outright by the blast. He found the children's bodies in Alia's bedroom. He recognized Alia only by the braces on her teeth. Later, Elvina told them that she was under Alia's bed when the bombardment began. She had wiggled beneath to retrieve her doll, which had fallen down behind it, and had simply lain there, her arms over her head, too frightened to move until she heard his voice calling her.

At first, he and Nadia tried to talk to Elvina about the deaths, but she would only look away from them and make no response, her eyes dull and fixed. If pressed too hard she would fall into a silence that might last for hours. That initial mute appeal to him continued, he sensed, but it was as if the hand once stretched out to him had fallen now to her side, as if she had lost her faith in his ability to save her.

At the thought of the terror she must have felt yet again

yesterday afternoon as she hung from that branch, waiting to fall, an anguish sour as vomit constricted his throat. Once more he had failed to protect her, this time from herself. Only chance and a stranger's courage had saved her.

He would do anything to keep his child safe, but he felt an impotent despair at the hopelessness of the task. If fate decided to take your child from you, he thought, there was nothing you could do. Twice now it had spared her. How could he hope for more?

Something touched his cheek. Startled, he opened his eyes, jerking upright. Karen stood laughing over him, a long stalk of tasseled grass in one hand.

"There was the weirdest expression on your face. Were you having a nightmare?"

He only grunted, and rubbed at his cheek, feeling the itch of the grass still on his skin. Before he could rise to his feet, she sat down beside him, her legs curled sideways under her. She smoothed the short dress across her thighs, then let one upturned hand rest in the hollow between her legs, like an invitation.

"I watched you playing Peeping Tom with those birds," she said, her face amused. "What're you going to do, sell the photos to the *News of the World*? I can just see the headlines. 'Turtle Doves' Love Nest pics.'"

"Yellowhammer."

"What?"

He shook his head. "It doesn't matter." He felt dazed and sluggish, as he always did when she was close to him. The clarity of the light failed him even as it intensified her flesh, glinting off the fine golden hairs of her arm. She smelled darkly of sandalwood and warm, slightly sweaty skin.

He gathered up the remnants of his resolve and blurted out that tonight was no good, he couldn't see her, then cursed himself for his clumsiness.

For a few moments she did not speak. She pulled another stalk of grass and sat hunched over, seemingly intent on splitting the end of the grass with the nail of her thumb. Her face was screened by her hair so that he sensed rather than saw her scowl. After a moment she looked slantingly at him through the cloud of frizzy hair.

"Why's tonight no good?"

He mumbled something about not wanting to hurt his wife. He was ashamed to use Nadia in this way, as a means of escape.

"Oh, right. Like she doesn't already know about me." She threw the stalk of grass aside and turned to contemplate him, a sarcastic smile on her face. "Or Solange."

He grabbed her arm. "What are you saying?"

"That hurts." She jerked back, shaking off his hand. "Come on, Mico, don't pretend." She spoke in the languid, bored manner she sometimes affected, as though each word were an effort. He found it infuriating but held his tongue, waiting until at last she went on, this time with a hint of impatience. "Solange told me she slept with you."

Stunned, he could only stare at her for a moment. "Why would she do such a thing?"

She looked amused. "Tell me, you mean? Or sleep with you?" Then, prompted perhaps by the anger he knew must show on his face, she added quickly, "She used to tell me lots of stuff. She said you were as jumpy as a rabbit. Like you expected Finn to walk in on you in the middle. Well, of course you must have been nervous, fucking your benefactor's wife."

Only once, he wanted to cry out like a child, *and I never meant to do it.*

It had happened days after their arrival at Kerreck Du. He had drunk too much one night, after the evening news, which had featured scenes of his devastated city. He was filled with shame for his cowardice in abandoning his stricken country, as well as a bitter resentment at all those who had persuaded him to leave, Finn most of all. Finn was away, Solange was obviously seeking distraction. It hadn't meant anything to her, he was certain. She might have done it merely for revenge; he'd suspected at the time that Finn was sleeping with Karen. Afterward, he was stricken with remorse. How could he have done such a thing to the man who had saved his family? From then on, he was very careful never to be alone with Solange. Her death had released him from terrible anxiety. It meant that Finn would never know how he had betrayed him.

But now, to learn that his secret was known . . . he groaned inwardly. Karen would tell Finn, sooner or later; it was a miracle she hadn't already.

"Oh don't look so gloomy," she said impatiently. "You think Finn's such a saint?"

He took this to confirm that she had slept with Finn. He gave a bitter laugh. "*La Ronde.*"

"What's that supposed to mean?"

"I slept with his wife while he slept with you. And now you and I, we sleep together."

She pretended astonishment. "I slept with Finn?" Then she smiled to herself, as though at some private joke. "I suppose you could say I did. At second hand."

Before he could ask her what she meant, she said, "Too bad about tonight." She arched her back, raking both hands up through the mass of frizzed hair, pulling it off her neck. He could see the outline of her nipples through the thin fabric of the dress.

She glanced at him, unerringly gauged his response, smiled. "You know what your trouble is, Mico? You take everything so fucking seriously. Including fucking. It's supposed to be fun."

That was how she thought; she felt no guilt. It was a large part of her appeal for him. That, and the way she made it clear there were no conditions to their lovemaking. Neither owed the other a thing, she had said at the start, as though she understood that he felt trapped in a web of obligation from which there was no escape. Each time he turned around he seemed to wrap himself more thoroughly in its sticky strands.

"Fun," she repeated. "Like this." She trailed one finger down his forearm, following the blue line of a vein through the dark hairs on the back of his hand, then smiled at his involuntary shiver of pleasure. "Only better."

"All the same . . ." His voice was thick in his throat; he coughed to clear it. "It's not only Nadia. Finn might . . ." He could see by her face that this was a mistake, and stopped.

"Jesus!" She flung his hand back at him. "You know, I'm getting fed up with the way we all act like Finn's the god and flame of his little world. All that crap about his brilliant perceptions. Sometimes I'd like to force his eyes open, he's so oblivious. He couldn't even see that Solange was—"

"Don't!" he said desperately. "You must not tell him. It would destroy his belief in her." And in me, he added silently. He could feel a hot breathlessness growing inside him, the vein in his temple throbbing. He forced himself to say calmly that if they were to continue seeing each other Finn would have to remain ignorant.

The corners of her mouth curled up. At that moment she looked to him like a predatory cat whose prey had gone limp. He felt diminished, and suddenly furious. Roughly, he pulled her to him and at the touch of his fingers on the soft flesh of her upper arm a small flame of excitement flared up in him.

Laughing softly, she tried to twist away, but he held fast to her shoulders, forcing her down to the ground. As she lay beneath him, her face flushed and eyes bright with expectation, he thought how easy it would be to ensure that she never told anyone what had happened between him and Solange.

Then she put her hands on his chest and pushed gently. "Not now. Tonight. Okay?"

He released her and rolled over, away from her. She smiled, an odd smile of satisfaction, as if she had proved something to herself, and sat up. He put his head in his hands.

"Okay?" she repeated.

He raised his head. "Yes. Yes, I will come."

She grinned, and stood up. "I'm sure you will. You always do."

As she turned away to leave, he almost called out to tell her that it was unwise to come out on the cliffs alone. But the words died in his throat.

Chapter 19

Dana stood in the wide doorway of the drawing room at Kerreck Du. She could hear voices coming from other parts of the house, but this room, where they were all to gather for dinner, was still empty. She was glad of a moment alone to take it in, undistracted.

Long and low-ceilinged, the wood-paneled room glimmered in the dusk with the cluttered, eccentric opulence of an Aladdin's cave. Scattered about on tables and on the top of a large piano were glass globes half filled with oil. The flames from their burning wicks, and from the log fire in the grate, cast a soft golden light on a profusion of objects large and small, ranging from the exquisite to the outright tacky or bizarre. Worn pink and blue Persian carpets covered the floor. Framed photographs hung on the walls. Surfaces were littered with fossils, small pieces of modern sculpture, stacks of magazines, and books lying open or marked with bits of paper. On the table beside her was a collection of paperweights whose glass domes enclosed the small polished skulls of birds. A life-size pink plastic flamingo stood on one leg in a corner, with cameras dangling from its neck. Flowers were everywhere, the massed heads of pink-frilled peonies, a cluster of yellow lilies, their perfume mingling with the scent of jasmine that drifted in through the French doors, open to the mild evening air.

Dana felt a small tingle of anticipation. After working all day alone in the glasshouse, she was ready for company, even company as contentious as Finn's other guests. And she was eager now to see Daniel again.

She tried to tell herself that she simply wanted to discuss Dr. Veasey's letters with him. But there was another, more powerful reason. She needed to know if she had imagined that seductive rapport between them yesterday.

All the while, a cautious inner voice warned her not to let emotions stirred up by Marianna's story infect her own life. She had finished with all that romantic nonsense. She had grown up.

But she couldn't suppress an excitement, and a contentment, unknown to her since the months of her pregnancy, the sense of possibilities and rich rewards. The pull of the future now seemed stronger than the pull of the past, and for that she had Daniel Finn to thank. Without him, she might never have come to Kerreck Du or discovered the truth about Marianna.

Today, sifting carefully through the rest of the documents on the desk in the glasshouse, she had found, among other items, Veasey's certificate of Marianna's death from "a seizure" as well as various notes of condolence and a brief, uninformative obituary in the *Times*. Nothing to equal the revelations of Veasey's letters. But those, taken together with the various photographs Henry had made of Marianna, surpassed Dana's most optimistic expectations for this visit. She now had material that, if Finn granted her permission to use it, would transform her article, might even form the foundation for the book whose vague outlines were already taking shape in her mind.

Pascale came into the drawing room with a heavily laden tray. Dressed in a white silk shirt and black trousers, with a choker of silver beads around her long neck, she represented the understated elegance Dana had always assumed was the unique province of Frenchwomen of her age and type. Refusing Dana's offer of help, she told her firmly to sit down, she would bring dinner to her. Swiftly, she began to set out a buffet of dishes on the refectory table that stood against one wall.

"I'm afraid I'm causing you a lot of extra work," Dana said. Pascale had also brought her lunch on a tray in the glasshouse, and had washed and mended yesterday's torn clothes, brushing aside her thanks with the wry observation that a visitor at Kerreck Du wasn't expected to risk her life or help with the dishes.

"A guest as invisible as you have been today can hardly be considered work," Pascale replied now. She glanced at Dana's dress, a royal blue mini-pleated tunic of a material that could be scrunched up in her backpack and emerge wrinkle free. "Your dress is lovely. That color suits you." As she turned away, she left Dana with the impression that her approval extended beyond the dress.

The others began to drift into the room. While they helped Pascale or stood together talking, Dana limped slowly toward one of the two sofas near the fire. If she'd had any lingering doubts, a random sampling of the books in a nearby bookcase, as well as the room itself, confirmed that Finn was a complicated man with eclectic interests. Sontag, Borges, Barthes, Foucault, Trollope, and Hardy stood cheek by jowl with collections of poetry and histories of photography.

As she sat down she saw Daniel talking to Pascale. He wore the wheat-colored jacket from the night of the auction, with linen trousers and an open-necked olive green shirt whose color brought out the deep auburn shade of his hair and the tan that had begun to darken his skin. From the way her body responded, she knew at once that she was already far past the point of being able to make calm judgments about their relationship, imagined or otherwise.

A glass of wine in each hand, he came over to her. "Pascale's sent me to ask whether you would prefer the cold veal or the hot crab casserole. Have both. They're delicious."

"Then I will. I'm very hungry."

"I'm not surprised. I hear you've been working hard." He pulled a sagging leather hassock nearer to place it under her foot, and asked with a small grin if the day had been productive.

She smiled back at him. "You know it was. Talk about infinite riches in a little room. I'm still recovering. The letters alone . . . when I read them I didn't know whether to shout with joy or cry. It's wonderful to have the answers to so many questions. But when I think of what Marianna went through so that I could have my thrill of academic pleasure . . ." She made a regretful face, and sipped a little of her wine.

He sat down on the sofa beside her. "You talk about her sometimes as though she's alive."

"Sometimes she seems that way to me."

"Why is she so important to you?"

"Her story's a godsend, professionally speaking. I'm a lecturer with an insecure future. And you know what they say, publish or perish." She wondered if someday she would be able to tell him the whole truth, the story of her miscarriage and divorce.

He glanced at her ankle, and then at the cut on her face. "Are things mending well?"

All sorts of things, she was tempted to say, but only nodded. "You've been taking very good care of me. All of you."

"It's only what a heroine deserves." He swirled the wine around gently in his glass, then added, more seriously, "It's a good thing you're brave. Anyone who stays at Kerreck Du these days needs a certain amount of courage."

Assuming that this was a reference to the Gull, she pointed to her ankle. "This will keep me from taking any risks. And anyway, I've had my fill of climbing."

"What I really meant was that the preparations for my father's exhibition make this a less than peaceable kingdom. That you should be prepared for a certain amount of uproar. Not," he added with a quick smile before he went off to transmit her dinner request to Pascale, "that it was so very peaceful before."

His words had sounded like a warning. But she had seen enough in her short time at Kerreck Du to know that the relationships among these people were volatile, as were the people themselves. And that Quentin Finn was perhaps the most volatile of them all. Only Pascale, and Daniel himself, seemed untouched by the turbulence.

He had called Kerreck Du a kingdom, and as she looked around it wasn't difficult to imagine Quentin Finn as the ruler of this miniature fiefdom, his own deliberately lost domain. Here were all the trappings of an autocrat, the idiosyncratic opulence, the stamp of personality on everything, the courtiers, some loyal, some, perhaps, disaffected. And that slight but unmistakable air of tension that must surely be always present at any court.

Her eye was caught by a pair of photographs hanging side by side on the wall to the right of the fireplace, a Victorian monochrome and a modern black-and-white, each roughly twenty-four by thirty inches. The earlier print was undoubtedly a Hobhouse. It showed a cloaked couple, their faces hidden, standing together under a vast, leafy tree in whose branches crouched the shadowy shape of an old man with a white beard. King Mark, she thought, eavesdropping on Tristan and Iseult in the orchard at Tintagel, hoping to catch them out as lovers.

Pascale set Dana's plate down on the table beside her. "That's Hobhouse himself in the tree," she said, noticing the direction of Dana's gaze.

"Who was out of his tree by the time he made that photograph," John Malzer added as Pascale moved away. He stood contemplating the print for a moment, then sat down on the sofa opposite Dana's on the other side of the fireplace, and began hungrily to fork up his food. He ate with focused concentration, slightly hunched over his place.

Estelle had taken the armchair next to Malzer's end of the sofa. With a jingling of gold bracelets, she spread her napkin across the lap of her full-skirted turquoise dress, speared a mushroom from her plate, and sniffed at it suspiciously. "Garlic. I do wish Pascale wouldn't insist on using so much of it. She knows how I loathe it."

Dana picked up her own plate. "Are you sure you're not confusing Henry Hobhouse with his first wife?" she asked Malzer. Nowhere in the accounts she had read had anyone accused the photographer himself of being less than sane. Arrogant, aggressive, self-important, even ruthless in trouncing rivals in print, but sane.

"I don't think so," Malzer replied through a mouthful of crab. "But Finn's the one to ask." He looked around, but Finn was still standing at the far end of the room by the refectory table, talking to Daniel and to Mico Tatevic, who had just arrived. Nadia might be along later when Elvina was asleep, Dana had heard Tatevic say. Lately, the child was restless and slow to settle.

Karen Cody sat down, with her legs tucked sideways beneath her, on the floor in front the fire. She had a plate with a roll stuffed with the veal in one hand and a large glass of wine in the other. "Finn shot another of his weird variations on Hobhouse yesterday," she told them. "Timothy and me stark naked cuddled up to a sword."

"We're lucky we weren't skewered," Sundy said irritably. He was wearing the pink blazer again tonight, and Dana wondered if this was partly in defiance of Thomas Attery's comment about it yesterday. When he pulled one of the hassocks over to Karen's side, she shifted away, only slightly but enough to make him scowl.

Attery overheard Karen's and Tim's last remarks as he joined Malzer on the sofa. The descriptions, he said tartly, made him think of a particularly unappetizing shish kebab.

"Unappetizing?" Karen glanced at him sharply. "I'll tell you what's unappetizing. Taking snapshots of dead people. That's unappetizing. Or maybe pathetic's a better word."

In the silence that followed this peculiar remark Dana asked if the photograph next to the Hobhouse, the modern black-and-white, was Finn's. It was certainly in his style, she thought. The upper torso of a nude woman was emerging, dryadlike, from a tree, pushing herself free of the trunk with her hands. Her long, dark hair streamed back into the bark so that it was impossible to see where the one left off and the other began. The uplifted face, which in profile had the delicate, finely etched beauty of a Botticelli, bore a striking resemblance to Marianna's.

Karen said, "That's Solange. Finn calls it 'The Green Fuse.' I call it 'Buggered by Beech.' "

Timothy Sundy gave a small snort of amusement, while Malzer looked mildly disapproving and Estelle smoothed out the turquoise folds of her dress with elaborate care. Dana noticed that Karen's outrageous remarks were always accompanied by a sly, sideways glance, like a child deliberately trying to shock. This time the glance was directed her way, but Dana's only response was to say that it looked like an oak to her.

Finn came over to sit down heavily by Dana. He didn't seem to be eating anything, but carried a large cut-glass tumbler of whiskey. Daniel, who had walked over with his father, leaned against a nearby bookcase, his plate balanced on one hand as he ate. In some undefinable way he seemed to be on guard, despite the outwardly relaxed manner. As though he were a type of guardian angel, Dana thought, keeping an eye on them.

That eye rested most often on his father. Finn sat sprawled beside her, legs outstretched. This evening there was a touch of the dandy to his dress. He wore a blue silk shirt with a wildly patterned tie in reds and purples, and shoes of burgundy leather. The fingers of one hand beat a restless tattoo on the arm of the sofa while the other hand moved the tumbler of whiskey regularly to his mouth.

When she said how much she liked the room, he turned his head lazily toward her, the blue eyes amused. "Could be used against me, all these things. My critics have always claimed I'm only interested in objects. 'Obscure objects of desire, with the emphasis on obscure.' That's how one put it." He gave a snort of contempt. "It's not the artist's job to resolve life's mysteries. Especially for critics."

"The Victorians would have sympathized," she said. "They loved curiosities."

"Surrogates for the real thing, that's why. The bloody Victorians saw the world as one vast exhibition created for their amusement and edification. All those nineteenth-century photographers trekking off into the unknown to gather images for the folks back home. Fenton, Du Camp, Frith. Bravest men that ever lived, some of them. Risked their lives time and again."

"So that a Nottingham mill owner could have his own Crystal Palace in a photograph album."

"Precisely. Booty in the eye of the beholder."

They smiled at each other. She could see Daniel's smile in his father's, and felt for an instant the same sympathetic current. But only fleetingly. Finn was not really her type. He was far too difficult, if difficult in an interesting fashion. Even the way he spoke was difficult, in short, sharp bursts, with a staccato assertiveness punctuated by humorous asides, dated slang, and the occasional obscenity. His speech could be salty and direct, or elliptical, almost a shorthand, so that occasionally she had to struggle to understand what he was getting at. Later, she realized that he had been well on his way to being drunk.

As she turned to pick up her wine, she caught John Malzer's eyes on her. He was staring at her with a meditative interest, but shifted his attention almost at once to some question Estelle was asking him, picking crumbs one by one from his black corduroys and navy pullover as he listened to her. Both trousers and sweater bagged loosely on his big frame, but something about him, a controlled stillness, suggested to Dana that he was not a sloppy person.

"Someone called photographs mock forms of possession. Forget who, but they were right," Finn was saying. Slumped down, he was looking now at the photograph of his wife, and his face seemed touched by sadness. In a voice so low it was almost a whisper, he added, "And how they can mock us."

He roused himself, setting the glass down on the carpet by his feet, and went on a stronger voice. "Speaking of forms of possession, you'll be interested to know that Marianna held her last seance here. May even have used that table." He nodded toward a round Victorian card table that stood by the French doors. "I bought this place lock, stock, and barrel from Henry's greatniece. Amazing old girl. Bit of a period piece, but all her marbles. She told me the table had belonged to Marianna."

Dana said, "You've put it in the right place. Marianna liked to hold her seances by a window or an open door. She wanted as much light as possible."

"I thought mediums worked in darkened rooms," Attery commented. His white silk turtleneck and gray jacket seemed to emphasize the pallor of his skin and the startling black pupils of his eyes. In a room so rich in color, his colorlessness seemed to Dana to set him apart. Or perhaps it was simply that he had such a cool reserve.

"Most did," she replied. "Marianna was an exception. She believed spirits were drawn to light. 'We are all connected by a bright cord of light,' she wrote once." Dana found this philosophy one of the most appealing aspects of Marianna's character.

"And she was afraid of the dark, wasn't she?" Daniel said, as he added another log to the fire.

She wondered how he had known, until she remembered that of course he had read Veasey's letters. "Yes, terrified. That was one of the things used against her when she was committed to the asylum, as proof that she was insane—the fact that she refused to enter a dark room."

"I don't see why you waste your time with such crap," Karen told her flatly. She yawned widely and pushed away the plate with her unfinished roll. "I mean, the woman had to be either crazy or a fake. What else could a medium be?"

Dana glanced over at Daniel, who gave a wry smile at this echo of his own words. She said to Karen, "That depends on your perspective. I think Marianna genuinely believed that she could communicate with spirits. Whether the spirits were real or not is another question. Marianna was probably an epileptic. Maybe epilepsy gives its victims a heightened awareness of things beyond our normal perceptions."

"What do you mean, probably an epileptic?" Tim asked her, a large forkful of salad halfway to his mouth. "Don't you know?"

Daniel spoke before she could reply. "There's no proof," he told the other man. "We can make an educated guess from the description of her symptoms, but people didn't admit to having epilepsy in the nineteenth century." Noting the "we," Dana gave him a grateful look.

"That's because epilepsy was thought to be caused by masturbation," Attery said, looking around at them all. Behind his gold-rimmed glasses, the curiously birdlike eyes were bright with amusement. "The cure for which could be castration, or whatever the female equivalent is. No wonder people kept quiet about it."

"Oh for Heaven's sake, Thomas. Do we really need to know that?" Estelle clattered her knife and fork together, her face screwed up, as at a bad smell.

Out of an obscure need to give Marianna a credibility by association, Dana told them that many famous Victorians had taken part in Marianna's seances, Elizabeth Barrett Browning among them, and that none had complained of being deceived by the medium.

"Did Marianna hold these seances in her own home or at her friends' houses?" Attery asked her. Both, she replied, knowing that he was going to point out, as he proceeded to, that this was clever on Marianna's part, for people would feel reluctant to accuse their hostess of fraud, or their friends of helping to perpetrate a hoax.

"And E.B.B. herself was rather gullible about spiritualism, wasn't she?" he continued, neatly wiping his mouth with his napkin. He placed his empty plate on the tray Pascale was holding out to him. "Of course, Robert Browning considered spiritualism a lot of nonsense. He wrote a satirical poem on the subject, 'Mr. Sludge, the Medium.' Browning says that it takes hysteric hybrids to make mediums."

"He has Sludge say that," Dana corrected quietly. "And Sludge goes on to say that, after all, well-balanced types don't usually 'yield the fire.' "

"She has you there, Thomas." Finn smiled as he stood up. He walked across the room to the piano, which was covered with framed photographs, took one from the cluster, and brought it back to them. He offered it first to Dana. "Hobhouse made this of Daniel Dunglas Home, the famous medium. Browning's real-life Sludge. I suspect it was meant ironically." It was a composite, he added, created from over a dozen negatives.

The small monochrome showed an effetely attractive young man surrounded by ghostly figures. They filled the air around him, floated above his head, lay on the carpet at his feet. One even spiraled out of his breast pocket. Visually lovely, with soft gray tones, it was also technically remarkable. As she passed the photograph to Thomas Attery, Dana remarked that it must have persuaded at least a few people into a belief in the reality of spirits.

Undoubtedly, Finn replied. But unlike genuine spirit photographers—he laid an ironic emphasis on the adjective—Hobhouse had never intended to dupe the viewer.

To Dana, the mocking photograph seemed to confirm her belief that all along, Henry's attitude toward Marianna's spiritualism had been one of cynical opportunism. Marianna had been useful to him at the beginning of his career, but once it was established, she became merely an embarrassment.

Pascale appeared with plates of dessert. If anyone preferred fruit or cheese, she said, they should help themselves at the buffet table. As Dana took her slice of cake she reflected that the Frenchwoman rarely seemed to sit down or to join in the conversation, but instead effaced herself, quietly seeing to people's needs. She didn't seem particularly shy, so perhaps it was simply that she preferred to keep aloof from Finn's guests. Dana could understand why.

"And those genuine ghost photographers," Karen was asking Finn, "how did they do it?"

He shrugged, "Conjuring tricks mostly." He described how some unscrupulous photographers would substitute a previously exposed plate or film for the original. Others would paint images on the background with sulfate of quinine diluted in sulfuric acid, which was invisible to the eye but would be recorded by the camera. Or they might take a very underexposed picture of the "ghost" against a dead black background and then use the same plate again for another picture.

"What did believers think was going on?" Tim Sundy asked through a mouthful of cake.

Finn glanced at Dana, as if to say, That's your department. She said, "I read a description once by a man who argued that spirits impressed their image on a photographic plate by depositing repeated layers of magnetism on it. Of course, the photographer needed to have an affinity with the spirits—to be a kind of medium—for this to happen."

"So why did Hobhouse bother to do this?" Sundy asked, holding up the photograph. There was a smear of chocolate on his upper lip, like a thin brown mustache. It made him look older, and faintly ridiculous. Dana saw Karen giggle as she noticed it.

Finn shrugged. "Who knows? I loathe the way we want to solve every mystery, expose every secret. Closure, that awful word. It's a symptom of our age's uncertainty. We want everything spelled out for us, don't want to think for ourselves. Art, thank God, is one of the few areas where there's more than one right answer."

"This is art?" Karen asked, looking down at the photograph, which she'd taken from Tim.

"Of its kind."

"It's certainly not straight photography," John Malzer said with a smile.

This provoked another outburst from Finn. "Straight photography! As though it's a virtue to be obvious."

"What the mob understands?" Daniel said, with a quizzical smile for his father.

"Daniel means I've been accused of elitism. But even the mob longs for allegory, symbol, myth. We all do. Most of us are just too bloody ignorant nowadays to recognize them."

"I agree," said Estelle vehemently in her piercing voice. She had said very little during this conversation, but from the way she had been listening, so intently that a frown marked the flesh between her eyes, it seemed to Dana that she was troubled by it. "We're so terribly materialist in every way. There's simply too little of the spiritual in our lives."

Karen stretched sleepily, then stood up. "I don't know why but that word always makes me want to pee."

As she left the room, Tim said. "I can't imagine anyone falling for ghost photographs today. We're too aware of the tricks cameras can play."

"I don't agree," Dana said quickly. "Most people don't know that much about photography and have no idea what it's capable of. Just the other day I was reading about an elderly couple in . . . Where was it? Oh yes, a place called Scunthorpe. How could I forget. They were completely taken in by a man who showed them photographs of their dead son's ghost. They gave him their life savings."

"People like that want to be fooled," Attery said contemptuously. "They'll believe anything that prevents them from facing the truth. When the conjuror does his job well, his mark is his co-conspirator. Mediums like your Marianna counted on that, of course."

Dana could feel her temper rise. "I don't think you can condemn the genuine simply because fakes imitate it. Anyway, there are limits to empiricism."

"But no limits to credulity," Attery quickly returned.

"Some might call it faith," Daniel said quietly. "And aren't we taught that there should be no limits to faith?"

John Malzer was helping himself to a second piece of cake. "That word terrifies most of us. We'll use any obscenity, but mention faith and we get all hot and bothered." At this, Estelle reached out to put her hand on his. He glanced at her with an oddly consoling smile.

" 'Faith is to believe what you do not yet see; the reward for this faith is to see what you believe.' " Finn had leaned his head back against the sofa cushions and was gazing up at the ceiling. "Wonderfully equivocal words." He closed his eyes.

"Are you still talking about ghosts?" Karen had come back into the room. She moved restlessly over to pick up one of the glass globes. Her eyes were glittering and the sleepy air was gone.

Thomas Attery leaned toward Malzer. With quiet malice, he said, "Amazing how a trip to the loo restores one. It must be that white cleansing powder." Tim's head snapped around and he told Attery fiercely to shut up.

Holding the globe of light under her chin so that it gave her features an exaggerated, masklike appearance, Karen began to chant, "Double bubble, toil and trouble . . ." Which made Shakespeare's words sound like an advertisement for chewing gum, Dana thought. Stumbling over the witches' incantation, Karen interrupted herself to suggest that they hold a seance. "We could raise the spirits of those women who were killed on the cliffs. Ask them whether they fell or were pushed."

"Really, Karen," Estelle said sharply, "it's not something to joke about."

"Don't tell me you're afraid of ghosts?" the younger woman asked her. In the thin diaphanous shift, with the metallic hair crackling about her head and the planes of her face thrown into sharp relief by the flame, she looked to Dana like the incarnation of some malign spirit herself. With sinuous deliberation she began to pace around the room, holding the globe of light before her like a priestess.

"She'll want the Ouija board out next, God help us!" Attery muttered, as he stood up to help himself to cheese at the buffet table.

Karen had paused in front of Daniel. "I'm sure there's a ghost you'd like to raise, Daniel." She smiled up at him, taunting. He shook his head slightly, and continued to lean against the bookshelf, his hands in the pockets of his trousers. His face expressed nothing more than a wary amusement.

"Too bad," the girl told him over her shoulder as she moved away. "I'll bet she'd come for you."

At this, Dana saw Daniel's eyes flick briefly toward his father. But Finn's were still closed. Dana wondered if he had fallen asleep or if he was simply choosing to ignore Karen's performance. She wished she could follow suit. The heat of the fire combined with the wine to make her feel light-headed. The room seemed to drift past her like some great cargo ship out of control, its somnolent captain asleep at the helm.

Karen next approached Mico Tatevic. He had been sitting so silently in a chair slightly apart from the others that Dana had almost forgotten his presence. As he watched Karen, his large hands rested on his knees, and the Easter Island face was expressionless, so that he looked like a figure carved from stone.

"I feel a spirit moving in me, Mico," Karen said, her voice thick with meaning. "Do you?"

As he sat there looking up at the girl it was clear to Dana that he was in some way fascinated by her. But there was an element of a bird's mesmerized compliance with a snake in that dazzled gaze, more fear than pleasure. The atmosphere in the room had changed, grown electric. Timothy Sundy stirred angrily. Beside her, Finn's eyes had opened just a fraction and he was staring at Karen through narrowed lids. Dana thought: I don't know these people. Suddenly, they seemed capable of anything.

Chapter 20

"Mico!"

The urgent voice broke across the silence of the room like the crack of a whip. They all turned to see Nadia Tatevic standing in the open French doors. Mico shook his head, as though to clear it, and moved past Karen toward his wife. He walked clumsily, like a sleepwalker waking in confusion. Nadia spoke to him in a low, bitter voice, her heavy face twisted with anger. He made no response but went silently with her out into the night.

"I didn't expect the devil herself to appear," Karen said, with a nervous laugh. She set the light down and ran her hands along her bare arms. A shiver visibly shook her, but whether of cold or fear or excitement Dana couldn't have said. Karen's behavior with Tatevic struck her as an odd mixture of provocation and nervous bravado.

Finn suddenly stirred and got to his feet. "For God's sake, Pascale, do we have to sit here in this gloom?" While she went around switching on the lamps he poured himself another drink, muttered something about needing fresh air, and went out onto the terrace. In a moment, Pascale followed him. Meanwhile, the others threw off the lethargy that seemed to have crept up on them all and wandered over to the refectory table to help themselves to more wine or dessert.

Dana wondered how long Nadia had been standing outside. She found it both painful and slightly unnerving to think of the woman hovering there in the darkness, watching them.

"Poor Nadia," Malzer said, like an echo of her thoughts. "Not a happy woman."

"Is it any wonder?" Thomas Attery swallowed a last bite of

cheese, then set his plate aside. He glanced pointedly at Karen, who seemed involved in some sort of argument with Tim in a far corner of the room. "The bombshells here come in a different packing. But I imagine she finds them just as destructive."

At that moment, Pascale reappeared to say that Finn wanted them all to come outside, that the moon was brilliant in an unclouded sky, its light unearthly. "He says you must see it. You know how Finn is about light," she added with a slight amused shrug of her shoulders.

Despite some grumbling, they roused themselves obediently. But when Dana started to get to her feet to follow the others, Daniel told her that she was excused. "Unless you're especially eager to see the moon . . . ?"

"I'll wait until the gallery's not so crowded." She sank back down into her corner of the sofa and stretched her left arm out along the sofa back.

He took his father's place beside her on the sofa. "I could arrange a private viewing." It was said lightly, but he put his own arm on the sofa back so that his hand lay close to hers, their fingertips almost touching, and his eyes were grave.

"The last viewing I went to," she said, her tone equally light but her eyes unable now to meet his, "I saw something I wanted. Unfortunately someone else wanted it, too." She was speaking now not only of Marianna's photograph.

"That doesn't mean you should give up on it." Something about the way he said this suggested to her that his words held the same double meaning as her own.

She looked directly at him then and said with a laugh, "Is this moonshine we're talking?"

"Only if you want it to be."

In the silence that followed, Attery's voice came back to them through the French doors. "Trailing clouds of whiskey do we come, Finn. I just hope you don't expect us to see the visionary gleam. We haven't your innocence."

Daniel raised an eyebrow. "Thomas has a cruel way with words. But he can be perceptive."

"About the innocence?" Dana tried to keep incredulity from her voice.

"Not a term that immediately leaps to mind for Finn, is it? But he does look at things with an innocent eye. Sees them fresh. Like a child."

"And the visionary gleam?"

"That's Finn's rainbow. He's always chasing it."

"Does he ever find it?"

Daniel's eyes slid to the photograph of Solange. "Sometimes. Then it's gone again."

"She was very beautiful."

"Yes." The monosyllable was flat. In a moment, he went on to say that Finn had given up photographing the human face until he met Solange. "She inspired a tremendous surge of creativity. Turned him in a new direction just as he was losing interest in the old."

Dana asked how the two had met, then immediately regretted the question for it was clear from the way his eyes clouded that it disturbed him.

"Through me," he said after a moment. "Solange and I, we were . . . friends. She came to visit me here, at the Schoolhouse." Then, as though it were important to him to be honest with her and that she understand, he said matter-of-factly, "The truth is, we were having an affair. Nothing very intense on either side. She was never in love with me, and Finn was everything she was looking for. Lover, husband, father figure . . ."

Rich and famous, Dana completed to herself. She was surprised by an emotion that might almost have been jealousy of the dead woman. And she wondered if Daniel's apparent detachment, his own seeming lack of jealousy, had been bought at a price that he was still paying. It couldn't be easy, she thought, to lose your lover to your father.

Before she could respond, however, Estelle came back inside, complaining that a wind had risen. She asked Daniel if he would fetch her jacket from the hall. As soon as he was gone she crossed the room to Dana and stood hovering over her. She seemed troubled, almost uncertain, her bustling, managing quality subdued. Even the bangles on her long, bony wrists were stilled.

"What you said earlier," she began hurriedly, "about keeping an open mind about spiritualism? I should so much like to talk to you about that. Will you have lunch with me tomorrow, at my house?"

Dana was grateful for the excuse of her ankle. The last thing she wanted was to have her work with the Hobhouse papers interrupted for a tête-à-tête with Estelle Pinchot.

The older woman frowned. "I quite forgot about your ankle. Then I'll come here. I'm sure Finn won't mind."

Forced to be explicit, Dana explained that as her time at Kerreck Du was limited, she felt she should spend it on her research.

"Yes, of course, I do understand," Estelle said impatiently. "But you see, this is important." She moved closer. Dana could smell the heavy perfume she wore, as oppressive as the woman herself, and a gust of stale breath. "That elderly couple you mentioned earlier," she went on, in a low voice, "the people who lost their life savings . . . I wanted to ask you—" She broke off as the others came back into the room.

"It's time we were going, Estelle," John Malzer called to her.

"Yes, yes, I'm coming." She gazed down intently at Dana. "Tomorrow, then. I promise I won't disturb you for long."

"Well, I . . ." Dana glanced at Finn, who had come up beside Estelle.

"Now, Estelle," he interposed smoothly, taking her arm, "you were going to give us a hand at the gallery tomorrow, remember? Around eleven?" Skillfully, he moved her toward the others, who were leaving the room. Karen and Tim offered Daniel a lift back to the Schoolhouse, but he shook his head, saying that he would walk back along the cliff path.

Estelle paused as she put her arms into the sleeves of the jacket Daniel was holding for her, and looked around at him. "Surely that's not wise?"

"Perhaps not on a dark night," he replied evenly. "But with this moon . . . And I know the track like the back of my hand."

"That's not what I meant," Estelle began.

Karen cut her off. "Why should Daniel stop using the cliffs just because people like to tell horror stories? I'm certainly not going to. Anyway," she added with a cruel smile for the older woman, "Daniel and I are too young for the Gull. He likes his meat well aged."

Finn told her sharply to behave herself, then chivied them all toward the hall, leaving Dana alone with Daniel and Pascale. "Karen is impossible," Pascale said, stooping to pick up a dirty glass from beside a chair leg. The French accent made the adjective sound doubly acerbic.

It would be better, Daniel agreed dryly as he began to help her, if Karen limited her talent with the needle to her work.

"Needles can also prick those who use them," Pascale observed. "Karen should take care."

Finn came back into the room loudly proclaiming his relief at the departure of his guests. Then he said off-handedly to Daniel, "Better if you stayed here tonight. Didn't like the feel of that wind."

Daniel seemed surprised by his father's concern. "In that case," he said, "I'd be glad of a bed at Kerreck Du."

"Good." Finn splashed more whiskey into his glass and sank into an armchair, setting the whiskey bottle on the table beside him. Dana saw Pascale's glance at Daniel, and his answering, almost imperceptible shrug. Finn must have seen it as well, for he said irritably, gesturing to the bottle, "Purely medicinal. Thomas and Karen together have given me a blinding headache."

Pascale was unsympathetic. "A self-inflicted wound. You would invite them to dinner."

He ignored this. "The milk of human kindness always ran rather thin in Thomas and what little of it there is seems to be curdling. He's very sour these days." With his free hand, he rubbed at his neck, and at once Pascale came around behind his chair to massage his shoulder muscles.

"He's unhappy in love," Daniel said.

Finn snorted. "Thomas's only love is money. And his collection. The other's a menopausal passion. Though what he sees in John is beyond me. The fellow looks like a large brown slug." When Pascale murmured something about the milk of human kindness, he laughed. "Yes, yes, I know. Pot and kettle."

"Anyway," she went on, "I don't believe it is physical. More like frustrated fatherhood."

"God knows I could tell him that fatherhood's a frustration in itself." Finn's voice was roughly humorous.

"Perhaps fatherhood's a skill like any other," Daniel said blandly. "Lack of practice might make it frustrating."

For a moment, the two men stared at each other. There was amusement in the younger man's eyes, but Dana thought she saw a dangerous light flicker in the older's. But Finn only laughed and told Daniel that he hoped he would get lots of practice when it was his turn. Then, in a voice grown suddenly serious, he said, "Karen's up to her old tricks, isn't she?"

"Drugs, you mean?" Daniel replied. "Judging by tonight, I'd say so."

"She's a fool. Talent but no self-discipline. I was no saint myself at that age, but I worked bloody hard. Nothing got in the way of that. Still doesn't. Apart from this exhibition." He scratched his beard fiercely, as though it irritated him, then twisted around in the chair to look up at his sister-in-law. "Remind me, Pascale, why I agreed to it."

"Because John flattered you until you couldn't say no. Now sit still."

"Ouch!" He glanced at Dana. "Was I right just now in thinking you wanted protecting from la belle dame sans merci?"

"I didn't mean to be rude. But since I don't have a lot of time here—"

"Nonsense! All the time in the world." The large gesture with his glass slopped whiskey onto the arm of the chair. He ignored it but Pascale left off the massage and went for a cloth. "Estelle seems to have taken a fancy to you," he added.

"She said she wanted to talk about spiritualism. She seemed upset about something."

"Estelle is always upset about something," Pascale said tartly as she blotted up the spilled whiskey. "Like Nadia."

"Never mind about them. Or that." Finn put his hand over Pascale's, to stop her scrubbing at the stain. He spoke curtly but left the hand on hers for a moment, and the gesture looked to Dana more tender than repressive. As Pascale moved away, he turned to his son. "You haven't told me yet about this new project of yours."

"I'm not sure you'll be all that interested. It's not really your sort of thing." Then, obviously catching Pascale's small warning shake of the head, he said quickly, "That is, it's boring if you're not—"

Finn slammed his hand down on the arm of the chair. "Goddammit! Don't tell me what my sort of thing is or is not!" He reached out for the whiskey bottle, knocking over his empty glass on the table. Pascale moved forward but he waved her away, righted the unbroken glass, then poured himself another generous measure. The Frenchwoman's mouth tightened.

Daniel's eyes were on some distant point, his face unreadable. After a moment, he said, "It's just that you've always been pretty unequivocal about digital imaging."

"Sure. Right now it's crap. That's not to say the manure won't produce roses someday. But they'll be scentless, those roses."

"I think it's partly a question of adjustment," Daniel replied coolly. "A hundred and fifty years ago, people complained about the change from the daguerreotype to the albumen process. They said the image wasn't as perfect, and they were right. But the albumen photograph has its own beauty. We need to develop an aesthetic for the digital process as well. That'll happen as the technology improves. Already color's more flexible."

"Color's the refuge of the creatively bankrupt," Finn said contemptuously.

Daniel smiled. "As in, 'If you can't make it good, make it red'?"

But Finn wouldn't be amused. "Black-and-white work demands an act of artistic transformation. If nothing else, color's distracting. Anyway, your technology will let you down. Ink-jet printing and dye sublimation will never give you the subtlety of the silver-toned image."

"Maybe not. But maybe it can give us something else as beautiful. Besides, aren't we supposed to express the meaning of our age in the modern medium? Digital's simply the new language."

"God help us."

While Dana listened to the verbal duel between father and son, she was interested to see that as Daniel calmly held his own Finn gradually lost his anger. It was clear to her that despite Finn's strong feelings on the subject he had a grudging respect for Daniel's persistence and for his opinions.

Finn drank some whiskey, then grimaced as though somehow

the taste of it had altered. He looked up at his son. "Sorry, Daniel. Your own work's not crap. In fact, it's very good. Technically astonishing."

"But fake?" Daniel did not sound angry or aggressive, merely curious, as though they were discussing an impersonal issue of minor importance.

Finn shook his head slowly. "If you're a fake, then I'm one, too. We only differ in our methods. And mine are doomed to extinction. I'm a dinosaur, you see," he said to Dana. He suddenly looked very weary and more than his age. The man she had seen in the clearing yesterday afternoon, she thought, had been a younger self.

"Black-and-white darkroom work is on the way out," he told her. "In a few years the manufacturers will decide that it's not profitable to make the supplies I use and that will be that. With luck, I'll be dead by then." He emptied his glass, then got to his feet. "Excuse me. The La Brea tar pits call. In other words," he added, turning to Pascale, "I'll be in the darkroom. I still have a few things to finish up." His gait was unsteady as he walked from the room. Dana wondered how he would manage in a darkroom.

"No matter how much he's drunk," Daniel told her, as though he had read her thought, "his hands are always steady." Then, to Pascale, he added enigmatically, "Signs and portents?"

"I think so," she replied with a small smile. "And I am happy you were here to see them."

Chapter 21

Karen stood beside the Rover in the drive outside Kerreck Du while Tim searched his pockets for the car keys and ranted at her in a low voice about her behavior with Mico. His angry face was so close to hers that she could see the swelling of a pimple on the side of one nostril. But his fury seemed to come from a long way off, too far away to touch her. The slight buzz in her head from the coke she'd done earlier pleasantly buffered emotion.

The gravel forecourt was lit by a fan of light from the open doorway behind them, where the others were saying good night to Finn. She heard Estelle's high, reedy voice thank him for the lovely evening. The evening had been very entertaining in its way, Karen thought, but hardly lovely. Though she'd had a good time tormenting Thomas with what she knew about him. He pretended to be indifferent, but she knew he was squirming inside. As if anyone cared about his disgusting little habits.

". . . make a spectacle of yourself," Tim was saying angrily. He couldn't quite get his tongue, thickened by wine, around the s's.

That was the point, she wanted to tell him, to make a spectacle, liven things up. But it was too much effort to explain. He was so conventional he wouldn't understand anyway.

The wedge of light contracted and vanished as the front door closed. In a moment footsteps crunched across the gravel toward John's Fiesta, which was parked next to the Rover. She glanced around and saw Estelle and Thomas with John between them. The love object. She giggled out loud.

Tim obviously thought she was laughing at him. Something in his face warned her, but before she could react he'd swung a hand up and slapped her face. Not hard, she barely felt it, but suddenly John was at Tim's side, his hand on the sleeve of the pink blazer.

"Don't do that!"

"Oh, bugger off and mind your own business!" Tim wrenched his arm away. But one of the blazer's sleeve buttons snagged on John's loose-knit cotton sweater, and the two men found themselves tangled together. Thomas stepped forward to help, only to get Tim's arm full in the face as the button suddenly pulled free of the fabric. With a cry of pain, Thomas clapped one hand to his nose.

Karen burst out in wild laughter. "The Three Stooges, that's what you look like! Curly, Larry, and Moe." Convulsed, she put one hand out to the side of the Rover to steady herself.

Momentarily sobered, Tim tried to apologize to Thomas, but the older man brushed him off and got into the back of John's car, where he sat holding a handkerchief to his nose. Estelle leaned from the open window of the front passenger side, beckoning frantically to Malzer. "Do come away, John. Can't you see they're both quite drunk?"

John hesitated beside Karen, chewing on his lower lip. In a manner so earnest that he might have been inquiring into the state of her soul, he asked her if she would be all right. "You could come with us, you know. It might be wise."

That was the last thing she wanted. She made her face as serious as his, put one hand on his shoulder to pull him closer to her, and whispered confidingly, "It's just sex, John. You know how it is."

The mud-brown eyes blinked. The expression in them was one she had never seen there before, and for an instant it caught her off balance, made her think that perhaps he was more interesting than he seemed, and that the weird story he'd told her was true. But almost at once the look she'd expected, the disapproving pout of the lips, replaced it.

Still he hesitated. She knew he probably wanted nothing more than to let her drive off with Tim, but was afraid his conscience would trouble him if they had an accident. She told him to run along home, she'd be fine. Tim was more angry with her than drunk. "We need to talk, that's all. He's okay." He nodded, clearly happy to accept this. Really, he was such a putz. His story had to be a fantasy he'd concocted to impress her.

Tim, meanwhile, had found his keys. As the others drove off, he removed the pink blazer and examined the sleeve buttons, then laid it carefully on the backseat. Even drunk and furious he treated his clothes with elaborate respect. More respect, she thought, than he showed her.

"You know, Tim," she said as she got into the car beside him, "I'll bet if we were on a sinking ship and you could save me or an Armani suit you'd have to think twice."

He gave her a savage look. "Don't count on it."

She laughed, then slipped off her shoes and propped her bare feet on the dashboard while he fumbled the key into the ignition. She ought to drive, he was so pissed, but he'd only get madder if she insisted, and she'd made him mad enough tonight as it was. Anyway, she wasn't in much better shape herself, despite what she'd told John.

"Put your seat belt on," he told her gruffly. He was meticulous about things like that: seat belts, smoke detectors, flossing.

She ignored the order. Rummaging through the box of cassettes he kept on the floor she found a Proclaimers tape and leaned forward to slide it into the player, turning the volume up. The Profaners, Tim called them. He preferred New Age music; his taste in music was one of the things that made it impossible to live with him. He pulled a face at the thudding beat that flooded the car, but did not protest. This was part of the pattern, the sudden capitulation. After a quarrel he was briefly sullen and resentful, then repentent, and finally—if she refused to forgive him—abject.

As they turned onto the road at the top of the drive, the Rover's headlights slid off a rolling wall of hedgerow. The overarching trees made a tunnel of the lane, damp and claustrophobic. It had a fungus smell, that peculiar smell mushrooms got when they'd been sitting around in the fridge too long. She hated these dark winding roads that took forever to get where they were going. They were slow, narrow, and secretive, like the people who lived beside them. It made her long for a bulldozer.

Tim was driving cautiously, thank God. His night vision was bad enough even when he was sober. She glanced at his silent, perfect profile, at the sleek blond hair. He was so beautiful that he assumed every woman wanted to sleep with him, but he put more imagination into dressing himself than he did into making love. He allowed himself to be made love to. At first it had excited her to be the aggressor, but the excitement soon wore off. He bored her now, except when she teased him. He was so easily provoked.

She craved variety, the sharp sexual thrill of the unexpected. A lover in college had once accused her of using sex like a remote control. As soon as she finished one orgasm, he'd said angrily, she was channel surfing for the next. Why not? she'd replied; guys did that all the time. And she could understand why. Stick with the same channel for too long and it got so you could predict what came next. Which was what had happened with Tim.

And with Mico. At first, his passion for his work had made him sexy. She was attracted to men who were possessed by their work. When she seduced them away from it she always felt that she'd won a victory. If, like Mico, they were married as well, it was a twin triumph. But it was only a game with Mico, some fun before she left.

She slapped her hand on the sill of the open window in time to the music. Some middle-aged men practically begged you to seduce them, she thought. It was like they suddenly became aware, in their forties, that they were mortal after all. They were going to get old; death would happen to them. They wanted to be with someone who would give them back that illusion of immortality. Of course, any man married to Nadia Tatevic might think death wasn't so bad after all. She gave an amused grunt as she thought of Nadia's face tonight. Poor Mico.

"You're finding a lot to laugh about," Tim said sullenly.

She turned and took his jaw in one hand, forcing his face toward her so that he had to look at the road ahead out of the corner of his eye.

"For Chrisssake, Karen, you'll have us off the road!" Then, when she persisted, "What?"

"Say you're sorry."

He tried to pull away but she held on, digging her fingernails slightly into his flesh. "Go on. Say it."

"I'm sorry. No, I am, really. I shouldn't have hit you, I know that."

It was his passive voice, the one with the whine in it, the one she thought of as housebroken. Satisfied, she released his face and leaned back against the headrest while he rubbed at his jaw.

"It won't happen again," he said after a moment, looking sideways at her, one eye partly hidden by the smooth fall of his hair. A geisha look. "I promise."

Too right, she thought. The Britishism provoked an inward smile, and so did the reason for it. He wouldn't hit her again because she wouldn't give him the chance. It was over, finito. She was leaving Trebartha. It had been useful as a place to start her career but it didn't make sense to stay any longer, not when she had a job waiting in London.

She would stay for Finn's exhibition only because it would be amusing to let him know the truth about Solange in front of everyone, a kind of payback for all the little humiliations he'd put her through. But the next day she was out of here. Tim would go berserk, but he'd have to accept it. Just like he'd had to accept it when she moved out on him.

As though he'd picked up on this last thought, he asked her abruptly if she'd had any word from Pippa, the friend whose place she was using.

"A postcard from Paris. She says she's staying an extra week."

"So you can go on living in her flat?" His voice was dull, with disappointment, she guessed. He counted on her being forced to move back in with him because she couldn't afford to pay rent.

She nodded.

"But you're not going to, are you?"

There was an edge to his voice this time that made her turn to look at him. To give herself time to think she cupped one ear with her hand, pretending she hadn't heard.

He reached over and punched the stop button on the cassette player. Silence rushed into the car with the wind but despite his comment he seemed reluctant to break it. Then at last he said, "It wasn't just a threat, was it, about going to London? You really are."

What was the point of pretending? If they were going to have a fight they might as well get it over with. "Tasha Delibe phoned. You know, the designer. She said she likes my stuff, wants me to work for her. I said yes." She hoped her matter-of-fact delivery would make him accept it. But she could see his knuckles whiten on the steering wheel.

"What about Sundy Best?"

"Look, I always said it was your baby, not mine. It's got your name, after all." This was a sore point, that he hadn't changed the name. She'd always thought it was a silly name anyway.

"That gives you the right to kill it?"

"Don't be so melodramatic. Anyway, it would be a mercy killing. You know as well as I do that it'll take a lot more money than either of us have to keep it going."

His driving, which had been gradually growing less cautious, now became erratic. The car swerved, then lurched back into place so that she was flung first against him, then against the door. She felt for the seat belt and strapped it around her.

"Come on, Tim. You knew it was ending, don't pretend you didn't."

"I didn't know any such thing. You made a commitment. I expect you to stand by it."

He could be so pompous sometimes, the stuffiest of Brits. A California haircut but underneath it the roast beef of old England, the product of a banker father and a mother who bred Borzois. When he was little, he'd told her once, his mother took him around on a leash, like one of her dogs. Proud of his good looks but continually critical, she made him feel like he was only temporarily "Best of Show." A better dog might come along. His father was so rarely at home that when he was, he would occasionally call Tim by one of the dogs' names. Money and good grooming, Tim said, that was what had mattered in their family. Well, at least he had a family, she'd replied, unsympathetically. Her own had consisted of guardians more interested in her bank account than herself; when their bad investments deprived even her money of their concern they'd faded away.

"You owe me a certain amount, after all," he went on, into her silence.

"There's nothing in writing. And I'm not a gentleman." The feedlot smell of manure and rotting hay was suddenly pungent on the air. They must be passing a farm, she thought.

"But I love you." He said it as though it gave him rights over her, as though it made a difference.

Exasperation, and the detached, floating sensation from the drug, made her reckless. "So what?"

His only response was to accelerate, hard. The Rover leaped forward and the seat belt contracted around her, snapping her back. As she opened her mouth to protest, the wheels hit a slick patch—oil or mud left on the road by a tractor—and the car slewed into a skid. It fishtailed across the road, the headlights splashing across a stone wall and into the wide entrance of a dark farmyard. She saw the black bulk of a tractor, with the curved spiky teeth of an upended harrow behind it, like the huge mouth of some nightmarish beast, into which the car was relentlessly sliding.

The cattle grid at the entrance saved them. With a clatter that drowned out her scream, the grid's metal bars gripped at the tires. She was jolted so hard that her teeth bit down on her tongue, drawing blood. The brakes kicked in, and the car came to rest in front of the harrow's prongs. Shaken, she and Tim sat for a moment in silence, too dazed to speak. Then there was a loud shout from the house and a lozenge of light as a door opened.

"Shit!" Tim threw the clutch into reverse and sent the car roaring backward over the grid and out onto the road again. When Karen screamed at him to be careful he slowed, shifted up, and accelerated only when they were safely past the slippery patch. As the car sped away, Karen twisted around to see the farmer's shadowy shape running after them, receding into the darkness as the distance between them increased.

"Okay, you can stop now," she told him when the man was out of sight.

He slowed and pulled the car into a passing place by the road. She unbuckled the seat belt. "I'll drive."

Without protest, he relinquished the keys and sat slumped silently in the passenger seat for the rest of the drive, his head turned away from her. When she pulled up in front of Sundy Best she told him that she wanted to keep the Rover a little longer. "I've got an errand to run. I'll bring it back in a couple of hours. I'll put the keys through the letter box. Okay? Since you almost killed me, you owe me that much."

She expected an argument, but he only nodded. Retrieving his jacket from the backseat, he looked like a sleepwalker, like someone in shock. As she drove away, she could see him in the rearview mirror, still standing there, looking after her. About as effective as that farmer, she thought.

Chapter 22

From the doorway, Daniel contemplated the living room at Kerreck Du, emptied now of all its guests but one. Peace had settled on the room at last. Finn had retreated to his darkroom, Pascale to the kitchen, and the others had driven off into the night quarreling like fractious children who had stayed up past their bedtimes. Only Dana remained, alone on the sofa, her gaze fixed on the embers of the fire. For the first time that night, the room struck Daniel as a place he wanted to be.

Dana seemed not to have heard him return, and he gave in to the impulse to gaze at her in silence, unseen. The light from the table lamp shone on her hair, streaking it with gold. Her hands lay folded in her lap. She sat without moving, the expression on her face thoughtful, the faintest of smiles curving her mouth. He found himself wanting to know what she was thinking.

After the turbulence of the evening, her contemplative stillness seemed to him more attractive than ever. It reminded him of Pascale's even-tenored composure, serene and restful. But he thought he saw something else in Dana, a streak of romantic impulsiveness, which was at odds with the tranquility. An image of a calm sea lying deceptively smooth under the full summer moon came into his mind, surface light above mysterious depths and currents, coolness and warmth. He imagined how easy it would be to immerse himself in her, to let himself drift with her until the past dissolved.

Some slight movement on his part must have made her aware of him. She turned her head, saw him, and smiled.

"You see what I mean about needing courage here," he said as he crossed the room to her.

She looked up at him. "How do you manage to stay so calm in all the hurly-burly?"

By ingesting large quantities of controlled substances, he was tempted to tell her. "It helps to focus on images, not words."

"You must have to use a close-up lens then. In order to ignore what's going on around the image." She unfolded her hands and held one out to him for help in rising to her feet.

He laughed. "A macro lens works best. It blocks out a lot."

His hand closed over hers, and he noticed once again how delicate the bones of her hand were, and how, despite this, her grip was strong and confident. As he cupped her elbow to steady her while she stood resting her weight on the stronger leg, he caught a trace of the perfume she was wearing, some flowery scent, mixed with the woodsmoke smell of the fire.

For a moment they stood like that, face-to-face, looking at each other. Somewhere in the room a moth was beating its wings against a lampshade, its soft, frantic blows loud in the silence. Under his hand the warm skin of her bare arm felt smooth, with a faint downiness, like a moth's wing.

Focus on the image, he told himself, the arm, not its owner. But it was no good, he was too aware that the arm was hers.

When her glance shifted to his hand as it held her, he was suddenly conscious that she really didn't need his help now that she was standing. He released her and took a step back, repressing the urge to apologize.

"I should help Pascale with the dishes," she said, a little awkwardly. She was fingering the blue pleats of her dress, smoothing them out one by one.

"I have strict orders not to let you in the kitchen. Pascale prefers to work alone."

"Like your father."

"In some ways, they're very alike."

"And you? Are you like your father?"

"God forbid." He said it so emphatically that they both laughed. "Well," he amended, "in some ways I suppose I am. But for my peace of mind I try not to notice."

She considered him, her head tilted a little. "You do look alike. Not obviously. But the resemblance is there."

To change the subject, which was making him increasingly uncomfortable, he said, "I hear the moon's worth seeing. And the gallery will be empty now. No crowds to block the view."

"I suppose we should look at it. To please Finn."

With a mild irritation that he did his best to disguise, he told her not to worry about pleasing Finn. "He'd be the first to tell you to please yourself."

"Then I will," she said, suddenly decisive, adding in mock command as she linked her arm through his, "So take me to the moon."

He raised an amused eyebrow. "It would be a pleasure."

As they went out through the French doors onto the terrace, he wondered if she intended him to read as much into her words as he would have liked to. But he didn't allow his thoughts to linger on this hope, as though she might somehow sense even the unexpressed wish, and draw away from him.

The moon's brilliance glazed the terrace's gray stone and the black grass of the garden with a slick of silver. In its sharp light, the distant outline of the cliffs looked to him like the crumbling ramparts of a walled city. Beyond their barricade he could hear the sea's muted thudding, like a battering ram manned by troops too sleepy now to force an entry. The wind had risen, as Finn had warned, and on the eastern horizon he could see a few tattered clouds scudding low against a sky with the sheen of navy blue silk.

"Marianna liked to hold her seances during a full moon," Dana said. "She said the spirits came to her more easily then."

"I once heard of a nurse at a sanitarium who marked the full moon on the calendar, to warn the staff. She said the patients always seemed worse when the moon was full. Not to imply Marianna was like them," he added quickly, noting the slight compression of her lips. "Only that we don't really understand the moon's power over us."

She nodded. "When I was a child, there was a rhyme my grandmother told me to say whenever I saw a full moon. 'I see the moon, and the moon sees me. God bless the moon, and God bless me.' Like a charm to keep me from being moonstruck. And I always said it, because I thought that if the moon could pull the sea toward it, it would have no trouble at all pulling me right up into space if it wanted to."

She gave a small, half-embarrassed laugh, then shivered. He was tempted to put his arm around her shoulders to draw her closer to him, but checked the impulse. Something, that element in her of reserve or uncertainty, some indecision of her own, left him unsure.

"Are you cold?" he asked her.

"I don't mind. It clears my head. I was feeling too warm inside. Even dizzy, once or twice."

"Kerreck Du can have that effect."

"And the people. Finn especially."

"A one-man heat wave, Finn."

The words were out before he could consider how they might sound, and immediately he regretted the sarcasm.

She glanced at him, as if uncertain of his meaning and hoping to find it in his face. After a moment, she said, "I meant, he's so quick, his thoughts, the way he speaks. . . ." She hesitated, searching for the right word. "It's not always easy to keep up. And yet he makes you want to."

He was annoyed with himself for feeling the tiny but recognizable prick of jealousy that her recurring references to Finn provoked. He had heard that mixture of curiosity and admiration in other women's voices when they spoke of Finn. It was too familiar; by now he should have ceased to react to it. Of course Dana found Finn attractive. Women did.

She was looking up at the moon again. The smooth, clear lines of her face seemed sculpted by the penetrating light. If he kissed her, he wondered, would that force Finn from her mind? He wanted very much to kiss her, and not just to keep her from thinking of his father. He was debating with himself whether simply to take her in his arms and do it, when she yawned widely. Clapping her hand to her mouth, she gave him a sideways, sheepish smile. "The sun can make you yawn when you look at it, but I never knew the moon could, too."

"We'd better go indoors before you're moonstruck."

As they crossed the threshold, she stumbled slightly. "Maybe I already am," she said with a rueful laugh.

He had turned instinctively to her, so that when she bumped against his side his mouth brushed across her hair. If she felt it, she gave no sign, and at the same moment Pascale came into the living room to say good night. After some desultory small talk the two women went off to their beds and left Daniel sitting alone, gazing into the fire.

Chapter 23

Estelle stared with dismay at her reflection in the mirror above her dressing table. The face that gazed back at her sagged, the eyes were bloodshot, the skin below them was dark and crepey. She looked, she thought, horribly like that snapshot taken of her shortly after Barbara's funeral, the one in which she'd seen herself transformed into an old woman by her daughter's death.

She scooped cold cream from a jar and worked it into her skin while her thoughts circled relentlessly around the evening's conversation at Kerreck Du. The ghost photographs; Dana Morrow's description of the elderly couple cheated of their savings; Thomas's revolting comments . . . She found it impossible not to think of these. It was like probing an aching tooth with her tongue, an irresistible impulse that only brought pain.

Her hand trembled as she cleaned mascara from her lashes. Above the whitened face, a large black smear streaked one eyelid. Now she looked like a clown. She could feel tears of self-pity swelling, tingling.

At that moment the phone on the nightstand beside the bed began to ring, its insect's chirr shrilling into the silence. Startled, she rose automatically from the dressing table to answer it, then paused with her hand hovering above the receiver, uncertain, almost afraid. At this hour it could only be John.

She and Thomas had driven back with him to Trebartha after the dinner party at Kerreck Du. As her house came before Thomas's, John had naturally dropped her off first, and so, to her mingled chagrin and relief, there had been no chance to speak with him alone. Although she yearned for his reassurance, she was terrified that he would not be able to resolve her doubts. If he could not, she would be truly lost.

Her warm, luxurious bedroom suddenly seemed cold. Under the thin silk of her dressing gown, her bare skin roughened with gooseflesh as she shivered. All the while the telephone continued to ring relentlessly.

This was cowardice, she told herself, the weakness that had cost her her happiness before. As her hand went down for the receiver, she swore she would not let it poison her life again.

But she was too late. As soon as she touched it, the telephone fell silent, as though to punish her. Misery and self-reproach thickened in her throat. She ought to have spoken to him. Why had she denied herself the comfort he would have given her? The tears that pricked her eyes now spilled down her cheeks.

Snatching up the telephone, she stabbed at the small square plastic numbers as if the force of her finger alone could annihilate indecision. After the third ring, the answering machine clicked on and she heard John's recorded voice telling her to leave a message after the tone. With a groan of despair, desolate and furious with herself, she disconnected, then threw the useless instrument onto the bed, and herself, sobbing, after it.

For a long time she lay there crying until, her nose clogged with tears, she was forced to sit up in order to breathe. In the bathroom she splashed cold water on her face and drank thirstily, careful to avoid looking at her reflection in the mirror over the sink.

She did not deserve to speak to John, she thought as she padded back across the thick carpet to her bed, a box of tissues in one hand. She had doubted him. Doubt was a terrible thing, insidious, destructive. It came, she knew, from her cowardice, her inability ever to speak up and say, This is what I believe.

To reclaim her happiness, to save the single most important relationship in her life, she must defy doubt and reaffirm her faith and trust.

Calmer now, she returned the telephone to its place on the nightstand, then went over to the dressing table and from the top drawer took out a small, flat, brass-hinged box. It was an antique daguerreotype case. With her eyes closed, she ran her fingers lightly over the worn blue velvet nap of the cover. The slight rasp of the velvet under her fingernails made her shiver again.

John had given her the case two weeks ago. It was his gift to her, he had said, folding her hands around it and placing his own over them. The act had the solemnity of a sacrament. As she leaned forward to kiss his cheek, she protested that it was too much, that he had already given her the greatest gift of all: the photograph now inside the case.

She sat down on the bed in the soft light of the nightstand lamp with its creamy parchment shade. Fearful, eager, she took a deep breath and opened the case. And once again the sick uncertainty of mingled hope and apprehension gave way to a vast peace as she gazed at the miracle.

The eerie infrared photograph inside the case was a portrait of herself sitting stiffly on a wrought-iron chair in the garden with her hands gripping the curved fronts of the armrests. A dark sky brooded overhead, filled with huge, ominous clouds; luminescent ivy writhed over the garden wall behind her like some living many-tentacled creature; to her left, a leggy bush of yellow rhododendron twisted upward with its vibrant blossoms exploding like Roman candles.

Beside her on her right—and this was the miracle—stood Barbara. Her shining, transparent figure was wraithlike and pitifully thin, but the large hollowed eyes, the clearest things about her, were laughing. One hand was raised above her mother's head, as though in benediction.

The photograph was less than a month old. Barbara had been dead for three years.

Shortly after moving to Trebartha, Estelle had found herself confiding to John her anguish and regret over Barbara's death. His sympathy and quick understanding, which amounted almost to an intuitive knowledge of her suffering, swept away all her reservations. Or almost all. She did not tell him of her own cowardice over the years, but instead said that Barbara had only revealed her father's behavior to her shortly before she died. When she described her visit to the medium, he did not laugh at her. In fact, to her joy, he told her that he himself communed with the spirits of his dead parents. More, that he had once succeeded in taking their photograph. It was, he said, his most precious possession.

Immediately, a wild hope had sprung up in her heart. It was days before she could bring herself to utter it to him, and it had taken many more days of persuasion before he would agree to try. He warned her that very likely nothing would come of it. He told her that he was afraid his failure would damage their friendship, and that her raised hopes would only be crushed again, making it worse for her. In turn, she assured him over and over that she would not reproach him or blame him in any way, that she would only be grateful to him for the attempt.

At last, reluctantly, he had acquiesced. He would try to capture Barbara's spirit on film. After countless photographs, taken indoors and out, in London and in Trebartha, when she had almost given up hope, he had succeeded.

He had taken the photograph with a technique developed by himself using a Polaroid camera modified to take an experimental form of infrared film. Infrared film, he'd explained, was commonly used to capture the glow of invisible life. Its special sensitivity saw more than the naked eye could. It could pick up certain auras, invisible rays that lay beyond violet, beyond the limits of the spectrum. Where the human eye found nothing but darkness, he said, the eye of the camera saw light.

Although he had done his best to explain the process to her, she found it ungraspable, and ultimately meaningless. All that mattered was the result, and that was indisputable.

She gazed at the photograph, feeding on the miracle. It was amazing how strongly she felt Barbara's presence with her now. She had only to look at the marvelous photograph to know that she had her child back. Not that she was so self-deluding as to deny the fact of Barbara's death. But surely this was the proof that she was right to believe that the dead left something of themselves behind to respond, if the call from the living was strong enough?

Now, when she remembered how John had always worked right in front of her eyes, the countless failures, her own insistence that he try again, his gentle persistence and faith, she felt ashamed of her doubt. He must never find out. She tried desperately to remember if he might have overheard her asking Dana Morrow about that elderly couple in Scunthorpe. Surely at the time he'd been outside with Finn and the others. When had he come back into the room? Afterward? Yes, afterward. Thank God Dana Morrow had refused to meet her tomorrow.

"I'm right to believe," she said to herself aloud as she closed the case and put it away in the drawer. Dana Morrow herself had pointed out that the work of a charlatan might tarnish but could not corrupt the truth.

Too restless for sleep, she went over to the window, pulled aside the heavy brocade curtains, and gazed out at the blackness. The lights of Trebartha at the foot of the hill seemed as remote as the stars. Despite everything, she felt the chill of loneliness. But today, when she had asked John to come and live with her, he had taken her hand in his, told her how wonderful it was she should want him, and promised to think about it very seriously. So there was hope.

As the wind moved rustling through the ivy, scraping a branch against the roof, night thoughts crept into her mind. She twitched the curtains together, to shut them out. Resolutely, she refused to think about the Gull. But that strange sarcastic comment of Karen's came back to her now, the one about photographing dead people. Karen had been speaking to Thomas, who had wisely ignored her. But the words, employed with all of Karen's considerable nastiness, had frozen Estelle, made her unable even to look at John beside her.

Was it possible that Karen somehow knew what John had done for her, knew about Barbara's photograph, and was laughing at them? If so, Estelle thought, her hands gripping her arms so tightly that the nails dug into the flesh, she didn't see how she could bear it. Karen's mockery would be a kind of sacrilege.

Barbara, she prayed, protect me.

Chapter 24

He was restless. Tonight nothing worked to release the pressure he could feel building in him. The day that had begun so well had ended disastrously. It seemed to him that as soon as he had dealt with one problem another was upon him. They were multiplying around him, forcing his hand.

Was it simply bad luck, Dana Morrow mentioning the couple in Scunthorpe, or had she done it deliberately? No, not deliberately; to think so would be the delusion of a paranoiac. Her research made it more than likely she would come across modern examples. The others' questions had elicited the remark; she hadn't simply dropped it into the conversation and watched for his reaction. In fact, she hadn't been looking at him at all.

Bad luck, then. Very bad luck. Already Karen was curious, and much too close to the truth. The only bit of good luck was that she had been out of the room when the Scunthorpe case was mentioned. But if she happened to learn of it, she might make connections back to Rita.

He had been walking down the street past Sundy Best, over a month ago, when it had begun to rain. Karen, who was working on the display in the window, saw him and beckoned him inside. He thought she was offering him shelter from the rain. She had a customer in the changing room, she told him in a whisper, a real provincial. "From Scunthorpe. And proud of it, God help her." Then, "You never told me you had friends in Scunthorpe."

Something, an intuition, or the spark of malice in Karen's eyes, had warned him. And so he wasn't totally unprepared when Rita came out of the changing room, holding a dress on a hanger. A Rita grown fat and gray in the five years since he'd last seen her, no longer pretty, but with the same sharp little eyes like small black currants behind her glasses.

"It's lovely, dear," she'd begun, "but a little too—" She broke off when she saw him but, never one to startle easily, went on to greet him quite calmly, as though it had been five weeks, not five years, since last they met.

"Hullo, love. I was just asking after you."

"I saw him passing," Karen had said. "Wasn't that good luck?" She smiled maliciously at him. "I couldn't tell your friend here—" She turned to Rita. "Sorry, I don't know your name—"

"That's right, dear, you don't," Rita had replied imperturbably, handing Karen the dress. To him, she said, "Fancy a stroll?"

Together, they had gone out into the teeming rain.

Rita, the senior partner in their former enterprise as well as his teacher, had told him that she had hunted him down with the intention of persuading him to become her partner again. She was living in Leeds now, and the pickings were good there. He might have replied that he was no longer in that line of work, but then she would only have insisted on sharing in the new line. He could not have that.

Knowing him to be malleable once, she had expected to find him unchanged. That made her careless and credulous. It was not difficult to lure her out onto the cliffs.

When he had next seen Karen, she asked him how his friend from Scunthorpe was. Sadly changed, he wanted to say. But, "It was a business relationship, not a friendship," was all he replied, and did not add that he had been forced to terminate the relationship. However, he had never been entirely sure that Karen believed him.

He'd had two bits of incredible luck. When Rita's body had finally been identified and the information released to the press, her address was given as Leeds. No mention was made of her Scunthorpe origins. The second break was the photograph published in the papers, an early, flattering one that looked nothing like the woman who'd come into Sundy Best, wearing glasses, hair flattened by the rain. This gave him a little time.

He went into the darkroom, intending to work. But his hands were trembling. Fingers spread, he held them out under the red glow of the safe light while he willed the tremors away. Capable of great skill and delicacy, his hands could also be brutal in their efficiency. At those times they seemed to him almost separate from his body. He rested them now on the large bottle of fixer that stood on the countertop before him. The cool curve of glass under his palms, the trickle of running water as it fed into the sink, the smell of developer, all these things served gradually to calm him.

There was no need to panic, to abandon his plans, when a single action might relieve him both of the pressure inside him and of the worst of the threats to his peace of mind. He would deal with others as they arose, as he had in the past. But he must act tonight.

He made the necessary telephone call. How simple it was. Yes, she was alone, she told him, and yes, she wanted to come; why had he waited so long to ask her?

Afterward, he changed into dark clothes, choosing a loose black sweater riddled with moth holes and a pair of old trousers, which he would not be sorry to burn. He put on his hiking boots, lacing them tightly. Then, with a theatrical flourish, he wound a long silk scarf several times around his neck. When he looked in the mirror, he saw that the scarf was wrong, not his style. She would find it odd. He took it off, folding it into a small square, and placed it instead in his trouser pocket. He would be able to get at it there more quickly anyway. Into the other pocket went a pair of surgical gloves.

He took his camera bag from the storage cabinet. Meticulous in this as in everything to do with his work, he kept the preloaded canvas inserts holding his cameras, lenses, flash units, battery packs, and films neatly ranged on a shelf, ready for use. He made his choices now and put them in the bag, then clipped the portable power pack onto his belt.

Before leaving, he wrote the first entry of this new record in his notebook. He liked to speculate before the act on the perfect shot, and afterward to compare the written account with the photographs themselves, to see how close his imagination could come to reality. The procedure gave a structure to the undertaking, which disciplined the energy that filled him at the prospect of all that lay ahead. He was like a skier, he thought, visualizing every twist and turn in the course of a race before launching himself down the slope.

Outdoors, the night was clear under the full moon. There was no need for a torch. A trace of creosote from a freshly stained fence came to him on the wind, a smell he loathed for its associations. It was the preeminent smell of his childhood in that dingy suburb where smears of dog shit fouled the pavement, where respectability was composed of starched net curtains and a neatly clipped privet hedge and never mind what went on behind them.

As he locked the door, the word they had bandied about at dinner came into his mind. Fraud. His fist clenched the key so tightly that its edges bit into his flesh. Such a crude word, much too crude to describe what had been in essence his first creative act. The old words were better: illusionist, conjuror, prestidigitator. Especially the last. For his fingers were nimble, almost as quick as his mind.

When fingers and mind worked flawlessly together, there was artistry, beauty even, in the construction of an illusion. The pieces then would fit seamlessly, all the joins hidden. His best illusions gave real happiness, as they were meant to. Why else had he been so richly rewarded?

To argue, as that idiotic niece had, that he had deceived and cheated was the self-serving nonsense of someone disappointed of their expectations. The last months of the dying woman had been filled with a happiness no one else had known how to give her. If that comfort came from an illusion created by a sleight of hand, was that so terrible? It had succeeded where the written and spoken word had failed. He had received only the due of all true artists, a tangible appreciation of his gifts.

Gravel crunched underfoot as he went down the path. His shadow stretched before him, elongated, with the camera bag's bulky mass protruding like a growth from a skinny giant's hip.

It would be interesting to talk to Dana Morrow about her work, he thought. She struck him as someone able to appreciate the more arcane forms of creativity. She had made no judgment on Marianna Hobhouse; to the contrary, she appeared to be in sympathy with the medium. There were any number of issues he might be able to discuss with her, as long as he was cautious.

And she was interesting because of the opportunities for

revenge she offered, if he was right in thinking that Marianna Hobhouse wasn't the only reason she was at Kerreck Du. He smiled to himself. It was a dangerous mistake, to care for someone. It made you vulnerable. No one had cared for him, and so he was free. He'd had to learn that lesson twice, as a kid and then again three years ago. The first time, when he was little, he'd been punished time and again for forgetting. But the second time he had been able to punish in return.

But his mind flinched away from that. He wasn't to know it would end that way. He hadn't meant to kill her, only to remind her that she needed him. He had truly loved her. Listening to her talk about her childhood, he had felt that somehow her suffering relieved his own. Still, she had deserved to die. She had made him ridiculous.

He entered the car park on the hill overlooking Trebartha. At this late hour it was empty save for the small, rusting caravan used to sell snacks during the day by a local entrepreneur who spent his nights at his house on the other side of the town. An empty crisps packet blew in front of him, carried by the breeze to join the litter in the undergrowth that fringed the lot. The surface of the tarmac was crazed with long cracks radiating out from a central drain. In the moonlight, they looked like the broken web of some enormous spider.

Karen was waiting for him by a cluster of stunted pines at the far side of the car park. The moonlight bleached the color from her face and made her eyes seem as huge and luminous as those of a lemur. Hands in her jacket pockets, she leaned against one of the pines, nonchalant, as if to flaunt her courage. But when he reached her, she said, "Thank God you're on time. I wasn't going to hang around here another second."

"Were you frightened?"

"No." The lemur eyes returned his gaze, unblinking. "Just wondering if maybe you'd made it up after all."

"Why would I do that?"

"To impress me?"

"Wouldn't it take more than that to impress you?"

"Depends." The way she looked at him, head tilted, reminded him of Estelle. "How impressed do you want me to be?"

"Why don't you let me know when I've succeeded?"

She gave a low, throaty laugh and linked her arm through his. Her touch revolted him, as did so much about her, but he endured it. In silence, they walked the several hundred feet to the footpath that ran along the clifftops. Somewhere a dog barked, its yap shrill as a fox's, but remote, no threat.

Her vanity was limitless, he thought. Together with a curiosity about the more perverse aspects of human nature it had brought her here tonight, as he had known it would. He suspected that to her this was merely a novel form of seduction. That was why she had been willing to keep their meeting secret. She liked secrets, shared or extorted.

Before they went through the gate onto the path, he asked if she was sure she wanted to come with him. He let anxiety shade his voice, contract his brow. "There's a very faint chance it may be dangerous."

That, for her, was the hook. "I wouldn't miss it for anything." Her eyes glittered with excitement. "Besides, I like the fantastic, you know that. And what could be more fantastic than you working for the—what did you call it?"

"Coastal Intelligence. But as I said, I'm just a volunteer."

He was angry, and then amused by his reaction to her tone, as though it mattered that she still found the idea ludicrous. All that mattered was that she believed him.

She hadn't, not at first. He'd had to show her proof: the official letter of confirmation, the booklets they had given him to identify the silhouettes of boats and aircraft, the secret code signal.

Smuggling was on the rise, he had explained, a result of the European Union's removal of most border controls. Cheap continental whiskey and cigarettes were flooding into England's black market, much of it brought back by holiday makers in cars, vans, or boats, and sold to pubs and shops. In an effort to combat this illegal traffic, customs officials had recruited what was in effect a home guard to patrol the coast and report suspicious boat landings at night, or aircraft flying without lights.

"Just like the Second World War," he had added, to help her understand. But her history did not extend beyond her own country's borders, and he'd had to explain the allusion.

She had found it all fascinating, and more than a little absurd. This very absurdity, he suspected, was what had convinced her, along with the documents. It was too ridiculous not be true. And he had taken care to make it seem that he was trying to impress her, just as she suggested.

When he had emphasized that it must remain a secret between them, she agreed readily enough. As far as he knew, she had kept her word. But when they were with the others she would glance at him with that look of shared secret knowledge that he found so annoying.

He had been forced to tell her because she had seen him one day, out on the cliffs, shortly before the first incident.

It seemed she liked to sunbathe nude, even in the winter, and had found a sun trap on the cliffs, sheltered from the wind and from view, where she would go with her sketch book. Her best designs, she had said, were created there. As she stood up to dress that afternoon, she'd seen him. She only told him this when it was too late, several days after the incident but long before the body was found. Luckily, the precise spot had not been reported in the papers.

"I watched you," she had said, quite casually. "You were behaving so strangely. Leaning over the edge, jumping up onto rocks. What were you doing?"

Scouting locations, he might have replied. Instead, feigning reluctance, he had told her about his work for Coastal Intelligence. The story had the virtue of being the simple truth. A newspaper article about the work done by the volunteers had caught his eye. Recognizing the perfect excuse to be out on the cliffs at any time of the day or night, he had offered his services at once.

Now he walked ahead of her on the footpath, a pale ribbon of pebbled earth that rose and fell as it snaked along Trebartha Point. There wasn't room to walk two abreast, and for this he was grateful. Her hand on his arm had felt like a trap.

On their left, huge outcroppings of stone thrust their way up from the mass of the point like lumpy fists under a thick blanket of greenery so dark it was black. The sea below in the shadow of the cliff was darker, the open mouth of some great beast gulping and lapping at the rock. A misstep here and one could so easily tumble into it.

A few minutes of steady hiking brought them to the end of the point, where they paused for a last backward glimpse of the town cradled in its cove. Lights spangled the harbor water, and to him those tawdry chips of color made the darkness beyond the point something pure and desirable, a place of peace.

"It looks like sequins on Lurex," Karen said suddenly, her voice harsh in the silence. "Talk about a fraud."

Startled, he asked her what she meant.

"It makes you think there's life in the place. But I didn't see a single person on the way tonight. Everyone's either asleep or drinking themselves blotto so they'll have the excuse of a hangover not to do any work tomorrow. Second-raters pretending they're geniuses."

He wondered which of their group she included in this bitter assessment. Perhaps all of them.

"So you're off to London then?"

If she said yes, she was leaving tomorrow as she had threatened, could he afford to spare her? No, he could not. She might harm him even in London.

She shook her head, pulling tendrils of windblown hair free from the lipstick on her mouth. "I was angry, that's all. I can't go yet, I've got some unfinished business. Besides," she glanced at him, "how can I leave when you're making things so interesting?"

Everything she said seemed ambiguous. But she would never have agreed to come with him tonight if she had any suspicions. He schooled his voice to speak calmly. "I told you, it's mostly routine checking. Nothing dramatic. Not yet, anyway."

As they followed the track around the promontory, the lights vanished from sight and the landscape became a study in monochrome. The moon bled silver over the mounded shapes of rock, stained the sea with a polished radiance, made metal masks of their faces. He felt its rays penetrate his blood like a needle's icy sting. Here, with the shelter of Trebartha Point behind them, the wind blew stronger. It fingered his clothes, plucking at him, imploring. Like those others, he thought, the ones who came into his dreams, even dared sometimes to visit him in daylight.

He pushed the thought away. He would not believe in ghosts. He was not Marianna Hobhouse; he never lost control, never confused illusion with reality.

When Karen touched his arm, he started violently, then whirled around.

She flinched back. "God, you look like you think I'm about to attack you! Didn't you hear me? You're walking too fast, I can't keep up. And I want to do something about my hair. It's driving me crazy."

He waited while she caught the blowing hair and expertly twisted it into a small knot. Her bared neck shone palely in the moonlight, bent with unaccustomed meekness as she worked. He looked away, afraid she might see his thoughts on his face. Far out, pinpricks of light from Channel shipping moved slowly west.

Then she lifted her head, eagerness once again in her eyes. "Okay, let's go. But not so fast this time. I don't want to break my neck."

He had told her that he'd twice seen two fishing boats meet at a certain place not far from Trebartha Point. If they were there again tonight, he intended to photograph them. Wouldn't the flash warn the people on board? she'd asked. It didn't matter, he'd replied; she and he would be safe enough up on the cliff, and if they hurried they would be able to alert the police in time to apprehend the boats.

"You know, you really surprise me," she said after they had walked in silence for a little way. "I would never have imagined you doing this sort of thing."

But then she had a very pedestrian imagination, he thought. Only in the clothes she designed did she show a spark of creativity.

"I'm no different from a train spotter," he said.

She laughed. "You're weird, you know that? But it explains stuff I wondered about."

He forced himself to walk on, to ask in an incurious voice, "Such as?"

"Oh, all sorts of things."

Now, he thought, now she'll say it: For instance, I wondered about the woman who was looking for you that day. What did she really want?

"All sorts of things," she repeated. "Most of all, why you seem different from everybody else. Like you had a mission or something. But I guess you do," she added with a laugh. He would be thankful never to hear that laugh again.

At last they came to the place where a deep fissure split the cliff face, opening a narrow wedge that forced the path to jog sharply around it. The crevice was obscured from above by overhanging bushes and from the sea by huge boulders that rose out of the water like a small stockade. No boat would come close in here, it was too dangerous. But she wouldn't know that. She professed to be prone to seasickness and bored by boats.

The loud susurration of the sea as it sucked in and out between the rocks excited him. Now that the moment was on him, he felt the familiar mixture of reluctance and fatalism, as though he were surrendering a part of himself to the inevitable.

She stood with her hands in her pockets, looking out at the sea, with her back to him. "So," she said, "what do we do now? Wait?"

No, he thought, taking the scarf from his pocket as he moved toward her, no, I don't like to wait.

Later, in bed, a small doubt began to worry him. If for some reason someone did decide to look down in just that place, could the body be seen? It seemed so unlikely. All the same, he must be sure. He would have to go back at dawn, before anyone was up, to have another look. If there was the slightest sign of the body he could disguise it easily enough with the gorse that grew there.

He set his alarm for five o'clock, rolled over, and went to sleep.

Chapter 25

A tolerance for chaos. Finn's words came back to Dana as she stood at the bathroom sink, preparing for bed.

A guest at Kerreck Du should have a tolerance for chaos, he had written in his letter to her, a caution that she had taken for a half-humorous warning of domestic disorder. But these past two days had shown her that it had nothing to do with erratic mealtimes and unmade beds or the cliché of artistic license concerning cleanliness. The chaos here was emotional.

It was also contagious. She felt herself infected with it, light-headed with her own emotional turbulence and her desire for Daniel. She held the hot washcloth against her face, breathing in the steamy scent of soap, then splashed cold water on her skin. Her hazy reflection stared back at her from the steam-misted mirror. What had Finn said in that hyperbolic postscript to his letter? Something about giving a bowlful of blood to a spirit to make it speak. She smiled. Any ghost drinking her blood tonight would get indigestion.

Her smile faded as she thought of Kerreck Du's spirits—Marianna, Solange Finn, and the two women murdered on the cliffs, their voices brutally silenced by premature death. And of her own familiar, whose image she always carried with her.

Slowly, she wiped the mirror clean, then turned and left the bathroom, switching off the light. In the bedroom, she opened the window, to breathe in the fresh night air. A cool wind stirred the heavy curtains and rustled some papers she'd left out on the bureau.

From her wallet, she took out the fetal photograph of her unborn child. She sat for a long time on the edge of the bed, staring down at that shadowy trace of a being whose life she had failed to sustain. Then she put the photograph away and began to undress, letting her clothes fall to the floor. With her eyes closed, she rested one hand against the warm, flat skin of her midriff, remembered it swollen and taut, protecting the quiet—then too quiet—life inside her. Remembered, too, how after the accident her own unwillingly reclaimed body had seemed unnatural to her, and a reproach.

A sudden noise from somewhere outside in the night caused the bare flesh to contract under her hand. It was an eerie, piercing cry, like the call of a loon she'd once heard as a child. Shivering, she pulled on the long pink T-shirt nightdress, then went to the window, leaning out to listen. When the cry came again she recognized it, unmistakably, as the voice of Nadia Tatevic, shrill with jealous fury.

She shut the window, pushing away a tentacle of ivy that had insinuated itself around a casement hinge. Maybe I should have howled like that, she told herself; if I had screamed at Stewart, thrown things, it might have saved us, and the baby. But it was not in her nature to scream or to throw things.

Despite the closed window, the misery in Nadia's voice penetrated the room. To escape it, she put on her sandals, strapped the support around her ankle, and took the key to the glasshouse door from her bureau drawer. She might not be able to work, she thought, but she could not stay here and listen to that pitiful sound. This time, there was nothing she could do to help.

When she went out into the hallway, she saw a faint lozenge of light shining onto the dark wood paneling from the open glasshouse door. She remembered Pascale's warning that Finn often wandered about the house late at night, and that she mustn't mistake his restless steps for those of some resident ghost. Perhaps, like her, he had sought the glasshouse as a refuge from Nadia's cries. If so, she would let him have it undisturbed.

Before she could retreat to her room, however, he appeared in the doorway. For a long moment they simply stared at each other. The man facing her looked like the fleshly embodiment of Nadia's howl of pain, his blue eyes bleared and bloodshot, his shoulders sagging forward while he clutched at the door frame as if for support.

In reaction perhaps to those desperate cries in the night or to his unhappiness, which was so patent that she sensed it as a palpable force between them, she took a step toward him and said without thinking, "What can I do?"

His mouth twisted in a smile like a grimace. He reached out for her hand to take it in his, clasping it tightly. There was nothing loverlike in his grasp; it felt more like the grip of someone at the edge of an abyss, terrified of falling.

In a hoarse voice, he said, "Just stay with me for a little while. Will you do that?"

She nodded. She felt as though her will were suspended, were temporarily his.

With her hand still fast in his own, he led her outside to the courtyard, its cobbled expanse blanched white by the moonlight. The night air felt cool on her flushed face, fresh with the scent of the sea. They had to move slowly, because of her ankle, but he seemed not to mind. His own gait was stiff, like that of a sleepwalker or someone made awkward by drinking or tears, and he walked with his head bowed. Apart from the sound of their footsteps, the silence now was unbroken. Neither spoke, until she glanced up at a lighted window in the near end of the converted stables, where the Tatevics lived.

He must have sensed where she was looking, because his head came up. "You heard?" he asked her.

"Yes."

"There's a saying, You've got to keep your eyes wide open before marriage but half-closed afterward. Nadia hasn't learned that." The bitter edge to his voice made Dana wonder whether he was speaking only of Nadia Tatevic.

"What do you do if your spouse forces them open?" she asked him, thinking of herself. "Look away?"

"Yes, goddammit!"

He had stopped abruptly and was turned to look at her, his gaze as fierce as his tone. She stared back, too startled to speak. Then he raised their joined hands and shook them gently at her, as though in warning, adding in a softer voice, "Yes, that's just what you do. If you're wise."

And if there's a child, she thought. But she hadn't been wise, and now there was no child.

They had come to a door in the far end of the stable block. He dropped her hand and took a key from his trousers pocket, unlocking the door, then went inside. When he switched on a soft yellow light, she saw that the shadowy room beyond was his darkroom, and almost drew back. It's late, she wanted to say, I'm tired. Instead, she followed him inside.

The large, windowless, oblong room seemed to her like nothing so much as the luxurious bunker of a reclusive scientist. A faint smell of chemicals, not unpleasant, reinforced this impression. More than a dozen enlargers were ranged along the countertops like giant misshapen microscopes; a pair of yellow rubber gloves lay limply over the side of the long metal trough, filled with a row of plastic sinks and trays, which partly bisected the room; bottles, pans, tongs, and instruments whose purpose she couldn't begin to guess at lined the shelves. There were several leather-topped stools, an armchair, a CD player, even a refrigerator. A thick carpet covered the floor, muffling their footsteps.

Finn made a flapping motion of one hand at the armchair, which she took as a command to sit down. When he closed the door, the silence was absolute. As the darkness would be, she thought, once the lights were out.

Wordlessly, he began to work. From a metal cabinet, he took a large glassine envelope and laid it beside one of the enlargers, then put on a pair of white cotton gloves. She was too tired to ask what he was doing, or to take it in if he had explained. She simply sat there in the dim warmth, suspended somewhere between sleeping and waking, while she watched him move about and listened to the soothing sound of running water. She was certain he'd forgotten her presence. Now, here in his realm, he seemed to reacquire the potency, the youthfulness, she'd seen in him yesterday when he was at work in the clearing. His movements were assured, fluid, precise, with the easy rhythm of long practice.

Hours might have gone by, she might even have slept. Every now and then a sound would startle her into focusing on him, the clinking of glass as he unstoppered a bottle or the slop of water in the trays, the click and whir of the enlarger at work.

It came to her that his darkroom was like the laboratory of a modern alchemist. In it, he had the power to manipulate light, chemicals, and paper into an alternative reality, to create facsimiles of life so true they seemed almost to breathe and reveal themselves. And so great was his skill that he persuaded the viewer to conspire with him in the illusion. Something he had quoted earlier tonight, at dinner, came into her mind. Photographs, he'd said, were mock forms of possession. But just who was being possessed?

She thought of her own sad facsimile, back in her room, the unreal reflection of a life no alchemist could resurrect, thought of how it possessed her.

Finn was carrying a print to the drying screen that stood near her chair. He placed the print on the screen, then pulled one of the stools forward to sit in front of her. "You look sad," he said. "Why?"

Perhaps it was his voice, its note of unfamiliar tenderness, which made her speak. Perhaps it was her sudden sense that she must tell someone, so why not this man who had suffered a loss of his own, and who had shown her his suffering? The darkroom, with its enclosed, hermetic silence, might easily have been a confessional.

"I was thinking of a photograph," she began, and then found herself telling him the story of her unborn baby's death and the end of her marriage.

It had happened in Connecticut, where she and Stewart had gone for a winter weekend. "Friends had lent us their house in the country. It was just the two of us alone, away from everything. We'd been so busy, we hadn't really seen much of each other. He was traveling a lot, and I was frantically trying to get as much work as possible done before the baby came." This state of affairs, in fact, had begun to worry her; she'd been the one to insist on a holiday.

"I was six months pregnant, but I still had a lot of energy. We wanted to do some hiking. We knew it might be the last chance for a long time."

The house had been an old Victorian with a high wraparound porch and steep flights of stairs. A winter storm two days before their arrival meant that they weren't able to do much hiking after all, for a thin crust of ice over the snow made walking treacherous. "Stewart was constantly warning me to be careful. Outdoors and in. He was so solicitous that finally I told him he must have a guilty conscience." She paused and looked up at Finn. "I meant it as a joke."

She and Stewart were in the kitchen at the time, fixing dinner. She was about to use the stepstool to get the olive oil down from the cupboard when he stopped her, told her he'd do it. He wanted her to sit down, he said, and let him wait on her.

"What's all this?" she protested, laughing, with one foot still on the bottom rung of the stool. "It can't just be the baby. You must have been up to no good."

Stewart's face went white. "Oh God."

The laughter drained out of her as she grabbed his arm. "What is it? What?" She thought for an instant he'd been taken ill, or that his heart was bothering him. He was in his late forties, much older than she was.

The relief she felt when he reassured her, said no, it wasn't that, passed almost at once. As though nerving himself to take the plunge, he added with a rush, "I don't want this hanging over us, Dana. I want to tell you the truth."

Once again, she glanced up at Finn. His gaze had grown somber and more acute. He looked at her now, she thought, as if her story meant something to him.

"Well, of course, Stewart had been having an affair," she said. A woman he'd met at a conference, no one she knew. It was over, he'd ended it, he said, as though that made it all right.

Stunned, she had stared at Stewart. It was at a conference that they themselves had met, while he was separated from his first wife. The irony made it worse, gave her a sudden vision of herself as simply one in an endless series of conference-going opportunities. Stewart, who was a star in his field, would be going to more conferences, many more. She turned and grabbed her coat and purse and left. She couldn't speak, couldn't stay with him another moment. All she wanted was to get away, as far away from him as she could.

"I was going to take the car and drive back to New York," she told Finn. "Just leave him there. Let him figure out how to get home. At that moment, I hated him."

She was so consumed by Stewart's confession and her own

emotional pain that she failed to pay attention. It was dark now. The porch light was off, the steps down to the walk lightly feathered with snow, which hid the icy patch. On the top step, as she reached out for the railing, one heel skidded out from under her. Unable to save herself from falling, she managed to twist so that she came down on her back.

Her scream brought Stewart running out to her. He carried her to the car, then drove the twenty miles to the nearest hospital like someone pursued by all the devils in hell. But it was too late.

"It's not your fault," the doctor had said, when she cried out that her own recklessness had killed the baby. There were complications; a miscarriage would have occurred sooner or later. She hadn't believed him, and she hadn't been able to forgive Stewart.

Her eyes met Finn's. In a low voice, she said, "I don't want anyone to confess anything to me ever again."

For a long moment the only sound in the darkroom was her own breathing; she was panting as if she'd been running. When at last he spoke he said, "And if he hadn't confessed? Would your child be alive?"

Slowly, she shook her head. "It wasn't the fall. I accept that now. It only made it happen sooner."

"So then?"

"I might still love him." For the first time, however, the words sounded false even to her. She was beginning to understand that the gap between her illusions and reality had been of her making, not Stewart's, and that this, as much as his infidelity, had ruined their marriage. She realized something else as well: she no longer felt the pain of that disillusionment.

Finn got to his feet, stiffly, like someone weighed down with a burden, and walked over to the rack of screens, where the prints were drying. He turned one face up and stared at it for a moment. Then glanced back at her, a sharp, almost clinical look. "So you could only love him as long as he spared you the truth? No, don't take offense. I'm interested.

"You see," he went on, before she could speak, "Solange told me the truth about herself. I didn't want to hear it either. I couldn't forgive her any more than you could forgive your husband."

The suffering had come back into his face. She began to wish, not so much that she had kept silent, for she sensed that her revelation had somehow mattered to him, but that the healing that had begun to work in herself from the moment of Elvina's rescue could be transmitted to him.

"My punishment is not knowing," he said, staring down at the photograph on the rack. "Whether her fall was an accident. Or . . ."

He left the sentence unfinished and shrugged. It occurred to her then that his unspoken suspicion of suicide might have been a fate he feared for himself, and that it was why he had wanted her with him tonight, a safeguard against his own impulses. When she got up from the chair and went over to stand beside him, she saw that the photograph on the plastic mesh screen was a barely recognizable study of Solange Finn. A Baconesque portrait of her face and bare shoulders, grotesquely distorted, her mouth open as though in a scream.

" 'My Last Duchess,' " Finn said with a short bitter laugh.

But the photograph, and the way he stared at it, made Dana think of a different Browning poem, "The Mesmerist," whose obsessive, tormented narrator calls up his dead mistress and by the strength of his yearning imprints her spirit "on the void," like a photographer.

Finn picked up the photograph. "I took it the day before she died. I told her I wanted her to think of her own death, God help me." With a violent gesture, he tore it in two, then moved toward the door, leaving the pieces where they had fallen.

They left the darkroom together. Dana felt as if she had passed through a transformation much like one of Finn's photographs, as if he had held a part of her self under his own eye's enlarger for scrutiny and metamorphosis. The picture of the woman who had walked into the darkroom earlier that night was changing. The pain, dark as a sunspot, was fading away.

As they went slowly back across the courtyard, arm in arm, she saw the shadowy shape of a man standing on the steps to the kitchen door. It was Daniel. Instinctively, she released her arm from Finn's, then realized, too late, how the action might appear to Daniel.

Silently, he watched them approach, his face impassive.

"Daniel—" Finn began.

But Daniel cut him off. "I've decided to go back to the School-house after all," he told his father curtly. With a single, unreadable glance at her, he said good night, then went past them and across the courtyard.

Dana watched him walk away through the gate that led to the path to the cliffs. She wanted to call after him, to explain, but he was already out of sight.

Chapter 26

Elvina lay sleepless on the cot in her bedroom under the eaves. Downstairs, her mother was shouting again.

She hummed to herself as she picked at the blistered skin on her palms, so that she wouldn't hear. It was the old quarrel, the one they'd had for months, maybe for years. She thought she remembered a time when they had never argued, but she couldn't be sure. All she knew was that her mother was afraid. Afraid of going back, of staying here, and of some other, more terrible threat. Her mother seemed to be afraid of everything now.

Pulling the sheet taut over her head, she made a tent with her knees. Inside, the dim space smelled of detergent, the touch of the iron, and her own warm skin. She panted openmouthed, to fill it with her breathing and leave no room for any other sound. But cotton also breathed, she remembered someone saying in English, and on its breath came the noises of the quarrel.

Sometimes her parents quarreled over her. At home, they had argued about her safety, about what to do with her when the schools closed because of the shelling, about the music she listened to on her Walkman, even about the photographs she had cut from magazines and stuck on the walls of her room. Here, they argued about who or what was to blame for the silence.

When the silence took her and she could not speak for hours on end, sometimes for the whole day, her father was patient with her, but her mother would plead with her or shout at her, accusing her of wanting to hurt them. What she didn't realize was that Elvina had no power over the silence. It controlled her.

Leave her alone, her father would say, she's okay, after what she's been through it's only natural she doesn't want to talk. At

229

those times, he would take her with him to photograph the birds, or into the darkroom, so that she would be out of her mother's sight. She loved her father then so fiercely that she would do anything for him. It didn't matter that they were far from home, from their family and their friends, in a place where everything was different. Here, he was safe.

The sounds of her mother's unhappiness filled the cottage, seeping like smoke under the door into her tiny bedroom. When she put her hands over her ears, the muffled noise might have belonged to some animal in pain, not to anyone human.

She let the tent collapse and turned onto her side to look into the closet, where Madonna sat on her pallet of straw. The soft glow of the night-light shone into the closet, whose door was always open. It was safer that way.

Madonna gazed back at her unblinking, the smile on her pink rubber face remote, the glassy blue eyes chilly, as if she disapproved of what was going on downstairs. She was dressed in one of Elvina's outgrown white T-shirts, with a string tied around her waist and her flaxen hair bound by a fillet of ivy Elvina had cut from a wall. An offering of wildflowers lay wilted on her lap.

The closet was Madonna's temple, and the night-light was the perpetual flame, which she tended for Elvina. If she allowed it to go out in the night, Elvina would have to seal her up alive underground. That was the punishment for vestal virgins, Elvina had read in a book about the Romans.

In turn, Madonna required ritual and sacrifice. Appeased, she would keep the shadows at bay and allow Elvina to sleep without nightmares. But when Elvina failed to follow the rituals to the letter, or when Madonna found the sacrifices unacceptable, the shadows and the nightmares came, and the silence took Elvina.

She thought she knew what her parents did when they were frightened. Her mother played the piano, and got angry. Her father worked. His darkroom was like his temple, where the magic happened only when the rituals were followed. She wondered if he, too, had nightmares when his rituals failed. She knew he made sacrifices. Both her parents did. They had told her so.

No sacrifice was too great, her father had said, to keep her safe. And her mother often complained of the sacrifices she had made to come here, to this doll's house in the old stables. That was what her mother called the cottage, its ceilings so low that her father's head almost touched them. But although he had to stoop going up and down the steep stairs, hunched like an old man, he never complained. He had his darkroom to make him happy.

Her mother was rarely happy, either with the house or with them. Elvina's newest fear was that her mother's anger would drive her father away. Sometimes it seemed that her mother feared that too, but instead of curbing her anger she became even more furious, as if the fear made her anger worse.

She remembered her mother at the piano alone or with her students in their old apartment, before, her face round and content. The apartment had been near the river, large and light, with high ceilings and a view of the hills. Elvina's best friend, Alia, had lived in the same building.

But she did not want to think of Alia, or go back to their old apartment, even if it had been there to go back to.

She wrapped herself tightly in the sheet, with only her face left bare. The swaddling always soothed her and helped her to sleep. This time, however, the quarrel was too strong to ignore. She began to worry that her mother's shouting would carry across the courtyard to the main house. No one would understand what they were arguing about because they were speaking their own language, but if the noise disturbed Finn he might become angry, too. He might even ask them to leave Kerreck Du. Then where could they go? They were lucky to be here, her father often said, lucky to have Finn as a friend.

All the same, sometimes Finn frightened her. She sensed that he had an anger like her mother's, although he tried to hide it with jokes and with kindnesses.

Shadows moved across the opposite wall as the curtains at her open window blew in the night wind. If she stared hard enough, faces began to form and out of the shadows came Alia and her family. The chalky taste of plaster filled her mouth, as it always did when they came.

She looked again at Madonna, begging with her eyes. But the doll stared past her.

Because she did not want to be alone in the room with those

others, she struggled out of the sheet and crept quietly into the hall where she sat on the top step, drawing her knees up to her chin. Her father's voice was a low rumble. He was saying something about London.

"You can't go without us, Mico," her mother interrupted, pleading. "How can you even suggest such a thing?"

"Why can't you be patient?" he asked her. "In a little while I'll send for you. In London you'll find friends, others like us, you won't feel so alone."

"No, no, I won't be left!" Her mother's voice grew frantic. "You must take us with you. I can't talk to anyone but you here, I have no work, nothing of my own. What would I do without you?"

"I have to go. Be reasonable, Nadia. The work Finn found for me can't wait. And we can't all live in London, it's too expensive. Besides, Elvina has to finish school for the year. But with luck, this will turn into a permanent job and then you can join me. A few months, that's all it'll be. Two at most."

"If you still want us."

Elvina flinched at the sarcasm in her mother's voice. Don't, she wanted to say, he hates it when you talk like that. But he said it for her.

"Don't, Nadia. There's no point—"

"Why not? Do you think I don't know why you want to go alone? She'll be there, won't she? That bitch Karen. No, don't bother to lie, of course she will, she—"

"For God's sake, shut up about that! I'm sick of hearing about it! You're like a madwoman with your jealousy."

As they argued, their voices rose until both were shouting. Elvina rocked back and forth on the step, clutching at her sides. It was bad enough when her mother shouted, but worse somehow when her father did, maybe because he so rarely raised his voice. She wanted to scream at them to stop or she would be sick. But then they would know that she had heard. Instead, she ran back to her room and found a scrap of paper and a pencil. "Dear Papi," she wrote, her hand so cold with fear that it could hardly hold the pencil. "Please don't leave us. I love you. Elvina."

She went into her parents' bedroom, to the chest of drawers, and pulled out the drawer where her father kept his socks and underwear, sliding the note into one of the socks. If he left, she reasoned, he would have to take socks.

As she got back into bed, her mother came running up the stairs. Elvina heard the slam of her parents' bedroom door, and then, through the wall, the harsh sound of her mother's grief, like someone choking to death. He wouldn't come to her, Elvina thought; he never did when she was crying. She didn't blame him; her mother's tears disgusted her.

Downstairs, the front door creaked open, then closed again softly. He's leaving without packing, she thought with sudden terror; he won't see the note. She threw back the sheet and ran softly downstairs, opened the front door, and slipped outside.

The moon hung in the sky like a cold white sun, huge and bright. It gleamed with a radiance that made the dark places blacker even as it lit up the house and the field beyond it so brilliantly that Kerreck Du seemed to lie in a puddle of silver.

Her father was already far away, his swift dark figure running up the drive with its long shadow dogging his steps. She could shout to him, but the others might hear and come out. In this place, her father always said, like a warning, their troubles were no one's concern but their own.

The drive curved up the black hill, taking her father out of her sight. She ran after him, keeping to the grass verge to spare her bare feet. But the damp, coarse grass was sharply stubbled from a recent mowing and thick with pebbles thrown up by cars from the drive. Once she stepped on a jagged stone that cut into her foot, although she hardly felt it. A stitch tugged at her side but she barely felt that either. When she got around the bend herself, she thought, where no one else could hear, she would call him back to her. He always came when she called to him.

But the curve unfurled to reveal her father standing beside a car with a woman. With Karen.

So her mother had been right to be afraid.

As she watched, her father got into the car, and then Karen drove off with him. When Elvina thought to scream after him it was too late.

Her head seemed full of blood, as though her heart had

nowhere else to send it. She could taste it at the back of her throat, could hear it surging in her ears. As she walked wearily back, she began to shiver, and her side ached.

In her bedroom, she crouched down by the open closet door and began to tear at the broken skin on her right palm until the blood ran from the wound. She let the blood drip onto the wildflowers on Madonna's lap as she prayed for her father's return. And for Karen's death.

Afterward, she lay in bed wishing she were back in their old apartment, where it had been so easy to die. But there were ways to die at Kerreck Du as well: the cliffs, for instance, or the chemicals in the darkroom. If her father did not come back . . .

Her thoughts changed to restless dreams. One dream, worse than the others, woke her before dawn. When she remembered, she scrambled out of bed and went quietly into her parents' room.

He was there, asleep beside her mother, one bare leg free of the covers. She watched for a while, to make sure it was him. He grunted once, half turning, as if some dream troubled him, while her mother lay motionless, her tangled hair fanned out on the pillow. The room smelled of them both, a mixture of their bodies and hair, their clothing, the safe smell of the familiar. Ordinarily, waking early, she would climb in bed with them, to burrow between them and fall back asleep. But now she turned away. They were together and she did not want to separate them. Before she left the room, quietly so as not to disturb them, she removed the note from the sock. It embarrassed her now to think of him reading it.

She knelt down in front of Madonna, to thank her. Rust-red drops of dried blood flecked the white T-shirt and the petals of the flowers. Somehow a drop of blood had fallen on Madonna's cheek. She licked her finger and rubbed it away, then put the finger in her mouth. The taste of it reminded her of her second prayer. But she would not think of that.

Instead, she asked Madonna how she could keep her father with her. At first, the doll did not answer. Only after Elvina found the right sacrifice to promise her, all her allowances for the next two months, did she reply.

She must take more photographs to please him, Madonna told her then, to show him that she was learning all he taught her.

If she took a picture that was good enough, perhaps he would stay.

There was one picture that would hold him, Madonna added.

To take it, however, meant going to the cliffs again, and her mother had forbidden that. But the bird was there. Her father thought that she had mistaken it for another, but if she could take its photograph he would know that she was right and then he would want to stay, in order to photograph the bird himself. There couldn't be any harm in walking along the path at the top of the cliffs. She would be home long before anyone was awake; her mother would never know.

She looked at Madonna. She would do it, she told her. In the gray light, the doll's smile seemed satisfied, her eyes now mild, the eyes of any doll. Elvina took the wildflowers from her lap, closed her eyes, and laid her on her side.

"Sweet dreams," she whispered.

After she had dressed, she pulled her suitcase out from under her bed. Her mother had confiscated the Canon as a punishment for climbing on the cliffs. But stored in the suitcase, along with some books and her winter clothes, was a disposable camera given to her as a gift for her birthday, with half the pictures left.

She took an apple from a bowl of fruit in the kitchen. Outside, the sky was beginning to lighten and the birds were loud in the trees. The long grass beside the path swept her bare legs with moisture, cold against her flesh, and her canvas shoes were soon wet through. The cut on her foot began to hurt again; she ought to have put a bandage on it, she thought.

She walked west, toward Trebartha. The sea was calm and gray in the early morning light, a milky mist at the horizon, ruffled into foam near the rocks. The rhythmic pulse of the waves as they curled and broke and slid away again made her think of the way her blood had sounded in her ears last night. After five minutes or so, she saw the bird. She expected to—Madonna had promised her—so it came as no surprise.

It was perched on a post, its back to the sea, surveying a field. Instinctively, she swung the camera up and snapped its picture. In the next instant the bird took flight. She photographed it again as it rose into the sky. On the long drooping wings and at the base of the tail she could make out the distinctive bars that marked it for what it was, a honey buzzard, just as her father had described one. Too high now for her camera, it soared in wide, lazy circles above the field in search of prey. Her eyes followed it as its hunting arc widened.

The buzzard must have seen something, some creature in the long grass, for it swooped, skimmed the grass, then rose again clutching a tiny shape in its talons. It made for a stand of trees in the distance and was soon lost to sight.

Suddenly hungry, she remembered the apple in her pocket, then found a spot in the shelter of an outcrop of rock near the path where she sat down to eat it. Afterward, peaceful in the knowledge of what she now possessed, she closed her eyes and slept.

The shrieking of gulls nearby startled her awake again. She stood up, stretching. Some hundred yards away she saw a man standing by the cliff edge, beside a clump of bushes.

Then he did an odd thing. He took a small saw out of his knapsack and cut one of the bushes, held it over the edge for a moment, then dropped it and cut another. This time, because he looked comical holding the bush that way, Elvina took his picture.

At that moment, as if he sensed her presence, he glanced around. She recognized him and waved. After a moment, he waved back. Then he dropped the second bush over the edge and came toward her.

Chapter 27

The sight of Dana and Finn coming out of his father's darkroom together last night had struck Daniel with the force of a powerful blow. The ache from it persisted this morning like a bruise in his chest. But it had left his head clear. He understood now the intensity of his feelings for Dana, and the need to sever his life from his father's.

He'd been a fool, he told himself, not to make his interest in Dana explicit to Finn. He had trusted too much to Finn's intuition and to his own belief that, after Solange, Finn would never again become involved with any woman even remotely connected to him. Finn's behavior with Lynn had seemed to confirm that belief.

He showered and shaved, dressed, made coffee, working with a city swiftness through the daily rituals over which, down here, he ordinarily liked to linger. But in an hour or two he was leaving for London, as soon as he'd closed up the Schoolhouse—was leaving, in fact, for good. He couldn't stay, couldn't go on pretending it offered him either a refuge or hope. It was tainted by too many ambiguities and defeats.

Once, as he'd signed the papers making the Schoolhouse his, he had dared to hope that its closeness to Kerreck Du would become more than geographic. The very fact of Finn's telling him the place was for sale had seemed to imply that he felt the same way. Now the mile of rocky coast that stretched between them was symbolic only of a mutual failure.

Methodically he noted minor repairs to be made before the building was put on the market, scribbled lists to himself, packed up his belongings. He tried to keep his mind on the job at hand, but beneath his determination to leave he felt a regret too powerful to ignore. Things might have been different, he thought, if not for Solange. If not, now, for Dana.

As he poured breakfast cereal into a bowl, it occurred to him that his reaction to the supposed loss of Solange might have misled Finn. The end of their affair had meant so little, apart from that tacit, reluctant consent to a lie. In fact, it would have been a relief if his rival had been anyone other than Finn. He had been able to yield with apparent good grace; too gracefully, maybe, in Finn's eyes. Finn might have persuaded himself that Daniel would always give way. If so, he would have to show Finn his mistake.

Suddenly impatient to be off, he tipped the untouched bowl of cereal into the garbage—he could eat later, somewhere on the road—then swept his shaving tackle into its case, stuffed the Yamaha's saddlebags with his camera equipment and the last of his clothes, and took a final look around.

A small manila envelope addressed to Dana lay on his desk. He picked it up and placed it in the inside pocket of his leather jacket. After locking the front door, he wheeled the motorcycle down the path. He refused to look back, or to acknowledge what the loss of the Schoolhouse would mean to him. At the moment, all he wanted was to get free of his tangled relationship with his father. He was fed up with silence and subtlety, and with the struggle to understand.

The Yamaha bumped from the path into the lane. He paused to put on his helmet and jacket, then swung one leg over the saddle and started the engine. When he adjusted the rearview mirrors, the right-hand lens briefly reflected the distant Schoolhouse, as though to remind him that the past would not disappear simply because he turned his back. He forced himself to drive on, slowly at first along the rutted track, then accelerating with a roar onto the main road.

He was on his way to Trebartha, to the Chapel Gallery. Finn had promised John Malzer at dinner last night that he would spend the morning there, supervising the installation of the exhibition. Daniel wanted to see Finn, to say good-bye to him in person. The parting might feel more final that way.

But he had another, more urgent reason. He intended to make his feelings for Dana unmistakably clear to his father. No matter what might or might not have happened last night in the dark-room, he wanted Finn to understand that much at least, beyond the possibility of confusion.

Finn's red Bentley stood next to Estelle's Rover in the parking lot opposite the gallery. While Daniel waited for the car ahead of him, which was hauling a trailer, to negotiate the turn into the lot, he contemplated Malzer's structural crossbreed. It had always struck him as one of those hybrid English buildings that are the architectural equivalent of a certain type of elderly eccentric. Out-landish, but somehow redeemed by age. Ordinarily, he enjoyed them as visual metaphors, symbols of a human complexity so often hidden in this country. But Malzer's gallery reflected its owner's peculiarities too strikingly. Daniel found it jarring both in its connections and in its inconsistencies, even devious.

He was reminded now of the glint of cold amusement he'd once or twice caught in Malzer's mud brown eyes as he looked at Finn, as though he harbored some grim little joke at Finn's expense. The sudden suspicion that Malzer's apparent goodwill toward Finn might be equivocal made him wonder if he ought to stay for a day or two more after all, at least to see the exhibition accomplished.

Dismounting from the Yamaha, he told himself impatiently that his doubts were absurd. Malzer might sometimes be less entranced by Finn and his work than he pretended to be, but hypocrisy hardly implied malignant intent. Anyway, Finn was more than capable of looking after himself. He swung the leather jacket over one shoulder and went across to the gallery entrance.

He found Malzer with Thomas and Estelle in the small foyer, a shallow bowl-like space around which curved the ramp leading to the viewing rooms. They were plainly in the middle of some dis-pute, or at least Thomas and Estelle were arguing while Malzer stood between them, consulting the piece of paper he held in one hand. Malzer glanced up and smiled, shrugging slightly as though to distance himself from his contentious friends. The other two barely acknowledged Daniel; they were too engrossed in their quarrel, which seemed to be about wine.

"Not Sauvignon please." Estelle tapped emphatically with one long orange fingernail at a spot on Malzer's paper. "I've ordered a case of that myself to serve later." She was giving a small party at her house after the preview, Daniel remembered. He would have to make his excuses.

Thomas's thin mouth tightened. He appealed to his friend. "I only offered to take care of the catering, John, because I was under the impression I would have a free hand. If I'm mistaken . . ."

Before Daniel could interrupt to ask where he could find Finn, Timothy Sundy came hurrying in and without preamble inquired if any of them had seen Karen. Daniel heard a genuinely worried note under Tim's habitual petulance.

Estelle and Thomas paused to stare at him, while Malzer, apparently intent on the list, merely shook his head. Daniel was the first to speak. "No," he told the other man, "not since last night."

"Why do you ask?" Estelle was frowning. She looked tired, Daniel thought, the gilt hair lifeless and dull, the bright orange lipstick like a gash against her sallow skin. But he noticed that the gold bangles had proliferated, as though to compensate.

"She never showed up at the shop this morning," Tim replied. "She had a fitting for a wedding dress at nine. The customer's furious. I've been round to her flat but she's not there."

With smooth malice, Thomas said quietly, "She did mention something about London once, Tim. If I remember correctly." He pushed his eyeglasses up his nose with one thin finger.

Sundy scowled. "We'd been arguing when she said that, but we made it up. If it's any business of yours." He looked miserable. Daniel had always wondered why Tim put up with Karen's treatment, but he realized now that he must love her. He was sure, on the other hand, that Karen did not love Tim.

"Did you look to see if a suitcase was missing?" Estelle asked him.

Irritably, Sundy turned on her. "She hasn't gone to London, I tell you. And anyway, she'd have let me know." One of the small photographs already in place on the wall behind Estelle seemed to catch his eye. He went past her to peer at it. It was a jokey piece, Daniel saw, a shot of a male nude done in the style of the sixteenth-century painter Arcimboldo, with certain but not all of the body parts replaced by vegetables that could be seen as comments on the originals. A large zucchini flanked by onions took the place of the head. Daniel seemed to remember Finn talking about it, and was fairly certain the torso belonged to Tim.

"I don't get it," Sundy muttered.

Thomas and Malzer exchanged glances. Thomas said, "I shouldn't worry about it, Tim."

"Well, I do," he replied, misunderstanding. "It's not like Karen to go off."

There was a silence. It occurred to Daniel that the same thought was probably going through all their minds: that it was precisely like Karen.

"Where's Finn?" Timothy asked loudly, perhaps sensing this.

"Here."

They all glanced up to see him standing at the top of the sloping ramp, where it curved away to the left. Dressed in a black sweatshirt and jeans, with his curling gray hair and burly shoulders, he looked to Daniel like an aging bull, pugnacious and full of the old edgy, aggressive energy.

Timothy repeated his query about Karen, but Finn replied indifferently that he hadn't seen her. Then went on, to Daniel, "I'm glad you're here. I was going to drop by and see you at the Schoolhouse later. Come on, I want to show you something." He turned and disappeared.

As Daniel went up the ramp and through the complex of little rooms, he told himself he was no longer concerned with what his father might have to say to him, or to show him. And yet he could not suppress the curiosity that Finn always aroused in him, or the conviction that if he listened more intently, saw more clearly, followed more closely, showed himself willing to meet his father more than halfway in understanding, the great riddle of their relationship would at once reveal itself. He wondered how long it would be before these old impulses died away from lack of nourishment.

He found Finn in the last and smallest viewing room, which gave onto the large open space of the old chapel, squatting in front of a stack of framed photographs propped against one wall. Daniel fought to control his annoyance—he wasn't about to play photographic critic with Finn.

Just say it and go, he told himself.

He spoke to Finn's back, keeping his voice matter-of-fact, uninflected. "I've come to wish you luck with the exhibition. I won't be here for it. I'm going back to London." Finn's only response was a grunt as he extracted one of the photographs from the stack and then, holding it by his side, stood up and turned to face Daniel. "There's something I want to say before I go," Daniel continued. "Something you should know."

"Oh yes?" Both voice and face held only a bland, almost benign interest.

"I'm attracted to Dana. More than that. I think I'm falling in love with her."

He hadn't meant to use the word love. It had slipped out automatically, naturally. He didn't regret it, however. It was, he acknowledged to himself, the simple truth.

The blue gaze was unblinking. "Yes, I thought so."

"You did? Then why the hell—?" Daniel forced the anger down and made himself speak quietly. "I just want you to know that after she gets back to London I'm going to do my damnedest to persuade her to fall in love with me."

"Good."

The monosyllable, uttered in the same pleasantly approving manner, momentarily threw Daniel, until it came to him that this was one of Finn's conundrums, the verbal equivalent of his photographs. Figure out what I'm up to, if you're clever enough. Well, he was finished with Finn's games. He drew the manila envelope from his jacket's inner pocket and held it out. Imitating Finn's own mild manner, he asked him politely to give it to Dana. "Tell her it's the last piece of the Hobhouse puzzle."

Finn raised one eyebrow, but did not take the envelope. "Maybe it's time I explained last night."

"Don't," Daniel said quickly, raising the hand with the letter to ward off whatever it was Finn wanted to say. "Obscurity has always had more appeal for you than for me, but for once I think I'd like things to stay unexplained." Immediately, he regretted the sarcasm. Its only effect was to make him sound like a sulky adolescent.

"All the same," Finn replied, without heat, "let's have a little clarity."

He walked over to the wall next to Daniel, lifted the photograph he was holding, and hung it in place. Then stepped back beside Daniel to contemplate it.

Daniel's brief glance took in two luminous, sinuous shapes on a ground so dark it was almost black, separated by a shimmer of silver straight as the blade of a sword. Small spheres, like tiny planets in the night sky, seemed to float around the larger bodies. The scene was shot from above, almost clinically, and the tones were silvery and very cold.

Clarity? This looked to Daniel like yet another form of obscurity, another of Finn's beautiful evasions. Furious now, he started to leave the room.

Behind him, Finn said meditatively, "I could call it 'Snakes in the Grass.' Or simply 'Solange and Karen.' What's your opinion?"

Shocked, Daniel turned around. To give himself time to think, he stared at the picture. Now he could see that the two largest shapes were female figures, S curves blurred and elongated until they seemed more serpentine than human. Each appeared to be lying on her side with her head, fused with the outstretched arm under it, at the other's feet. The other arm lay along the hip, palm curved upward, and he noticed then that in each upturned palm lay the indistinct image of an apple core. The tiny globes that littered the ground might have been windfalls.

"Solange and Karen?" He looked back at Finn. "Karen?" he repeated, not quite able to believe it.

"Among others. Solange's taste was catholic. Maybe you knew."

Their eyes met. "Not about Karen," Daniel replied after a moment. Something in his father's face, an invitation at last to the truth, prompted him to go on, to reveal what he knew. As gently as he could he described his discovery of Solange's infidelities. It was only at the end of their affair, he explained, that he had learned how she had betrayed him, when it was too late. "It seemed to me the only chance we had, you and I, was if I kept silent. And I hoped . . . well, that she might be different with you. That she loved you."

With his head bowed now, like someone absorbing a blow, Finn rubbed wearily at the back of his neck. "I think she did. In her fashion."

"How did you find out? About Karen."

"Solange told me. I thought she wanted forgiveness. I realize now she wanted to leave."

Although he pitied his father, Daniel couldn't help but wonder if Finn had suffered as much from the wound to his vanity as from the sense of betrayal. Tolerant of amorality in others, and largely indifferent to shadings of what was or was not permissible in matters sexual, he might have found it easy to be that way simply because he was always the one who left.

Daniel thought, too, of the months in which the unspoken truth had stood between them like a wall. There was so much he wanted to say, to know, but he could only bring himself to ask about the thing that had least to do with himself. "All this time, Karen's continued coming to Kerreck Du," he said. "You've gone on seeing her, using her as a model. Why?"

Finn shrugged. "To punish myself? To find a way to take revenge? God knows. Maybe simply to try to understand. In the end, that," he gestured at the photograph, "seems to be revenge enough." He stared critically at it for a moment, then went up to adjust the balance slightly.

"I finished it last night," he said over his shoulder to Daniel. "Dana kept me company in the darkroom while I worked. She seemed to understand that I needed someone to be there." He turned around, his face lighter now, almost smiling. "Go and see her, Daniel. Give her your puzzle piece yourself." When the smile appeared, it was sardonic and slightly mocking. "And don't tell me you don't have a taste for enigmas."

Before Daniel could reply, Malzer came into the room with Thomas and Estelle on either side of him, as if each were determined not to yield the other any advantage. "Look, Finn," Malzer began, "about that change we discussed. I really don't think . . ."

Grappling with the implications of Finn's revelation, Daniel was almost grateful for the interruption. He needed time to think. Questions could wait; it was more than likely Finn wouldn't answer them anyway. At the moment, he felt a profound relief, which told him just how little he'd wanted the break with his father, and how happy he was to find the way to Dana free of Finn's complication.

"I don't give a damn about the catalog," Finn was telling Malzer as they all left the room together. "People don't come to read a catalog, they come to look at the pictures. They're what matters, not some bloody catalog. If I want to replace one photograph with another, I'll do it."

Attery turned to Daniel and said in a mocking aside, "Turner was still touching up his paintings after they'd been hung. John's lucky Finn hasn't got a darkroom set up in here."

When Daniel came out of the gallery, he was surprised to find Tim waiting for him. He began to speak as soon as he saw Daniel. "I'm not going to get an honest answer out of anyone in there," he said, jerking his head toward the gallery. "But I know you'll be straight with me."

"About what?"

"Karen. She took my car last night, said she was meeting someone. Did she go back to Kerreck Du?"

Daniel didn't need to ask why Tim thought Karen might have returned to Kerreck Du. "If she did," he replied cautiously, "I never saw her. Is your car missing?"

Tim shook his head. "Someone brought it back. Left the keys in it, if you can believe that?" Outrage crept into his tones. "It could have been stolen, for God's sake."

Daniel noted the hint of paranoia. Someone, not Karen herself. When leaving the keys in the car was so typically Karen's style.

"I'm not blind, you know," Tim went on intently. "I saw what was going on between Tatevic and Karen. I know she went to meet him last night."

It was probably true, Daniel thought, remembering the scene at dinner. He felt a spasm of pity for Tim, and a rueful amusement. Tim's jealousy might have been an ironic commentary on his own.

Abruptly, the other man burst out, "Why do we pretend to ignore what's right in front of our faces? Just look at what's happened since Tatevic came here. Solange, those two women, now Karen."

"Come on, Tim," Daniel said, half incredulous, half appalled, "you can't honestly think Mico and the Gull are—?"

"Why can't I? I do! I know what you're all thinking, that

245

Karen's just taken off. Well, I don't believe it. Something's happened to her. And I know who's responsible. What's more, I'm going to the police." With that, he strode off down the hill.

Damn, Daniel thought, as he watched him go; he'd handled that badly. But the allegation was so unexpected, so absurd, that he'd been caught off balance. He'd never taken Tim very seriously, the man was too vain and too obtuse, but he did sympathize with his anxieties about Karen. Fear of the Gull made any inexplicable disappearance sinister. But to believe that Mico . . .

Well, the police were trained to handle wild accusations; with luck they would calm Tim down and make him see reason. Briefly, Daniel considered whether he ought to tell the others, then rejected the idea. It would only add another unstable element to an already volatile situation. He would, however, have a quiet word of warning with Mico when he reached Kerreck Du.

Chapter 28

"Elvina."

Dana was sitting on the terrace in front of Kerreck Du, eating breakfast, when she saw the child. She had overslept and waked to find the silent house apparently deserted. A note left by Pascale in the kitchen announced that she and Finn were going into Trebartha—shopping for her, the Chapel Gallery for Finn—and might be back late; Dana should help herself to whatever she liked for breakfast and lunch. Scones, eggs, a bowl of stewed fruit, and half a dozen different kinds of cereal were set out on the countertop, but tea and toast were all she could face.

The sun was already high. A drowsy warmth, very faintly humid, suffused the air, stirred by the gentlest of breezes. Across the sky lay a thin transparent wash of gray, like a veil, dulling the blue. Lethargy settled over her, a disinclination to work, even to think.

She crumbled her toast, tossing crumbs to a sparrow that patrolled the flagstones. Her head ached, partly with the residue from the night's excesses, partly perhaps from the weather, but more profoundly with her struggle to understand that last brief scene with Daniel and Finn. Its ambiguity perplexed her. Had Daniel misunderstood, had he thought she and Finn . . . ? And if he had, did it matter?

Yes, intensely.

It was then that she saw Elvina walking slowly across the lawn from the garden end of the house, her doll clutched to her chest.

When she called her name again, this time more loudly, Elvina raised her head. Dana was struck by the look of almost ferocious concentration on the wan little face. The hollow-eyed gaze stared with such fierce obliviousness that she sensed she was virtually invisible to the girl. She noticed that the doll had leaves and dirt clinging to its yellow hair, and was now missing an arm. For some reason, this disturbed her almost as much as the sight of Elvina's face.

"Elvina, are you all right?"

Without responding, the child went past her and through the gate into the courtyard. Dana bit her lip, uncertain whether she ought to follow, to find out what the matter was. Not that she couldn't guess easily enough. The mother's unhappiness was so clearly reflected on the troubled surface of the daughter's face.

"Don't be hurt. It's not you."

She turned around in her chair to find Daniel coming down the portico steps, a mug in one hand. The relief she felt at the sight of him was almost as great as her happiness. He hadn't misunderstood then, after all. She had simply read too much into the scene at an hour when perceptions were naturally skewed.

"Every now and then Elvina goes silent," Daniel went on in explanation, "refuses to speak, sometimes for days. Her parents blame the war, but I doubt that's the only reason." He pulled out the chair beside her and sat down, placing the mug on the table. Although he spoke with detachment, his face was sympathetic.

"You think she knows about Karen and her father?"

"How could she avoid knowing?"

And what, Dana wondered, could anyone possibly say to comfort her? That the war would end, someday? That the woman her father was infatuated with wasn't the faithful type? Someday might as well be never to a child, and that first consciousness of love's betrayal wouldn't be forgotten.

Daniel's voice broke through her thoughts and she glanced across at him. He was sitting with his legs stretched out, cradling the mug in his hands, his blue eyes narrowed against the sun. The light burnished the dark auburn hair and tanned skin so that they seemed to glow against his white shirt.

"Your ankle," he repeated. "How is it?"

"Fine." She smiled, and moved her leg out from under the table, pulling her trousers up slightly to show him. With a sideways glance, mock flirtatious, she wiggled her foot. "Look, no cast."

"Great," he replied lightly, falling in with her tone, "because I'm here to corrupt you."

"And I have to be mobile for that?"

"For this particular form of corruption, anyway. I want you to play hooky today. I thought we could visit Tintagel. Nothing too strenuous, no hikes up to the castle ruins. Just a look at what's become of Beacon House."

The idea immediately appealed to her. She was curious to see where Marianna Hobhouse had spent her last days, especially now, in light of Theophilus Veasey's letters. And she was eager to get away from Kerreck Du, if only for a few hours. Distance might give her a perspective on the place she seemed to lack.

Daniel's proposal was attractive for quite another reason as well. It meant time alone with him in a different setting, one where his father's shadow would not fall. She would see him distinct and separate from Finn, as she'd first met him, in London at the Kazanjian Gallery.

When she replied that, yes, she'd like to visit Tintagel, he warned her not to expect too much. There would be the tourist hordes, he explained, the King Arthur car park, Lancelot's Bed & Breakfast, all the trappings of a thriving commercial enterprise to frighten away the ghosts of the past. "But with your back to the town, the site's evocative. Even if you strip away the Geoffrey of Monmouth and Malory fantasies and accept the castle as simply a medieval earl's effort to impress the locals."

"Strip away, if you like," she said blandly, "but leave me my fantasies."

He gave her a startled look, then grinned. "Which are . . . ?"

"The Tennysonian sort of course. 'Mystic, wonderful.' " Her smile was teasing. "What other kind could we have at a place like Tintagel?"

A faintly speculative amusement crinkled his blue eyes. "I'd like to think that we have the same fantasies, you and I."

Beneath the bantering, she sensed a deeper implication, an invitation to be serious if she wished. The possibilities this evoked took her breath away.

"There is one slight problem," he continued. "The way we get there." Would she mind traveling by motorcycle?

Mind, she was tempted to ask him, when it gave her an excuse to put her arms around him? She smiled at the thought but aloud said only that as she'd never ridden on a motorcycle she was looking forward to the experience.

Good, he replied; he hoped it would be the first of many she would let him introduce her to. Again she heard that seductive nuance in an otherwise conventional politeness, the latent suggestion of pleasures to come. It made her shy, unable to sustain his gaze. He gestured at the plate of crumbled toast. "If you're finished, we should leave now, while the day's reasonably young."

"I'll get my jacket and meet you at the front of the house." She tossed the toast to the sparrow and went inside to leave a note, saying where she'd gone, beside Pascale's in the kitchen. When she came out a few minutes later, he was standing next to a large red motorcycle, pulling on a leather jacket. As she strapped on the helmet he handed her, she thought to ask if they should bring lunch with them.

"Tintagel has restaurants. But if you'd prefer to picnic, I know a place that makes a good take-out Cornish pasty." He swung one leg over the saddle. "Or you could have Star-gazy Pie. It's made with whole pilchards. Their heads stick up through the crust so their eyes stare at you as you eat them. Or Muggety Pie. . . ."

"Maggoty?" she asked in disbelief as she climbed on behind him.

"Muggety." He grinned around at her. "It's filled with sheep's entrails and cream—"

"If you go on, I won't want any lunch."

They rode at first along lanes that dipped and rose through wooded valleys and over rolling hills, past worn Celtic crosses at lonely crossroads and isolated farmhouses where dogs rushed out at the sound of their passing. But as the road climbed to the edge of Bodmin Moor the landscape emptied, shorn of habitation and trees, and became a vast billowy yellow-gray sea speckled with islands of heather and bright green moss. When Daniel opened the throttle on the long empty stretches of high road, the motorcycle surged forward, racing toward a horizon hidden by waves of grass and rock. Later she would remember the journey as pure sensation, the engine's roar drumming against her ears, the torrent of gorse-scented wind cool on her face, and Daniel's body a promise of pleasure under her hands. A glorious, wordless, speed-filled rush toward the unknown.

They stopped several times so that Daniel could take photographs. "Still okay?" he would ask before they set off again, meaning her ankle. "Perfectly," she would reply, meaning more than her ankle. The moorland at last gave way to the harsh, jagged rock of the coast and they passed between high black cliffs to emerge in a litter of modern bungalows and caravan sites. The first signs appeared, advertising Guinevere's Cream Teas, The Round Table Café, Gawain's Gifte Shoppe, the Hall of Chivalry.

Leaving the Yamaha in the public lot, they walked along the straggling main street. A line of diesel-belching tour buses disgorged passengers onto a sidewalk already cluttered with ice cream sellers and stands displaying postcards and plastic armor, all the bric-a-brac of any seaside town. Dana began to wish they hadn't come. No fantasy could survive this much realism.

A large tour group milled about ahead of them, blocking the pavement, spilling out onto the road. A sweating, red-faced man with a can of soda in one hand and a cigarette in the other bumped into Dana, jostling her sideways. Her ankle gave a sharp twinge and she gasped. Daniel put his arm protectively around her shoulders, forging a way through the crowd with the edge of his body.

Ahead, a massive crag with black precipitous cliffs shouldered its way out of the sea, thinly covered by a worn pelt of grass through which poked the bones of ruined walls. It was loosely bound to the mainland by a cord of crumbling stone so narrow that a season of violent storms might shatter the tenuous hold and allow the island to drift free of its mooring.

From the top of the stony track, she and Daniel watched the sightseers making their way down toward the castle entrance, like a line of ants on holiday. She tried and failed to place Marianna's cloaked and bonneted figure among the modern crowd, to imagine that nameless lover at her side, the buffeting wind and the unseen spy, Mrs. Biddicombe, the keeper, hovering indecisively where she and Daniel now were standing. The anachronism was too pronounced. A flutter of black cloth wisped briefly across her mind's eye and was gone.

She caught Daniel's rueful look, and shrugged. "You did warn me."

"Come back some stormy November afternoon, just before sundown," he said. "When the ghosts come out."

"I'll bet the ghosts emigrated years ago." Under her breath she added in a murmur, "On a dusky barge, black as a funeral scarf." She had once memorized all 354 lines of the "Morte d'Arthur," partly to impress an English professor she'd had a crush on at the time, partly out of a genuine passion for Tennyson's poetry.

Yes, she thought, something lingered here; if only in words.

"Talking to yourself. A bad sign," Daniel said gravely. He linked his arm through hers. "I think it's time I took you to the asylum."

An elderly woman standing nearby gave them a startled glance, then a sweet smile. As Dana smiled back at her she noticed the woman was carrying a Penguin paperback copy of Beroul's *Romance of Tristan*. For some reason this made her feel better about the hordes. She mentioned Beroul to Daniel as they walked through the rest of the village. He hadn't read the Norman's twelfth-century saga of Tristan and Iseult's passion, but he knew that it named Tintagel as King Mark's stronghold and that the poet himself had traveled around Cornwall. Beroul might have seen the Tristan stone, he said. He explained that this was a sixth-century memorial stone roughly eight feet tall with Tristan's name on it, which stood now at a roadside not far from Kerreck Du.

"The inscription's in Latin. It says Tristan was the son of Cunomorus. Which, apparently, was another name for Mark."

That put an interesting spin on the story, she told him—not uncle and nephew, but father and son fighting over the same woman. "All those fascinating Freudian implications." Then she bit her lip and flushed, wishing the words unsaid, as the parallels with his own story of filial conflict struck her.

He flashed her an ironic, amused glance but only lifted one hand to point out a large Victorian house set back behind a low stone wall on the outskirts of the village. Beacon House. Beyond it, treeless, stony fields grazed by sheep stretched away to the cliffs' edge.

Theophilus Veasey's asylum was now the Pendragon Hotel. A paved forecourt filled with cars fronted the red brick facade, which looked recently cleaned, its trim freshly painted white. Ornamental orange trees sat in tubs on either side of the door. The place had a prosperous, slightly pompous air that hinted at expense accounts and champagne weekends. No ghosts here, either, Dana thought, as she gazed at it.

Daniel bought them take-away pasties from the back of a bakery where the line of customers was reassuringly long. They ate the fragrant meat-filled pies, along with some apples and a shared bar of chocolate, sitting on a bench in the sun. By now her early lethargy had been transformed into a pleasurable contentment, an expansive, leisurely anticipation, still vague but unmistakably finding its source in Daniel. She watched a young couple approaching along the road, proudly cooing over a baby the father was pushing in a stroller. Her once habitual reaction to such a sight, that small dart of pain, was absent. Unable quite to believe it, she probed for any lingering tenderness. But there were no sore places left, only a slight scarring to tell her where the wound had once been.

"Ordinary human happiness," Daniel observed quietly, as the trio went past them. "It almost seems out of place here, doesn't it, where the passions were all on the grand scale?" He offered her the last square of chocolate.

"Especially when they were mostly the nastier ones," she agreed. "Lust, ambition, jealousy, betrayal, fury. And vengeance, the nastiest of them all." She ate the chocolate, and then said reflectively, "I'm beginning to believe *that*'s the root of all evil. Not money. The urge to punish, to take your pound of flesh."

Then, as she watched the couple disappear down a side street, she found herself telling Daniel about her miscarriage and its consequences. He listened in silence, half turned toward her with his left arm resting on the back of the bench. She felt the tips of his fingers touching her sleeve, the lightest of pressures but as comforting as if his arm were around her.

"I suppose it was one of the reasons I was drawn to Marianna," she said, when she'd finished. "Though you mustn't think I have some sort of obsessive overidentification with my subject. At least," she acknowledged with a rueful laugh, "not anymore."

After a moment's silence he said matter-of-factly, "I know what it's like to feel betrayed. To be that angry. I wasn't honest, the other night, when I told you that my relationship with Solange wasn't serious. In the beginning, at least, it was."

And then my father came along, she thought he was going to say. But instead to her surprise he said, "And then I found out that she was sleeping with an acquaintance of mine. Several acquaintances, in fact," he added dryly.

"I was furious, of course, for a lot of different reasons. Hurt pride was probably the strongest. But I realized pretty quickly that I was also relieved, that I'd been wanting to end things, and here was my reason on a platter. Hard to digest but good for me.

"Solange was in Paris at the time," he went on. "When she came back, she said she'd been with Finn. That they were getting married. She pointed out that if I told him about her affairs it wouldn't make any difference to him. He would either think I was lying from spite, or he'd shrug it off. He never cared much what women had done before they met him. Only afterward."

She thought of what Finn had revealed to her. Did Daniel know that Solange had also been unfaithful to his father? An instinct told her that he did, and that the questions remaining would someday be answered, but now was not the time to ask them.

"So there you are," he added with a humorous look. "The saga of the Finns." He stood up, as if he'd had enough of the subject, holding out a hand to help her to her feet. It seemed inevitable that her hand should remain in his while they walked back along the main street.

They were passing an old hotel, a white, two-story building with a large bow window, when she happened to notice the name written in gold lettering above the door. The Shorncliff Arms. It was the inn where Marianna had met her lover on that blustery October afternoon in 1870. Dana gaped, astonished. "It's still here! Oh Daniel, it's still here." She turned to him, grasping his arm. "You see what this means, don't you? They might have the old guest registers. Then we'd know . . ."

It seemed too much to hope but when, breathless, she told the pleasant young woman behind the reception desk what they were after, the woman replied that yes, she believed their old records had been kept. What date were they interested in? 1870? She wrinkled her forehead when she heard it. "So far back? I'm not sure . . . Oh, Joseph," she suddenly called to an old man who was shuffling along a passage from the back of the hotel. "If anyone will know," she told them, "it's Joseph. He's worked here for years."

Consulted, the old man said with slow courtesy that so far as he knew nothing had been lost, even in the fire of '57, although of course he couldn't be certain the very register they were after would still be there. However, he would go and have a look if they liked. Mind, he warned, it might take him some time; not everyone was careful to return things to their proper places.

"Why don't you go and have tea in the lounge?" the receptionist said, when Joseph had shuffled off again. "And perhaps some sandwiches or cakes?" They glanced at each other. In light of what was being done for them, they could hardly say they didn't want any tea and were too full for cakes.

They sat drinking their unwanted tea in a small sitting room crowded with stuffed armchairs upholstered in the same bottle green velveteen. There was a small footstool, which Daniel insisted Dana put under her leg. She found she was glad of the excuse to rest her ankle, which had begun to ache slightly.

After what seemed to her an interminable wait but couldn't have been more than twenty minutes, the old man returned. To her relief and delight, he was carrying a worn leather register. He placed it on the table in front of them and opened it, stooping over and peering at it nearsightedly. "Now, what day precisely would you be looking for?" She watched with mounting excitement as he paged deliberately through the book. At last he turned it around so that the list of names was facing her.

The combination of spidery handwriting and faded ink might have made it difficult for someone else to decipher the list, but she was used to reading old documents. Her eyes went down the page looking for any name that might have the initials P.B., then stopped as one name leaped out at her. She stared in amazement, unable to trust her eyes. It seemed at first almost impossible, but as her mind ran swiftly over all the facts that might confirm it, she knew it could be true.

It was. It had to be.

"There," she told Daniel exultantly. She pointed to the name.

"Robert Wiedemann Barrett," he read aloud. When he glanced up at her there was a puzzled look on his face, which she interpreted as an understandable failure to comprehend why the name should excite her so. After all, in his letters Dr. Veasey had referred to Marianna's lover as P.B., not R.W.B.

"Is there some way we could make a copy of this page?" she asked Joseph.

He looked doubtful. "Well, I don't know...."

"Would you let me photograph it?" Daniel said, holding out the camera that was slung from its strap around his neck.

"I can't see the harm in that," the old man replied.

Quickly, Daniel switched films and made the necessary adjustments, then snapped off several shots of the page, the one beside it, as well as the register cover. When he'd finished and Joseph had gone, taking with him the register and their thanks as well as a generous tip, Daniel turned to her. "So what makes you think this Robert Barrett is the one?"

"Because his full name was Robert Wiedemann Barrett Browning."

One eyebrow lifted quizzically, but again he seemed more puzzled than astonished. "The poet?"

"His son."

"What about the initials? R.W.B., not P.B."

She disposed of that. "He was known as Pen. It was a nickname—short for Penini—that his parents gave him when he was a baby in Italy." She leaned forward in her chair, toward him. "Don't you see how it makes sense, Daniel? They knew each other, Marianna and Pen. We can be certain of that much from the photograph with Elizabeth Barrett Browning. It's not inconceivable that somehow they met again when his father brought him to London after his mother's death. In 1870 he would have been twenty, and a student at Oxford."

Warming to her thesis, she went on eagerly, "Not that his studies lasted long. He dropped out and began to run with a wild crowd, had affairs. He became an artist—he'd always had talent—a painter and sculptor, mostly of nudes. There's a story he kept a ten-foot python in his studio which he used to drape around the necks of his models until one day it began to strangle one of them and he had to shoot it.

"He did settle down eventually, got married at thirty-eight to a rich American wife, and lived in a beautiful palazzo in Venice. But it wasn't a happy marriage and it broke up fairly quickly. There were rumors that a young servant in the palazzo was either his mistress or a daughter by an affair he'd had in the late 1860s. . . ." She stopped, struck by a sudden thought. "What if—? No, that's too farfetched. How could Marianna have had a child without anyone knowing?"

Still consumed by her inner debate she went on, "You know, it always seemed to me a sad life, Pen Browning's. Blighted somehow. I thought it was because he suffered from being the only child of not one but two famous people. Famous as much for their love affair as for their work. Now I wonder . . . Maybe he never recovered from losing first his mother and then the woman he loved."

Daniel had listened without interrupting, obviously interested but almost, she thought now, like a teacher with an apt pupil, curious to know if the speculation would lead to a conclusion already drawn by the teacher. It came to her that he was accepting it all too easily, as though it confirmed something he'd already suspected.

Accusingly, she said, "You knew, didn't you? Dammit, Daniel, you might have—"

"Suspected," he said calmly. "There was no proof. You've provided that." Reaching inside the leather jacket, which lay over the arm of the chair, he drew out an envelope. When he handed it to her she saw that it had her name written on it. "This was always the joker in the deck. It was with Veasey's letters but I took it out before you came."

"Why?"

"I told myself I was curious to see what sort of theory you'd come up with without it. But it was more than that." He paused. "The truth is, I wanted to have an excuse to see you again. If . . . well, if things had turned out differently than I'm hoping they have."

Wordless now, she looked into his face. On his mouth was the same slow-dawning smile that she knew must be on her own. The waitress's arrival to inquire if they wanted anything more broke through their absorbed contemplation of one another. While Daniel paid for the tea, she took out the letter that the envelope contained.

My dear Friend,

How can I express to you the depth of my gratitude? All I have to offer you is my simple thanks—but they are of the sort that one can only give once or twice in a life. You have restored to me one whom I believed lost.

I shall never forget the inexpressible joy I felt when I again saw her precious light shining through your blessed medium. To be alone with her, and with you, was an incomparable happiness. And yet I felt a sadness, neither hers nor mine but rather belonging to the one whose gifts had compassed our reunion. I would give all I possessed to heal that sorrow, as mine has been healed.

Perhaps you will feel it presumptuous in me to address you in this manner. I have however the example of one much greater than I to spur me on, my father. He would not be prevented from fulfilling his vow to liberate an imprisoned spirit whose muted radiance deserved to shine out in its full splendour, and no more shall I.

I will be with you tomorrow, as promised. Until that happy hour, May God bless and keep you.

Ever and increasingly yours,
Robert Wiedemann Browning.

When she looked up at Daniel, he said, "He's obviously referring to a seance, isn't he? He must have come to Marianna hoping she would get in touch with his dead mother for him. And she succeeded, or at least persuaded him that she did." He smiled. "I think it wins the prize as Most Bizarre Seduction Scene. Though who was seducing whom isn't clear."

"It's really not that bizarre," Dana replied, "given the times. And Pen Browning's past. His mother took him to seances when he was a child, until his father put a stop to it. When he was an adult he did say that spiritualism was nonsense, but that may have been to please his father."

She went on to describe the hothouse atmosphere in which Pen had been raised, the way he was doted on, dressed in ribbons and satin, his hair in long curls. And how, at twelve, when his mother died, his life, even his appearance, had changed completely. "His father cut his hair, threw away the lace jackets, and took him off to England, away from everything he'd ever known, including the Italian nurse who'd cared for him. Not that Robert Browning didn't love him—he did—it was just that he was so devastated by Elizabeth's death he couldn't bear the thought of staying in Italy without her. And he wanted Pen to have an English upbringing. But England must have seemed cold and gray after life in Italy. Pen must have longed for his mother."

"All those fascinating Freudian implications," Daniel echoed with a grin. Then went on, "So, to put it crudely, Marianna's beautiful and unhappy. Pen's confused and passionate. Both are vulnerable but he's made of coarser stuff. And in the end he saves himself."

"In the short term. And he was only twenty," she reminded him, struck with a sudden sympathy for Pen as well as for Marianna. After all, he might have given her, if fleetingly, the only real happiness and love she had ever known.

As she slowly folded up the letter and returned it to the envelope, she realized that she had come to the end of Marianna's story. She felt strangely bereft, as though the shadowy companion who had been beckoning her forward for the past two years had abruptly vanished. But she reminded herself that the telling of the story lay ahead, with all its rewards, and that Daniel's collaboration inevitably would play a part in it. She watched him as he got up to walk over to the window, and was suddenly filled with the hope that she now had another companion, somone solid and real this time, to give her that sense of a promising future.

He turned back to her. "The weather's changing. It looks as if we might get rain. We'd better go."

Outside, the thin gray film across the sky had thickened. Over the sea, to the north, a line of clouds was advancing steadily toward the land, driven by a sullen wind that sent bits of trash swirling up the street. On their way back to the car park, Dana's eye was caught by the headlines of a local paper displayed in front of a news agent's shop. "Gull claims another victim," screamed the bold-faced type. She was about to point it out to Daniel, then thought better of it. Why let a tragedy that had nothing to do with them spoil a day so rich in pleasurable surprises that it seemed she would never come to the end of them?

While they put on the rain gear he took from the saddlebags, he asked if they could stop in at the Schoolhouse on their way back to Kerreck Du. "There are one or two things I need to do there. It won't take long."

"Take as long you like. I'm in no hurry."

He helped her free a zipper that had stuck on a bit of cloth, his head bent close to hers. Their eyes met. "What I asked you earlier," he said, "about our fantasies—"

"They're the same," she whispered, her throat suddenly dry. "I'm sure of it."

"Good. Then I *will* take my time."

Chapter 29

The clouds from the sea caught them while they were still on the high road over the moors. A slanting rain drove against the Yamaha's windshield and dulled the muted colors of the moor to a faded monochrome. Mist rose from boggy ground. It turned large outcroppings of rock to vague sinister shapes that seemed to bar the road ahead, which wove and feinted around them. But Dana was too happy, and too confident of Daniel's skill with the motorcycle, to mind the rain or to feel anxious. Their isolation only made certain sensations more intense: the metallic taste of the rain on her tongue; the slick wet feel of Daniel's raincoat against her cheek as she leaned into him on a curve; and the sweet conviction, now, that she knew what lay ahead. She had the surreal impression that at any moment they would burst through the fog into some light-filled valley islanded among the moors.

By the time they rode down the Schoolhouse lane, the heavy rain had turned to a soft drizzle that dripped listlessly from the trees into puddles below. Mist stretched boneless fingers toward them. Without definition or boundary, the landscape seemed to hold a menacing uncertainty, and when a gull drifted past on a silent swoop of wings as they walked up the track, bringing to mind the newspaper headline she'd seen in Tintagel, Dana felt fear like a feather brush lightly over her spine.

The Schoolhouse stood foursquare and solid as a beacon in the mist. Inside, while she stripped off her sodden rainclothes and hung them to dry, Daniel switched on a space heater, then knelt to lay a fire. These simple domestic actions, cheeringly prosaic, seemed to shut out that amorphous world beyond the walls.

Dana went over to warm herself in front of the heater. She

looked around, curious, and was struck by the almost monastic restraint of the clean, spare space, emphasized by the great arched window, and by the paradox that while outwardly the Schoolhouse seemed firmly rooted, inwardly it looked impermanent, the dwelling of someone prepared to strike camp at a moment's notice. Everything here, she thought, could be packed up in less than an hour.

"You keep this place very tidy," she told Daniel dryly.

The fire leaped into life with the touch of his match. He stood up, closing the screen, and smiled as though at some private joke. "I plan to be messier in the future," he said. "You could help."

Now she smiled. "Is that why we came back here? So I could untidy you?"

"No. But it's a fine idea."

He noticed then that she was shivering, and put his hand on the sleeve of her jacket. "It's damp," he said, frowning. "You should have told me." Rummaging through the saddlebags, he produced a T-shirt and a navy blue wool fisherman's knit sweater, which he insisted she change into. He would make coffee. As she pulled the sweater over her head in the spartan bathroom she could smell his scent in the wool, like the imprint of his skin. That and the sweater itself, which was far too large and enveloped her like a blanket, were immediately comforting.

"I'm sorry, I'm all out of milk," Daniel called as she came out of the bathroom. "Is black okay?"

She preferred it that way, she told him. She leaned across the wooden counter that separated the tiny kitchen alcove from the rest of the room, resting her arms on its wooden surface, hands clasped. On the other side, he set two empty mugs down on the counter. Then, facing her, took her hands in his.

"Good," he said, "you feel warmer now."

She looked down at their linked hands. "That helps."

"And this?" Slowly he slid his palms along her bare flesh inside the loose sleeves of the sweater until his fingers curled around her elbows, cupping them. Joined, but separated by the counter, they stood looking at each other. The query lingered in his eyes, multiplied, grew insistent.

Before she could give him his answer, the espresso pot boiled over. "Damn," he said with a rueful smile, then turned to deal with it. She sat down on the sofa in front of the fire, slipping off her shoes and damp socks, and drew her left knee up to her chin so that she could rub her ankle, which had begun to ache again.

"Here, let me." Daniel put their coffee down on the small end table. Settling cross-legged on the floor in front of her, he took her bare foot onto his lap and began to massage the ankle. As she gave herself up to the feel of his hands on her skin, warmth flowed through her like brandy, while the coffee, untouched, grew cold beside her.

An explosion of sparks from the fire threw off rainbows of light behind him. Through half-closed eyes she gazed down on his bowed head, remembering the way he'd looked that first time she'd seen him, at the auction. A man at his ease, determined to get what he wanted no matter how long it might take. But not, she now knew, no matter the cost. He had his father's determination but not Finn's ruthlessness.

Desire for him flushed up in her. Her throat, her flesh, were suddenly thick with wanting him. Hoarsely, she said his name, and when he looked up, she saw an equal desire in his eyes. Kneeling, he put his hands on either side of her head, threading his fingers through her hair, and gently drew her face toward his. He began to kiss her mouth, the lids of her closed eyes, her neck, with the deep, passionate kisses of someone as hungry for her as she was for him. She moved her hands down his sides to bring him up to her until the pressure of his body crushed hers back against the cushions.

Turning her head aside, she rested it against the cool skin of his neck, felt the muscle there hard against her cheek. She whispered, "I haven't got anything—"

"I have. Shall I . . .?"

She nodded. While he found what he needed, she stood up, so that when he came back to her she was waiting for him, passive now. She let him undress her in front of the fire, his hands skillful, deftly stripping away the sweater, pushing aside her clothes so that he could move his mouth across her body. It excited her to be naked while he was clothed, to feel the rough cloth of his jeans cool against her hot flesh. She knelt over him in turn and together they tugged off his clothes, each made impatient, almost clumsy, by longing. During the brief moment when he half turned away from her to sheathe himself, she felt as if she stood on the brink of some great gulf, unafraid. Then he took her in his arms, urgent yet tender too, delaying his own pleasure to minister to hers. When they came together the blackness that for so long had shadowed her soul at last dissolved and light flooded into her.

Spent, they lay watching the fire die away. As she looked down at his hand resting on her hip, she thought of how he had reached out to help her, both literally and figuratively, on the cliffs, in her search for Marianna, and in her loneliness. A cord of light now bound them to each other, a connection glowing and unbreakable. She turned to put her arms around his neck, to tell him how he had saved her.

With her mouth against his hair, she added softly, "You asked me once which way we should go together, up or down. On the cliffs, when you rescued me. Remember?"

"I remember that you didn't seem to need much rescuing."

"Oh, but I did. And you've taken me in the right direction."

He glanced down at himself, at what was stirring again between them, and smiled. "I think it's obvious that I can say the same."

And then he told her—both in word and, at length and with variations, in deed—that the salvation was mutual.

They returned to Kerreck Du shortly before six to find Finn and Pascale in the kitchen eating an early supper. The two were talking intently together, intimate, almost conspiratorial, across the table. To Dana, they looked like a long-married couple, comfortable together and deeply connected.

When they saw Daniel and Dana a swift covert glance passed between them, some sort of inquiry on Pascale's part to which Finn gave an almost imperceptible shake of his head, before Pascale rose to her feet, insisting that they join them for dinner. They should leave for the preview in less than an hour, she continued, glancing at her wristwatch, earlier perhaps because of the fog. She began to move around the kitchen, taking plates from the cupboard, dishing up a casserole of lamb and mushrooms. Her usual calm demeanor had a brittle edge, Dana noticed, and all the while she kept up a steady stream of comments, as if she were afraid of what might be said in the silence.

Finn rose to pour wine into their glasses. A dry smile twitched one corner of his mouth. "I think Pascale is more anxious than I am about this bloody exhibition. So tell us about your day. We could do with a diversion."

As she and Daniel described their discoveries at Tintagel, Finn and Pascale listened intently, seemingly taken with the story of Marianna and Pen Browning. At one point, Finn told them that old Miss Hobhouse, from whom he had bought Kerreck Du, had once referred to a suppressed scandal, which if revealed would have destroyed the family's peace forever. "Victorian vapors, I thought at the time. Henry in his dotage taking nude photos of shopgirls. Or liking to dress up in private as Queen Victoria. She might have told me, I suppose, if I'd pressed her, but I wasn't much interested. Daniel tried to get me interested, but ferreting out the sordid details of people's private lives . . ." He shrugged and pushed his empty plate away. "Waste of time, if you ask me."

Perhaps that was one of the explanations for his success, Dana thought. A single-minded focus on his work. Living or dead, other people simply didn't matter that much to him, apart from those he permitted into his life. And even those chosen few would not be allowed, ultimately, to distract him from what truly mattered.

Despite their apparent absorption in the tale, Dana had the strong impression that Finn's and Pascale's questions and responses masked a deep unease that had nothing to do with the preview that night. Once she saw Finn's eyes rest momentarily on Daniel, and in them a look that might almost have been anxiety. All through the meal she sensed an inhibition in their manner, something held back. It was clear from several glances Daniel sent her way that he too had sensed this.

Her intuition was confirmed at the end of dinner. While they discussed whether to take two cars or one to the preview—the Tatevics were going with them—they carried their coffee into the living room. Finn settled onto the sofa, and when Pascale sat down beside him there was something in the way she placed her body, curved toward his, that seemed to Dana protective of him. She and Daniel sat in neighboring armchairs.

A silence fell as they drank their coffee. Pascale then glanced at Finn, who nodded. Turning to Daniel, he said that they had bad news. "We didn't tell you before because"—he paused and looked quickly from Daniel to Dana, and an expression both wry and indulgent briefly flickered across his features—"well, I thought you might as well eat your dinner first." Then in a somber voice he went on to say that the police had been at Kerreck Du earlier that afternoon. "They found Karen's body on the rocks below the coastal path. She was murdered last night."

Dana felt as if an icy hand had gripped her heart. For a dizzying moment the room spun on its axis and she seemed to see Karen once again circling before them, the glass globe in her hands casting its shadows up onto her face while she taunted them to raise the spirits of the Gull's victims and ask them how they'd died. A spirit had been summoned forth last night, she thought, an evil one. It had brought Karen's death with it.

Daniel asked how she had died. Strangled, Finn replied. The ugly word seemed momentarily to hang in the air above them. "Not raped, apparently," he went on. "But of course they won't be certain until the autopsy's complete."

Although Pascale's face remained impassive, the restless stirring of her spoon in the coffee betrayed her nervousness. She said, "They wanted to know about dinner last night."

"What did you tell them?" Daniel asked her.

"That it was a pleasant gathering of friends." When Finn snorted with obvious derision Pascale turned to him, "Yes, very well, but what would you have had me tell them? That undoubtedly Karen gave more than one of us who were present good reason to wish her dead?" She set the spoon down in the saucer with a little clatter of silver on china. "The wish is not always father to the deed."

"Do they know about Mico and Karen?" Daniel asked.

This time it was Finn who replied. Tim had taken the news of Karen's death badly, he said, and had made some unfortunate accusations to the police. "Told them Mico was mixed up with her. Even said I'd slept with her, the damn fool, though eventually he agreed that Karen herself had never said that. Luckily, Nadia swears Mico was with her from the moment they left together.

And I have an alibi." He glanced at Pascale, who, astonishingly, blushed like a girl.

Daniel pointed out that as Karen had gone home with Tim, and as Tim had been overtly jealous of her, Tim himself must certainly fall under police scrutiny as a suspect.

Finn muttered an assent. "He says she borrowed his car and went off with it to meet someone. But apparently she was seen later by a couple out walking, returning it alone. Which must leave Tim as much on the hook as anyone."

"The police asked about you, too, Daniel," Pascale said. "Naturally I told them you spent the night here." When Finn quickly interjected to say that this was the truth as Pascale understood it, she gave him a puzzled look, clearly not understanding.

Daniel enlightened her. "I decided to walk back to the Schoolhouse after all. About one in the morning. After you'd gone to bed."

The reminder chilled Dana. Not because it raised questions in her own mind—it was impossible that Daniel should have anything at all to do with Karen's death—but because it might in the minds of the police.

"I hope you're not thinking of telling the police that," Finn said harshly. "Why complicate things? Who's to know?"

"You and Dana, for a start," Daniel pointed out in a reasonable tone of voice. "Pascale believed she was telling the truth. But if the police ask any of you directly now . . . And they will, you can be sure of it. We were the last people to see Karen alive. Eventually we'll all have to sign written statements."

Finn drew a hand wearily over his face. He was sitting hunched over now, his head bowed. Beside him, Pascale said in a fearful voice that was little more than a whisper, "The police also asked us again about Solange's death."

"As though it had anything to do with Karen's," Finn flared out, raising his head. "Christ, if they start looking into every accidental death along this coast they'll have their work cut out for them!" His face was flushed with anger, the blue eyes so vivid they seemed electric.

A frown furrowed the skin between Daniel's eyebrows as he leaned forward in his chair, toward his father. He seemed about to speak but hesitated, turned to set his cup aside, and stood up. "I'll go and see them now. Get it over with." He looked and sounded perfectly calm, as though it were a minor nuisance, nothing to worry about.

Finn stared up at him, his face suddenly stricken. For the first time, Dana thought, he looked like a father simply concerned about his child. "In God's name, Daniel, what's the rush? It can wait until tomorrow."

"I don't think so. They'll only want to know why I didn't come forward at once." He smiled, a little grimly. "And I don't want them turning up at the gallery tonight to question me."

Dana stood up. "I'll come with you."

He gave her a grateful look but shook his head. "I'd rather you didn't. Go with Finn and Pascale to the gallery. I'll meet you there." Then, taking her hand, "But you could walk me to the door."

She stood on the steps in front of the house, watching the Yamaha's taillight fade as he rode away. When the light was gone the gray mist closed in on her, chilling her to the bone.

Chapter 30

When Estelle's telephone call came late that afternoon, John Malzer was alone in the gallery. There were one or two details that only he could attend to, minor but essential adjustments to the lighting that were necessary if he was to achieve the degree of success he was counting on tonight. He resented the interruption and found it difficult to keep his annoyance out of his voice.

He assumed at first that she was calling simply for reassurance. Together with Finn and Thomas, he had been told of Karen's death when one of the local painters had stopped in at the gallery shortly after midday, ostensibly to offer his help. His real purpose, Malzer suspected, had been to retail the terrible news he'd just heard from his brother-in-law, who worked with the local rescue unit. Hikers, noticing an unusual number of sea birds flocking to a certain point at the foot of the cliffs, had seen a bit of bright cloth under some bushes where the birds were busiest. The police were still out on the cliffs with Karen's body, he told them. It looked like the work of the Gull.

Estelle had immediately collapsed, recovering only when Thomas placed a dripping cloth on her face. The painter, readily accepting their assurances that his help was not needed, went off like the town crier to spread his grim tidings. Finn left with him. He would go to Sundy Best, he told them—Tim ought not to hear the confirmation of his fears from a stranger or over the telephone. Thomas, perhaps remembering last night's brief tussle with Tim outside Kerreck Du, did not offer to go along.

Malzer had found it difficult to gauge Finn's reaction to Karen's death. He had shown very little emotion, merely a deepening abstraction, which could easily be his habitual self-absorption.

Perhaps he had been wondering what effect the death would have on his plans. Neither he nor anyone else had suggested that the preview, or Estelle's party, be postponed. An indication, if such was needed, Malzer thought, of Karen's unpopularity.

Thomas and Estelle had remained with him at the gallery and had worked on in comparative silence, apparently too stunned by the murder to continue sniping at each other. Malzer had the impression that Thomas intended to outwait Estelle, but eventually he too had left, promising to return early to ensure that the waiters they'd hired for the preview understood their duties.

At last the press of her own preparations for the post-preview party had forced Estelle to depart. Mrs. Pargeter would be waiting for her, she said, and for once she would actually be glad to have the woman in the house.

Shortly afterward the police had arrived at the gallery to take a brief statement from Malzer. He had kept it simple. Yes, he had been at Kerrreck Du with the others and had seen Karen leave with Timothy Sundy. He himself had driven Thomas Attery and Estelle Pinchot to their houses, and had then gone home to bed. No, he knew of no reason why anyone should want to kill Karen.

All the while, he had monitored his emotions, pleased to find himself well in hand. He had felt as though he were at a slight remove from everything, suspended above events that he alone controlled. He would allow nothing, not a death, not the police, to interfere with the smooth proceeding of the evening's events, the culmination of three years' hard work and meticulous planning.

Now Estelle's voice came down the wire, obviously excited, so shrill that he had to hold the receiver away from his ear. "I've just spoken with Marcus Kitaen." This was a drawing teacher at Quarles who had used Barbara as a model; Estelle had once told him that Kitaen had been very kind to her after Barbara's death. "Did I mention that I rang him the other day, on the spur of the moment, to invite him to the preview as my guest?"

Malzer's grip on the receiver tightened. "No, you didn't." At first he could not speak, and when the words came out they sounded hoarse in his ears. Sweat pricked under his arms, between his legs; he was sure she was about to tell him that the man had accepted.

To his relief, she said that Kitaen had refused, pleading the pressure of work. But in some old portfolios at the college, she went on, Kitaen had found a number of sketches his students had done of Barbara. He thought she might like to have them, and had sent them off to her express mail.

"They should arrive with the late afternoon delivery. I want you to be with me when I open the package, John. You're the only one who can truly understand their significance." Her voice was softer, almost shy. "You may even be able to help me see her again."

Malzer's first impulse was to refuse, to say he was too busy. However, an instinct warned him that he would be wise to go. "Of course, Estelle. I'm on my way now."

"Good. Park by the back door. The caterers will be bringing the food and I don't want the drive blocked." Now that she had accomplished her purpose she reassumed her imperious manner.

He was about to hang up when he thought to ask if the police had been to see her yet. Yes they had, she replied. "They wanted to know if I knew of anyone with a grudge against Karen, someone who might have wanted to kill her. Dozens, I wanted to say. Karen was someone who liked to set the cat among the pigeons. And to her we were all pigeons." This was more astute than Malzer would have expected of Estelle. "But of course I didn't tell them that. They would only have wanted examples and I really didn't have time to go into that. And what would be the point? This is clearly the work of a madman. A madman," she repeated, and the brisk voice became suddenly tremulous, as if the word itself terrified her. "I can't stay here, John. Not after this. I'm going to make arrangements tomorrow to return to London."

He replied with the usual reassurances, adding that as she never went out on the cliffs she had nothing to fear. But she only reiterated her determination to leave. Reproachfully, she said that she might feel differently if he would agree to come and live with her. To distract her, he asked if she had mentioned the business between Mico and Karen at dinner to the police.

"No, I did not. The poor man has quite enough to endure with that wife of his. And I'm sure someone will tell them. Thomas, probably." More likely Tim, he thought. She waited and when he did not respond, continued, "But you can't think Mico had anything to do with Karen's death. Nadia had far more reason to kill her. And I hardly think she's the Gull."

"No, I don't see Nadia as the Gull."

After he'd said good-bye, he stood for a moment unmoving, willing himself calm, but the dark thoughts stirring inside him were stronger than his will. He began to feel the first tremors of a desperation that he knew could be lethal. He must not panic.

Before he left, the same instinct that had persuaded him to agree to Estelle's request prompted him to fetch his camera, as well as two other items. The camera he would leave in the car, but the two last he tucked into his jacket pocket. On stepping outside he was shocked to discover that fog was lying thickly over the town. He'd heard the rain on the roof but hadn't bothered to think about the weather once it stopped. His initial anxiety dissolved, however, as he told himself that if anything the fog would help rather than hinder his plans.

Cautiously, he drove the half mile to Estelle's house. As he approached, he saw the courier delivery truck pulling away, its taillights soon lost to sight in the mist. The tall hedge of escallonia and the overarching branches of trees and shrubs hid the large white house from the road and turned the drive into a tunnel. The house seemed especially isolated in the fog. No wonder Estelle felt nervous here at night.

Estelle must have heard or seen his car for she was waiting for him at the kitchen door. She waved a large padded envelope as he walked across the gravel toward her. "Perfect timing. It just arrived."

In the kitchen, the overhead light was so bright it hurt his eyes. Plastic-covered trays of hors d'oeuvres were laid out on the countertops, small pieces of salmon on puff pastry, stuffed mushrooms, fruit kebabs, and petits fours. Glasses stood on trays, shining under the ceiling light, and through the open pantry door he could see bottles of wine and mineral water cooling. He had the beginnings of a headache and the smell of the food sickened him.

The caterers and Mrs. Pargeter had come and gone, Estelle told him. "Mrs. P. was full of Karen's murder, of course. Took a positively ghoulish pleasure in talking about it. Finally I couldn't bear it any longer and told her to go home. You know I was never very fond of Karen, but to die that way . . . I wouldn't wish it on my worst enemy. I've been absolutely terrified ever since I heard. And with this fog . . . thank goodness I've had the party to think about." She led him into the living room, talking all the while about the horror of Karen's death. She sounded to him more excited than horrified.

They sat together on the sofa, the gold bracelets on her wrists clashing loudly as her hands struggled to remove the tape that sealed Kitaen's package. Malzer looked around the room, thinking how much he disliked it. It was a woman's room, he thought contemptuously, a woman like Estelle, overdecorated, stifling, with too much surface glitter. He particularly hated cream chintz, the slippery feel of it, the pasty color. There had been a forbidden room in his childhood with untouchable furniture covered in the stuff; secretly, he used to smear raspberry jam from his bread on the undersides of the cushions, until one day his crime was discovered and punished by the woman who pretended to be his mother.

Estelle sat back with a little exclamation of dismay. "I can't open this. I'm far too nervous." She held out one trembling hand to show him.

"Let me." He took the padded envelope from her and expertly ripped off the tape, then gave it back to her. She would want the pleasure of removing the contents herself.

As usual, she made a production of the business. First, she pulled apart the envelope and peeked inside, almost coyly. Then with an anxious glance his way, she slowly drew out the small sheaf of drawings. Christ, he wanted to say, just get on with it. But before she allowed herself to look at them, she reached out and squeezed his hand. "I'm so glad you're here, John. I wouldn't have the courage for this otherwise."

The first half dozen sheets were exercises in pure draftsmanship of varying degrees of competence, studies of Barbara both nude and clothed. Estelle held each drawing up close to her face; naturally, she would not put on her eyeglasses in front of him. She exclaimed over them, gently touching her fingers to the paper as though it were her daughter's flesh. Malzer had to force himself to look at them, to say the expected words of admiration, while a storm of pain slowly gathered in his head, swelling until he felt the blood beat against his temples with such force it seemed about to burst through the bone and flesh.

Estelle was laying aside one drawing in order to look at the next beneath it when her hand abruptly checked. He felt her stiffen beside him, heard her gasp. And when he, too, looked down at the drawing on her lap he knew why he had been wise to come. The excess blood ebbed from his brain, leaving behind a crystalline clarity, the knowledge of what he had to do.

On the paper were a number of small sketches of male and female heads, five or six of them, seen from various angles. One of these heads was Barbara's, half turned. Another, full face, was that of a young man with long, tousled hair, sleepy eyes, and a heavy, pouting underlip. Himself.

Estelle picked up the sheet of paper and stared at it, then slowly turned to Malzer. "This is you," she said wonderingly. She looked down at it again and confusion grew on her face. "But how—? You said you didn't know her."

"No, I never said that. You assumed it."

The bangles slid down her wrist as one hand plucked tremulously at her throat. "I don't understand. How could you have known her? When?"

He thought of lying to her again, of saying it was a coincidence, that the artist must have seen him somewhere, on the tube, on a bus, and sketched his face from memory. But he couldn't summon up the energy. And he wanted, finally, to tell her how he really felt.

He said, "I was a student at Quarles. We met there, Barbara and I. We shared a room in the squat. Oh, we weren't lovers, nothing like that. We both knew how sex could foul things up. But I did love her. She was important to me in ways you could never begin to understand." Those tales of her father's abuse, whispered late into the night, had been like a drug to him; he had savored each. Sometimes he had wondered, however, if, seeing the pleasure he took in them, she had dressed them up a little for his sake. She had needed him, too, then. "We looked after each other. And she was getting better, she really was. Until Finn destroyed her."

She stared at him wildly. "Finn? What do you mean?"

"What I said. If he hadn't slept with her she would never have died. He confirmed what she already knew. That sex is just someone strong using someone weaker for their pleasure, that it's ugly, that the power's always on one side. . . . Finn didn't make love to her, he just fucked her."

"Don't!" Estelle's face contorted. She held up her hands, as though to ward off his words. "Don't tell me any more. I don't want to know."

But he was determined to spare her nothing. She would at last hear and understand. He would sit in judgment, he thought, not shrink from it as so many did, all those cowards who looked the other way and permitted the wicked to flourish, to hurt the weak. He would punish. "Finn seduced her for his own amusement. She was vulnerable, he would have known that if he'd bothered to find out. But he never cared about her. Only about what he wanted. Just like her father."

Estelle sat as if transfixed. One hand opened and closed convulsively on the drawing and in the silence the crumpling paper sounded to him like a flame crackling. Her eyes, wide as a mesmerized rabbit's, were fixed on his face.

He went on, relentless. "She told me you never once intervened, never protected her. You just let him do what he liked. You would go into your bedroom and shut the door—"

"I didn't know," she moaned. "I didn't think—"

"No, you didn't think. Or if you did, it was only about yourself."

"But I did care," she protested, imploring. Tears were running down her face now and she raised her hands to her cheeks to rub them away.

"Too late," he pointed out coolly. "Tears at her funeral. Like now. They don't do any good."

She took her hands away from her face and looked up at him. "You weren't at the funeral."

"Of course not. Why should I have listened to a lot of lies? I mourned Barbara in my own way."

Shuddering, she stared down again at the drawing on her lap. Then back at him, flinchingly. "The photograph—"

"Was one I took of her when we were together. You wanted it to be more than it was. I obliged. With tricks any knowledgeable photographer could have used." Proud of his talent he described the tiny interior pivoting lens he'd rigged up, but he could see she wasn't listening. She never listened.

"But how could you have done that to me?" It was a cry deep from her own egotism, he thought.

"Perhaps I simply wanted to make you happy, Estelle."

He could see her wanting to believe this, the pitiful signs of her vanity struggling with the conviction that he was lying. Finally, she shook her head, then violently crumpled the drawing and threw it at him.

"You mean you wanted my money! Well, I'll see you pay every bit of it back with interest. My lawyers will know how to handle this. And if you think I'll let Finn have Barbara's picture now, you're very much mistaken. I'm going down there this minute and bring it back with me."

He picked up the crumpled ball and smoothed it out. Slowly, he shook his head. "No, I can't let you do that. This exhibition is important to me." Then he smiled and perhaps it was something in the smile, or in his voice, so cool and gentle, that made her face change, grow fearful. "You talk as if what I did was a crime, when it gave you nothing but happiness. It was really Finn who harmed you. After what I've told you, the destruction of his work should please you."

This shook her, he saw. Her throat moved convulsively as she swallowed and when her words came out they were thin and fearful. "Destruction? What do you mean? What are you going to do?"

"I could punish Finn. His arrogance makes it easy. He fancies himself a great artist, wants his prints to be unique, like a painting or a statue. So he's vulnerable, too. Don't you see? A fire in the gallery now, tonight, would be devastating. Everything he's worked for, gone up in smoke!"

Her face was frozen with disbelief. "You're not serious?" she interrupted. "This is some sort of fantasy, what you'd like to do!"

"Perhaps. But it would be a fitting revenge, don't you think?"

"Revenge?" The word seemed to frighten her. He could see her struggling to calm herself. "Listen, John," she said at last, pleadingly, "taking revenge is madness—" She stopped abruptly, choking a little on the word, then in a rush went on. "If you're afraid I'll tell anyone—or go to the police—you needn't be. What I said about my solicitor, that was anger speaking. But I'm not truly angry with you, really I'm not. I can see how you cared about Barbara. Well, it's obvious, isn't it? Besides," she added with a nervous little laugh, "do you think I want people to know how gullible I was?"

He gave her his most appealingly boyish look. "You mean you could forgive me, Estelle? That would make me very happy."

"Of course, of course." Relief made her voice foolish. One hand reached out, as though to pat his knee, but drew back. "After all, you only did it because you . . . you loved Barbara."

"And Finn? Are you going to forgive him as well? Don't you think he ought to be punished?"

She stared helplessly at him, as if she were trying to figure out what he wanted her to say. "Well, yes, of course. But perhaps not so . . . so harshly. Why don't we wait, discuss it. Together we'll come up with something I'm sure."

He pretended to think this over. "I suppose it is a bit extreme, my idea. Maybe you're right. Maybe the best punishment might be if you took Barbara's photograph away from him in front of everyone tonight. Let the world know what a callous bastard he is."

Her face blanched, possibly at the thought of this scene. "No, no, I've changed my mind. I won't go to the preview. I don't want to see him again." Or you, was implicit in her voice. "You do it. You take the photograph down and send it back to me. I'm leaving Trebartha. I'm going back to London."

"What, tonight?"

She licked her lips. The orange lipstick looked dry and caked on her mouth. "Yes, I'll go tonight. That would be best."

"What about the party?"

"I'll cancel it." Her eyes were feverish. She looked around the room as though it were already full of the expected guests to whom she owed an explanation. "Tell them . . . Tell them the truth, that Karen's death has frightened me so badly that I've gone back to London."

It was like playing a fish, he thought. You had to stay calm, in control, with the gentlest touch to guide it in. He thought of the camera in the car; he had been right to bring it.

He said, "Better send a note. Tell Finn yourself." While she sat dumbly watching, he went over to her desk and took out the pen and a piece of writing paper he found there. He placed them on the coffee table in front of her.

Her hands were still trembling as she moved the drawings from her lap onto the coffee table, then leaned forward to write the note. When she finished and stood up, he could that see it was taking all her willpower not to bolt from the room. "I think I'll go upstairs and pack," she told him.

He was standing now too, chewing on his lower lip. "Very well. I suppose I'd better go and see to things." He moved a little away from her, as if to leave.

"Yes, yes, you really must get back to the gallery." She panted the words out eagerly and he could see a kind of sick relief in her eyes.

"Oh," he said, "I almost forgot. The note." He glanced back at the table.

Even as she turned away he was drawing the leather cord from his trousers pocket. The bangles on her wrist made more noise than she did. He was glad when at last they were stilled.

Some fifteen minutes later, he finished taking the last of the photographs. Wearing latex gloves, he dressed Estelle's body in her coat and then picked her up. She was as difficult in death as she had been in life, unwieldy, her head flopping back instead of resting against his chest as it was meant to do. He struggled and failed to open the kitchen door, and was momentarily overcome with a strange exhaustion. Sweating, he sat down for a moment to rest on one of the kitchen chairs with the body in his arms. Estelle's open eyes were fixed on him, reproachful.

"You deserved to die," he told her. "You're the one who killed Barbara, not me. You and Finn. She would never have been on drugs if you'd looked after her the way I did." He had meant only to make Barbara sick, he explained, so that she would need him again. But he had misgauged the power of the drug. "I wasn't to blame. I loved her."

She still wasn't listening. He could see that.

As he stood up again, he considered taking the body to the

cliffs. But there wasn't time and, despite the fog, he might be seen. The best course was to leave it here. The note would give him a little time. Enough time.

He was barely outside, however, when he had to go back into the house to switch off the porch light. Then, on the gravel drive, he stumbled over a bit of uneven ground and almost fell. Estelle's head and one arm lolled free and for a moment she seemed to smile up at him giddily, like a woman too drunk to walk. He began to talk to her again, not loudly but conversationally, describing in detail what he intended to do tonight. The way he'd wired to ensure the flames would spread quickly, the cheap, flammable carpeting, the deliberately faulty sprinkler system, the old insulating material in the ducts primed with cleaning fluid. It was a relief to tell someone.

Still talking, but more to himself now, to remind himself of each step of the operation, he placed the body behind the steering wheel of her car, which was garaged at the back of the house, then went back inside for her suitcase and purse. He'd already packed the suitcase with clothes she might be expected to take with her for a few days away. The suitcase went in the boot of the car, the purse on the seat beside the body. He closed the garage door and stood leaning against it for a moment, dizzy with fatigue.

Back inside the house, he returned all but one of the drawings to their envelope, which he put with the papers on her desk, carefully wiping off his fingerprints. The study of male and female heads went into his pocket for burning later along with his clothes. After this, he picked up the telephone and dialed the gallery. He waited until the message machine clicked on and let a minute go by in silence before replacing the receiver in the cradle. British Telecom would confirm his statement that Estelle had called him at—he glanced at his watch—5:26 to say that she was going back to London immediately.

It would have to do. At the very least, it should give him the time he needed to see to his affairs. The gallery in London was obviously not to be, he realized that now. But it was not too much to hope that with careful planning he might achieve a similar success elsewhere. Under a new name, of course.

Before he left, he looked around to make sure he had not

forgotten anything. Then, locking the door behind him, he went out to his car and drove slowly away. He took the longer circuitous route back, to avoid being seen. Only when he was out on the road some distance from the house did he switch on his headlights.

Chapter 31

Thomas shivered. The fog's gray light, filtered through the rice paper shades, penetrated the study with a wintry chill. The room seemed cold, colder even than the low temperature at which he normally kept it for conservation purposes. Perhaps, he reflected, it was simply that the murder of someone familiar was inevitably chilling, regardless of whether the dead person was liked or hated. Karen's death did not grieve him, but neither did it relieve him of the tensions she had played upon so expertly. The threat she had embodied continued to hang over him, more amorphous now but equally intense.

He paced from photograph to photograph, staring at each as if it could tell him why he was so afraid. But for once his collection failed him.

One threat at least was temporarily in abeyance. Finn, thank God, had agreed to give him time to repay what he had taken from the accounts. Of course Finn could well afford to be reasonable, thanks to the level of financial security that he, Thomas, had helped him achieve.

More immediate concerns troubled Thomas now. He had no alibi for the time of Karen's death, had not, in fact, been at home as he'd told the police. A compulsion, undoubtedly foolish, to talk to John, to find some sort of comfort there, had interrupted his preparations for bed. Failing to reach John by telephone, he had walked over to the Chapel Gallery. Either John had been so deeply asleep that he hadn't heard Thomas's repeated knocks or else—and this was the real reason for his concern—John had not been at home. Driven by a need to confirm his suspicions, Thomas had rung Estelle as soon as he'd returned to his own house, but she hadn't answered either. There could only be one reason why.

She must have persuaded John to return to her by exploiting her fear of the Gull and then, when he was with her, exerted other pressures. Estelle was voracious in her need and demands. Thomas's mind swerved away from any detailed imagining of the form those demands might have taken. But he had to know if John had been with her.

He considered ringing her now, to question her about last night, then rejected the idea. She might refuse to discuss it, or to see him if he asked to come round to talk to her. Better simply to show up, to give her no chance to put him off. He would know by her face if she lied to him, for Estelle was not a skillful liar.

As his car was still in the shop, he would have to walk. In a fog this thick, however, it was almost safer to walk than to drive, and the exercise and fresh air might clear his head, which felt clogged with a dull oppression, as if the fog itself had penetrated his skull.

He put on his tweed cap and overcoat, turning up the collar, then went out into a colorless, undifferentiated world. The neighboring houses, set back like his own from the road behind hedges and walls, were little more than vague shapes. As for the town below, that was utterly lost in the fat gray cloud pressing down on it. Like a swollen sponge, the fog seemed to have sucked water up from the sea and was now oozing the excess moisture drop by drop over the hidden landscape.

Thomas pulled his cap further down on his forehead and buttoned his overcoat up to his neck. He did not want to catch a chill. Walking well to the side of the road, for there was no pavement for pedestrians, he kept a sharp ear out for approaching cars. Here on the high road above the town there was little traffic, but two cars did go slowly by, their headlights a dull smear against the wall of mist. And once a boy on a bicycle rang his bell behind Thomas, startling him so that he leaped aside to land in the ditch as the boy cycled past, laughing at his shout of outrage.

"Cheeky bugger," a man who happened to be passing by with his dog said sympathetically. "But you want to be careful. In that coat of yours you're not easy to see." He himself was wearing a bright yellow anorak.

The fellow was right, Thomas thought as he wiped the mud from his shoes on the long grass that fringed the ditch; he ought to have worn something more visible than gray tweed. However, Estelle's wasn't much farther now. He hurried on, cursing the boy, for the shoes were wet as well as muddy from the ditch. He cursed the compulsion, too, which had forced him out on what might well prove to be a fool's errand.

A few minutes' brisk walking brought him to Estelle's house, invisible from the road behind its high hedge. As he turned in at the drive, he paused to push aside the thick foliage of the bushes that screened the drive from the house. A pale light glowed from the living room window. But his relief changed to chagrin as the light suddenly went out. Was she leaving already? He must catch her before she got into her car; it was urgent now that they talk.

As he let the branches fall back into place, a stray tentacle from a wild rose bush brushed against his face, knocking his eyeglasses off. He looked down, but could not see them in the thick tangle of grass and shrubbery at his feet. Kneeling, he groped with his hands in the wet undergrowth and found the glasses caught in a cleft at the base of the rosebush. The lenses were smeared and his hands were scratched from thorns and nettles. As he stood up, feeling for his handkerchief, he heard the sound of the door at the back of the house opening. Damn, he thought, she's going.

Hastily, he tried to wipe the lenses clean. Squinting down the misty length of the drive to the back steps, faintly illuminated by the porch light, he noticed that a car was parked there. At the same moment a man came out of the house, carrying a large object in his arms. When Thomas shoved the eyeglasses back onto his face, he saw that the man was John and that the car was his.

Then, with a shock of fury, he realized that the object in John's arms was none other than Estelle, her blond head resting on his chest.

He could only stare through the smudged lenses, paralyzed by the blow, unable to move or call out. He felt as if those unimaginable suspicions had suddenly taken shape to confront him with his own folly. As he watched, he saw John stop abruptly on the bottom step, then turn and go back up into the house, leaving the door open.

Sick with a mixture of jealousy and rage, Thomas wanted desperately to give way to his fury, to confront John and Estelle. But a wiser self urged caution. Watch first, it told him; act later. Quietly, he crept closer to the back door.

Almost at once the porch light went out and John reemerged, still carrying Estelle. Hiding among the branches of a huge rhododendron that grew against the house some fifteen feet from the door, Thomas watched him walk slowly down the steps. John was looking down, concentrating. Estelle's left arm hung limply, swinging slightly with each step that he took. The pair struck Thomas as strangely silent. Estelle looked asleep, or unconscious. Her body seemed to sag like . . . Before he could fully formulate the thought, Estelle's head fell back and he saw the livid face with its slack mouth open in a soundless cry, the eyes bulging from her head, staring upside-down at him. It was the face of death, more real than any photograph.

Thomas's first clear thought was: John must have hated her all along. A shameful surge of triumph coursed through him, replaced almost at once by a second wave of nausea as, rooted there and powerless to move, he watched John walk past his car across the lawn to Estelle's garage. Startled, he heard John speaking to Estelle, although he could not hear the words themselves. For a confused instant he thought he must have been mistaken, that she wasn't dead at all. He didn't know whether the emotion he then felt was relief, or regret.

But when John heaved the body over his shoulder in order to open the garage door, Thomas knew without doubt that Estelle was dead. The knowledge terrified him.

As soon as the grotesque pair disappeared into the garage, he was released from the nightmarish impotence that had kept him immobile. Gagging, he turned and stumbled away, then began to run wildly, without looking back. His cap flew off at the end of Estelle's drive, but he left it there. Amid the chaos of his thoughts was an overmastering, desperate determination. He must destroy those snapshots, burn them all, and sell off his collection. Get rid of everything. Only then could he think what to do, who to tell.

The blood was pounding so fiercely in his head that he did not hear the car coming around the bend behind him, too fast, until it was almost on him. He looked back in time to see a haloed yellow light shining full into his face, obliterating everything.

Chapter 32

Dana wandered restlessly through the Chapel Gallery's crowded labyrinth of rooms. It was close to ten o'clock, long past the time she had expected Daniel to return from the police. She'd seen every photograph in Finn's exhibition twice over and had by now grown too anxious even to pretend to take them in.

She was wearing last night's short blue tunic, and now found herself playing restlessly with its tiny pleats. To still her hands, she accepted a glass of wine from a passing waiter. Her stomach was tight with a nervous energy, which the wine only intensified as she moved through the throng, searching for a sight of Daniel.

A middle-aged couple pushed past her, talking loudly. "Far and away the best show I've seen this year," the man was saying to the woman with him.

Comments like this, and the numbers eager to pay homage to Finn, told her that the retrospective was an enormous success. But she wondered how much pleasure the triumph was giving Finn, for it was obvious to her that he was as worried about his son as she was, and that the same question troubled him. Why were the police keeping Daniel so long?

She set the half-empty glass down on a table. In an effort to distract herself, she watched faces observing the photographs, or one another, and followed the path of the large heating duct that ran from room to room along the ceiling. It looked sinister, she thought, hanging there overhead like an enormous bloated snake.

Through a gap in the crowd, she saw Mico and Nadia, arm in arm. Nadia looked almost pretty tonight, with her hair piled neatly on top of her head and a dress patterned in pale green leaves which flattered her figure. When Nadia caught sight of Dana, she beckoned her over.

Earlier that evening, Dana and the Tatevic family had driven to the gallery with Finn and Pascale in Finn's Bentley. No one had said much on the way—they were too preoccupied with the dangerous road conditions and with Karen's murder. But Dana sensed that Karen's death had somehow brought the Tatevics together. The possibility that the police might consider Mico a suspect seemed to have roused Nadia's protective instincts. She was much calmer now, perhaps because the threat to her marriage was gone. And Mico seemed gentler with his wife. It was impossible to know from his granitelike face, however, how he felt about Karen's death.

"Where's Elvina?" Dana asked as she joined the couple.

"With her book," Mico replied. "She refuses to come with us, and there is no point trying to persuade her." He shrugged and spread his hands wide. "She can be very stubborn. As you know."

On arriving at the gallery, Elvina had at once sat down on a bench in the foyer and taken a book from her pink knapsack, ignoring everyone and everything. Dana had tried to talk to her, admiring the pretty flower-printed dress she was wearing, asking after her doll, whose flaxen head was visible inside the open knapsack, but each attempt was met with Elvina's wordless, apologetic smile or a helpless shrug of the shoulders.

"She does not mean to be rude," Mico continued. "We have told her she should speak to you."

Dana shook her head, sympathetic. "Not if it's hard for her."

Nadia murmured a few words to her husband, in a voice softer than Dana had yet heard her use. When she finished, Mico said solemnly, "My wife wants you to know that although Elvina will not speak, she is very grateful to you. Elvina has told us that she wishes she could do something for you, to show her appreciation. When we are living in London we hope you will come to us for dinner."

Surprised, Dana said that she hadn't known they were going to London.

"Finn arranged it. We will go as soon as Elvina's school finishes. Nadia hopes to teach again in London."

His wife nodded and smiled, as if she understood some of this. Given how unhappy she'd appeared twenty-four hours ago, her cheerfulness struck Dana as remarkable. Perhaps there was hope for the Tatevics' marriage after all; she began to feel slightly better about Elvina. As they walked into the main exhibition room, she told Mico that she would look forward to the dinner.

While the Tatevics went over to the small wine bar set up on one side of the room, Dana found herself drawn once again to Finn's unsettling photograph of Barbara Pinchot. She took it as a sign of Finn's genius that the photograph conveyed so powerfully the peculiar combination of narcissism, self-doubt, arrogance, and fragility characteristic of certain young women. On seeing Dana's fascination with the picture, Pascale had told her who the model was and how she had died. But Dana didn't have to know that Barbara Pinchot had overdosed, or recognize the symbolism of the headless shadow, to realize that the woman in the photograph was no survivor.

But then, Dana thought, how could you really be sure who would survive? Karen had seemed so tough and astute, yet apparently she had gone walking alone at night with a murderer, which meant that the killer had to be someone she knew, someone her instincts had failed to warn her about. For Elvina's sake, Dana hoped that someone would not turn out to be Mico.

Finn's sudden bark of laughter rose above the hubbub. Dressed in a striped black-and-gray jacket over black jeans and a blue tie the color of his eyes, he was holding court in the middle of the room with Pascale at his side. From his boisterous manner, an observer might have concluded that he was enjoying the attention he was receiving. But Dana saw him put his arm out to Pascale, to draw her closer to him, as if he needed the reassurance of her calm presence.

"Finn's certainly in his element," a voice beside her said.

She turned to find John Malzer also watching Finn. He wore a dark suit, which made him look more grown-up, and carried a small pile of exhibition catalogs. She congratulated him on the evening's success.

He lifted his free hand, as though to ward off bad luck, then ran it nervously through his tousled hair. "I hope it ends more smoothly than it began. It's just a pity so many of last night's dinner companions at Kerreck Du aren't here to enjoy it. You don't happen to have seen Thomas, have you?"

"Not yet." She found it strange that both Attery and Estelle had failed to show up; each had seemed so involved with the exhibition. Estelle's short, cryptic note had plainly baffled Finn, who had tried without success to call her, to persuade her to change her mind. Dana wondered now if Barbara's photograph had as much to do with Estelle's abrupt decision to leave as her fear of the Gull. The murder of a young woman, even one whom Estelle had plainly loathed, might have reminded her too painfully of her child's death. It might have been easier simply to leave than to come here tonight, where she would be obliged to confront those revealing images.

"Mind you, in this crowd it's difficult to see anyone," John was saying. "People certainly haven't been put off by the fog."

"Or by Karen's murder."

He gave her a sharp, almost contemptuous look, and his smile was sardonic. "Oh, I'd say her murder helped bring them out, wouldn't you?" Without waiting for a reply, he moved away to adjust a photograph that was hanging slightly askew.

Dana told herself that it couldn't be easy to orchestrate an exhibition, work with an ego as temperamental as Finn's, and cope with unexpected complications, like fog and murder. John might be edgy because of his responsibilities, or because he was upset about Estelle and Thomas letting him down at the last minute. On the other hand, John was the one who had suggested that in Estelle's absence, her post-preview party be moved down the hill to the Pickled Herring, and had himself contacted the pub to organize things when Finn concurred. So perhaps he thrived on complications.

Anyway, she thought, looking around the crowded room, he was probably right about Karen's death. The combination of fog and murder made people want light and companionship more than ever. Better to be here, where there were warmth and laughter and the diversion of Finn's brilliant photographs, than to be alone thinking about the Gull. And, judging by the raucous laughter of the noisy group next to her, provoked by macabre speculation about the Gull, violent death only heightened some people's determination to enjoy themselves.

As Dana moved away, her uneasiness about Elvina revived. There must be something she could do to reach the child, some way she could help her. Determined to try again, she made her way back to the gallery entrance.

Elvina's bench was empty. From her vantage point at the top of the ramp, Dana slowly scanned the crowd of people in the foyer, some of whom were struggling into coats as they prepared to leave, but Elvina was not among them. Somehow she must have missed her on the way.

She was about to turn around and retrace her steps when the main door opened and Daniel walked in. The look on his face immediately checked her relief and delight, and banished all thought of Elvina, for he had the grim air of a messenger bringing bad news. During the few moments it took her to reach him she felt as though a cold hand were squeezing the breath from her lungs.

When he saw her, his face cleared and he extricated himself from some people who had stopped him to praise the exhibition. Barely acknowledging others who called out to him, he took her arm and drew her to the small area behind the reception desk, where they would not be overheard.

"Are you all right?" she asked.

Something in her voice, her obvious fear, caused his face to cloud over again, this time with contrition, as though he hadn't realized until then how much she would worry. He touched her cheek. "The police know I'm not the Gull," he said, and the breath came back to her body in one long sigh of relief. But before she could speak, he added quietly, "They think it's Thomas."

In a low voice, he went on to explain that Attery had been hit by a car not far from Estelle's house earlier that evening. He was unconscious and his chances for survival weren't good. "The driver of the car said Thomas was running down the middle of the road like a madman. The police found his hat by the side of the road just outside Estelle's driveway, and his footprints in the mud of the drive.

"That's not the worst of it, I'm afraid." He paused and looked around, to make sure they weren't overheard, then told her somberly that the police had found Estelle's body in the garage. "She'd been strangled. Like the others."

Dana's hand went to her mouth. Her horror was mixed with an immense pity for Estelle, so frightened of dying in just this way, and with a bewildered, incredulous astonishment that a man who had shown nothing worse than a cutting way with words should all the while have been capable of murder.

"I have to tell Finn and John," Daniel was saying. "Do you know where they are?"

"In the main exhibition room. Pascale's there too."

They started up the ramp, but so many people stopped Daniel to tell him how wonderful the retrospective was that they made very slow progress. Every time he managed to shake one off, another would catch hold of him. Finally, they agreed Dana should bring the others to him.

She managed to signal to Pascale, who detached Finn from his admirers. "Daniel's fine," Dana said quickly to reassure them, and saw Finn's face relax. "He's here now, down in the lobby. The police know he's not the Gull. But he needs to talk to you. And to you," she added, as John Malzer came up to them. He gave her a queer, almost frightened look, and she winced inwardly with the knowledge of the blow about to fall on him, and on Finn.

Before Malzer could question her, however, Finn was hurrying them along through the crowd, brusquely deflecting efforts to waylay them. Daniel met them in the foyer. The briefest of looks passed between father and son, a recognition of their mutual relief, and then Daniel asked John if they could use his office.

"Yes, of course." He put his hand to his trousers pocket, frowned, and added, "That is, if we can get in. I seem to have mislaid my keys." He strode ahead to try the handle of the door that led to his private quarters. When the door opened, he looked alarmed but said nothing as they all went inside. While Daniel closed the door behind them, however, he began to search the surface of the desk, pushing aside the litter of papers and empty coffee cups.

"Relax, John!" Finn said irritably. "The damn keys are sure to turn up. We'd better hear what Daniel has to say." When the other man ignored him, Finn shrugged and told Daniel to go ahead.

Succinctly, Daniel told them what had happened. Finn and Pascale's shocked distress was obvious, but John was turned away, looking down at the contents of a drawer. Then he wheeled around to face Daniel, breaking the brief, stunned silence with a string of urgent questions.

"How is he? Will he live? What are his chances?"

"Not good," Daniel replied calmly. If he was taken aback by the onslaught of questions, or by Malzer's failure to show emotion over Estelle's death, he disguised it. "He's in intensive care now."

"Have they talked to him?" Malzer shed his jacket and threw it over a chair, and the pungent smell of his body filled the little room. Dana saw that the armpits of his shirt were damp with sweat. "How do they know he's the Gull? Did he admit it?" Despite the intensity of his voice, the flat brown eyes were opaque and unrevealing.

"The police haven't been able to talk to him," Daniel told him. "He was knocked unconscious by the car. As far as I know, all the police have is circumstantial evidence. But that looks bad enough. And when they searched his house and saw that collection of his . . . Well, you can imagine what they thought."

Finn groaned, rubbing at the back of his neck. "I've always known that in some ways Thomas is a weak man. That he has a nasty tongue and some strange tastes. But I'm damned if I understand how he can be the Gull. And as for Estelle, and Karen . . . Christ! It doesn't bear thinking about."

Beside him, Pascale said softly, "She must have been leaving, believing she would be safe. It's too cruel."

Malzer meanwhile had begun searching again for his keys, checking through his jacket pockets for the third time. Then abruptly he halted and said, almost to himself, "Shit, I must have dropped them somewhere." This fixation with the keys in the face of the terrible revelation of Estelle's murder and Thomas's metamorphosis into the Gull was so extraordinary that Dana could only assume he found it impossible to come to grips with the news.

Finn was slumped against the door. He looked up at his son, his eyes dull with fatigue. "What should we do, Daniel?"

Dana sensed rather than saw Daniel's almost imperceptible

start of surprise at his father's question, as if he were unused to having Finn ask his advice. "That depends. Do you want to stay on here, or go back to Kerreck Du? Or would you like to go to the hospital?"

"Show support for Thomas, you mean?" Finn looked surprised, but it was obvious the idea appealed to him.

"At least give him the benefit of the doubt."

The blue spark was back in Finn's eyes. He straightened and moved out into the room with his old pugnacious energy. "Daniel's right," he told Pascale. "There's not a thing we can do for Estelle, but I'm damned if I'll be stampeded into judging Thomas until there's solid proof."

Pascale gave a faintly ironic, affectionate smile. "And when have you ever been stampeded by someone else's opinion?"

"I'll take you to the hospital then," Daniel said. "The Yamaha's outside. Pascale, will you drive Dana and the Tatevics home in the Bentley? Now that a wind's come up the fog's not so bad." When she agreed, he suggested she let a little time go by after his and Finn's departure. "People might start asking questions if we all leave at once. If anyone does want to know where Finn is, just tell them part of the truth. That Thomas had an accident and we've gone to the hospital. The news about Estelle will get out soon enough."

"What about you, John?" Finn asked the gallery owner, who was still standing by his desk, head bowed, as if lost in thought.

"What?" He looked up with a distracted air, then said slowly, "Oh, I'll do my best to join you at the hospital." He jingled a set of keys, which he'd taken from one of the drawers. "My spares. Locking up's no problem, but I don't like to leave the place as long as the others are missing. Don't expect to see me till I've found them."

A look passed between Finn and Daniel. Dana wondered if they were finding Malzer's abstraction, his seeming lack of emotion at the news of Estelle's death and the discovery that his friend was the Gull, as disconcerting as she did.

John opened his private outer door to let Finn and Daniel leave unnoticed. "I'll try to clear the gallery as soon as possible. Encourage people to head down to the Pickled Herring. Of course, they're bound to hear there what's happened." The caustic smile Dana had seen earlier on his face returned, with a cruel edge. "But I don't imagine it'll put anyone off their liquor, do you?"

Dana walked with Daniel and Finn to the parking lot. She said she wanted a breath of fresh air, but the truth was she found herself reluctant to part from Daniel. Her uneasiness hadn't left her, even now, when she knew he was safe. If there had been room for her on the Yamaha, she would have asked him to take her with them.

A light wind from the sea was slowly shredding the fog, swirling it up out of the town in milky currents that surged silently around the gallery's buildings. Lights from the invisible town below would flicker briefly into life as the fog thinned, then vanish when it thickened again. Overhead, the raveled, salt-laden strands parted to reveal the occasional glimpse of a clear night sky bright with stars. On the wind, Dana could hear the sound of the sea, a restless, low-pitched susurration that seemed full of sorrow. It made her shiver.

"Are you warm enough?" Daniel asked, slipping one arm around her waist. He wore his leather jacket, but she had left her own coat behind at the gallery.

She nodded untruthfully, leaning into him, glad of his body next to hers.

The motorcycle was parked on the far side of the lot, beside a wind-crippled pine. While Finn strapped on his helmet, Daniel drew Dana aside and put his arms around her. His eyes looked down into hers, gravely smiling. "This is a hell of a time to say I love you. But I love you."

"It's the perfect time," she whispered against his mouth. His words, and his body, were like a shield suddenly held up in front of her to keep the horror at bay.

Afterward, as she walked back across the road to the gallery, she remembered Elvina. At the same moment, she noticed a dim light showing through the shutters that covered the single window in the last cottage. Like the other two cottages in the row, it was a small cube of gray granite with a steeply pitched slate roof and a squat, massive chimney set into the valley between the roofs. In the fog the three roofs looked like a child's drawing of mountain peaks rising through the tidal cloud of mist.

Perhaps it was the juxtaposition of this image with her thoughts about Elvina that made her curious, made her turn left along the path in the front of the cottages instead of walking up to the gallery entrance. As she passed John Malzer's private quarters, she noticed his light was off. Then, when she was a few yards from the door of the last cottage, she saw Elvina's small pink knapsack sitting near the drainpipe that ran down the facade. Protruding from the knapsack opening was the doll's head.

More puzzled than afraid, she tried the knob of the worn wooden door and found it unlocked. Leaving the door open behind her, she stepped down into a large unfurnished storage room lined with metal shelving and dimly lit by a single bulb hanging from a low ceiling. It smelled of mildew and damp, and faintly of chemicals. She looked around. A small whirlwind seemed recently to have passed through the place. Boxes and containers stood open, their contents exposed; packages of paper were ripped apart; a large plastic carton was upended on the rough flagstone floor beside one set of shelves, as though used for a stepstool.

On the far side of the cottage she noticed another door, which might have belonged to a closet or a small inner room. Framed on either side by high steel shelves, it stood partly open.

"Elvina?" she called softly.

A soft noise, like a shuffling of feet, startled her. Before she could move, the door to the closet swung wide and she saw Elvina standing silently on the other side like a tiny apparition, with a white, pinched face and enormous eyes. Wordlessly, the child turned and switched on an overhead light.

As Dana hurried over to her, she saw that the inner room wasn't a closet after all but Malzer's darkroom. Windowless and almost clinically neat, it wasn't much larger than a small pantry. Bottles, beakers, and other equipment were lined up in rows on the counter, and in one corner was an old porcelain sink half covered in trays, with a red hose attached to the spigot. Elvina now stood at the counter with her back to Dana, stretching up on tiptoes in an effort to open the cupboard above, which was just out of her reach. The fist resting on the counter was curled around a bunch of keys.

Dana touched her shoulder. "Elvina, what are you doing?"

Mutely, Elvina shook her off. She reminded Dana of some small busy animal, a mouse or a mole, so intent on its task that it was oblivious to danger. In an effort to hoist herself up onto the high countertop, she knocked against a bottle, which fell with a clink and began to roll toward the edge. Dana caught it just in time.

"Please, Elvina," she pleaded as she set the bottle back in its place, "tell me what you're looking for. I want to help you." When the child continued to ignore her, Dana grabbed her upper arms, forcing her down to the ground and around to face her.

"Your parents said you wished there was some way you could show me your gratitude. Well, there is. Talk to me! Tell me what you're looking for!"

For a long moment, the child stared back at her; there was such fear and confusion in her eyes that Dana felt her heart turn over. Just as it seemed she would refuse, she said, "My camera."

"But why do you think you'll find it here?"

"Because he took it."

"Who? Mr. Malzer?"

Elvina nodded, then frantically clutched Dana's arm. "You must not tell! He will send us back!"

Fighting to control her impatience, Dana made herself speak with deliberate calm. "I don't understand. You've got to explain what all this means. Please."

Haltingly, Elvina described how she had photographed John Malzer on the cliffs, how he had taken her camera from her, telling her he would have her family sent back to their own country if she mentioned to anyone what he had done. "He said he can do that. He showed me a paper from the government." Her voice was the voice of an old woman, weary and fatalistic.

Too baffled by this to understand its implications, Dana could only point at the keys, presumably Malzer's. "How did you get hold of those?"

Elvina gave a faint, pleased smile. "I saw him drop them on the floor. He didn't notice, he was busy with some people. So I took them." Then, as if afraid Dana would snatch them from her, or accuse her of theft, she clutched them to her chest, adding defensively, "He stole my camera. Why can't I steal from him?"

Dana had no answer for that. "But what made you look in here?"

"My father, he brings me to the gallery sometimes. Mr. Malzer won't let anyone come in here. So I know it's private, where he would put secret things."

"Weren't you afraid of what he said he'd do?"

Elvina shrugged. "I don't know. Yes, a little." She was turning the keys over in her hands and at first would not meet Dana's eyes. Then she raised her head and said in a rush, with a peculiar, shamefaced look on her face, "Madonna told me to find the camera. It's my punishment."

Dana was about to ask who Madonna was when she remembered the doll. "Is that Madonna outside?"

The girl nodded. "She's supposed to watch."

"Why would she punish you?"

"Because I made her die."

Dana felt as if she were stumbling through a maze; each question, each answer, only led to a deeper confusion. What she was hearing seemed incredible: John Malzer stealing a child's cheap camera, threatening her with deportation; a doll as night watchman and judge combined; Elvina believing she'd killed someone. None of it made sense.

"Made who die?" she asked, somewhat desperately. "Madonna?"

"That Karen."

Speechless, Dana could only stare at Elvina. At the thought of all the misery that must burden the girl's mind, she felt sick at heart. She took her in her arms and told her firmly, "You didn't make Karen die. She was murdered. The police think Mr. Attery did it."

"But you don't understand," Elvina said despairingly. "I asked Madonna to kill her and she did." The bony little body convulsed with shuddering sobs.

Help me say the right thing, Dana prayed as she held the crying child. She stroked Elvina's hair, murmuring in her ear, "We all wish for bad things sometimes. That doesn't mean if the wish comes true that we made it happen." But she knew even as she spoke that it would take more than words to convince Elvina.

She wondered if it was possible that Elvina had misunderstood

Malzer? If not, what on earth could possess him to behave that way? If the Gull hadn't been caught . . .

Suddenly Elvina twisted free, and before Dana could stop her had scrambled onto the countertop, reaching up for the shelves above. As Dana grabbed at her waist to pull her back, the counter began to move, rolling toward her. Caught off balance, she stumbled backward with Elvina wriggling wildly in her arms. Somehow she managed not to fall, but the strap of her purse slipped off her shoulder and the purse dropped to the floor, while Elvina lost her grip on the keys.

Furious, Dana set Elvina down. She was about to demand that the child leave with her immediately when she noticed the small two-drawer filing cabinet that had been hidden beneath the counter. Elvina saw it, too. She snatched the keys from the flagstones, then shoved the counter completely aside, crouching down in front of the filing cabinet. Her eyes glittered with excitement as she looked up at Dana. "Please," she pleaded.

Dana wanted to say no. But the camera seemed to matter so much to the child, and Malzer's inexplicable behavior made her resentful on Elvina's behalf, as well as curious. A quick look, she thought, then they could leave. Against her better judgment, she nodded. "But I'll do it," she added before Elvina could do more than smile with gratitude. "You're in enough trouble for taking Mr. Malzer's keys."

Docile at last, Elvina stood up and gave her the keys. Dana tried each one on the lock of the filing cabinet. She knew what she was doing was not only foolish but illegal, but when the smallest key turned in the lock, she felt a surge of illicit excitement.

Both the top and the bottom drawers proved to be full of hanging files, which seemed to contain only photographs. She was shaking her head, about to tell the child that there was no point searching further, when she glimpsed something in a partly open file that made her lean forward for a closer look. With a galvanic shock, she realized that she was looking at a photograph of Karen Cody's dead body.

Turning, she shoved Elvina away so roughly that the child stumbled against the wall. "Go to your parents!" she shouted at her. "Go on! Run!" But Elvina stubbornly kept where she was by the door, watching Dana as though she'd suddenly gone mad. Frantically, unable to credit her eyes, Dana opened other files, and saw more photographs of women's bodies. A battered face in bizarre close-up stared back at her. It was Solange Finn's.

She slammed the drawer shut and shoved the rolling counter back into place over it. She had to leave it unlocked for her hands were trembling so violently that she could never have fitted the key back into the keyhole. Then she snatched up her purse and dragged Elvina out of the room, pulling the door closed behind them as if to seal in the terrible truth that the darkroom contained.

Tugging at the child, she hurried her across the cottage. But it was too late. They were only halfway to the door when a man's figure loomed up in the open doorway. With Elvina clutched to her side, she stood transfixed as John Malzer stepped over the threshold.

Chapter 33

"I found Elvina in here looking for her camera," Dana blurted out as Malzer closed the door behind him. Despite her terror, she knew it was crucial that she persuade him to let them go before something was said that would make it impossible. "I realize she's confused but I think we're all too tired to try to sort it out now."

She sensed rather than saw Elvina's look of outrage. Under her protective arm she could feel the small body trembling—but with anger, she guessed, rather than fear. She tightened her grip in warning, and fought the dread that was rising through her own body like a deadly nausea.

He simply stared at them. Jacketless, his cuffs unbuttoned and rolled back on his wrists, he stood blocking the door while he cracked his knuckles, one at a time. At the sound, nausea rose into her throat. She swallowed it down and made herself meet that brown unreadable gaze, suppressing an overpowering urge to bolt past him to the door. He might put her nervousness down to the fact that he'd caught them trespassing, but he would know by her fear what she had seen.

Then his eyes flicked behind them, and in that glance she thought she read his own dilemma. He suspected they'd gone into the darkroom, but he couldn't be sure. To check, he would first need to lock the main door, to keep them from escaping. But a move like that would panic them, and it might be difficult to kill them both before someone leaving the gallery heard their screams.

For a long moment they stood there, wordless, equally at an impasse. Then he held out his right hand, palm up. "My keys."

To refuse would only make him more suspicious. She forced her leaden limbs to move forward, to hand him the keys at arm's length, then return, without turning around and with her eyes still fixed on his face, to Elvina's side.

"How did you get them?" he asked as he put them in his pocket.

"It's not her fault," Elvina muttered sullenly. "I took them. I wanted my camera." Straining against Dana's grip, she suddenly shouted, "You have no right to keep it!" To Dana's relief, she looked furious rather than frightened, resentful of his inexplicable theft instead of terrified at finding herself with a murderer. From her face, at least, Malzer might conclude that his secret was safe.

Quickly, before he could respond, Dana said, "We can talk about that later, Elvina. Right now your parents will be looking for you. Pascale's waiting to drive us all back to Kerreck Du." She wanted to remind him that people would notice their absence, especially Elvina's. With one hand on the child's back, she urged her forward, fighting the need to scream at her to run. As long as there was the slightest chance of his believing that his secret was safe she mustn't give way to her terror.

He did not move aside to let them past but stood like a stone in their way, stolid and inscrutable. Although he was breathing heavily, his face revealed no anger at their trespassing, nor any anxiety at what they might have found. He had seemed more upset by the loss of his keys.

He stared down at Elvina and said quietly, "I'm sure you know Karen Cody was killed last night. The police think they've caught her killer, but they aren't certain. We wouldn't want them to start wondering if someone else might have done it. Someone who had strong feelings about her." He paused, and now the ditch-water eyes narrowed and became very cold. "Do you understand what I'm saying?"

Elvina nodded. The thin body under Dana's hand was as taut as a bowstring.

He gave a faint smile. "Good. Then you know it's important for you to cooperate with me?"

"She won't say anything about being here, if that's what you mean," Dana said hurriedly, to prevent Elvina from bursting out at him again. Her voice sounded high and thin in her ears. To Elvina she added, "It's better if your parents don't know about this. We can work something out about the camera later, but now's not the time." She stopped, frightened that she sounded too conciliatory. Oh God, she prayed, not daring to look at Malzer, please don't make him wonder why I'm so eager to oblige him.

Elvina gave a reluctant nod of assent, although the stubborn set of her face said clearly enough how she felt about this capitulation.

"I can see you were busy in here," he said. His glance took in the welter of boxes and papers, then went once again to the closed darkroom door behind them, before returning to Elvina's face. "Where else did you look?"

Dana dug warning fingers into the child's shoulder.

She shrugged and in a colorless, indifferent voice replied, "Only in here."

"We'd better go now," Dana told him, forcing herself to sound firm. "After Elvina's fall on the cliffs, her parents will be frantic if they can't find her. I'm sure she'd be happy to come back tomorrow to clean up the mess."

To her horror, this roused a glint of amusement in his eyes, as if he understood what she was trying to do. But she hoped he understood, too, that he had no choice but to let Elvina go. Keeping her would only provoke a search which would inevitably bring people here to the cottage.

What he said next implied that he understood more than that.

"Run along then, Elvina. Miss Morrow and I will come in a moment. There's something she and I need to discuss first."

Elvina was looking up at her, obviously unwilling to leave without her. Dana saw confusion in her eyes but also the glimmering of a suspicion that she must not be allowed to give voice to, at least not here in this room. Not until she was safe. For Elvina's sake, she had to keep calm.

She made a last desperate effort. "Can't it wait?" she asked him. "I . . . I'm really too tired to talk now."

"No, it can't wait. Otherwise, there might be consequences." His face remained impassive, but his head tilted slightly in Elvina's direction, as if to say, Consequences to her.

Dully, Dana nodded. Then gave the child a gentle push forward. "Do as he says. Go back to your parents. I'll come soon."

Elvina moved reluctantly toward the door. Although Malzer now stood to one side to let her by, she made a wide circuit around him. He said her name as she put her hand on the knob, and she looked warily back at him.

"Tell your parents whatever you like. But don't tell them you were here. Or that Miss Morrow was with you. That way I won't have to inform the police that both of you were trespassing. They might let you off, but they'd have to charge Miss Morrow." He turned to Dana. "Isn't that right?"

She could only nod. But as soon as Elvina was safely through the door she would shout, Run, Elvina, run for help! He's the Gull!

As though he sensed her intent he moved quickly to stand directly beside her, facing the door now. Slight as it was, the touch of his arm on hers made her cringe. Turning to look at her, he shook his head imperceptibly in warning and inaudibly mouthed, "Don't." Then called to Elvina to shut the door behind her.

Before the door had closed completely, he clapped one hand over Dana's mouth and pulled her violently against him with the other, pinning her arms to her sides in an unbreakable grip. "Don't struggle," he whispered, "or I'll have to strangle you."

It was easy enough to obey; fear had dissolved every bone in her body.

"You know something, don't you? But she doesn't. I wonder what you saw." His breath felt hot and moist on her skin. She gagged from the fetid smell of it and from the taste of his hand on her mouth.

Suddenly he forced her back with him toward the rear of the cottage and shoved her up against the wall outside the darkroom, wedging her so roughly into the angle formed by the wall and one end of the steel shelf beside the darkroom door that the edge of a cross-brace bit cruelly into her cheek. The hand over her mouth pressed her head back, exposing her neck. Using his body to hold her in place, he tore her purse from her shoulder and threw it to the floor, then dropped his hand to his pocket. All the while his eyes never left her face.

Terror squeezed every conscious thought from her mind except the certainty that he was reaching for a weapon and would kill her now. When she heard the jingle of his keys, the sound came as a fleeting reprieve.

Perhaps he assumed that the darkroom door would be locked, or perhaps he didn't expect it to open so easily. When it swung forward at the touch of his key, he turned slightly toward it, as if surprised. This relaxed the pressure of his body on hers, and gave her the chance she needed.

She wrenched her left arm free and brought it up in an arc at his face, jabbing hard with her fingers toward his right eye. He jerked his head sideways in time to avoid the worst of the blow. But his temple hit the end of a steel shelf with such force that he shouted out in pain and lurched back, reaching up to his head with the hand that had muffled her mouth. Released, she threw herself to the left, into the narrow space of the open door, grabbing at the doorknob to pull it toward her as she fell back into the darkroom. Somehow, before he had time to react, she managed to find the bolt on the door and drive it home when the door slammed shut.

She had an instant of terror as the darkness closed down on her before she remembered the light switch by the door. Groping, she found it and flipped it up. Now she could see that the bolt looked miserably weak, no match for a man determined to force it. Terrified, she gripped the knob fiercely with both hands, kicked off her shoes, and braced her feet on either side of the doorframe. At any moment she expected to feel the pull from the other side that would signal the beginning of an unequal, deadly tug-of-war. Instead, she heard the key in the lock.

Of course. Why should he waste time trying to get to her now, when he could keep her trapped and come back at his leisure with an ax or a sledgehammer to break the door down?

The scream bottled up inside her burst out in a long shrieking cry for help. She shouted until at last her voice gave out and she sank exhausted onto the stool, breathless and sick with despair, cradling her head in her arms on the countertop.

In the silence, his muffled voice came to her from the other side of the door. "No one outside can hear you, you know. Not with the double walls. You ought to save your breath. You'll need it." His voice held a bizarre sympathy. He might have been offering advice or wishing her well.

She lifted her head to stare at the thin slab of dark wood that separated them. "What are you going to do?" She hated herself for asking, for giving him the satisfaction of hearing her fear, but she had to know. There was another long silence, and when at last he spoke his enigmatic answer told her nothing.

"Heap coals of fire on my enemy's head. But not with kindness." He gave a soft laugh and then, in a graver tone, went on to say that she needn't worry about Elvina, that he wouldn't hurt a child. "I admire what you did for her. Really. Some people would only have thought of themselves. You're not like that."

"Then let me go." Even as she spoke, she felt the humiliating futility of her plea.

"I can't." And then, in a curious repetition and with a tinge of pity, he added, "I'm sorry, truly I am. Because you're not like the others."

Despite his tone, the words themselves were comfortless; they told her that her difference would make no difference to her fate. Despair sucked at her strength, draining it down into the icy black pit in her stomach. And now, while she listened to the sound of his footsteps retreating, followed by the outer door opening and closing, image after photographic image rose up like wraiths emerging from the hidden filing cabinet to float across her mind's eye in grim warning. He did this to us. He will do it to you.

How long did she have? One hour, two? Less. Malzer had told them he intended to close the gallery early, and with Finn gone and the liquor supply cut off, people would be happy to head down to the pub. He would make up some story to explain her absence, perhaps that she too had decided to walk down to the Pickled Herring. It was useless to hope that Elvina would tell her parents what had happened. Fear of what Malzer had implied he would do—to her father, to herself, even to Dana—would keep the child silent.

A terrible fear and the claustrophobic sense that the walls of the tiny room were converging on her made her suddenly sick with dizziness. She buried her head in her hands, pressing the palms fiercely against her closed eyes as she moaned in terror. Behind her lids, light fizzed and sparked in an electric aura of color.

Oh God, she didn't want to die, not here, not like this, not when happiness had seemed hers for the taking. She loved Daniel; she wanted children, a home, the long conversation of a lifetime with him. She had work to finish, Marianna's story to tell.

Marianna. Whose own life had been destroyed just as it seemed poised on the verge of happiness.

She had a vision then of Marianna's luminous, oval face gazing at her, so intensely real that it might have been in the room with her. In the medium's eyes she saw an urgency that seemed a warning. Passivity had shaped her gift, Marianna seemed to say, but she had not let it determine her life; she had struggled against her fate, and against death. Act, her eyes told Dana. So long as you live, you must not give in to death.

A strange ecstasy seemed to possess Dana as a current of renewed strength and determination flowed through her veins. Roused from the stupor of despair, she began to rummage furiously through the cupboards and drawers, looking for weapons among the plastic beakers and bottles, brushes, and print tongs. A pair of scissors and a sharp-edged T-square, as well as a set of sturdy metal measuring spoons with long flat handles, were all she could find. They would have to do.

As she ranged the capless bottles of chemicals along the counter, more weapons in her pathetic arsenal, the extractor fan set high on the wall caught her eye. The fan's mounting plate was barely eighteen inches across, but the large metal apron surrounding it led her to think that the opening behind must be considerably bigger than the fan itself. Malzer might have simply fitted the fan onto one of of the big yellow ventilator ducts that snaked through the gallery. If so, she might have a means of escape.

Feverishly, she shoved the counter over to the wall below the fan and climbed up onto it. The fan was now at eye level. Using the flat end of the metal tablespoon, she attacked the screws of the mounting plate. It was slow, laborious work but eventually the last screw spiraled out into her hand. She removed the fan and let it dangle against the wall from its electric wires. Jubilantly, she saw that the circular ventilator duct behind the fan matched those in the central part of the gallery. Roughly two feet in diameter, it was just large enough for her to wriggle through.

She set to work on the metal apron. Her fingers were bleeding, her arms ached from reaching up, and a sharp twinge in her bad ankle told her that it could give way at any moment, but at last, triumphantly, she felt the final screw in the apron begin to turn. Wrestling the heavy piece of metal out of the opening, she set it down on the countertop, then looked through the hole.

The duct stretched away into an impenetrable darkness. She did not let herself think of what might be living in it, the spiders, centipedes, even rats, of the decades' accumulation of dirt and dust, or of the real possibility that she could be trapped and killed in its narrow lightless tube. It was her only hope.

She was about to hoist herself up when the thought of the photographs stopped her. Unless she took them with her, Malzer would destroy them, and then there would be no proof.

Ignoring the urgent voice that warned her not to delay, she climbed down from the counter and opened the filing cabinet. While the grisly images sent shock waves of terror and pity coursing through her, she forced herself to select a dozen or so of the most incriminating. She wondered how on earth she would carry them without her purse, until she thought of her panty hose. Stripping off the hose, she stuffed the rolled-up photographs into one nylon leg, which she she knotted at the top, then tied the stockings around her waist like a belt. She was barefoot now, but that would give her feet a better grip.

The duct's narrow circumference forced her to lie flat on her stomach with her arms stretched out in front of her while she wriggled forward, pushing with her knees and toes and pulling with the palms of her hands. She listened for a noise behind her that would warn her of Malzer's attempt to break through into the darkroom, but heard only the rasp of her own breathing loud in her ears and the rustle of her body as it snaked over the curving metal surface.

A sudden draft of cool air on her head made her pause to look up. Above, another section of ductwork rose into the gloom, forming an upside-down T with her own. She twisted her body around, arms held overhead, and inched her way up into it, then stood up. Abruptly, her hands slid off the metal onto stone. After a moment's confusion, she realized that the duct must be set into the disused chimney between the middle and end cottages.

Several inches wider than the duct, the chimney shaft had crannies for finger and toe holds. To climb it would take all her strength, however; and even if she reached the top, the opening onto the roof might be too small for her to squeeze through, or might be capped to keep the rain out.

Better to save her energy, she told herself, easing back down into the horizontal duct. This should bring her eventually to the central section of the gallery; if anyone was lingering there, a tenacious guest or two, or caterers clearing up, she would hear their voices and scream for help. In the meantime, she knew she must be careful to make no noise, for sounds would travel along the duct to tell Malzer at once what she was doing.

Silently, she propelled herself forward like a mole in its tunnel, blind in the darkness, her hands and body shoveling up the great mats of dust and dirt that were clinging to the sides of the duct. Dust thickened the stale air, filling her nose and throat. Tears ran down her cheeks as she stifled the urge to cough and her parched tongue longed for a taste of the water back in the darkroom. The curving metal seemed to squeeze the breath and the life from her body. But she could not go back, only forward.

As if to refute her, a soft bulky mass met her fingers. She recoiled with a gasp, terrified, until reason told her that whatever it was, it wasn't alive. She reached out gingerly to move her hands across it. Pungent with a chemical smell like cleaning fluid, it seemed to be some sort of insulating material. Its dense mass filled the duct, like cotton wool plugging the neck of a bottle, resisting all her efforts to push it away, blocking escape.

Her only hope now was the other duct.

She tucked the skirt of her dress into her underpants, to prevent it from getting in her way, then wriggled backward until she reached the junction with the vertical shaft. It was here that a terrifying realization struck her. The tunnel's darkness was unrelieved; no light shone into it from the darkroom. This meant either that Malzer had cut the power, or that he had broken into the darkroom and switched off the light. And was waiting there, like a monster in a nightmare, to grab her legs and pull her out to him.

Instinctively, she turned her head. It was then she smelled it, smoke, the faintest whiff but unmistakable, drifting from somewhere behind her. In the roiling turbulence of her thoughts, Malzer's strange reply to her question came back to her. He was going to heap coals of fire on his enemy's head, he had said. Now, horrifyingly, she knew what that meant. He had set a fire in the darkroom to burn the evidence of his crimes, and with it the gallery, Finn's work, and herself.

Fear as galvanizing as a fire set under a chimney sweep sent her scrambling up the vertical duct, fingers and toes scrabbling for the crannies in the stone, her back braced hard against one side, her knees against the other. Consumed by the urgent and overwhelming need to escape the smoke, and the flame that at any moment might start licking at her heels, she barely felt the stone scraping away her skin, or her muscles screaming for rest.

The chimney shaft was mercifully short, seven feet or less. At the top, her head hit a screen, which gave way at the blow of her fist and fell with a crash onto the roof. Gathering the last of her strength, she levered her body up over the edge of the chimney and into the night, then lowered herself to the valley between the roofs. A loose tile broke free and clattered down beside her to fall into the metal gutter that ran along the cleft.

She rested there with her back against the chimney stack, head turned up to the sky, too weak and exhausted to move. Her desperate need for rest was momentarily stronger than even the terrifying thought of the fire that might be burning beneath her. After the suffocating dark, the cool, misty air met her face with the blessing of baptismal water, sweet with the smell of the sea.

An uncontrollable shiver swept over her. Numbly, she crouched down, pulling her dress free to wrap the torn and dirty cloth around her knees. Here in the trough between the roofs, she was partly protected from the worst of the wind, but the cooling sweat was already chilling her body, and beneath her cut, bleeding feet, the wet slate felt as cold and as slippery as ice.

She had to keep moving, as much to stay warm as to make her escape. But where could she go?

Like black glaciers, the slate slopes of the steeply pitched roofs rose high on either side, impossible to scale without falling, trapping her here in the narrow valley. A few feet beyond the chimney was the roof's edge, at the back of the cottages, but when she crawled over to it she saw a twelve-foot drop to rough and possibly stony ground. To jump down would almost certainly injure her in some way, if it didn't cripple her already damaged ankle. She would never escape him then.

Through the wind-torn fog, faint pinpricks of light shone from distant houses in the town below, dazzling beacons of hope to eyes dulled by the darkness. She wanted to scream out to them, but the wind was blowing away from Trebartha, and at this hour and in this weather people would be indoors with their windows closed. No one would hear her. Her screams would only bring Malzer.

As she turned around on hands and knees, rainwater glittering in the gutter caught her eye, a silvery trail that led to the front edge of the roof, some fifteen feet away. She remembered the downspout that descended there between the cottages. Would it take her weight?

She never found out.

The sound of the falling screen or slate must have told Malzer where she was, for she saw with a shock of horror the indistinct outline of his head rising over the edge of the roof where the gutter ended. He had put a ladder up against the facade so softly that she hadn't heard him. If she hadn't happened to look in the right direction, she might never have seen him until it was too late.

Snatching up the fallen slate, she hurled it at him like a knife-edged discus. A loud curse as his head disappeared from sight suggested she'd given him something to think about, and herself a little time, but she knew that the slate hadn't hit him. He would soon be back.

She ducked behind the chimney stack, trying to summon up the courage to face that twelve-foot drop to the ground behind the cottages. The panty hose belt snagged on a piece of rough stone and the nylon, already ripped to shreds by the climb, gave way. She grabbed at the unfurling roll of photographs as it spilled out, and thought she'd caught it in time. Unnoticed, a lone photograph escaped from the rest to fall to the roof beneath her. Held in place by the moisture, it stuck to the wet slate like a stamp. When, unwittingly, she put her foot down on it, it slid out from under her, and she saved herself only by clutching at the chimney beside her.

Heart pounding, she clung to the stone and glanced back along the roof. Malzer hadn't returned. But her narrow escape had given her an idea.

Swiftly she plastered photographs over a tiny section of slates that rose from the gutter behind the chimney, close to the edge of the roof. She kept two photographs back, tucked inside her dress. They would be evidence, if she survived. Crouching over the photographs on the slates, to hide them from Malzer, she peered around the chimney stack again. This time she saw the humped outline of his body swarming like a huge, dark spider up over the front edge of the roof.

When he caught sight of her, cowering there behind the chimney, he straightened and switched on a flashlight. Now she could see that in his other hand he held what looked to be some sort of stick or metal bar. He aimed the flashlight beam at her face and came at her along the valley, balancing on the gutter, the bar held partly in front of him to ward off anything else she might throw at him. She began to scream, to distract him, to make him hurry, but most of all to release the pent-up terror that threatened to undo her.

In the converging shadows, his body bore down on her, lethal and relentless. Now she could make out his face, could see how his murderous rage had changed his features to a madman's, mouth wide and grinning, eyes dark as a swamp determined to suck her into its lightless depths. He had her, the eyes seemed to say. Why bother to struggle?

Then, through her screams, she heard the distant roar of a motorcycle's engine and, farther off, the sound of a siren. Daniel! Hope lit up the gathering darkness inside her, restoring her strength and the will to resist that deadly urge to give up.

Malzer broke into a run. The flashlight's beam bounced crazily over the shining black slates while his harsh grunting breaths seemed to drown out all other sound. Despite her terror, she kept still until the last possible moment, to hide the photographs. Only when he was almost on top of her did she scramble backward up the sloping roof, using the chimney as a brace to keep from slipping.

When he lunged at her, swinging the iron bar around at her

head, she fell flat on her back. The bar cut through the air above her, as his foot came down on a photograph and slid out from under him. For a horrible moment, she thought he was going to fall on top of her. Instead, the bar's momentum carried him sideways to slip on other photographs as he toppled to the edge of the roof.

He dropped the bar, but could not recover his balance. For a split second he wavered there on the edge, his arms windmilling furiously against the night sky like a scarecrow blown by a hurricane, while the flashlight arced from his grip to go hurtling into the mist. Then, with a shout of mingled fury and incredulity, he fell.

Dana heard the impact of his body hitting the ground. At first she was too stunned to do more than gape at the place where he had been, not quite believing that she had really been spared, that he wouldn't suddenly reappear like some wicked jack-in-the-box. Released at last by the motorcycle's ever-strengthening roar, she slithered down the slates and crawled to the edge, and forced herself to look over.

Spreadeagled below on the ground at the back of the cottages, Malzer's body lay facedown and motionless. She turned then, and not yet trusting her legs to hold her upright, crawled to the ladder and climbed unsteadily down. As she gained solid ground, she saw a powerful beam of light come up over the hill, piercing the fog and the dark. The motorcycle slewed to a stop in a skidding turn and Daniel jumped off, shouting her name above the wail of the siren as the police car pulled in beside him.

She couldn't move, could only wait for him as he ran to her in the dazzling spread of light from the headlamps. Dazed by the light, and by the astonishing fact of his presence and her own survival, she saw him shining with the brilliance of an archangel. But the shock on his face told her what she herself must look like, filthy and bleeding, barely able to stand. When he caught her up in his arms, she held on to him with all the passion and thankfulness of someone reborn to life.

She could feel the last of her strength swiftly ebbing away as the light began to flicker and fade in front of her eyes. Somehow, in those few moments before she lost consciousness, she managed to tell Daniel about the fire and about Malzer's body behind the cottages. Only then, safe in his arms, did she allow the peaceful darkness to take her.

Hours, or perhaps only minutes, passed.

Groggily, she heard Daniel's voice, speaking low, and another man's, gruffer. She opened her eyes. It took her a moment to realize that she was sitting wrapped in Daniel's leather jacket in the back of a police car, with Daniel beside her and his arm around her. Someone had treated and bandaged her cuts, and placed a blanket around her legs. A policeman stood next to the car, bent over to talk to Daniel through the open window. Beyond him was a long fire engine with a revolving blue light flashing on its roof.

She jerked into full consciousness. "The fire! Oh Daniel, was there anyone in the gallery? Was Finn's work—?"

"It's okay," Daniel said soothingly. "They got to the fire in time. No one was in the gallery, and Finn's work is safe. Here, drink this." He held a thermos to her lips.

Obediently, she sipped the hot, sweet tea, then sank back against his arm. "And John Malzer?"

The policeman's deep voice answered her. "The bastard broke his bloody neck. Pity. There are questions we'd have liked to ask him."

Stiffly, for the slightest movement hurt, Dana drew out the hidden photographs, badly crumpled but with their hideous revelations intact. She handed them to the policeman, explaining where she'd found them. "There are more up on the roof, and in his darkroom. If they survived the fire."

He rushed off, photographs in hand, with the muttered assurance that he would return later, after she was rested, to question her.

Then she told Daniel haltingly that she had discovered Solange's pictures among those of Malzer's other victims. She couldn't see his face, but when his grip tightened around her shoulders, she knew he must be thinking of the pain that faced his father. And when she came to Malzer's final effort to kill her, he drew her closer to him and swore violently under his breath. He took her face gently in his hands and moved his mouth over the swollen places, softly, tenderly, as if he longed to heal them.

"But how did you know—?" she began, when they drew apart at last.

"Elvina told her parents what had happened, when they got home. They told Pascale. She called us at the hospital as soon as she heard. The police were there too, of course. Thomas was drifting in and out of consciousness and most of what he said wasn't making much sense, but put together with Pascale's call it was enough to suggest to the police that they might have the wrong man."

Somehow, then, all the damage done to Elvina had not destroyed her courage. Perhaps the child had her own Marianna, some being or vision urging her through the darkness toward the light. Dana tried to conjure up that ecstatic, hallucinatory moment in the darkroom when Marianna had come to her, but she could no longer see the medium. Only her words lingered: We are all connected by a bright cord of light.

Dana gazed up at Daniel's face. And knew, with a certainty equal to Marianna's own conviction, that the cord now binding her to him for all time was no false light, but the true, enduring light of love.

Acknowledgments

Professor Peter Bunnell's friendly advice and his fascinating course of lectures on the history of photography were invaluable to me in the writing of this book. I am grateful, too, to Alison Speckman for illuminating her darkroom for me.

For their patient, perceptive criticisms and encouragement, my thanks to Sally Branon, Flora Davis, Hanna Fox, Irene Lynch, Meg Pinto, Janet Stern, Virginia Stuart, and especially Maggie Sullivan and Ted Champlin, who also read and commented on the final draft of the manuscript.

Marianna Hobhouse's story was partly inspired by the account of the life of the spiritualist Louisa Lowe in Alex Owen's stimulating book *The Darkened Room: Women, Power and Spiritualism in Late Victorian England*. I have given some of Louisa's own recorded words to Marianna.

CAROLINE LLEWELLYN is the daughter and granddaughter of writers. Her mother was a Virginian and her father was half-Welsh, half-English. Born in Singapore, she grew up in Canada and as an adult has lived in England, Italy, Germany, and the United States. The foreign settings of her novels—*The Masks of Rome* (Italy), *The Lady of the Labyrinth* (Sicily), *Lifeblood* (the English Cotswolds), and *False Light* (Cornwall)—reflect her peripatetic life. Her books have been translated into German and French.